# Gloria Goldreich

# Walking
# HOME

MIRA

**MIRA**

ISBN 0-7783-2109-6

WALKING HOME

www.MIRABooks.com

**Printed in U.S.A.**

First Printing: January 2005
10 9 8 7 6 5 4 3 2 1

# GLORIA GOLDREICH

### Leah's Journey

Winner of The National Jewish Book
Award for Fiction

"An absorbing and often moving narrative,
written with sensitivity and compassion."
—*Publishers Weekly*

"A blockbuster."
—*San Diego Evening Tribune*

"A superior reading experience."
—*Best Sellers*

"A reading adventure, weaving together excitement
and compassion, drama and tenderness."
—*Hadassah Magazine*

### Mothers

"Dramatic and moving…"
—Helen Del Monte, fiction editor, *McCall's*

### Leah's Children

"[A] compelling sequel to *Leah's Journey*."
—*Publishers Weekly*

"Written in clear, almost poetic prose…
This delightfully entertaining family saga
should win Goldreich many new fans."
—*Booklist*

### Years of Dreams

"A rich and satisfying tale…
written by an adroit raconteur."
—*Publishers Weekly*

For Harry and Allison

## ACKNOWLEDGMENTS

The author wishes to acknowledge, with thanks, the kind advice of Judith R. Greenwald and Sheldon Horowitz, Esq.

# CHAPTER ONE

I was always amused, during those long strange seasons of my discontent, at the reaction I received when people at parties asked me about my job and I told them that I was a dog walker. I was prepared for the surprise that flickered across their faces, for the disapproval, however tolerant, that shadowed their eyes. I knew that I didn't look the part. Dog walkers are marginal, grungy types and I still wore the short leather skirts and long silk chemises that had been my standard corporate uniform during my years at BIS, Business Industry Systems, a public relations agency specializing in high-tech accounts. And then there was the Phi Beta Kappa key that dangled from a thick gold chain. I didn't wear it to show off. I wore it because my father had had the chain made especially for the key (he was prouder of it than I was) and it would have been a betrayal of a kind to remove it. I waited for them to ask the obvious—why would a Phi Bet spend her days leading a herd of canines through Central Park? I scripted clever answers to parry back and I was always a little disappointed when I didn't get to use them. It meant that the questioner (usually a yuppie guy on the make) was not really interested in me, that his eyes were already raking the room in search of someone who might be a little more interesting, a lot more appropriate.

Such disinterest startles me still, jostling the conditioning of my childhood. I grew up with the expectation that everyone would be deeply concerned about me, that I had an inviolate claim to their attention, a right to their immediate involvement.

I was, after all, the only child of Holocaust survivors who had married late and then remained childless for almost a decade. I was the miracle in their lives, the wonder child whose very existence was a marvel. When their cousins, Morrie and Zelda (our sole claim to extended family) spoke of me, their voices trembled with disbelief. Who would have expected Lena and Isaac Weiss—she so fragile and pale and he stooped beneath the burden of memories—to ever have a child? And such a child. I listened greedily as they spoke of me—"a face like a flower, hair the color of fire, tall and so smart—you should know from such smartness." They kissed their fingers into the air and smiled at me, in adoration, in gratitude. My parents' luck brushed their own lives with hope. "Ah, Ruchele," they whispered. My name is Rochelle but my family always used the Yiddish diminutive, which sounded to me like a loving prayer.

It seemed only natural to me that I should be the focus of my parents' lives, the sole claimant of their affection, their aspiration. From grade school on they pelted me with questions; every minute of my day away from them was subject to their scrutiny, their hungering anxiety. My mother packed my book bag each morning, checked that I had my homework, my notebooks, my texts, a sweater, a neatly wrapped lunch. She unpacked it again when I returned, sniffed the sweater and folded it, talking and talking as she moved from room to room in our quiet and orderly Queens apartment. *How was school? A test—was there a test? Did I eat my lunch—both halves of the sandwich? That nectarine—it was good wasn't it, and juicy? Maybe I shouldn't have bought nectarines—they're still not in season, but I read that they have a lot of vitamin C and you get so many colds...* My mother's voice would trail off, lost in worries about my cold, memories of her younger brother who had died of pneumonia that had developed from a cold during a cold Polish winter, concern that she had spent too much for the nectarines when my father was struggling to meet the bills. Still, maybe business would get better, maybe my father's investment in the new buttonhole machine would work out.

My father did not ask about my lunch. He wanted to see my notebooks. He wanted to know if the teacher had liked my composition. He examined my book covers, and if they were at all frayed he immediately sat down at the kitchen table with brown wrapping paper and scissors and fashioned new ones. He studied my test paper, passed his callused fingers across the shiny gold stars and asked how many other children had received stars. He visited his cousins and brought me their discarded *National Geographics* for my "extra credit" projects. When I entered high school he bought a set of the *Encyclopedia Britannica* in a gold maple bookcase, which was the bonus gift that year. I keep it still in my apartment, much to the bemusement of my friends who point out that you can do whatever research you need on-line and my computer is a state-of-the-art Apple, my signing-on gift from BIS.

My mother monitored my social life. *Who did you sit with lunch-time? Who did you play with at recess? Maybe you want someone to come home with you after school? I'll make cupcakes.* She wanted me to have friends. She did not want her own solitude to be a curse upon my childhood.

"When you raise your hand in class, don't wave it around," my father counseled. He had attended night school. He understood the American classroom. He wanted me to volunteer the correct answer with dignity. He did not want me to call attention to myself. My mother would nod. She too understood the danger of making oneself conspicuous. They had survived by willing themselves to invisibility in that netherworld from which, against all odds, they had escaped. This I guessed because they never spoke of it.

They both hovered over my bed when I was ill, proffering glasses of juice, bowls of apple sauce, their trembling fingers and moist lips pressed against my forehead. When I fell roller skating they both examined my skinned knee and, each night until it healed, they studied the scab, waiting impatiently for it to fall off, for the new soft pink skin of healing to emerge. My body was their responsibility and they could not, would not, relinquish dominion over it. When I was an infant, I think they must have spread open my diapers, examined each moist stool, perhaps even bent their heads close to sniff my body's mysterious excretions, to inhale the miracle of my existence. I know that they never slept when I was awake and although I sometimes resented their absorption and wondered how such devotion could be repaid, for the most part I reveled in it. More dangerously, with the casual narcissism peculiar to children—or at least to the child that I was—I assumed that everyone else would share that intense interest in my life, my world.

And for a long time that assumption, that expectation, was reasonably fulfilled. I was smart without being snotty, a precocious child who skipped a grade and brought the teacher sweet poems, but who never, never jumped up and down in her seat squealing, " I know. I know." And I was pretty—auburn curls tumbling to my shoulders, my hazel eyes long lashed, my features delicate, my neck strangely long. By adolescence I was taller than most of my classmates, always slender and a natural athlete. High-school audiences cheered as I leaped for baskets on the polished floors of gymnasiums and sped to the finish line at track meets.

Being a star athlete and an academic achiever kept me the focus of attention in high school and then at Collins, the small, excellent New England college where I majored in English, made dean's list effortlessly, was elected captain of the track team and editor of the yearbook and then glided into Phi Beta Kappa. During those student years everyone seemed as interested in me as my parents had been—my coaches, my teachers, the recruiters who descended on campus our senior year to pluck up talent ready for ripening. I got the key interviews and the BIS rep offered me the job and the computer without even contacting my references. I accepted without reservations. It was at a top firm, pioneering in public relations for computer companies.

And when you're pretty and smart and geared for success, you're a magnet for friends. Classmates flocked to my dorm room, called on the phone, courted intimacy. They peppered me with questions the way my parents had. *Where did you get that dress? What are you reading? What are you doing Saturday night? What are you writing your soc paper on?* I answered their questions with the same equanimity I had offered my mother when she had asked me about sandwiches and nectarines, my father when he asked me about my schoolwork. I accepted their interest as my due. It took me a long time to realize that not everyone really cared that much about my answers, that most people were too wrapped up in their own lives to care at all. The questions were merely pro forma. It wasn't until my second year at BIS that I noticed that occasionally people barely listened when I replied. My parents would never have believed it and for a long time I had trouble believing it myself. This was me, Rochelle Weiss, sharing information about her life. How could they not be interested? It was difficult to abandon the certainty of childhood, to recognize that I was not, after all, the center of everyone's universe.

But that was not the only reason why I was disappointed when people failed to ask me how I got hooked on dog walking, which was, admittedly (even I admitted it), a very weird job for someone like me. I wondered how it was that my listeners didn't share my fascination with the serendipitous ways in which people find their professions, how they stumble onto their life's paths. That was something that always intrigued me, that compels me still.

I remember how, as a small girl, I tingled with excitement when we visited our cousin, Morrie, and his family in their spacious Washington Heights apartment. Morrie was a tall, bald man with thick chestnut-colored eyebrows who checked the time on a gold watch that advertised his wealth and authority. My parents deferred to him. He was in import-export. The words sang. Import-export, export, import. I chanted them as I jumped rope and treasured the stamps he gave me. Merchants in Pakistan and China wrote to him. He dealt in spice and leather, chemicals and steel. His was a mysterious and dramatic profession and I wondered how he, with his pronounced accent, so much thicker than my father's, and his too-loud laugh, had managed to find his way into such a complex world.

My father explained that when Morrie came to America after (there was no need to ask "after what?"), a cousin found him a job as a bookkeeper in an import-export firm. Why not? In Cracow he had been an accountant. Numbers were numbers and Morrie was smart. Soon he learned the business, made suggestions. Soon the owner's son went off to Mexico to study art and the owner got sick. Morrie ran the business, found an opportunity here, a good deal there. It was pure chance that a job had been found for him in import-export. It could just as easily have been a bakery or a dry-goods firm and there would have been no stamps from Pakistan, no envelopes from China.

I asked Mendy, my American-born cousin, with his sweet breath and long fingers, how he had happened to become a dentist.

"It was something I always wanted to do," he said. "I was a good science student, and I was good with my hands. That's important for a dentist, you know. But I couldn't have afforded to go to dental school. Where would my family have found the money for tuition? But Elias, my mother's uncle—maybe you remember him—he was a dentist. His son Aaron was developmentally challenged and he worried about him. So he made a deal with me. He would pay my tuition and take me into his practice when I graduated. In return I would always take care of Aaron. A good deal for both of us. So that's how I became a dentist and that's why Aaron lives with me and Selma."

I knew Aaron. He was a gentle man with a vacant smile who sat in a corner at family gatherings wearing an oversize grey cardigan that matched his smooth, pebbly eyes, and endlessly playing with a ball of string. If Aaron had been average he might have gone to dental school and Mendy would never have studied at NYU, never have earned the right to wear a starched white jacket and look into my mouth with a silver-backed mirror, his breath wafting sweetly across my face.

My own father had become a buttonhole manufacturer because of his aunt Rose, his mother's sister, who had a buttonhole machine in her kitchen. It was her therapy, recommended by the psychiatrist who guided her through a nervous breakdown after her only son was killed during the Battle of the Bulge. It's mechanical. It will calm her, soothe her, the doctor told my uncle, and he had been right. Plump Aunt Rose, with her pale blue eyes, sat in her kitchen and made buttonholes for small manufacturers. The garments arrived in soft piles, flannel pajamas, cotton blouses, shirts, the buttons in place. She bent over her small machine and carved out the holes while her radio played the soap operas she did not understand and the kitchen grew steamy with the scent of thick soups always simmering on her stove. When my father came to stay with her after the war, she taught him to operate the machine. He liked it. It was warm and pleasant in his aunt's kitchen. It was a long time since he had known warmth and pleasantness. His fingers flew. The pile of garments grew smaller.

The machine was logical, methodical, reliable. So little in his life had been logical, methodical, reliable.

"I got interested. I began to learn more about buttonholes," he told me.

He learned that some were finished with neat stitching and some remained raw, slits in a cheap fabric that would soon unravel. Some were rounded in satin and some in grosgrain. Each job lot had to be carefully measured. Make the hole too small and the button is forced through, which is no good. Make it too big and the button will pop out, which is also no good. It was necessary to be careful, precise. I thought my father a magician of a kind as I watched him study fabric and button, make his calculations and his decision. This machine gauged just so. That machine for a more elegant job.

He bought his own machines, rented a loft. He had a small factory and after a few years my mother no longer had to worry about the price of out-of-season nectarines.

I would wonder what my father would have done if Rose's son had not been killed, if her psychiatrist had been less wise or had suggested a different form of therapy. What if she had been crafting baskets or sewing beads onto purses when he arrived, so exhausted, so untrained. Would he have busied himself with strips of wicker, gleaming bits of jet? Life's course I know was uncharted, chance and choice rising and ebbing in uneasy, unpredictable currents.

I think of my own friends, of Carl who is studying for a Ph.D. in philosophy at Berkeley. NYU Med wait-listed him for a year and he took a job at the register at Barnes & Noble. Someone returned a philosophy text and because it was a slow day, he read it through, his mind and heart racing. By the time NYU found a place for him he was already packing his bags for California. Then there's Brett, who is in the window-sash business because his girlfriend got him a job with her uncle who manufactured them. Brett had majored in architecture and graduated just as the economy and construction ground to a standstill, so he was glad of any job at all. He figured out a new design for window sashes and presented it to her uncle, who bought it and eventually made him a partner. Brett broke up with the girlfriend, but he's now a window-sash magnate. Cousins Mendy and Morrie redux. Chance, circumstance and suddenly a life.

Then there's my college roommate, Melanie, a psych major who hated psychology and had no idea how she would live after graduation. Now she runs a flower shop on the east side, not far from my apartment, haunts flower shows and speaks knowledgeably about stargazers and jonquils. All because her mother befriended an elderly neighbor who, for years, had brought her a small bouquet from the flower shop where she worked. When the old woman became ill, Melanie's mother managed her mail, rationed out her painkillers, set up a buzzer system between their apartments. Each morning she brought her a bowl of oatmeal, each evening she carried in a bowl of soup and spooned it into the old woman's mouth. Acts of loving-kindness. The neighbor was widowed, childless, utterly alone. What else could one do? When the old woman died it was revealed that she had owned the flower shop and had willed it to Melanie's mother. The deed was transferred the week that Melanie graduated, the timing fortuitous, almost magical. Melanie's mother, a divorced woman, was a teacher who loved her work. The decision to offer Melanie the shop was obvious. And so, because her mother carried bowls of soup across a dimly lit hallway, Melanie spends her days arranging long-stemmed roses and advising brides-to-be about their flowers.

When Melanie tells the story of how she came to be a florist, she makes it sound like a fairy tale with her mother the beneficent queen and she herself the fortunate princess. It is a conceit for which I forgive her, because she is Melanie who dyed her hair magenta and because she understands why I spend my days walking dogs and even approves of my decision.

"It's not forever," she said once. "Nothing's forever. Was BIS forever?"

My answering laughter was tinged with bitterness. Once I had thought so, that is if I'd thought about it at all. I liked my job, my successes were easily achieved as they always had been. Like an accomplished swimmer, I knew how to overcome the occasional cramp of discontent. After ten years I was scooting pretty rapidly up the corporate ladder, going straight from the training program to assistant manager of a key account and later, when Ellie the senior manager had the requisite nervous breakdown after a bad divorce and an even worse love affair, I slipped easily into her job. It was supposed to be temporary, but Ellie's recovery was slow and I came up with ideas that the client loved and that actually worked. I really peaked when I organized the sponsorship of a Special Olympics event for one of our clients, orchestrating a press conference at which the CEO stood in the midst of a group of kids who were all wearing sweatshirts with the company logo. The wire services picked up the photo, the client was in heaven and I received a dozen yellow roses and a terrific bonus check from Brad Forman, the BIS vice president in charge of my division. I knew there was no way Ellie was ever going to reclaim that account.

My professional success neither surprised nor thrilled me. It had come as easily as the medals I had won at track meets, as the Phi Beta Kappa key that my mother still insisted on polishing. And I wasn't smug—at least no one ever accused me of that. It was noted that I worked hard, said the right things at meetings, smiled at the right people. What did give me great pleasure each week was my paycheck. I loved being a high earner. I was the daughter of parents who had endured poverty and now everything I wanted was easily affordable.

I had a jazzy one-bedroom apartment on the Upper East Side and an easy friendship with Lila and Fay, two aspiring actresses from New Orleans who shared an illegal studio sublet down the hall—

and Melanie's flower shop, which had become a drop-in place for college friends, was only a few blocks away.

Lila and Fay, both very thin and very blond, dashed about town, waitressing between auditions and acting lessons, entertaining at kids' parties and earning a couple of extra dollars walking Thimble, the miniature white poodle that belonged to the elderly widow who lived in the penthouse. I had noticed, with some amusement, that the white curls that clustered on her head exactly matched Thimble's and that she matched the satin ribbons on Thimble's collar to her own pastel cloches.

I also had a boyfriend named Phil Gold who was tall and dark haired, large featured and flat assed, addicted to tennis and regular workouts at the health club. Phil took me out to dinner three times a week to restaurants where the headwaiters knew our names and told us confidingly what was really good that night. He always had tickets to the top shows two weeks before they opened. He was a stock analyst for an investment-banking firm and he had graduated from Dartmouth with Melanie's brother, Warren, which is how I met him. He came to the party Melanie gave to celebrate the opening of her flower shop and since he was the tallest man there and I was the tallest gal we smiled at each other over the heads of the other guests. Minutes later we were together at the punch bowl and he offered me a rose-gold gladiola.

"It matches your hair," he said and I smiled although I did wonder if he had thought to pay Melanie for the flower. Not that it would have bothered Melanie that night. She was too busy dashing through the shop in a pink leather minidress that, oddly enough, did not clash with her magenta hair, hugging her friends and adjusting the garlands of baby orchids that dangled from the fixtures, her laughter trilling above the soft music and murmuring voices.

Phil and I left together, had the first of many dinners that we would share over the years, found out that we were both into running, classical guitar and sunsets. It took us several more dates to discover that we were both the children of Holocaust survivors and after that we never spoke of it again. There would not have been much to say. My parents never talked about their experiences during the war and probably Phil's didn't, either. Of course, we might have talked about their silences, but it was easier to focus on the play we had seen, the new film that was a must, the vagaries of our friends, the stock market (which dominated Phil's life and vaguely interested me) and the pros and cons of the Fire Island beach houses we took shares in for three consecutive summers. I suppose that eventually we would have gotten around to talking about engagement rings and weddings. I remember that he did once discuss a wedding in a Stonington vineyard that he thought was really classy. *Classy* was a word he used a lot. But we were careful to keep our boundaries defined. We made no demands and scrupulously respected each other's independence. We were, we told each other in congratulatory tones, a thoroughly modern match.

Phil only met my parents a few times, although almost every Sunday I rented a car and drove out to the retirement community in Suffolk County where they had been living since I finished college. My father had closed his business, retaining only the first buttonhole machine he had ever purchased. They kept it in the bedroom and my mother fashioned a chintz cover for it that matched their bedspread and draperies.

Those Sunday visits pretty much followed the pattern of my childhood. Visiting relatives—like Cousin Morrie the importer-exporter who now leaned heavily on a cane, or Mendy, the dentist who still opened his office twice a week for the elderly patients who feared to reveal their ground-down teeth to youthful strangers—marveled at my success. They told me how pretty I was, how clever, and asked jokingly when I would marry. "A princess needs a prince," Mendy's wife, Selma, said and I smiled. Once again I dominated the orbit of their affections.

My mother was much diminished by age, her skin waxen white,

her hands gnarled and twisted by arthritis. She worried that I was too thin, too pale—even when my skin was burnished by the Caribbean sun after a week-long company junket.

My father asked about my work and dutifully I showed him storyboards for campaigns in progress, news releases I had written, even the occasional memo of commendation. He read them with the same rapt attention he had once devoted to my book reports, and handed them back to me with great care. I replaced them in my briefcase with equal care. They were, after all, my weekly offerings on the high altar of parental affection.

Each week our conversations were the same.

"So you're doing well. They like you?"

"I'm doing fine. They love me." I would pat his hand and please my mother by eating everything she set before me, always vaguely worried because she seemed to eat nothing at all.

Once I brought Lila and Fay with me and my two blond southern friends watched our little family as though they were at the theater engrossed in an ethnic drama. Lila took a picture of my father seated beside me on the sofa, turning the pages of a proposal I had written. He turned the pages with one hand and rested the other hand on my head. Because I was taller than he was, he had to arch upward against the cushion, an awkward and endearing posture, but it would not have occurred to him to shift position. I warranted his discomfort. In the background my mother, wearing a flowered cotton dress that hung too loosely, balanced a plate and smiled shyly at my friends.

"I never saw anyone get as much love as they give you," Lila said, not even bothering to mask her envy. She had been raised as a foster child, shunted from home to home in a New Orleans parish. Her parents were alive, but they lived down in the bayous and now and again sent her an incoherent letter, always with postage due. Clearly, Lila had never been at the epicenter of anyone's life.

"I know. I'm lucky," I said truthfully.

On those Sundays I appreciated their love and my centricity
in their lives as I never had during my childhood and adolescence.
Driving away, I would watch them in my rearview mirror as they
stood side by side, my little mother in her neatly ironed, ill-fit-
ting cotton housedresses and my gaunt, weary father in his baggy
trousers and oversize cardigans. They waited patiently until my
car disappeared around the bend in the road, drinking in that last
glimpse of me as they had always drunk in every aspect of my
existence.

When I ate dinner with Phil on Sunday nights, I toyed with my
food and imagined my mother urging me to eat, coaxing me to finish my salad. Phil did not notice what I left on my plate, was indifferent when the waiter carried away almost a full serving of arugula
and yellow peppers. He was my lover, not my monitor—as, of
course, he should have been.

We were both in the habit of taking work home and we would
sit in the deep armchairs in my living room, pecking away at our
laptops. Phil worked with great absorption while I was alternately
amused or irritated by the projects at hand. His seriousness, his
concentration, annoyed me. Once, on a wintry afternoon, I clicked
my laptop shut and thrust my files out of the way. I went to the
window and watched as Lila, wearing a bright green parka and yellow Lycra tights, walked Thimble across the street. I tapped lightly
on the pane, but I knew, of course, that she could not hear me. Phil
looked up.

"Something wrong?" he asked. The pleasantness of his tone
shamed me. It seemed to me that the darkness of my sudden and
inexplicable mood hung like a cloud over the pleasant room, dimming the soft lamplight, dulling the music that wafted out of the
CD player. It was Mahler, I think. *The Song of the Earth.*

"I don't know. It's just that it all seems so stupid to me. This
whole damn business. Hours and hours of work for a two-minute
sound bite—maybe. Or maybe the release will make it into some

syndicated column so that someone can dump their coffee grounds onto it. And what do I have to show for all these hours?"

Carefully, he closed his own laptop, slipped it into its case. He had been working all that long day on an analysis of a stock option offered by a company that, within another month, would slither off every screen into the obscurity of a well-planned bankruptcy.

"Well, we do have our paychecks to show for it," he said and he poured each of us a glass of white wine.

He too loved payday. We had that in common. He had confided to me, with boyish embarrassment, how he loved holding the crisp check in his hand, the small surge of pride he felt when he deposited it. Once he had asked the teller to cash it for him in singles and he had carried the small mountain of bills home and spread it across his bed, even tossing some of it into the air and laughing as it drifted down. He offered an apology for such odd delight, relying on my understanding.

His parents had been poor. Only a generous scholarship and participation in a work-study program made it possible for him to go to Dartmouth and then to Columbia for an MBA. His father owned a small newsstand and Phil had watched each evening as he sat at the kitchen table and separated the coins into piles—nickels, dimes, quarters, pennies. He wrapped them in paper rollers for deposit in the bank. His gnarled fingers were soot stained with the filth of the coins, his palms blackened by the newsprint. Phil never kept change. Any coins he received he dropped into the paper coffee cup of the first homeless person he passed.

"I want to have more to show for my work than a paycheck," I said.

I sipped my wine and remembered the piles of garments on the long wooden worktables in my father's factory. I had loved sliding my fingers across the neat buttonholes, the thrill of responsibility as I buttoned each garment, readying a lot for delivery. Oh, what useful work my father had done. Dressed in his overcoat, he swept the floor of the loft each evening and studied the long empty room with worried satisfaction. I myself dashed out of BIS at the end of the day, never looking back.

I chided myself for stupidity, irrationality. My job was great, I assured myself, my life terrific. Phil and I both earned gloriously and spent gloriously——ski vacations in the winter, beach-house shares in the summer. My work was reasonably creative, my colleagues pleasant, the perks bordered on fantastic. I even enjoyed the moments of crisis, mostly because I knew the crisis to be transitory and because I had learned to cope so well. I knew how to trace a storyboard lost in transit, how to reschedule when a client spot was preempted by real news, how to dash off a swift release to fill a last-minute hole in a professional journal. In moments of stress I acted as concerned as everyone else——concern and sincerity were greatly valued at BIS——but I knew that basically I didn't give a damn.

I made fun of office emergencies as Lila groomed Lucky, the golden retriever owned by a lawyer and her ophthalmologist husband who lived across the street.

"Major distress. The *Times Circuits* page didn't run our 'Game Girl' story. The whole office is in sackcloth. The flag at corporate headquarters is hanging at half mast. Brad didn't open his office door all day." I laughed, although at the office I had maintained a pained expression and had even knocked tentatively at Brad's door and in my most sympathetic tone had asked if there was anything I could do.

"Alas, cruel world," Lila said. I had gotten her some temp work at BIS and after a week of answering the phone and typing up presentations she had sauntered into my office one day and asked, in her languid southern drawl, "This here company, Rochelle baby, do they actually make anything happen?" Her eyelids, beneath their heavy coating of violet shadow and pressed powder (she had an audition that afternoon), had drooped as I explained the relationship between public relations, name recognition and sales. "It's all bull-shit, ain't it?" she said when I had finished and we had both shrugged our shoulders and laughed.

Melanie smiled when I visited the flower shop and imitated a client who had asked me in all seriousness if I could arrange a photo op for him with the President.

"What did you say?" Deftly she added a white camellia to the wreath she was weaving. She had just discovered that funeral flowers were a big moneymaker.

"I said that I'd check it out with my Washington connections." I snipped off a flower and sniffed it. It had no aroma. "How long do these things last?" I asked.

"There's a preservative spray. Hey, Rochelle, did you ever see anyone at a funeral actually stop to smell the flowers?"

Melanie loved her shop, loved thinking up new ideas, new arrangements. Baskets of rosebuds to celebrate a baby's birth, photo frames rooted in the earth of flowering plants for doting grandmothers. She had also placed a small red rail outside the door so that her customers had a place to loop their dog's leashes while they shopped. Dog lovers, she told me, bought a lot of flowers. Fay, who often left Thimble outside Melanie's shop, did not buy any flowers. Instead, she went to the coffee shop on the corner, ordered a cappuccino and read *Variety,* twirling a strand of her long milk-white hair around her finger while the poodle entangled itself in its narrow red leather leash.

But of course, I did not mock my job when I visited my parents. My professional success sustained them, validated their suffering and their sacrifices. They asked hesitantly about Phil, but they never pressured me, never mentioned marriage. Their lives had taught them never to up the ante, to be resolutely grateful for what was given to them. I was happy. I was doing well. All right. Enough. They dared not ask for more.

I loved them for their forbearance and rewarded them with

tales of my exorbitant bonus, a substantial raise, a working trip to the Bahamas. BIS had just landed a huge account and there was a good possibility I'd be asked to manage it. Brad had intimated as much over a long lunch at the Brasserie. "You're a real asset to the company, Rochelle," he had said. "You don't push too much and yet you always get the job done." I didn't tell him that I didn't push too much because I didn't care enough.

"The manager of such a big account."

They spoke in unison. My father beamed. My mother clapped and I struggled to think of something else to report that would please them, that would cause my father to nod in amazement, my mother to clap even harder.

I kept my doubts about my career at a low pitch when I was with Phil. He was proud of my achievements, proud to drape his arm about my shoulders when his company gave a dinner, held a party. His fingers toyed with the silk collar of my tunic as he introduced me to his colleagues, chronicling my credentials.

"Rochelle is a mover and shaker at BIS—their youngest account manager. How many people on your team, honey?"

I would smile, knowing it was unnecessary to answer a question like that. By then I had learned that no one really cared. It was easier to reach for a glass of wine and toss my head back so that my auburn hair caped my back, a gesture Lila had taught me.

Perhaps my life, so reasonably lived, so pleasant and comfortable, troubled only by my own wry cynicism and my infrequent and inexplicable dark moods, might have continued on its relatively placid course, if not for the phone call that Thursday morning.

"A Dr. Manganaro on three," Cheryl, my admin assistant said.

"Who is he? I can't talk now." I was irritable. I had two ad campaigns to review and a conference to prepare for and I didn't know any Dr. Manganaro.

"He's from the Harlen Hospital, he says." It was Cheryl's turn to be irritated. She didn't want to screen my calls. She wanted to be me.

I reached for the phone. Harlen was the hospital my father had checked himself into the previous week. *Just some tests, he had said. Routine. Overnight I'll stay. Maybe two nights. It's nothing.* I had gone to Chicago for a meeting and he was in and out of the hospital before I returned. When I called he assured me that everything was fine. *These doctors. For everything they want a test. That's how they make their money. These doctors.*

"Dr. Manganaro, this is Rochelle Weiss."

"Miss Weiss, I'm glad I got through to you. I have a meeting set up with your parents next week. I think it would be helpful if you came with them."

"Do they know you called me?"

"No. And of course my intervention is somewhat unorthodox, but they seemed reluctant to discuss the situation with you, to upset you."

That, of course, was the understatement of the year. My parents would have elected to be burned at the stake if it meant sparing me any distress.

"Is everything all right?" I asked, although I knew the answer. This doctor would not opt for "unorthodox intervention" if everything was all right.

"There are diff-i-cul-ties." He pronounced each syllable very slowly. It was a word, I supposed, that he often used. "I think it important that we meet."

"I can be at your office this afternoon." I knew that I could not bear to wait a week and I knew that I wanted to see him alone. I glanced at my watch. There were appointments to be canceled, a car to rent. Phil had theater thickets for that evening. Could I be back in time? My palms were damp, my throat constricted. I feared that the phone would slip out of my grasp.

"I suppose I can fit you in." I heard the reluctance in his voice, but he was a kind man. He gave me the address, offered directions, warned me of a speed trap at a particular junction—an odd caution, I thought, all things considered.

Three hours later I sat opposite him in an office furnished in pale gold wood with drapes of a geometric design drawn against encroaching sunlight. I noticed that the hems of the drapes were frayed and this annoyed me. I did not want my parents to see a doctor who maintained a shabby office. He sat slouched in his chair, his sad gray eyes trapped behind very thick rimless glasses, thin strands of silver hair pressed against his pale skull. His gray suit was well cut, although the cuffs of the jacket were too short and revealed thick red wrists. He offered me coffee, which I declined. He fingered the folders on his desk. *LENA WEISS. ISAAC WEISS.* He did not open them. He cleared his throat but, still, when he spoke his voice was hoarse.

"I'll come right to the point," he said. "Your father has pancreatic cancer. It's a fast cancer, even at his age. He'll probably go before your mother."

"My mother?" His words shocked me.

He stared at me in surprise.

"Your mother has non-Hodgkins lymphoma. You didn't know?"

I heard the accusation in his question. How could I not have known? How could they not have told me? I could not explain to him how they had cushioned me always with their love, how they had bought me nectarines out of season, willed me to happiness.

"I thought—I knew she had tests last year—she said it was because she was anemic. That was why she was so thin, so tired. The doctors said she needed more iron. That was what she told me."

And I had believed her because I wanted to believe her. I bought her a large bottle of ferrous sulphate pills, shaped like ruby-colored bullets. I imagined them exploding within her frail body, swimming into her bloodstream, invigorating it. I smiled bitterly at my naiveté. Non-Hodgkins lymphoma. A college friend had died of it as had poor retarded Aaron, his vacant eyes quite suddenly filled with a pain he could not comprehend. *Lymphoma*. And I had offered her pills the color of Christmas candy.

"What do we do now?" I asked.

Dr. Manganaro stood and paced briefly. His socks were also gray, his shoes charcoal-colored loafers with rubber soles. He dressed for obscurity, trod lightly, spoke softly. He knew what to tell me. He had given these instructions so often before, would offer them so often again.

A program would have to be put into place immediately for my father. Chemo. Radiation. Any shrinkage of the carcinoma would buy him more time, relieve his distress. There would probably be daily trips to the hospital. And then, of course, pain monitoring. At the end. Someone always there, always with them.

He did not speak of my mother. We both silently acknowledged that when he died she would swiftly follow him.

"It's a demanding regimen," he said apologetically. "Do you have other siblings who might help?"

"I'm the only child. They married late. They were—they are—Holocaust survivors." I invited his pity. I wanted him to recognize the uniqueness of their tragedy. The pain of their youth should have guaranteed them an old age free of suffering. It was unfair, so unfair. I wanted to stamp my feet in fury.

"I can get you the names of some excellent caregivers. People who would stay with them, sleep in the apartment." He strained to be helpful, but I saw him glance at his watch and then at the pictures of a bespectacled small boy and a thin-faced girl that stood on his desk in tacky gilt frames. He was in a hurry to get home to his children, to shed the gray uniform of his death-haunted professional life and dress in a kelly-green sweat suit, a bright red T-shirt.

"No," I said firmly.

Live-in help was not an option. I could not bear the thought of a stranger living in my parents' neat little retirement apartment, touching their things, perhaps moving the crocheted white circlets so precisely centered on the cushions of the textured gold easy chair, the newly reupholstered peacock-blue sofa. My mother had never allowed anyone to help in her kitchen. There was always the danger that they might mix up her meat and dairy dishes, place cutlery in the wrong drawer, pots and pans in the wrong cupboard. She had never even had a cleaning woman to help her prepare for Passover. She guarded her table linens, her silver, her gilt-edged china with intense zeal, perhaps because for years she had not owned a single utensil, had spooned her food into pitted aluminum bowls, taking her ration from a communal trough.

And I knew that it would be difficult for my father to accept the care of an aide. He would not allow a stranger to touch his body, someone whose hands might reek of disinfectant, whose clothes might have an alien scent. He was excruciatingly sensitive to smells, leaving windows open even on wintry days, inviting fresh air to do battle with household odors. Proximity to strangers made him gag. More than once he had bolted from a crowded train or bus, repelled by the stench of sweat or even the not unpleasant aroma of cosmetics or perfume. That sensitivity, I had read somewhere, was peculiar to those who, during childhood, might have inhaled fecal stench and the malodor of decaying garbage. It was, of course, a description that fitted my father.

"I'll manage something," I assured the doctor.

"Yes. I'm sure you will. Give it some thought."

He escorted me to the door, shook my hand, but even as I walked down the path to my car, I knew that I did not have to give it any thought. My decision was made. It was I who would take care of my parents, I who would live in their apartment, wash their bodies, cook their meals, drive them back and forth to the hospital. How could I do otherwise? The ledger of their love would be balanced, the great debt of their devotion repaid.

I would take a leave from BIS or perhaps arrange to work from home. That night I drafted a memo to Brad. My request seemed sensible and reasonable. I called Phil, but he was not at home. He had, of course, found someone else to use my theater ticket and I thought, resentfully, that it was easy enough for another person to slip into my niche. I hung up just as Lila knocked at my door. She was scheduled to walk Thimble. Did I feel like joining her?

"Sure," I said, but because the evening was cool and Lila had forgotten her sweater, it was I who held the slender red leather leash and started down the street. Thimble turned to look at me and I scooped her up and buried my face into her furry white head, my tears falling onto her floppy ears.

# CHAPTER
## TWO

Brad Forman did not think my request sensible and reasonable. My carefully worded memo reached him late Friday afternoon. On Monday morning he called and asked me to have lunch with him. It was not an invitation, I knew, but a command. His voice was grim and the restaurant he picked was Barbetta's, an expensive, dimly lit trattoria with recessed booths. It was not a place to see and be seen like the bright and buzzing Union Square Cafe or Shun Lee East, Brad's usual choices on more expansive days (and Phil's favorites as well, a not very mysterious coincidence). Barbetta's was a place where serious and often somber business could be conducted without fear of awkward interruptions.

On my way to the restaurant I stopped at a boutique and bought a copper-colored silk scarf that closely matched my hair, twisted that day into the sleek chignon that Phil hated but Brad favored. It fell in loose folds over my severe black turtleneck dress and I fingered it as I walked, taking comfort from its cool, light-as-air smoothness.

I allowed it to brush my wrist as I slid into a red leather booth and smiled brightly at Brad. He nodded, but did not smile back. Instead he studied the oversize menu with great concentration, as though it were an intricately detailed campaign proposal, and then ordered what he always ordered—a cup of minestrone and a chef's salad.

"I'll have the same," I told the grave-eyed waiter. "And a glass of white wine," I added too quickly. I needed the wine, I knew, to keep my smile fixed firmly on my face. Brad had told me more than once how much he liked my smile, how terrific it was that I could remain so upbeat even in moments of professional crisis. Clients felt relieved and reassured when I smiled, he had said, and I trained that smile on him now so that he too might feel relieved and reassured. His expression did soften and for the first time he looked directly at me.

"I want to tell you how sorry I am about your parents. It's a tough hit. I wanted to send them flowers or a fruit basket or something like that, but my assistant didn't have their address."

"Oh, that's all right," I said hastily. "Please don't send them anything."

I imagined their bewilderment when the huge basket of flowers or the wicker hamper filled with out-of-season fruits, cheeses they had never heard of and packets of gourmet cookies and crackers wrapped in bright crackling cellophane arrived and overwhelmed their small orderly apartment. My mother considered the purchase of fresh flowers a waste of money and instead patiently rubbed oil on the misshapen leaves of her ancient rubber plants, which, as she pointed out, did not litter her carpet with fallen petals. Food was a serious matter to both of them, not a frivolous gift to be encased in a gleaming metallic-paper tent.

"But I would like to do something," he said. "Any suggestions?"

Our soup arrived and we ate for a few minutes in silence. He had given me my cue. The next line, we both knew, was mine and

I rehearsed it mentally before delivering it more softly than I had intended.

"What you could do, what BIS could do, would be to give me a leave for a few months. I didn't mention it in my memo, I didn't want to go into detail, but it would, of course, be a leave without pay. If you wanted me to work at home I could do it on a freelance basis at an hourly rate."

"Rochelle, this isn't a question of money." Brad looked vaguely offended as though my reference to pay was crude, inappropriate. Surely, his reproving glance seemed to say, he and I were above such coarse considerations. "It's about priorities." He broke off a piece of bread and smiled, as though pleased to have happened on that word. "I would like to think that you have your priorities in order."

"I think I do," I said evenly and I allowed my smile to fade even though I had emptied the glass of wine the attentive waiter was scurrying over to refill.

"I'm not sure that you do. Look, you're asking for this leave just when we've landed the Longauer account. It's the biggest baby we've ever reeled in and you know how important it is to the firm. And when I say the firm I mean everyone—the partners, the senior managers, creative staff, support staff, every assistant, every messenger."

He paused and I nodded. This was a theme that Brad, with his lean and sensitive face, his cultivated intensity, emphasized at every staff meeting, every office gathering.

"We are more than fellow workers and colleagues," he would say, smiling benignly. "We're family, each of us responsible for the others. We're a caring community—we're connected."

I acknowledged that he was not far wrong, but BIS was not unique in that. Most of my friends felt more involved with their colleagues at work than with their own families. Some had parents in distant cities and they traveled home wearily and reluctantly during the holiday season, carrying gifts purchased too hastily and without enthusiasm. Lila was uncertain of her parents' address and Melanie did not speak to her father. There were those who had a father in one state and a mother in another; they spoke of sisters and brothers with whom they had quarreled with inexplicable bitterness. Family homes had been sold and aging parents wore pastel pantsuits and lived in cleverly designed retirement villages in Florida and Arizona where there was little room for a visiting adult child.

Their own relationships were fragile. Few of my married friends had children; two or three years into their marriages they spoke darkly of trial separations and spent fifty-minute hours weeping on their therapists' couches. My single friends spoke of "significant others" with almost clinical detachment. The "other" said it all.

Our brightly lit offices replaced our vanished homes, teams of co-workers became families, fax machines and computers were an electronic hearth and the coffee machine and microwave a substitute for the familial kitchen, an island of intimacy where confidences could be exchanged.

We watched reruns of *The Mary Tyler Moore Show* and, without embarrassment, identified with that mythical workplace family— accepting Ed Asner as the cynical patriarch, Betty White as the ditzy mother and Mary as the perky all-American girl, always heading for a fall. We understood those falls all too well and we knew too that when real families disappear into the mists of dysfunction and distance, the families of "must see" TV take on a virtual reality. Everyone I knew, even Phil, who prided himself on his independence, wanted to be a member of Jerry Seinfeld's family of friends. We stayed up too late when *Nick at Nite* featured *Cheers* because we longed to escape our own urban anonymity and be in a place where everyone knew our name.

At our offices we reconfigured into new adopted families and often we reinvented ourselves. When Brad spoke with such paternal concern of his BIS "kids" he achieved what his sexual proclivity denied him. He was gay; not flamboyant, but open about his life. His companion, Julian, a portly music editor and gourmet cook, accompanied him to the BIS annual Christmas bash. Their life together was very private and, in all probability, very solitary. But at BIS, Brad was the head of a large and noisy family, a proud parent who beamed at his children's achievements and urged them to care for each other as much as he and BIS cared for them.

My colleague, Suzanne, an only child herself and a single mother, brought her daughter, Cassie, to the office on her birthday and we, like doting aunts and uncles, converged upon the little girl, sang "Happy Birthday" and bombarded her with clever gifts. Cassie and Suzanne were not alone. They had us.

We circulated get-well cards when a receptionist or assistant was ill, flocked to the hospital when Brad broke his leg. Experience and affection bonded us and now I, who had basked in the radiance of Brad's approval and been singled out for an office with a window (more prized than any coat of many colors), was about to betray that bond by opting for a leave and abandoning my company, my family, at a moment of crisis.

The Longauer firm was large and successful, slated to grow even larger and more successful. Its billing potential was enormous enough to double the yearly profits of BIS, profits that would be shared with the entire staff in accordance with the generous program that was already in place. Jeff, who ran the copy room, could buy a condo in Florida for his aged, ailing parents. Suzanne could write a check for Cassie's tuition without juggling her bills. Matt, our messenger, would have enough to replace the down jackets he routinely lost each winter month.

"You do understand what the success of the Longauer account will mean to everyone?" Brad asked.

"Of course, I understand that," I said. "But I don't think my taking time off exactly puts the account in jeopardy. I can work at home on the campaign and someone else can handle the client contact. Suzanne or Lloyd. They're both good. Or maybe you can bring Ellie in." My own daring surprised me. Ellie was my predecessor who, in her own time, had betrayed the BIS family by having the temerity to have a nervous breakdown in the middle of a spring campaign.

"The management at Longauer, in fact Eddie Longauer himself, was particularly excited about having you on board. They've been tracking you and you're one of the reasons they came to us. They saw that profile on your public service campaigns in *Computer Age* and that hooked them. Rochelle, I'm seriously concerned that if you leave BIS we may lose the account." He set his knife and fork down as though the very utterance of those words made it impossible for him to finish his meal. His throat constricted in horror at the thought. He would choke on the garlic-soaked greens.

"But I'm not leaving BIS," I protested. "I never even mentioned the word. Look, maybe I can work something out. Maybe I can arrange to come in half time—two, maybe three days a week. I think I could manage that."

My mind raced furiously as I plotted a schedule. I would have to get a car—I would have to get one in any case to drive my father to his treatments—I could get up at dawn on the days I spent in New York, hiring one of Dr. Manganaro's trained caregivers to take over while I was gone. It would be tough, but I could do it and it would be a relief to have some money coming in. I had looked at my bank account the previous evening and the balance shocked me. It was amazing how little could be saved from a six-figure income when a six-figure life was lived. I would have liked to talk to Phil about managing my money better, something I would do when he returned from his business trip. He had left a message on my machine telling me that he would be away for a couple of days and asking me to try to switch two sets of theater tickets and cancel our Saturday-night dinner reservations. "I love you," he had added, but he had not asked about my parents, an omission that wounded but did not surprise me.

"Part-time. Three days a week." Brad repeated my words through puckered lips, as though they had turned sour in his mouth. "Rochelle, think of BIS. You really must prioritize." He loved that word and would not let it go. I imagined it appearing on my evaluation. *Rochelle Weiss is an excellent and creative account manager, but she is unable to prioritize.* Suddenly it angered me and I leaned across the table, clutching a heel of the still-warm Italian bread and crushing it into a hillock of snowy crumbs.

"I have my priorities in order. I am the only daughter of two old people who have been through hell. They were lucky. They came to this country and managed to build a new life. And I was more than lucky because they loved me and cared for me every single day of my life without ever asking for anything in return." I paused and saw that his gray eyes were marble hard, his lips compressed. He understood that I was really saying that I had a flesh-and-blood family of my own, that I didn't need the invented family ties of BIS or the parental authority he would arrogate on my behalf.

"And now they are sick and they are going to die. Maybe this month, maybe next month, maybe not until the winter. But no matter when, I want to take care of them. They are my priority, Brad. And yes, I think that they're more important than BIS and the Longauer account. Which is not to say that I don't care about BIS, that I won't do a good job for Longauer. If you want me to I'll call Eddie Longauer myself and explain my situation. I'll do whatever you want, but I must have this time with my parents." I kept my voice low but firm. My cheeks were flushed, but I took another sip of wine and forced myself to smile and lower my eyes.

"Let me think about it," Brad said. "In any case it's a board decision and the board doesn't meet until Thursday. Let's see what we can work out."

I was relieved because he began eating his salad again, chewing carefully and deliberately. We did not speak of my parents. Over cappuccino he told me that he and Julian were planning to take a long vacation in Tuscany. Julian had an idea for a cookbook that could be copied onto discs and given to BIS clients as a Christmas gift.

"I don't think any of our clients know how to turn on their restaurant quality ovens," I said.

"And I'm not sure any of them can read," Brad added and we both laughed. Ridiculing our clients was a small professional luxury. Brad ordered chocolate liqueurs for both of us and we walked back to the office very slowly, even stopping briefly at the boutique where I had bought my copper scarf, so that Brad could pick up an ascot for Julian.

"How did it go?" Lila asked me that evening as we circled the block with Thimble and Lucky in tow.

"Okay, I think. In the end I got good vibes from him. I'm pretty sure he'll agree to some part-time arrangement."

I spoke with certainty. I had, after all, marched through life getting my own way. Brad would agree because I was right and because I had earned his agreement. I was not asking for anything that was not due me.

I spent the rest of the week researching the Longauer account and chronicling the history of the company. It had begun in Eddie Longauer's MIT dorm room and rocketed into a multi-million-dollar international with his development of a software program that could wipe out bugs in a variety of programs. Eddie Longauer had never finished his degree. "What would be the point?" he had asked in an interview.

Instead, he had traded in his bottle-thick black-framed glasses for contact lenses, adopted a wardrobe of pastel-colored silk shirts and loose moleskin slacks, and fashioned his long unkempt hair into a saurian cap that hugged his rather small head. His company was now housed in a Hoboken complex where he developed new projects that sent the industry reeling.

Marketing was not his problem. Customers flooded him with faxes and his order department worked overtime. Eddie did not need BIS to improve his sales. He needed us to make him feel admired and loved. The sleeves of his silk shirts covered the skinny arms of a boy who had been the high-school nerd and it had been noted that he often riffled through his alligator wallet, counting the wad of bills and snapping his credit cards as though to assure himself that he had left the poverty of his childhood far behind. I thought of Phil lying on his bed tossing dollar bills into the air and I knew that I understood Eddie Longauer.

"Any ideas on the Longauer account?" Suzanne asked me late on Wednesday afternoon. She leaned over my desk, holding her happy-face coffee mug, appealingly waiflike in the gauzy light-blue dress that matched her pale-lashed blue eyes, sucking on a strand of black hair.

I sympathized with Suzanne. Her husband had walked out on her during the eighth month of her pregnancy, but she had forged ahead—slowly rising in the company, dealing with boring minor accounts, coming in early and working late. But I didn't trust her. I had seen her eyes narrow when I returned from a three-day Caribbean junket with a major client, when Brad gave me an office with a window. Her envy exhausted me, made me wary.

"I'm working on it," I said.

My phone rang just then and I listened as Dr. Manganaro outlined the program he had scheduled for my father's radiation and chemo treatments. The first appointment was in a week's time. Was I sure I could manage the driving and the home care?

"Of course," I assured him. "I'm trying to work something out with my office."

Suzanne wandered over to the window, that envied window, with its uninspiring view of slowly moving traffic.

"Thanks for everything, Dr. Manganaro." I hung up as a wave of grief washed over me. Briefly, I covered my eyes.

"Problems?" Suzanne asked.

"My parents. They have cancer. Both of them." I offered her my sorrow and invited her sympathy. I wanted her to understand that we were perhaps equally balanced on the seesaw of sadness and loss. She had her pain and I had mine.

"Oh, Rochelle, I'm so sorry."

"Thanks." I wanted her to leave so that I could either surrender to my grief or lose myself in my work, but she lingered on.

I sighed and picked up the Longauer file again. I had outlined a plan for inner-city scholarships to be endowed by the company, for internships to be awarded to minority kids. Eddie Longauer may not have finished his own degree, but he was an outspoken supporter of stay-in-school programs, crediting his shortened time at MIT as his inspiration. I could have him travel from school to school with follow-up appearances on talk shows. First, however, I needed a catchy title for the presentation. I stared at my computer keyboard and typed in "Longauer Leads" and then "Education: A Longauer Legacy."

Suzanne glanced at the screen.

"That's good," she said. She put a hand on my shoulder, sympathetic, protective. "What are you going to do about caring for your parents?"

I knew then that Brad had spoken to her.

"I'm going to be there for them, of course," I said. "If you can take care of Cassie, I can take care of my mother and father. I've spoken to Brad about flextime, about working from home."

"You'll never be able to do that with a client like Longauer. He's supposed to be really demanding—the 'I needed it yesterday' type-A personality. You'll have to be hands on. And Rochelle, I never took flextime to look after Cassie. I made child-care arrangements. I was here, no matter what."

"Suzanne, I appreciate your interest, but really, it's not your concern," I said in the flat monotone Melanie calls my "drop-dead" voice. "In any case it's up to Brad and the board when they meet tomorrow. They'll take a vote." The BIS directors prided themselves on their democratic and benevolent attitude toward employees, their carefully considered discussion of any extraordinary problem. But I did not consider my problem to be extraordinary. There was nothing extraordinary about a daughter wanting to care for her dying parents.

I reached for the phone and asked my assistant to connect me with Eddie Longauer. I did not look at Suzanne as she glided from the room.

"Good luck," she said at the door.

"Good luck comes with hard work," I replied coldly. "Haven't you noticed?"

She closed the door very softly behind her and it angered me that she did not slam it.

My assistant buzzed me. Eddie Longauer was not in his office. He would call back. I thought for a moment of how much time I spent playing telephone tag. High above the city, with fax machines running and printers regurgitating page after page, we played children's games.

I called Phil and got his voice mail. It wasn't that unusual for him to leave town without telling me. I occasionally did the same. We were both in high-pressure jobs and things came up suddenly. And we were, after all, strictly independent operators. He would be away for the rest of the week. His message offered a series of phone numbers in an area code I didn't recognize to be used in case of an emergency. I wondered how Phil would define an emergency. Perhaps a sudden sharp plummet in the NASDAQ, a margin call in a high-risk company. I knew that he would not see my parents' situation as an emergency and if I told him that I had awakened the past three nights in a cold sweat, my mouth dry and my heart hammering, he would say, "Come on, Rochelle, baby. Get a grip." I did not call the numbers he had left and when he called my apartment that night I kept the conversation light. He was, it turned out, in Vail, meeting with corporate investors who played tennis in the morning and talked venture-capital schemes in the afternoon. He missed me. The weather was terrific. There were predictions of early snow. We should make plans to get some skiing in.

"I'll think about it," I said and wondered if my parents would die before the winter snows began. The casualness of my thought frightened me and I began to cry. "I miss you, too," I said and tasted a hot salt tear on my tongue. But I didn't miss him. I just wanted someone to touch and someone who would hold me close and tell me that everything would be all right. Although it wouldn't be. I knew that.

I slept that night curled into a fetal position and dreamed that I was in our Queens kitchen. My mother was broiling liver and my father was listening to the radio. In my dream they were both very young and their feet were bare, their toenails strangely long.

Thursday morning Eddie Longauer called. He wanted to meet with me. I called Brad and told him that I was going out to Hoboken. As I left the office I saw members of the BIS board file into the conference room. Brad, in a new khaki suit that he wore with a light green shirt and dark green tie, kissed my cheek as I walked by.

"Good luck with Longauer," he said.

"Oh, I think I've got some ideas that will turn him on." I smiled my famous confident upbeat smile. "Have you got a minute to look at them?"

"No time today. Big issues to discuss. Big decisions to make." He smiled at me and I felt a surge of relief. Everything would work out. He would go to bat for me, arrange for a part-time schedule. My words to Suzanne had been prescient. The board would understand my value to them. Eddie Longauer had asked for me specifically, after all.

Eddie Longauer had converted the top floor of his Hoboken factory into a glass-enclosed penthouse that overlooked the faded red brick chimneys of the adjoining buildings. Thin wisps of smoke drifted skyward and factory workers paused briefly to stare out of windows encased in rusting mesh netting. In contrast, Eddie's office was brightly lit, with halogen lamps that trained pools of light onto his black malacca desk and the black leather chairs and sofa that comprised what upscale decorators called "the conference corner." Abstract paintings in recessed black lacquered frames hung on the stark white walls, and when I walked across the room the sand-colored woven carpet that covered the polished wooden floor was soft beneath my feet.

Except for a telephone with an intricate control panel, the desk was bare, and then I glanced across the room and saw a battered old maple desk with an unmatched ladder-back chair, weighed down by a state-of-the-art PC and littered with printouts. I understood that it was at that desk that Eddie Longauer did his work. It was his good-luck station and it was more than probable that on its scarred and ink-stained surface, he had developed the computer chip that had brought him fame and fortune. It commanded his loyalty. He would not walk away from an island of familiarity, not even after he had landed on a mainland of glitz.

It occurred to me that the desk could be the focus of a human-interest story and I imagined a photographic spread with Eddie working at his computer, shifting the light of his gooseNecked student lamp, with the rest of that sleekly designed room shrouded in shadows. Old furniture symbolized old values—hard work, tenacity, fidelity.

Eddie rose to greet me. Perched on black platform shoes of soft leather, he moved awkwardly, and at that moment I forgot that he was the biggest client BIS had ever landed and that my own professional future was in his hands. I just wanted to reassure him, to tell him that it was all right to be short—that he didn't need those stupid shoes—that he would probably look better in horn-rimmed glasses than the contact lenses that made his eyes water and caused him to blink nervously.

"Hey, Rochelle Weiss," he said. "I've heard a lot about you. We've been following your stuff and it's terrific the way you get your clients on the map."

"Well, you're already on the map, Mr. Longauer." I smiled my client smile and he smiled back, a shy parting of his lips that revealed the brightest white caps I had ever seen.

"Eddie. Call me Eddie," he said. "Let's see what you've got for me."

"Don't you want your PR person in on this?" I asked. Most of our clients had an in-house public relations director with whom we worked.

"I'm the PR person," he replied. "Beam me up."

I was not surprised. Clearly, he was a hands-on CEO who controlled every aspect of his business and relied minimally on subordinates.

I flipped open my laptop and watched as he studied the screen that outlined my campaign to focus on inner-city schools with a program of scholarships and internships.

"It's an indirect approach," I explained. "It emphasizes the program rather than the product, but the message gets through. We're reinforcing the idea that the Longauer name is associated with good works, with community awareness. Of course, I have to flesh it out. I've just begun working on it."

"Good. Fine." He nodded approvingly. "We can sponsor contests, have the kids compete. Maybe a computer-game competition. And then we can do in-depth interviews with the winner. What motivates them, who inspires them."

"Meaning you?" I asked.

"Maybe me, maybe someone else. Einstein, Bill Gates. It won't matter. What will matter is that Longauer is sponsoring and underwriting the whole effort. Can you work that up?"

"Yes, of course."

"Good. Give me a call in a couple of weeks."

In a couple of weeks I'd be out in Suffolk County, driving my father to his chemo appointments, cooking and shopping and re-assuring my fragile, silver-haired mother that everything would be all right when we both knew that nothing would ever be all right again—my father would die and she would die and I would be alone. A wave of self-pity washed over me and, fighting it, I turned back to Eddie.

"Sure, we'll be in touch."

Time for the smile again, for the well-rehearsed tossing of my copper curls, for the handshake with the lingering pressure of my fingers intimating the promise of good times ahead.

It was too late to return to the office, but I imagined my report to Brad. "Eddie Longauer really loved my presentation. He defi-nitely wants to work with me." At BIS it was seldom an embarrass-ment to blow one's own horn.

Phil called that night. His deal was going well and he would probably sew it up over the weekend. The weather was terrific.

"How about hopping on a plane and joining me?" he asked, and I knew that even as we spoke his eye was fixed on the latest CNBC market update, although he'd had the sense to mute the volume. There was nothing strange about his suggestion. Over the years we had often made last-minute plans to meet in distant cities, jetting off to catch the Mardi Gras in New Orleans because Phil was meeting a client there, deciding on a Friday evening to catch an early-morning flight to Bermuda. Cruising through cloudless skies, nursing our drinks, soothed by the hum of the engine, we reveled in our independence, in the freedom that made it possible for us to pack a bag at a moment's notice. We celebrated our abil-ity to pay for whatever we wanted, to seize the day and fly through the night. We soared on the wings of privilege, fortune's favorites, destined from earliest childhood for the ease and success that had so cruelly been denied our parents.

"Not this weekend," I said with a regret I did not feel. I did not tell him that among the things I had to do was arrange for the purchase of a secondhand car, nor did I tell him that I likely couldn't afford the ticket to Vail.

"How are your folks?" he asked just before we hung up.

"Oh, you know," I answered, reasonably certain that he did not know and did not care. I tried to remember the last time Phil had mentioned his own parents and could only recall how he had told me that he hated to visit them because of the cooking odors in the hallways of their apartment building.

"I hate smells," he had said with sudden vehemence and I realized that he also hated the harshness of a raised voice, dirt beneath his fingernails, the touch of rough fabrics on his skin. He favored cashmere sweaters and silk scarves, shirts of combed cotton. Bottles of Drakkar stood on his Lucite bathroom shelf and on his rosewood bureau.

Lila knocked on my door then and I murmured a swift good-bye. She had a new dog with her in addition to Thimble and Lucky, a moist-eyed cocker spaniel named Goldilocks although he was clearly male.

"He belongs to this old couple, the Eliots," Lila told me as we followed a path into the park. "They're customers of Melanie's. He buys fresh flowers for her twice a week—a bouquet of lilacs and tulips in and out of season. I want to be an old woman just like her, with a silver-haired husband who brings me beautiful flowers for no reason at all. Anyway, I like working for them and I can use the extra cash. Faye and I want to go to the Cape for a couple of months. A lot of stock companies are starting up along the coast. No reason why we shouldn't be in on the action."

"That should be fun," I said wistfully and I wondered what it would be like to drift through life as Faye and Lila did, making do with very little money and a lot of hope, always waiting eagerly for the magic break—the voice-over or the bit part in a soap—

and shrugging off disappointment with the ease of those who have never really anticipated success.

Later, in Melanie's shop, we sat in her workroom over mugs of coffee, breathing in the moist fragrance of a new delivery of dark-hearted red roses. The ultraviolet lamps that Melanie trained on her plants bathed our upturned faces in a gentle lavender light. The three dogs who crouched at our feet breathed heavily, rhythmically as the long melancholy twilight deepened into the darkness of a starless night.

"Have you decided what you're going to do about your parents, Rochelle?" Melanie asked.

"I'm going to take care of them," I replied. Those words, spoken to Brad, to Suzanne, to Dr. Manganaro, had become my mantra and I was irritated that Melanie, who knew me so well, had even thought to ask such a question.

"What about your job?" Lila stroked Lucky's neck, put Thimble on her lap.

"I asked Brad for a leave or a freelance arrangement. Maybe flextime, which I think I can work out." How reasonable my request sounded, how plausible and responsible. A solution to my problem and a solution to Brad's concern about the Longauer account.

"What did he say?" Melanie toyed with a long-stemmed daisy, scattering the white teardrop-shaped petals across the scarred surface of her work table. She had met a new man, I realized, and she was playing our old game—will he call, won't he call, will he love me, won't he love me—her lips moving silently until she was left at last with a crumbling yellow center that she crushed between her fingers.

"He didn't say yes and he didn't say no. He talked a lot about how I had to get my priorities in order, but he softened. He said that he would bring it up at the board meeting, which was actually today, so I guess I'll get the news tomorrow. And he did go ahead and turn a big new account over to me. I met with the client today and he liked my idea, which means that BIS will probably want to keep me working with him."

"What if they turn you down?" Lila asked. She was used to rejection, conditioned to the brittle voices of unloving foster parents, the casual dismissals of agents and casting directors. "Don't call us, we'll call you."

I, on the other hand was the miracle child, born to parents who had survived against all odds. My life, like my birth, was charmed, the ease of my serial successes a magical gift to them, compensation for all that they had endured.

"They won't turn me down," I said. "I'm pretty sure I'm protected by the Family Leave Act if it comes to that. But I don't think it will. That's not what scares me."

I could not and would not speak of my fear of my parents' pain, of my terror at the thought of their losing each other, of my losing them.

"Good for you," Melanie said, handing me a small pink cactus plant that we both knew would please my mother. It was a hardy, diminutive survivor, barely filling its small ceramic pot, determined not to take up too much room in the world.

I arrived at BIS early the next morning, eager to tell Brad about my meeting with Eddie Longauer, to receive his congratulations and his assurance that the board had agreed to my request. The door to his office was open, which meant that he was in, but when I called his name he did not answer. I walked down the corridor to my own office and smiled at Frank Adams, the stocky security guard who was standing just outside my door. I liked Frank, who was always helpful and always grateful to me because I had arranged for his son to work for Melanie, delivering flowers. But that morning Frank did not smile back at me. Instead, he averted his eyes and his fleshy face crumpled into a mask of misery.

"I'm sorry, Rochelle," he said. "I'm supposed to go into your office with you." He kicked the carton at his feet. "I'm supposed to watch you pack up your personal stuff and make sure you don't touch the computer or the files. I don't want to do it—you know that—but it's my job. It's what they told me to do."

"I understand," I said softly, although my hands trembled and my heart plummeted. I dared not raise my voice, fearful of the rage it would betray.

Frank's directive was standard operating procedure at BIS. An employee who had been terminated might commit acts of vandalism and theft. Computer systems could be sabotaged, files stolen. Through the years I had seen Frank posted outside other offices, an unwilling and embarrassed sentinel. I had watched former colleagues slink out, their faces pale, their eyes dull with disbelief, hugging a carton similar to the one I now held, clutching the white envelope that contained their last paychecks and severance payments that were, invariably, generous.

BIS prided itself on its fairness. Even a rejecting parent was concerned with the survival of a child who had disappointed. BIS took its paternalism very seriously, within limits. Occasionally, I had stepped out of my office to extend a hand or offer an embrace to a colleague with whom I had shared coffee or lunch breaks, week after week, year after year, whose deepest professional and personal secrets I knew.

"Call me. Let's stay in touch. We'll get together." Lips brushed cheeks, arms rested lightly on shoulders.

We mouthed all the requisite words, but we knew that we would not call, we would not stay in touch, we would not get together.

Such farewell gestures met with Brad's disapproval. He perceived them as a betrayal of his judgment, a lack of loyalty. More recently, on such mornings, I had simply remained in my office with the door closed, until I heard the maintenance crew descend on the abandoned office or cubicle, urgently vacuuming away all signs of the vanished occupant.

I was not surprised then that every office door remained closed, that no one ventured out to the coffee or Xerox machines, that no one dared to step into my office to express regret or sympathy.

Numbly, as Frank watched, I placed my blue ceramic coffee mug, my plastic bag of emergency cosmetics, my black cardigan (worn at the elbows, but undeniably a double ply cashmere) and my sneakers into the carton. I removed the plaque that proclaimed me "Idea Gal of the Year" from the wall. It startled me that after five years and thousands of working hours at BIS, there were so few items that defined me. I would leave no mark, and within weeks, Rochelle Weiss, "BIS Idea Gal of the Year," would join those shadowy former employees whose names would eventually, and without regret, be deleted from the Christmas-card list.

My throat grew tight. I went to the window and looked down at the street below, where a man was running frantically to catch a bus. It pulled away just as he reached the corner and he slammed his fist against his attaché case, his face distorted with rage. His haste, his anger, saddened and mystified me. I watched men and women hurrying down the street, dashing out against the light. Some hugged phones to their ears and talked urgently as they walked. A dark-haired girl carrying an oversize black leather portfolio consulted her Filofax without breaking pace. Their world, which for so long had been my own, seemed strangely alien to me. I took my brave African violet plant from the windowsill and turned away.

"Please, Frank, don't look so grim," I told the security guard. "It's not the end of the world."

"I know," he said, but his voice was heavy with sorrow.

Frank, at least, would remember me, would think of me with affection. Perhaps I could turn to him for a reference. A vague hysteria gripped me and I struggled not to laugh aloud.

"Rochelle."

Brad Forman stood in the office doorway. His timing was perfect, I reflected. Experience had probably taught him how long it took an employee to recover from the shock of being fired and to regain enough composure to clear the office of personal possessions.

"Hi, Brad. Do you want this?"

I held the African violet out to him and wondered if he would wince. His expression did not alter. It remained serious, mingling polite regret and sympathy.

"No, thanks," he said. "Rochelle, you know this is not personal. The board was unanimous in its approval of your work, its estimation of your talent. You could have gone very far at BIS, but it's policy that account executives must be available full-time. We're a full-service organization."

"Oh. I thought we were a family. A concerned and caring family," I replied, keeping my voice even. "I suppose I overestimated BIS. I definitely overestimated you."

"There's no need for sarcasm." He held out a white envelope. "You'll see that we've been very generous."

I made no move to take it.

"You understand that I have a cause of action against BIS under the Family Leave Act," I said. "You do remember that seminar you sent me to when we were pitching the Women's League account? It was about protecting the rights of employees, particularly the rights of women, and the lawyer who spoke said that employees were entitled to leave if they had to care for a parent with a serious health problem. That's what I'm asking for—leave to care for two parents with serious health problems."

"It's the Family and Medical Leave Act," Brad corrected me smoothly. "And I did ask our attorney about it. There's a clause in that act—something about the necessity for that leave being foreseeable. You hardly gave us thirty days notice, Rochelle."

"How could I have? You know the situation." My cheeks were hot, my voice rising.

Brad closed the door.

"Our attorney said that we have no obligation to hold your position if doing so would cause us what the law calls 'grievous economic injury.' And I think we can safely argue that we would, in fact, suffer such injury. Of course, you're welcome to enter into a lawsuit—if you can afford it. And, if you can afford a reputation as a litigious employee, which I don't believe will aid your job search. I'm only thinking of your own good." Effortless sincerity oiled his voice.

He was right, of course. I reached out and took the envelope from his hand.

"Rochelle, I do hope your parents will be all right."

"They won't be."

"I'm sorry. Really. You'll keep in touch?" He was uneasy. He would have been more comfortable with tears or anger, but I offered him neither. I had spent to many years giving him what he wanted, pleasing him, flashing my too-bright smile.

He held out his hand and I shook it, but when I turned to Frank I kissed him on the cheek.

"Can I help you with your stuff? Maybe get you a taxi?" Frank asked.

I shook my head and left, hugging the carton that was surprisingly light. Suzanne hovered in the hallway holding her happy-face mug and a tulip plant that I knew would not get enough sunlight in my office windowsill. I thought to tell her so, but instead I waved and glided into the elevator.

I stepped out of the building into the harsh sunlight, uncertain for perhaps the first time in my life about where to go and what to do next. A taxi zoomed up and, like a sleepwalker, I stepped into it and gave the driver my address. My cell phone rang as he jerked forward and I plucked it from my bag. My mother's voice quivered.

"Ruchele, can you come—today—soon? Papa, he's not feeling so well."

"Mama, yes. I'll be there as soon as I can. I just have to rent a car. Don't worry, Mama. I'll take care of you." Her words become my own.

"I know."

Her voice was a whisper, a muted prayer of gratitude. I clutched the phoned and dialed Phil's voice mail, telling him not to call me, I would call him. And then I sank back against the cracked leather seat, my heart hammering, but my eyes dry. I did not look out the window, nor did I look back.

# CHAPTER THREE

My father did not die that day. He had experienced an angina attack, caused by stress.

"Cancer is a very stressful illness," Dr. Manganaro confided mournfully, and his words triggered that recurrent internal hysteria. Stress, I thought, was the least of the side effects of that thuggish disease, which clutched its victims between claws of unrelenting pain.

But it was that day that my new life began. I consigned my laptop to a corner of my bedroom closet in New York and arranged to have my calls forwarded to my parents' number. I changed into jeans and a T-shirt and swiftly packed a bag, remembering at the last minute to toss in my black TravelSmith dress. I might need it, I told myself, although I knew, in fact, that I would wear it to the funeral. I closed my mind against the image of myself in that very smart dress—ordered from a *New Yorker* advertisement in those vanished days when I ordered clothing as casually as I ordered pizzas—standing beside a freshly dug grave.

I arranged to rent a car and then called Phil who, miraculously, was at his desk.

"Hey, babe, what's going on?" he asked.

"I have to go out to Suffolk, to my folks' place. My dad is really sick so I'm driving out and staying there for a while. I thought that maybe you could come out one night this week." I doodled as I spoke to him, question marks intertwined with flowers, a heart perched on top of a telephone. I hated my hesitant tone. I wasn't sure why I couldn't tell him what had happened at BIS that morning, why I hid my fury and sorrow from him.

"You're going to stay there?" he asked.

"Yes. Phil, my dad is sick. Very sick." My heart hammered, but my voice was calm. I spoke slowly, as though explaining a complex situation to a small child. "I really want to see you," I added, softening my tone so that the words became a plea.

"I want to see you, too, but this is a crazy week. I'm juggling two deals. But let's see. How's Thursday? We can have dinner on Thursday night. I'll pick you up at your folks' place. There's this fish place I heard about in Bridgehampton——a really terrific menu. A guy in the office was telling me about bluefish he ate there—— cooked in lemongrass or something."

I wrote Phil's name on my pad, first in oversize cursive script, then in tiny block letters, crossing out each effort with angry slashes. Phil's discussion of restaurant food had always irritated me. I looked away when he pondered a menu and discussed the relative merits of seared tuna steak and salmon en croute with sneering waiters who shared inside information with him. *The salmon was not Alaskan but pond-grown, the tuna steaks had been frozen. But the red snapper was freshly caught and prepared with a wonderful sauce.*

The concentration on food that obsessed so many of my friends and colleagues, their long discussions of broccoli sprouts and wild-mushroom sauces, seemed to me to be the peak of narcissistic entitlement. They were convinced that their bodies were conditioned to ingest only the most expensive, the most unique, the most intricately prepared food.

"Do you have anything really good tonight, really special?" Phil would often ask a patient waiter and I knew that he was thinking, "If so I will order it because I am really good, really special."

"Bridgehampton sounds fine," I said. "I'll see you on Thursday night—around seven I guess." *If my father does not die before then,* I thought to add. *And if my mother's condition remains stable.* But of course I said nothing.

I wrote Phil's name again, this time in lowercase letters, and waited for him to say that he hoped that my father would be all right, that I should drive carefully, that he missed me. But his buzzer sounded and I heard his assistant remind him of a meeting in that peremptory tone peculiar to valued employees who address their superiors as they might speak to recalcitrant adolescents, forcefully persuading them to complete the tasks set before them.

"I really have to run, Rochelle," he said. "Hey, babe, you'll be okay, won't you?"

He was redeemed. I allowed his name in lowercase letters to remain intact on my pad. I even circled it with a heart.

"I'll be fine, Phil. See you on Thursday."

"Until soon," he said. Our loving words of leave-taking.

"Until soon," I replied.

I put my house plants and the few perishables in my refrigerator into a carton, the second carton I had packed that morning, and carried it down the hall to Lila and Fay's studio. They were not home, but I had a key. I put the food in their refrigerator, which smelled dankly of dog food, and arranged my plants on their windowsill, careful to place my office African violets in a particularly sunny spot. Like myself, it had been twice displaced that day. The phone rang and when I answered it, a woman introduced herself as a friend of the couple who owned Goldilocks, the golden-coated spaniel. She too had a dog and she wondered if I could somehow manage to fit her into my walking schedule. I took her number, explained that I was only a visitor who had picked up the phone by chance and assured her that either Lila or Fay would call her. As I hung up, I wondered absently how much my friends charged their clients, and I realized that it was not a question that would have occurred to me a week earlier.

I returned to my apartment, disconnected all the appliances as my parents always had when they left their apartment for a mere overnight journey. I was heiress to their anxieties, vigilant against unseen and perhaps unlikely dangers. I did not know the source of their fears, but that was irrelevant. I was enfolded in the mysterious shadow of a past they would not, could not, share with me. I locked the door behind me and wheeled my suitcase down the hall and out of the building to Melanie's flower shop.

The small store was very busy. The door chimes jangled as customer after customer entered, spurred by the brightness of the day and the hint of warmth in the air. Young east-side mothers with very clean hair, wearing very white sneakers and pastel sweat suits, examined pots of forced daffodils and paper-white narcissi as their toddlers prattled happily to each other. They would rush the season, these young women, so used to having their own way, so eager to speed away the hours, the days, the years, until they could reclaim their own lives. A white-haired woman in an elegant teal silk suit carefully selected irises. A tall, middle-aged man, his cheeks as pink as the bouquet of roses he had selected, thrust his credit card at Melanie.

"I'm in a hurry," he said.

Melanie nodded, caught sight of me and winked. I winked back. We both understood that he was buying the roses for his mistress, that he was perhaps speeding across town for a swift assignation, that he was petrified that one of his wife's friends would enter the shop. We knew that we could be wrong, that probably we were, but it was a game of speculation that had amused us since our college days, and more than once we had discovered that our imagined scenarios actually proved true.

A tall man whom I did not know stood beside Melanie at the cash register. Slightly balding, his avian features creased with amusement, he watched as she rang up the sale and flashed a brilliant smile at her departing customer. I took note of his tweed jacket, his pale blue shirt, his wool tie of a darker blue, his gray slacks. An academic, I decided. A historian. Maybe an anthropologist. He plucked a vagrant sprig of fern from her hair, carefully, tenderly. Good for Melanie. A gentle-fingered man.

"Rochelle, this is Leonard Quinton," she said, taking his large hand and placing it in mine, decreeing with this gesture that we should be friends. Melanie wore a bright yellow smock with flaring sleeves that contrasted happily with the dots of fuchsia rouge that dotted each cheek.

"Hi, Leonard," I said. "What do you teach?"

He and Melanie laughed in unison, an intimate companionable laughter. I thought of the smiles my parents exchanged when my father told my mother a story in Yiddish. How excluded I felt then, a small trespasser hovering on the edge of the closed circle of their togetherness. How excluded I felt now. I drew back, my smile fading, but Melanie reached for my hand.

"Rochelle, that's exactly what I asked Leonard the first time I saw him. What do you teach? It's weird that you should ask the same question," she explained.

"And she was standing right where you're standing now. I just came in to buy a crocus for my mother," Leonard added.

"A blue crocus. Actually, a violet one. Anyway, as it turned out, Leonard doesn't teach anything. He's an electrician."

"An electrical contractor," he corrected her patiently. "Don't call me if your toaster is broken. Call me if you want me to bid on the wiring in the apartment complex you're building. I keep trying to explain the difference to your friend here, but she refuses to understand."

"Oh, I'll explain it to her," I promised. "And I will call you when I build my first apartment complex. Which won't be any time soon because I'm a little short on capital. I got fired today."

"You didn't," Melanie said as she rang up two sales. "Those bastards."

A blond young mother had bought the narcissi and a not-so-young dark-haired one had bought the daffodils.

"Not your kids. I didn't mean your kids," she assured them and put a daisy into each child's hand.

"We know you didn't," they chorused. "See you soon, Mel." Skillfully, they maneuvered their Perego strollers through the door.

*Mel.* I had never called her Mel. It angered me that they should use a nickname for my best friend that was unfamiliar to me.

"They are real bastards," Melanie continued. "After all you did for BIS."

"Rotten bastards," I said and the words tasted good on my tongue. "I hate them. All of them. Especially Brad. And Suzanne."

"The bitch," Melanie agreed happily, although she knew Suzanne only through my tales of office politics.

"Anyway, that's not even the worst news of the day. My mom called. My dad is feeling lousy. I'm driving out there as soon as the rental agency delivers my car here."

"Oh, Rochelle, Shelley, I'm so sorry." Melanie hugged me, kissed my cheek. She smelled of all the flowers in her shop. "You talked to Phil?"

"Not about everything," I said cautiously, warningly.

Melanie nodded.

"I'll call you. Fay and Lila have the keys to my apartment if you want to use it." It would be convenient, I thought, for midafternoon trysts. Melanie grinned and I knew she was thinking the same thing.

"I have your folks' number. I'll call. Is that your car?"

A white Neon had pulled up in front of the shop, followed by a similar car. The driver beat down on the horn, producing urgent staccato blasts. He had no time to waste. He was a busy man in a busy city. It occurred to me that everyone in the city was busy except for me.

"It must be. I'm going to shop around for a secondhand deal when I get out there. This renting is too damn expensive."

Melanie stared at me in surprise. I had never before been concerned about money. But then never before had my parents been deathly ill and never before had I been without a job. Swiftly and without warning my life had veered off course, its conventional plotline abandoned. Here I stood, at the very beginning of a work week, wearing jeans and a pink T-shirt, about to drive out to Suffolk County in a car I wasn't sure I could afford to rent.

"Let me take your bag out," Leonard said.

He stowed it in the trunk as I dealt with the paperwork. I scanned the agreement and the rental fee, paid with my credit card and wondered if I had enough money in my account to cover the charges.

Melanie raced out of the shop with a pot of red tulips that she placed carefully on the floor of the back seat. She kissed me, her eyes bright with unshed tears. Leonard Quinton placed a comforting arm on her shoulder. I remembered the daisy petals Melanie had scattered across her worktable and hoped she had murmured "loves me" as the last one fluttered down.

"I'll be fine," I assured her and I almost believed it. Wasn't I fortune's favorite, conditioned for success?

I drove off, and when traffic ground to a halt, on the Long Island Expressway, I opened the white BIS envelope. Brad had not lied. BIS had been generous, very generous. My salary, vacation pay and sick leave had been factored into one check, with a month's salary added in lieu of notice. A second check represented a decent bonus. Conscience money, I decided. I felt no gratitude, only a sense of relief.

It was early afternoon when I reached my parents' apartment. My mother's eyes were red-rimmed and my father stood in the hallway, his arms fluttering in the sleeves of a plaid shirt suddenly grown oversize, his gray corduroy trousers falling too low over his shoes. Frail, and angry at his frailty, he reminded me of a small sulky boy, dressed in too-large clothing handed down from an older child. His eyes, hazel in color like my own, appeared to have sunk deeper into the walnut wrinkles of his angular face, and when he spoke, flecks of snowy spittle formed at the corners of his mouth. I longed to wipe them away, but I dared not.

"This is foolish," he said. "So I felt a little sick. Now I feel better. Mama shouldn't have called you. Why should you come all the way out here? It's a workweek. Why did you come?"

"I came because I wanted to come," I replied briskly. "And what's more, I'm staying because I want to stay."

"But your job? The presentations, the clients, the directors?" He used the vocabulary of my workplace, the words that I had tossed out so carelessly over the years and that he had committed to memory, although what I actually did, the substance of my work, eluded his understanding. He had confronted mountains of fabric each working day and patiently, systematically, had gauged his machines to carve out circlets of space through which buttons might slide. But I, he knew, created something out of nothing. Ideas blossomed into being as I pecked away on my computer. I flew to distant cities to explain what I envisioned. He imagined me standing in wide-windowed rooms, speaking clearly, confidently to those mysterious, important people: *clients, directors, managers.* How he loved to use those words. It pleased him that my work earned me a huge salary. That salary validated my success and because I had succeeded, he and my mother had succeeded.

"I've made arrangements to stay out here for a while. It's company policy to give special leave in certain situations. They expect it of us." My voice was matter-of-fact, my implication clear. To refuse that compassionate leave would be a flagrant violation of company policy, an act of disloyalty that would surely be frowned upon by those directors of whom he spoke with such respect, such deference.

"Well, if it's the policy of your company." He shrugged in defeat and my mother sighed.

"So, come. You should get settled," she said.

The very tiny room, which the developers euphemistically called a den and which she had used as a sewing room, became my bedroom. I crammed my clothes into the shallow maple bureau that had stood in my girlhood bedroom in Queens and hung my black TravelSmith dress in my mother's closet. It was a somber presence amid the neat cotton housedresses in plaids and florals, and the two or three good suits in pastel shades reserved for synagogue or her rare journeys into the city. My mother had never worn dark colors. Once, as we shopped together for dresses for a family wedding, I had taken a navy blue silk dress from the rack and held it against her. Angrily, she had pushed it away.

"But what's wrong with it? It's your size. A perfect style," I had protested.

"I don't wear such colors. Black. Navy blue. They remind me."

I had not asked her of what, but then I had never asked my parents questions about their haunted pasts, about the dark and terrible years they had survived. Their new lives had sprung into being with my birth. My heart twisted as I realized that my own new life would begin with their deaths.

That afternoon we drove out to Dr. Manganaro's office and I listened, nodding knowingly at appropriate intervals, as he explained the implications of the angina attack. He gave my father nitroglycerin patches, cautioned me to be sure that he used them properly, and asked the nurse to bring me the schedule of appointments for the treatments at the oncology unit.

"You're going to be keeping a lot of people busy, Isaac," he said, and it angered me that he should use my father's first name. It seemed to diminish his dignity, to imply a nonexistent intimacy. But my father nodded appreciatively.

"I don't want to give anyone any trouble," he said. His life had been consecrated to an avoidance of trouble—his bills paid on time, his deliveries made on schedule, his demands minimal—each small comfort a wondrous luxury. He had wept when beige wall-to-wall carpeting was installed in our Queens apartment. He, who had walked barefoot on splintered barrack boards, something he had mentioned only once, felt a yielding softness beneath his feet. But as always, his pleasure was focused on me. "You see, Ruchele," he had said, swinging me across the beige expanse, "your feet won't be cold. They'll never be cold."

Dr. Manganaro looked at him and smiled.

"You wouldn't know how to give trouble, Isaac," he said and the sharpness of his insight startled me.

Indeed, during the difficult days that followed, my father did not give any trouble. He protected us from his discomfort and pain. He had his first treatment the next day and I sat with my mother in the waiting room, my hand covering her thin fingers, both of us silent because we feared to speak the words that weighed so heavily upon our hearts. We drove home with the windows open because my father craved air, because he feared that if he did not breathe deeply of the fresh sea-scented breeze, he would drown in a wave of nausea brought on by the odors of hospital corridors and illness.

And so it was again the next day and the day after that. I was learning that illness has its routines, its daily rhythms, its unvarying and constant demands. I was learning to greet the receptionist at the oncology unit with false cheer, to speak softly to the nurses, deferentially to the technician. I spoke a language newly learned, using the words *tolerance* and *reaction* with increasing frequency. My father had an amazing *tolerance* for pain, I told Dr. Manganaro. He did not seem to be having an adverse *reaction* to the rays and chemicals that bombarded his fragile body. He emerged from each session pale and withdrawn, but we celebrated the fact that he did not vomit, that he even managed to eat the broth my mother prepared, salting it carefully, as though each measured grain was drawn from the vast mine of her love.

On Thursday morning Phil phoned to confirm our dinner date. He might be late, he warned. His computer had crashed and he was desperately trying to retrieve data, to re-create a file. I imagined the frenetic atmosphere in the office, the urgent calls, the worried cluster of consultants circling the ailing computer, like physicians surrounding the hospital bed of a very ill patient.

"Poor Phil," I sympathized and struggled to keep the indifference out of my voice. I held a bottle of pills in my hand. My mother was asleep and my father was moaning softly. "You don't have backup?" I asked, jiggling the pill bottle, and I listened absently as he launched into a discussion of programming errors and systems failures. I realized that he was describing precisely the kind of situation Eddie Longauer's product was designed to prevent, but I said nothing. Eddie Longauer had disappeared from my life.

"So you'll understand if I'm late?"

"I'll understand."

But he was not late. I was still dressing and he arrived and I did not rush out to greet him. I draped the copper-colored silk scarf over my shoulders, pleased with the way it offset the austerity of the simple black dress. I brushed my hair so that it fell loosely and smoothly to my shoulders, as Phil liked it. I wanted him to lift the fiery tendrils beneath his fingers, to press his cheek against the fragrant folds. I wanted him to reclaim me, to assure me that I still belonged to his world of dimly lit rooms where slow music played and fragrant candles burned. I wanted to sit beside him in his low-slung car and inhale the brisk night air, free of medicinal odors. I wanted him to be my Prince Charming and wake me from this nightmare of impending death, to spirit me back to our shared domain of intensive, exciting work and luxurious leisure.

As I dabbed perfume on my neck, behind my ears, he and my mother spoke softly. It took me a few seconds to realize that they were speaking in Yiddish. I had heard Phil speak it only once before, in an exasperated telephone exchange with his father who could not, would not, understand an investment plan Phil had devised. But now his words were gentle and I was grateful to him for recognizing that my mother needed to hear the sad, sweet syllables of her distant and terrible girlhood.

My mother smiled as I came into the living room, that familiar smile of pride and wonder, and Phil smiled, too; his a smile of approval and a different kind of pride. With my well-chosen dress, my subtly made-up face, I reflected his own success, his discernment.

He kissed me on the cheek in welcome, in appreciation, and I touched my hand to his lips. Odd, tentative gestures. We had, after all, been lovers for more than four years and we had been apart for over a week. But so much in my life now seemed odd and tentative. I had been wrenched from all that was familiar and had not yet mastered the cue cards of this new, interim scenario.

Phil asked after my father, who was asleep in the bedroom.

"The cure makes him sleep a lot," my mother said. She insisted on calling his treatment, designed only to shrink the tumor and perhaps slow the progress of the disease, a cure and I did not have the heart to correct her.

"I understand," Phil said. "Please tell him I asked for him."

"I'll tell him. For sure I'll tell him." My mother liked Phil. He was a good man, she said. Perhaps almost good enough for me. Always she said this wistfully and always I gave no answer, nor did she press me for one.

I bent to kiss her and she touched my scarf, her gnarled fingers lingering on the fine silk.

"You'll have a good time," she said, repeating the monitory words worriedly repeated when I left for birthday parties, for high-school sleepovers, for dates. Not a wish, but a command. My good times were recompense for all that had been denied her.

"Of course I will," I promised and put my hand on Phil's outstretched arm.

He surprised me then. He turned and kissed her cheek. Her hand flew up to the spot his lips had touched. Her thin face was flushed and I knew that I was seeing her as once my father had seen her, first as a young girl, emaciated but still beautiful, in Europe and then again, in the chance encounter that had led to their marriage, in New York. I smiled at Phil and together we walked into the cool dusk of early spring.

"Did you speak Yiddish at home?" I asked him as we walked to the car.

"Yiddish. English. Whatever." His lips clenched and I knew that I had come too close to a forbidden border.

The restaurant in Bridgehampton was a long ride, but worth it, Phil assured me. He looked wonderful that night, his lean face bronzed by the Vail sunlight that had also lightened his chestnut-colored hair. His turtleneck was startlingly white, his dark green jacket and gray flannel slacks comfortably loose.

"Great jacket," I said.

"I picked it up in Vail." He touched the soft wool lovingly and it occurred to me that I had never seen him wear anything so daring before. I also realized that the color almost matched his eyes.

When we reached the restaurant at last, it was, in fact, worth it. Drinks were served on a deck of bleached wood that overlooked the water. Candles flickered on the tables, defying the encroaching darkness. We watched as a flock of gulls scissored their way across the sky onto a barren beach where they shrieked wildly. A lone heron watched them, now and again fluttering her wide white wings, but making no move to fly away.

Our drinks arrived, a very dry martini for Phil who had explained to the waiter that he preferred vodka to gin, but only if they had Absolut. If they did not have Absolut, he would take gin after all, but only Gordon's. He smiled engagingly as he spoke, acknowledging that he was demanding, that he was spoiled. It was all right, he had told me once, for him to spoil himself, certainly his parents had never spoiled him. They had been too busy scurrying to make a living, stacking the coins tossed onto the splintered wood of their newsstand into neat piles, to worry about their son who had demonstrated very early that he could take care of himself.

My own drink was white wine, served in a long-stemmed glass of delicate crystal.

Phil lifted his glass.

*"L'chaim,"* he said. "To life." His invariable toast.

I grimaced.

"It's a little hard for me to drink to life these days," I said. And then, to my surprise and shame, I began to cry.

"Rochelle, don't." He covered my hand with his own, moved his chair closer and passed his fingers through my hair, as I had wanted him to. I leaned toward him and slipped into the comforting cave of his embrace.

"I try," I said. "But it's not easy. None of it's easy."

"I know." He spoke soothingly, and suddenly the gulls flew off, their angry screams swallowed by the wind. The heron, alone on the beach, strutted bravely toward the surf.

We sat on in silence for a while, breathing in the scent of the sea, watching the darkening horizon, pointing together at the evening star. We had, after all, shared so many sunsets, sat together through so many twilight hours, patiently waiting for that silver shard to appear.

We went into the restaurant at last, walking hand in hand through the beautiful, wood-beamed room that was aglow with the golden light of hanging lanterns. Because it was so early in the season there were relatively few diners, but Phil spotted at least two celebrities—a famous film producer sitting too close to a very young woman who was definitely not his equally famous actress wife, and the vice president of an advertising agency whose photograph appeared regularly in the business section of the *New York Times*. He was alone, a gray-haired, gray-faced man, cutting and forking each bit of fish with great concentration. I wondered if he ate alone because he could not bear to be diverted from the meal set before him.

We listened to the waiter's requisite recitation of the specials, Phil with rapt attention and I with an indifference I did not bother to hide. In the end, Phil ordered for both of us, as he often did. Bluefish, which was the catch of the day, the fish chowder for which the restaurant was famous, radicchio and endive salads.

Once the waiter had left, Phil leaned across the table and smiled at me.

"I know you're going through a rough time," he said, "but it's short-term. You'll stay with your folks for a few more days, get them organized, arrange for help and then you'll come back to the city."

"But that's not the way it's going to be," I protested. "I'm staying with them through it all." I did not say "until they die" although the words formed in my mind. I was not yet strong enough to say them. He was not yet strong enough to hear them.

"But what about your job? BIS. Did Brad give you a leave?"

"No," I said flatly. "He fired me."

The words fell heavily between us. Phil blanched and his eyes narrowed.

"You don't mean it. BIS would never fire you. You're too important to them. Didn't they just name you exec on the Longauer account? There was a squib about it in *Advertising Age*."

"Yes. Well. I had the Longauer account for roughly seventy-two hours. Until I asked Brad for a leave, until he referred my request to the board, until the board turned me down—even though I had said that I would work on it at home or arrange to come in part-time." I spoke in a monotone, but the explanation soured my mouth; I tasted again the biliousness of betrayal.

"Bastard," Phil said, and his anger pleased me.

I dipped my spoon into the chowder and saw that the advertising executive, his plate empty, was watching us. On another evening, I might have smiled at him, perhaps even encouraged Phil to invite him to our table for a drink. He would be a useful contact, a name for my Rolodex and perhaps for Phil's, as well. Men who ate alone surely had a lot of money to invest. But right now, I realized, I had no Rolodex and no need for contacts. I concentrated on the chowder, which was, indeed, very good.

"Still," Phil continued, "I can see their point. It's a big account. They definitely need someone to service it full-time. The scuttlebut is that Eddie Longauer's a kook—a brilliant kook—but like all kooks probably incredibly demanding. I can see what the BIS priority would be."

"Funny you should use that word. It's Brad's new favorite."

"What word?"

"Priority. Is that the big theme in B-school journals these days?"

"Come on, Rochelle, you're not the new kid on the block. Don't be sarcastic. Maybe you should examine your own priorities."

"Like I told Brad," I said evenly. "My priorities are my mother and father. Who are both dying."

"What about me?" Phil asked. "Where do I rank among your priorities?"

"High," I said. "But not as high as my mother and father. And not as high as death."

He flinched. "All this has really gotten to you, and I can understand that. It could make anyone lose perspective. But look, you can still work something out. If you went back to Brad and told him that you'd reconsidered, you've thought it through and you can see where he was coming from, where BIS was coming from, and you're prepared to recognize that they were right…" His voice trailed off. He was formulating his argument, struggling to find the right phrases for the pitch that seemed so reasonable to him.

"But I don't see that they were right. And I don't want to work for a company that can't make room for a human dilemma, that can't understand that there are more important things than launching a campaign. Let's juggle the equation, Phil. BIS can always get a new account executive. My parents have only one daughter." I did not add that I had only one mother, only one father, but I set my spoon down with such force that it clattered against the cunning china soup bowl, shaped like a gull. The film producer and the young woman who was definitely not his wife looked at me and then looked away.

"You're going to throw your career away? Everything that you worked so hard for?" Phil was incredulous.

"Actually, I didn't work very hard for it. It sort of came naturally, which means that maybe it wasn't worth having. Anyway, I just did what was always expected of me."

"You'll never get another job in the field," he warned. "Word will spread. You'll be considered capricious, unreliable."

"Maybe I don't want another job in the field," I retorted. "Maybe I want to do something else with my life."

"Like what?"

"Like I don't know what." Suddenly the conversation, my future, overwhelmed me, and I longed to think about something else. "Let's not talk about it. Tell me about Vail. Tell me what's happening with you."

"Vail was great," he said. "It was terrific to get away from New York, to get some R and R." I was grateful to him for changing the subject.

I knew what he meant. We who listened to the news of a distant war and worked in our wounded city were nervous invalids, slowly recuperating. We were in need of the magic mountains of Vail, of release from the urban landscape of stone and steel that had proved itself so vulnerable. I envied Phil his time away, but I did not begrudge him that respite. But swiftly he began to speak of his job.

I deboned my bluefish as he spoke of bear markets, of losses, of the opportunity to make a killing if one invested with care, even now. He complained about his computer, one glitch after another, and I suggested that he check out the Longauer system.

"I'll try it," he said. "Listen, our Circle Repertory subscription is up for renewal. Should I go for it?"

"I'm not sure I'll be able to get to the performances, but sure, renew. You can always go with someone else. Melanie loves that company." But then I remembered Leonard Quinton and I realized that Melanie would no longer play the role of the easily available single friend. She had, I was certain, reached the safe haven of permanence. Lucky Melanie, lucky Leonard Quinton. My heart was weighted with a new sadness. I had without warning drifted into a season of loss—and change—and I was prepared for neither.

"I'll renew," Phil said. "You can't tell. You may get back to the city sooner than you think. You can still work something out with Brad."

I did not answer. There was nothing left to say. And Phil would only hear what he wanted to hear.

We ordered dessert, strawberries in crème fraîche carefully selected by Phil from a laden trolley, and talked about the new Philip Roth novel that Phil had just finished and that rested, unopened, on the buttonhole machine that I had appropriated for use as a bedside table. Phil mentioned the surprisingly bad review of a play we had both liked when we saw it in preview. We spoke easily, relieved to be back on familiar terrain, bonded by shared interests, shared pleasures.

The bill came and Phil slapped his credit card down and factored in the tip using his pocket calculator. He smiled happily as he did this, reminding me of a child delighted to be playing with his favorite toys. I smiled at him, pleased at his pleasure, and sipped the last of my cappuccino, dipped the last strawberry in the thick white pool of melting cream.

We drove back across a network of country roads, avoiding the main highway. A warm breeze rippled through the open windows of the car and, above us, smoke-colored clouds were threaded with silver starlight. On the radio, Toni Braxton sang her desperate hymn of love and pain. We added our voices to hers and then Phil drove deep into a meadow. We got out of the car, leaving the radio on. We danced. The high sweet grass scratched my bare legs, and Phil's chin rested on my head. When the song ended, he switched the ignition off, took a blanket from the trunk and spread it on the ground. We made love then, tenderly, sadly, our bodies arched against each other, lips brushing skin as though in search of an elusive memory. And then Phil covered me with my own dress and ran his fingers through my hair. With my head resting on his bare shoulder, we looked up at the star-crested sky, at the sliver of a slowly vanishing moon.

"What would you do," I asked, "if you were in my place? If your parents became ill?" I spoke slowly, almost dreamily, because I was so very tired and because my question was not a challenge.

Phil hesitated, but when he spoke, his words were deliberate, his meaning clear.

"I would hire the very best caregivers I could find," he said. "I would visit them regularly, make sure that they had everything they needed. But I would not do what you are doing. It's..." He fumbled for the word and found it. "Masochistic," he said finally. "Don't you see that?"

I shrugged. I had forgotten his two years in therapy, his obsessive reading of pop psychology and self-help books. Lightly, too lightly, I kissed his cheek, struggled to my feet and dressed, aware that the gentle wind was now edged with a chill. I tied my hair back and slid into the car. Phil got in beside me, his white turtleneck shirt faintly stained by the wild young grass. We spoke very little on the drive back.

He kissed me goodbye at my parents' door, twisted my hair free of the scarf.

"I'll call," he said and glanced at his watch. It was late and he had a long drive to the city. He wanted to be at his computer when the opening prices on the Tokyo exchange flashed across the screen.

I closed the door very softly behind me and tiptoed across the darkened room. I did not want to wake my mother and father, but I need not have worried.

"Ruchele, is that you?" They were vigilant sentinels, wearied and weakened, but unable to sleep until they knew that I had arrived home safely. In a few months' time, there would be no one to worry about me, no one to leave a lamp dimly lit and murmur my name softly, lovingly. I swallowed hard, as though I could ingest the lump of self-pity that seemed to well up in my throat.

"It's me," I replied. "Go to sleep. It's very late."

I did not go to their room. I did not want them to read the sadness on my face.

Phil did call during the weeks that followed, as did Melanie, Lila, Fay and other friends. Even Brad left a message on the answering machine, which I heard when I returned from a trip to a therapist who supposedly had techniques for dealing with the side effects of chemo and radiation. In my father's case, he could do nothing, he admitted, and both my father and I nodded. We had expected nothing.

I seldom returned the calls. The pace of my father's illness had accelerated and my mother was running a low-grade fever: her lymphoma was no longer in remission. I drove back and forth to the oncology unit, did laundry, cooked and shopped, a daughter mothering her parents. I served tea to Morrie and Zelda, who made the long trip to Suffolk County, chatted cheerfully with my parents and retreated into the small kitchen to weep. I never went beyond the first chapter of the Roth book. Its title "Death," plucked from a Yeats poem, hit too close to home. Instead, I turned the pages of an Oscar Williams poetry anthology, reading and weeping through the long evenings, springing to my feet to bring my father a painkiller, my mother a glass of hot water and lemon. Their soft moans haunted me, even when I slept.

*How much longer can this go on?* I asked myself and immediately I broke into a sweat, shamed that I should wish for their deaths because I yearned for a swift end to their pain and my own.

The days grew warmer and my secondhand car trailed optimistic beachgoers jumping the season. I glanced curiously into the windows of minivans packed with children and laughing young mothers. Their childhoods were foreign to me. I had never known what it was like to have a mother who was so young, who laughed with careless spontaneity.

One afternoon Dr. Manganaro asked me into his office. His tone, as always, was sad and calm. He told me that it was time to begin home-hospice care. My father's condition had proven unresponsive to treatment. A visiting nurse would come daily to regulate a morphine drip.

I nodded my agreement. I had watched, day after day, as my father deteriorated. The pain overwhelmed him, the agonizing treatments assaulted the last remnant of his strength. Each morning he seemed thinner, wearier. Pale skin dangled from his bones, his eyes were deeply sunk into a face the color of parchment. My mother wept. His skeletal form had to be a replay of his past and her own. They must have looked like that at the war's end, starved adolescents, orphaned and racked with grief. Miraculously they had been liberated, plucked from the edge of death and nourished back to life. She knew that there would be no similar rescue this time and, of course, I knew it, too. Death was not a malevolent historic caprice now, but a biological certainty.

The hospice nurse came the next day, Jessie Taylor, a smiling black woman who spoke in the lilting accents of Jamaica.

"Not to worry. We'll be fine," she said comfortingly, but my mother, my little mother, so neatly dressed that day in a freshly ironed pink plaid housedress, her thin gray hair twisted into a bun, fainted because Jessie Taylor wore a uniform, a flowing dark cape, a jaunty hat. Uniforms had always frightened my mother. She drew back at the sight of the letter carrier, the Con Ed meter reader, crossed the street to avoid a group of Boy Scouts walking three abreast. But never before had she fainted.

Jessie Taylor and I rushed to her side, crouched beside her, and together we lifted her onto the sofa and covered her with a blanket. I knelt beside her, my hand in hers as Jessie tended to my father. Through the open door I saw her lift him as she might lift a child. She sponged his fragile limbs, his distended abdomen, pregnant with death. She threaded his pale shrunken veins with the clear tubes filled with substances that would nourish him and kill his pain.

I closed my eyes and sat back against the couch, my hands plunged into the pockets of my jeans, a scab of my father's vomit clinging to my long loose blue shirt, and fell asleep. I awakened, perhaps minutes later, from that shallow sleep because Jessie Taylor was kneeling beside my mother, desperately searching for a pulse that she did not find.

"Mama!" I screamed, and my father called to me from behind the closed door of their bedroom, Yiddish and English melding.

"*Vis iss?* What's happening? Ruchele. Lena *mine*. Ruchele. Lena." Our names were his mantra and he repeated them again and again as the nurse dialed Dr. Manganaro's office and told him what had happened.

"Time of death?" she said and glanced at her watch. "Nine-thirty, I think. Perhaps nine-forty."

I went to my father then, crept into the bed beside him, rocked him in my arms as, in my childhood he had rocked me, and told him that my mother had died. I pressed my face to his so that our tears mingled and, it seemed to me, that our hearts, so newly broken, beat as one.

"Oh, Papa. I'm sorry. So sorry."

My words reached him, penetrating his pain, piercing his sorrow. And he, so desperately in need of comfort himself, comforted me.

"You will be all right, Ruchele," he murmured through parched lips, as though he understood my deepest fear. "We were blessed. Me and my Lena. You were our blessing. Ach, my Lena. My poor Lena."

I wiped his eyes with my fingertips and held them to my tongue, tasting the bitter salt of his sorrow.

"She didn't suffer, Papa." My voice cracked, but I spoke the truth. "She just closed her eyes and left us."

My words were grief-thickened, alien. Leave-taking implies an act of volition, but my mother had dressed carefully that morning, rising early to iron her cotton dress, to arrange her thinning gray hair, to place the drops of lilac toilet water my father favored behind her ears. She had prepared for another day of life, not its swift and always inexplicable ending. But I had known for weeks that she was slowly drifting away, her movements slowed, her voice growing wispier and wispier, her dreams more vivid than her thoughts. And so, yes, she had left us, perhaps not willingly, but inevitably. She had fainted, closed her eyes against the darkest of past memories and the iridescence of present pain. She had drifted from consciousness into a gentle death.

I helped my father from his bed and, supporting him, walked him into the living room where capable Jessie Taylor had spread a clean white sheet across my mother's body, leaving only her face and her feet exposed.

My father bent and kissed her pale forehead, touched her hair and then slowly, slowly, stroked her small and slender feet with his gnarled and twisted fingers.

"Lena, my Lena." Love trembled in his voice, and Jessie closed the drapes against the intrusion of the sun's brightness.

Drained of energy, my father did not leave his bed that afternoon, but I stood in the doorway as Dr. Manganaro, sadder and wearier than ever, filled out my mother's death certificate. I watched as he motioned to the attendant, who lifted her body onto a gurney and wheeled her through the front door, past the rosebush that she had planted with such tender care.

The doctor examined my father, spoke softly to him.

"She suffered no pain," he said.

"I know," my father replied, adrift as he was on the magical drug that eased his own agony.

"It won't be long," Dr. Manganaro told me, following me into the kitchen where I sat at the table, my head lowered. "Be strong."

"Do I have a choice?" Resignation, not bitterness, edged my words.

He left and I made the necessary phone calls. Relatives. Friends.

"I'm all right," I assured them.

*And your father?* The question was asked softly, cushioned by compassion.

"The doctor says it's just a matter of time." Tears fell as I spoke, but my voice did not tremble.

Jessie Taylor left as darkness fell and I sat beside my father's bed until his eyes closed and his breathing became regular. I went into the living room then and, sitting in a circlet of lamplight, I took up pad and pen and wrote four lines of a poem. The words danced through mind and memory. *"My mother's feet, my father's fingers…"* I put the pad away and fell into a light sleep. I dreamed of my little mother dancing barefoot and of my father holding her hand. Music played. A violin, its strains plaintive and slow, then slower still until the dancers melted into silent darkness. I jerked into wakefulness and heard my father's voice.

"Lena," he gasped. "Ruchele. Lena."

I hurried into his room, checked the morphine drip and wiped his brow with a damp cloth. My lips brushed his cheek, passed across the stiff silver bristles of his unshaven chin. I knelt beside the bed.

"I'm here, Papa. I'm here."

He stroked my head.

"My Ruchele. My Lena."

Again and again he spoke her name and mine, his voice keeping rhythm with his touch. Then his hand grew still and, although his fingers were luminous sticks of bone and his palm a flat cushion of wizened flesh, that hand was heavy on my head. Weighted with love. Stiffened by death. My father died with a tendril of my copper hair forming a wispy bracelet on his narrow wrist.

My parents' joint funeral was a simple graveside service. The rabbi offered the traditional prayers. Morrie spoke. He came from the Polish town where they had been born. He had known each of them separately *before*. *Before* the war. *Before*. The code word that had divided their lives. He spoke of how beautiful they had been, how brave they had been. His voice broke and he wept as did that small congregation of bewildered mourners, uneasy in their black suits and hats, the red clay of the Long Island cemetery clinging in clumps to their polished shoes. My mother's friend, Bella, who had been interned with her and liberated with her, moaned softly.

And I wept because I was alone and because I knew so little of the *before,* and my ignorance, so benevolently and protectively imposed by them, was also my loss, my unclaimed legacy. I recited the Kaddish and the women lifted their handkerchiefs to their eyes. The men stared grimly skyward. Murmurs rose and fell.

"To lose two parents like that. Poor girl."

I was a child to all of them, their tears and words chorus to my prayer.

My friends were there. Melanie, carrying a single white rose, standing beside Leonard Quinton who pressed his white handkerchief into her hand. Lila and Fay in dark skirts and high-necked white blouses. They had worried, I knew, about what to wear to a Jewish funeral. Phil arrived late and he did not move to stand beside me although his eyes never left my face. Brad and Suzanne, oddly, represented BIS and I supposed that Phil had called them. They stood awkwardly amid the small group of mourners and stepped back as friends and relatives moved forward to lower shovels of earth onto the two pale pine coffins. Suzanne air-kissed me and Brad pressed my hand as they left, climbing too rapidly into the black limo that BIS hired for late-evening meetings and early-morning funerals. Phil took his turn, spoke briefly to Morrie and put his hand on my shoulder.

Melanie handed me the white rose. I pressed it to my cheek, inhaled its melancholy fragrance and watched my tears fall like dew upon its heart. I dropped it into the grave, saw the petals flutter loose and settle in odd formations. A strangely shaped star. An infant's soft white fingers. The images comforted me.

I observed the traditional week of mourning at my parents' apartment. Melanie, Lila and Fay split the week, each staying over for one or two nights, waking when I awakened, preparing pots of herbal tea. They served the few elderly relatives and friends who came to offer comfort and memories, things I had not known. As a boy, my father had played the violin. As a girl, my mother had memorized and written poetry for competition. Of course, all that was *before*. Bella remembered my mother reciting poems in the darkness of the camp barracks.

"You used to write poetry. Read it, Ruchele," she said.

"I still do. Or I would, if I had the time." But now, of course, I would have all the time in the world. No parents. No job.

"You'll call. Come for a shabbos dinner, Ruchele." Morrie's invitation was a plea.

"I'll try," I promised.

My friends helped me to fill cartons with my parents' modest possessions to be donated to charity thrift shops.

A moving van arrived to cart the furniture to the Salvation Army. I watched as they carried my past into the huge padded compartment—the kitchen table on which my father had covered my schoolbooks, the maple bureau for which my mother had made a white runner, embroidering my initials in pink satin thread, (Who had taught her to embroider? I wondered, pierced with grief that I had never thought to ask her), the coffee table on which my college-graduation portrait and my athletic ribbons and academic awards had stood. They were packed away now in a sealed carton that I would keep, but probably never open.

Phil came on a Sunday afternoon and helped me box linens and blankets for newly arrived Russian families. He was apologetic. He wished he could do more, but he was so damn busy at work. There were new accounts, a venture-capital deal. Melanie's brother, Warren, had already made a fortune. Even in these crazy times, with the economy still struggling, there were deals to be done, money to be made, if you were careful, if you knew what you were doing.

"The trick is to diversify," he said.

"All right," I replied indifferently. I felt removed from the world of faxes and deals, of careers that spiraled and plunged, of profits and losses mysteriously recorded in electronic accounts.

Phil offered to drive back out when I was ready to return to the city, but I shook my head.

"I still have the car," I said. "I'll sell it in the city. And I sort of look forward to driving alone. It helps me to get my head together."

His face went slack with disappointment and I turned away. I was done, for now, with deferring to the needs of others.

Three weeks after the funeral, I swept the empty apartment clean, loaded the buttonhole machine in its chintz cover onto the back seat of my car and drove very slowly back to the city. I was in no hurry. No one awaited me. I was released from all obligations. Now and then, during that lonely ride, tears streaked my cheeks, but I did not wipe them away. It was all right to cry. With my parents' deaths, all expectations had been canceled. My tears were my own, affecting only myself.

My cell phone rang, but I did not answer it. Instead, at the Nassau border, I pulled over and parked on the grassy verge. I stepped out of the car and kicked off my sandals so that I stood barefoot, my face brushed by sunlight and a gentle breeze.

# CHAPTER
## FOUR

I returned to a city dizzied by a fierce and unseasonable heat wave. In the small garden at the rear of our apartment building the petals on the newly blooming daffodils were ribbed with scorch scars. Mario, the superintendent who cultivated the patch of urban earth so tenderly, stared sadly at the short-lived flowers. Tulips blossomed beautifully and then drooped with heartbreaking swiftness. I stood by my window at dawn and at dusk and watched Mario nurse his plantings. He hosed the friable ash-colored soil, spooned fertilizer into the roots, snipped the dead leaves that sapped the strength of healthier plants. Occasionally, he looked up at me, lifted his hands in defeat and shrugged. I, in turn, smiled sadly and nodded. Silently then, he in his garden and I at my window acknowledged that we were powerless against the inevitable.

My phone rang sporadically, but I ignored it. Instead, I listened as the answering machine picked up. Phil's voice was alternately optimistic and concerned.

"Rochelle. Where are you, baby? Give me a call."

"Rochelle, this is crazy. I want to see you, speak to you."

"Rochelle, I have tickets for the Met this Saturday night. Get back to me so we can make plans." He was tempting me, cajoling me.

"Rochelle, why don't you get back to me?" He was plaintive.

I wondered how long it would take for his anxiety to evolve into anger, for anger to fade into disinterest. I was being unfair, I knew, and once I did call him back, but he was not at his desk and I did not leave a message.

Melanie called.

"Hey, Shelley, I know you need time, but whenever you're ready, give me a call."

"Listen, I think you've had enough time. Have dinner with me and Leonard tonight. We know a really grungy Chinese place with great sesame noodles."

"Rochelle, call me. Now." Melanie's voice was threatening, but her anger did not unnerve me. I knew that my silence would never invoke her indifference.

Fay and Lila called, knocked tentatively at my door, left small gifts. A pizza. A Greek salad. A pound of Fairway's Colombian coffee. I heard them retreat down the hall and I waited for the phone to ring.

"Hey, Rochelle, honey, we know you're there, but that's okay. Alone time is good. But open the door. We don't want you to starve to death."

Lila's southern accent was strangely comforting. Listening, I imagined myself as Scarlett O'Hara, preparing to reinvent herself.

I ate the whole pizza at one sitting. I pecked at the Greek salad. I ground the coffee beans while watching a rerun of ER, but I stopped because an old woman died of cancer on that episode and I began to cry.

Slowly, methodically, I cleaned my drawers and closets. I relined my kitchen cabinets, vacuumed my hardwood floors, my russet and gold Rya rug. Each spring I had rolled that rug up and tossed batik throws across my chairs and sofa, because that was what my mother had done, but this year I left the furniture unprotected, the rug in place. I lived in New York and had no need to fear the harsh Polish sunlight. My furniture did not have to last forever. It could be replaced. I imagined my mother sighing wearily, saying, "Whatever you want, Ruchele." That was what she had always said, and I had repaid her by doing what she wanted, what I thought she wanted, passively obedient to her passive wishes. *Oh, Mama.* I lay down on my red-and-gold rug and fell asleep.

I created a space for the buttonhole machine in my bedroom, where it stood incongruously draped in flowered chintz between my futon and my long teak worktable. I filled cartons with clothing I no longer wore, but in the end I gave nothing away because I did not know what my life would be, what costume I would need for that next unnecessary stage, whose setting still eluded me. Wise Scarlett, I thought, to have held on to those green velvet drapes.

I was waiting, during those heat-heavy days, cocooned by my solitude, for a new emergence, as yet undefined. Encased within a silent, orderly chrysalis of my own weaving, I awaited a morphology independent of the expectations of others. In the interim, I kept my radio tuned to the classical music of WQXR, watched old movies late into the night and immersed myself in poetry anthologies, unread since my undergraduate days. Poetry had been my passion then, a secret indulgence, economics my practical major.

Occasionally, in the early evening, I left my apartment to shop for groceries or to pick up videos. Always, I exited through the rear of the building, reluctant to face my fellow tenants who would be returning home at that hour. Dressed as I usually was in those days—sandals, an oversize T-shirt and jeans—I felt myself a deserter from that army of urban professionals in their well-pressed suits, armed with laptops and attaché cases. "The yuppie mafia," Lila jokingly called them, and when I protested that I too belonged to that mafia, she shook her head. "But you're not really like them, Rochelle," she had said and I wondered then, as I wonder now, what, in fact, "I was really like."

At that twilight hour, Mario sat in his garden on a faded cloth beach chair, sadly surveying his dying garden. Tomato plants, still in their flats, sat in a corner, shaded by a canopy of newspapers. He would plant them, he had told me, when the heat wave ended.

"It will rain. Things will get better. Things always get better," he said each evening, when the violet-colored air was still thick with the heat of the day that had passed. His undershirt clung to his muscular body and his dark hair was matted with sweat.

"Yes. Of course they will," I invariably replied and willed my-self to believe that he was right.

I returned from the video store one evening, hugging *A Night to Remember* and *Four Hundred Blows,* neither of which I really wanted to watch, and found Phil standing outside my apartment door. He had come straight from the office, I knew. Fatigue lines curled about his eyes and mouth. His blue cord suit jacket was slung over his shoulder, his narrow tie unknotted, his pale blue shirt darkened by circlets of sweat. He looked at me warily.

"I hope you don't mind, Rochelle, but what else could I do? You didn't return my calls. Fay buzzed me in. Don't be mad at her. I told her we had a date." He smiled disarmingly, his sad, familiar après-sex smile.

I smiled back. Smiles were my secret talent, carefully prac-ticed, carefully cultivated. Smiles for clients. Smiles for lovers. Shy smiles. Bold smiles.

"I don't mind," I replied. But I did. I minded terribly. I was not yet ready to see him. I did not know what I wanted to say to him. I knew only that, as everything else in my life had changed, so too would my relationship with him. I needed more than he offered. "I'm glad to see you."

And that, surprisingly, was true. I pressed my fingers to his lips, fumbled with my keys and motioned him inside.

He sank into the black leather chair and, following the habit of all our shared hours, I brought him a tall gin and tonic. That had been our pattern, our pseudo-domestic routine—gin and tonic in the summer when heat pressed against the windows, short scotches against the chill of autumn evenings, of cold winter nights. We were skilled at protecting ourselves against the small terrors of oncoming darkness.

"Thanks," he said. "I need that. You're not having one."

"No," I replied. "I sort of got out of the habit."

The before-dinner drink, the programmed moments of unwinding, fingers curled about a cold glass, thought and fear suspended, had become both irrelevant and impossible during the weeks I had spent with my parents. After the funeral, I found I did not want to drink alone. It was soothing enough to stand at my window and look down at Mario's forlorn garden.

"You seem to have dropped a lot of habits." Phil sipped his drink and flicked his fingers against his glass. Soon, very soon, he would pluck out the ice cube and suck it.

"Such as?"

"Such as leading a directed, organized life. Such as caring about what happens to you professionally. Such as returning phone calls, honoring commitments."

"I honored my most important commitment," I replied stiffly.

"Rochelle. It's time. Your parents are dead. It's sad, it's terrible, but it's over. You have to get on with your life. We have to get on with our lives. Summer's around the corner, the best shares in beach houses are gone."

"Our lives?" I repeated. "Meaning what? Shares in beach houses, ski lodges? Dinner and theater? Good food, good seats, good sex."

The bitterness in my voice surprised me and I lowered my eyes in shame.

"We had more than that," he said calmly. "But let's say that's all it was. What do you have in its place?" He glanced at the videos I had tossed on the table. "Hours in front of the VCR. Chinese take-out? Cold pizza?"

"Maybe. For a while. For now." I went to the window. A red tulip that had blossomed that morning drooped on its tall stalk. Blood-red petals littered the dry earth.

"All right. Let's get practical. How long can you afford to live like this? How are you going to pay your bills?" There was a new hardness in his voice. Perhaps he addressed clients in such a tone. *Do you want your money to work for you? How much can you afford to lose?* Such a competent objective professional had no need for a bedside manner.

I went to my desk, removed my checkbook, my bank statement. My last deposit was for the money I had received when I sold my battered car. Hardly enough to cover my rent and expenses for the month. There was still a balance from my last BIS checks, but I had a sheaf of bills and I knew that I would soon have to do something about my health insurance. I was coasting, but I could not coast for much longer. Perhaps I could apply for unemployment, but I may have waited too long. There would be some money in my parents' modest estate, but it would not be a significant amount. My cousin Morrie, that kindly old man who no longer imported or exported, had told me this, his voice heavy with concern.

"But don't worry, Ruchele. If you have any problems you're not alone. You have a family. You have friends," he had assured me sadly. "You understand that?"

I had nodded, but of course I would never approach my weary, elderly relatives for financial assistance. Not I, their golden girl, their American princess, forever poised on the springboard of success, skillful swimmer through the mysterious corporate waters of this their wonderland.

Once my picture had appeared in *Time* magazine. I was photographed making a presentation, my pointer authoritatively thrust at a diorama. They had ripped the page from the magazine, carried it about in their wallets, their faces bright with a pride that embarrassed me although I had enlarged that same page and given it to my parents, knowing what it would mean to them. No. I could not, would not disappoint them by confessing my need. It would not be right. It would not be fair. It would not be necessary.

I rummaged in the drawer, found my canceled checks, my income tax schedule. Wordlessly, I handed everything to Phil. He riffled through them, pulled a pad out of his attaché case, clicked rhythmically away in his pocket calculator and made notes, his mouth pressed in disapproval.

"You're not in good shape," he said.

"I know."

"If you cut back you can manage your rent and utilities for another three months at least. Counting in unemployment insurance. Your parents didn't leave anything, I take it?"

"Not much. A little."

"Rochelle, you've got to think things through. Look, give Brad a call. BIS made a terrific investment in you. They'll want to recoup. They'll find a way if they know you want to come back. They might even give you the Longauer account again."

"No," I replied shortly. "I don't want to talk about it anymore. I'll manage. Let's have some dinner. I have eggs, mushrooms. I'll make an omelette."

"Let's go out."

But I was already in the kitchen, dicing mushrooms and garlic, cracking eggs. The melting butter swirled in the skillet, the vegetables sizzled. Energized, I rummaged through the refrigerator. There were carrots. There were onions. *If you have onion and car-*

*rots you have a meal.* My mother's mandate, the credo of the poor and dispossessed, reliant always on vegetables that grow within the darkness of the earth.

"I have onion, I have carrots, Mama," I whispered.

She would have approved of this swift and simple meal. But then, when had she not approved of me? I grated the carrots and onions, tossed in some parsley and mayonnaise.

We watched the evening news as we ate. Refugees drifted across the screen. Weeping women. Sad-eyed children. Strong men bewildered by their powerlessness. Another suicide bombing. A mother cradling her lifeless child. Grim medics lifting stretchers.

"I can't bear it," I said.

Phil's face was tight, his hair wet. He had taken a quick shower as I cooked. We sat in silence, flinching as the day's horrors were chronicled, bonded by our dark present and our parents' even darker pasts. But we said nothing, partners in a silence that was not of our making. Phil turned the television off, made coffee.

"So what will you do?" he asked, setting the brimming cups down.

"I don't know. I need time."

"Please, please don't say that you need space. That's what the women in my office say when they explain why they left their husbands, why they broke up with their lovers, why they need time off. Time, okay, but not space."

He smiled. I smiled.

"All right," I said. "No space." I sipped the coffee, burned my tongue, winced. "Do you think I should invest some of my money?"

"You don't have anything to invest. Not in this market. You have enough to live on for a while, until you get another job or go back to BIS. Then we can talk."

"We have to talk about more than my financial situation." My voice dropped. "I think we both know that things have changed. For me. For you."

"Nothing's changed for me." He strode to the window, then back to the couch.

"I don't think that's true. Phil, who helped you pick out that green jacket?" My question came unbidden, surprising me, surprising him.

He was disconcerted, as I had wanted him to be. He did not meet my eyes. My question was an unexpected challenge. But when he spoke, his voice was steady.

"It was a woman I worked with in Vail. Nothing serious. Two nights. Two days. I was lonely. She was lonely. It wasn't important. It had nothing to do with us. With you and me."

"How can you separate it from you and me?" I asked harshly.

He set his coffee mug down, his face pale. "Look, Rochelle, I thought we had an understanding. We never talked about exclusivity, at least not when we were in different cities. I didn't want to pressure you and you didn't want to pressure me. I thought we were on the same wavelength. You're important to me. If you want to change the rules, that's something we'll talk about. It's been a rough couple of months, I know. I just don't know where you're coming from, where we go from here. Spell it out."

"I don't know what I want. Maybe we need some time apart. At least until I know what I'm going to do, what I want." I was trembling, my head was hammering.

"What *you're* going to do. What *you* want. It's all about you, isn't it? Your parents are dead but you're still the miracle girl. You're still the center of the universe. Everything revolves around you. What about me? What am I supposed to do while you decide what you're going to do, what you want?" His face was pale, his eyes dangerously bright.

His anger ignited my own.

"I don't know, Phil. Find someone else to go shopping with. Someone else to play tennis. Someone else to take to dinner, to split a share in a beach house. Someone else to sleep with." The cruelty of my own words caused me to tremble. My lips clenched, locking themselves against the flow of my fury. And yet I felt a cleansing relief. Never before had we quarreled, exchanged angry words. This exchange of angry honesty validated us, vested us with a new reality.

But he was standing now, pulling on his jacket, fumbling for his attaché case, his laptop.

"Listen," he said. "All this is crazy talk. All of it. I'm leaving. I'll do what you want. I'll wait. I won't call you. At least I think I won't call you. But Rochelle, don't take too much time."

How tired he sounded, this tall lean man who had been my lover for four years, whose thick dark hair was spackled with silver.

I went to the window. Mario was deadheading the red tulip, tying the stalk down. I put my hands to my eyes, staunched the hot tears that soon would fall. Phil moved across the room, stood behind me, his hands on my shoulders. I thought to lean back, to surrender my sorrow, to claim his support. Instead, I spoke very softly.

"I'm sorry," I said.

"I'm sorry, too."

He left then and I remained at the window. Mario knelt before his tomato plants, then folded his beach chair and stood it against the fence. I went to clear away the dishes and saw that Phil had forgotten his tie, a narrow navy blue knit that I placed in my bottom drawer beside my copper-colored scarf.

I was washing the last mug when there was a knock at the door. Lila's knock, light, tentative, implying forgiveness if it went unanswered. But I did answer it, relieved to have company, to be released from reviewing the words I had spoken to Phil. He was not at fault. We had not entered into a contract; we had pledged ourselves only to a mutual exchange of pleasure, to the casual compatibility that had kept us together for so long. My anger had been unjustified. I hadn't the right to taunt him with his failure to meet expectations that I had never articulated.

"Stupid," I muttered to myself as I went to the door.

Lila and Fay both stood there, Lila holding Thimble's red leather leash while the small white dog happily licked her leg.

"Come on in," I said.

"Phil's gone? I hope you don't mind that we buzzed him in, but he sounded so sad." Fay's was a kindness born of the unkindness she herself had suffered.

"No. He's gone. And I don't mind. I should have seen him long before this. I should have seen everyone. I've been a little self-indulgent, I suppose."

They followed me into the living room, watched as I plucked a napkin from the table. I was the daughter of a woman who had never left a dirty cup in the sink and this learned passion for order persisted. It was an antidote against the disarray that affected every aspect of my life. My parents were dead, my job had vanished and my lover had just left, closing the door too softly behind him, but my apartment would remain well kept, everything in place. Almost reflexively, I centered the ceramic bowl, flanking it with the two terra-cotta figurines Phil had bought me during a vacation in Mexico. Perhaps this was how my mother had fought the turmoil of memories.

"Well, you have every right." Lila, wearing white shorts, and a blue tank top, her long blond hair twisted into a single braid, crouched on the floor in the lotus position with Thimble settled happily beside her.

"Nothin' wrong with a little self-indulgence," Fay agreed. She plunged her hands into the wide pockets of her sleeveless yellow shift.

"I suppose not. I guess I'm just not used to it. Having depended always on the indulgence of others." And I had. In that, Phil had not been mistaken.

They laughed. Fay had read for a revival of *Streetcar* months ago and we had all taken turns as Blanche DuBois.

"Coffee?" I offered, suddenly feeling as though my anger with Phil had broken something loose inside me, allowed me to reclaim part of my life.

"Nope. We had coffee over at Melanie's shop," Lila said.

"And where is Melanie? Or are you her ambassadors?"

"Melanie is out with her Leonard. Her nice Leonard. Her lovely Leonard." Fay smiled. "I guess he's the one she's been waiting for. Although she couldn't have known that."

"No. It's hard to know what we're waiting for." Perhaps I would wake up one morning and know exactly what I had been waiting for during these hot spring days. Perhaps I'd find a map—no—a game board beside my pillow neatly labeled: *Rochelle Weiss—Personal and Confidential. Do not pass Go. Advance three squares. Buy that property. Take that course, that job, that plane, that bus.* I relaxed, happy for Melanie, suddenly optimistic for myself.

"Well, Lila and I think we may have what we've been waiting for. Or at least a chance at it," Fay said.

"Hey, let me hear." I leaned forward expectantly. For the first time in weeks, I felt the stirring of excitement, the contagion of joy.

"Well, y'all know that we've both been talkin' about doin' summer stock on the Cape this summer. So I auditioned for a company that's doin' repertory in Wellfleet, and so did Fay—and we both made the cut. It's not just a gig for a couple of nights. It's a whole summer with a great director and some real interestin' plays. A Williams, a Pinter and two new playwrights." Lila's face glowed with pride and anticipation.

"I guess they want you guys for the Pinter on account of your impeccable English accents," I said and we all laughed. "Anyway, this calls for a celebration."

I opened a bottle of white wine, poured three glasses and proposed a toast.

"To the Wellfleet Rep and a glorious summer."

We clinked our glasses and sipped the wine.

"Well, we got to deal with just two problems," Fay said, refilling her glass.

"And they are?"

"Number one—our apartment. We'll have to rent a place on the Cape and I don't think we can swing the rent on the studio here as well. But we don't want to give it up. We'll never find another deal like it in this neighborhood, illegal or not. And problem number two is the dogs."

"The dogs?"

Lila scratched Thimble's neck, allowed the small dog to crawl onto her lap.

"Walking Thimble, Lucky and Goldilocks has become pretty much a regular gig. Old Mrs. Clark could never manage Thimble on her own. And the Eliots might have to give up Goldilocks if they can't find anyone to walk her, which would really be hard on them. I'm not too worried about Lucky, but the Catons pay us pretty well and I'd really like to have that job when the summer's over. Just in case we don't get Hollywood contracts," she explained.

"How much do you charge for walking the dogs?" I asked.

"We have a sort of sliding scale. Five dollars a walk for Thimble and Goldilocks, which isn't much but it's a lot for Mrs. Clark and the Eliots. We charge ten bucks for Lucky because the Catons can afford it. A doctor and a lawyer with a three-bedroom co-op on Park," Fay said without embarrassment. "We're kind of the Robin Hoods of dog walking."

"How many times a day do you walk them?"

"Twice. Morning and evening usually unless we're working somewhere else. Then we get high-school kids who take them out for a couple of bucks."

"So then you average like forty dollars a day for three dogs? And that's all cash? No taxes?"

"Do we look nuts?" Lila asked. "We're going to pay taxes on that?"

"So if you added a couple more dogs, working in the afternoon on a couple of circuits, you could be clearing a hundred, two hundred a day?"

"Probably. But we've always needed the afternoons for auditions. For voice and acting lessons, sometimes for a restaurant job or a kid's birthday party. Even, miracle of miracles, a gig, maybe a TV walk-on. And now we can't even handle the mornings," Fay protested.

"But I can," I said.

They stared at me in surprise.

"Rochelle, you mean you'd take the dogs over for the summer?"

"That's what I mean. Why not?"

The idea seemed logical. I had no plans and I had always enjoyed trailing along with Lila and Fay when they walked the dogs. I knew that I could recruit as many new clients as I could handle. After all, I had organized campaigns for multimillion-dollar high-tech companies. I could certainly launch a small dog-walking agency. And I would be my own boss—no false paternalism, no office politics, no phony camaraderie, no spying and competing. It would be a painless way to generate income while I decided on my next step. And the idea of walking delighted me—walking and walking in rhythmic pace, destination unnecessary.

Fay and Lila looked at me and nodded. Lila planted a kiss on my cheek.

"Great. A break for us and everyone else. Thanks, Rochelle."

"Thank you." We hugged each other like schoolgirls bonded by a happy secret.

I went to sleep smiling that night. I had become a dog walker as serendipitously as my father had become a buttonhole manufacturer, as Morrie had tumbled into import-export. Against all odds, without a plan or a game board, I was breaking into a new life.

# CHAPTER
## FIVE

I christened my new enterprise Dog Daze and designed a flyer with a stick figure of a young woman dangling several leashes and cuddling a puppy. The message read, Let Dog Daze Guarantee You Peaceful Nights. I ran them off on pastel paper at Kinko's, stapled a business card with my phone number to each one and pinned them to bulletin boards at strategic locations—pet stores and gourmet delis, Barnes & Noble, the Fairway grocery store and the Food Emporium. Melanie displayed one prominently in her flower shop.

"Flower people are dog people," she said.

"Okay. So much for our target audience," I said. "Now we wait." I repeated the words that I had so often spoken to reassure BIS clients, the same words that I was sure Suzanne had, by this time, used to soothe an impatient Eddie Longauer.

It didn't take long. My phone rang so often that within days I had a full roster and apologetically took names for a waiting list. By the time Lila and Fay left for Wellfleet I had ordered stationery for billing and T-shirts in the same pastel colors as the flyers, with the drawing and logo screened across the back.

"My work clothes," I told Lila and Fay as I tried the pink one on in their studio. "And a walking advertisement. How economical can you get?"

"You're goin' real corporate on us," Lila said. "Hey, maybe you're onto somethin'. Maybe we'd be better off walkin' dogs than struttin' the boards."

"No way we're givin' up the Cape," Fay retorted.

She was right: they'd worked hard to find this opportunity and they would have a good summer. I had taken over their dogs, they had found an affordable apartment in Wellfleet, and Leonard Quinton had sublet their studio, an arrangement that seemed to suit everyone.

"Convenient," he explained. "And cheap enough."

"And temporary," I thought uncharitably, worried for the first time about Melanie. Leonard still went home to Queens several times a week to be with his mother, a frail diabetic widow.

"She depends on him a lot," Melanie said.

"Is that good?" I asked, and she stared at me in surprise.

"A funny question coming from you," she said, and I turned away in silent apology. "Besides," she added, "Leonard and I met because he came in here to buy his mom a crocus. So I owe her one."

During those first few weeks, however, as I struggled to get my new life in order, to establish a routine, I had very little time to worry about Melanie and Leonard. I juggled my dogs' schedules, figured out how to team them up, negotiated fees. I would build up gradually, I told myself. Go slowly, gather momentum. I approached Dog Daze as I had approached every account—psyching out my clients, figuring out time-savers, gauging my energies against the demands of the job, estimating my profits. I was, it occurred to me, as meticulous as my father had been when he accepted a job-lot of merchandise.

I was out of bed at dawn and I dressed swiftly, pulling on jeans and the ubiquitous T-shirt, strapping an oversize money belt to my waist that I filled with plastic bags, the bright green tennis ball that playful pups were partial to and a tangle of clearly marked keys to the dog owners' apartments, surrendered to me with a notable lack of hesitancy. I had tried to offer references but my new clients were largely dismissive. It seemed that security-obsessed New Yorkers were oddly trusting of dog walkers, thinking of them perhaps as eccentric eclectics, as innocent as the dogs in their care.

I gulped down a cup of instant coffee, nibbled at a piece of dry toast and picked up the four dogs whose owners all lived on Eighty-second Street. Two in the same apartment building and two others in adjacent brownstones. They were all small dogs, two terriers, a Chihuahua (appropriately named Diego Rivera) and a plump ash-colored pug. They were always yelping plaintively at the door when I arrived, their owners at the ready with outstretched leashes. Our interchanges were pleasant and superficial.

"Terrific day, it looks like."

"I hope this weather keeps up."

"Have a good one."

We smiled cheerfully, indifferently at each other.

"Gee, I wish I had your job," the owner of the pug confided one morning. She was tall and auburn-haired, the owner of an expensively reconverted brownstone and an account executive at a major advertising agency. At seven in the morning she was already dressed in a lavender linen power suit, her face made up in the careful tight mask that would sustain her through the day. In the room behind her a fax machine hissed. I stared at her and realized that I was looking at a mirror image of myself in ten years time—if, after all, I had remained at BIS and was still scrambling up the corporate ladder.

"Well, I can't say I'd want your job," I replied. I had learned that I could say almost anything with impunity, that my words were unimportant to her (as they were to most of my clients) and would barely register. Who was I, after all?

Still, she did glance at me curiously. I wore a green T-shirt that morning, and my hair, brighter and thicker than her own, brushed my shoulders. Her gaze lingered on my Phi Beta Kappa key and then she shrugged and turned away. Smiling, elated by a malicious pleasure, I headed for the park with my impatient charges, their tails wagging excitedly, their paws beating softly upon the sun-streaked pavement.

I loved the park at that hour, veiled as it was in the mists of early morning. Joggers sprinted past me, their bright tank tops pocked with circles of sweat, their nylon shorts clinging moistly to muscular thighs, their sneakers as blinding white as newly fallen snow. The women swept their hair back in dank ponytails, slipped terry-cloth sweatbands over their foreheads, smeared balm on their lips as they ran. They lifted their arms, rotated their shoulders, murmured to themselves, sometimes singing in accompaniment to a Walkman, sometimes conducting furious silent debates with themselves. One morning I saw a tall blond girl weep and talk to herself and weep again, never breaking pace.

The men ran with their heads bent low, their lips pursed, intent on completing their mileage, indifferent to the long dark shadows their bodies cast on the pathway, the comical cawing of crows quarreling atop an overflowing trash can. Nervously, they glanced at their watches, increased their speed and exited the park, sometimes waving to each other, more often heading home, glancing neither to the right nor the left.

I too ran briefly, my small dogs yelping at my heels, the pug snorting with delight. Exhilarated, my heart beating wildly, I delivered each dog and headed back to my own apartment building, where I ran Mario's hose across the small shovel and pooper-scooper I carried. Mario watched me sadly.

"What kind of a job is this for you?" he asked one morning.

He would not want his own small daughter to grow up and shovel dog shit. Each morning he walked her proudly to the Catholic school five blocks away. Black ringlets framed her chubby face, her plaid school uniform was neatly ironed and her black oxfords polished to a high gloss. Schoolbooks covered in brown paper peeped out of her bag. Had Mario himself covered them? I wondered. My father would have agreed with Mario. He had not covered my own books so carefully so that I might grow up and shovel dog shit. But I no longer had to answer to my father. My debt of gratitude, the bill of his expectations, had been duly met. I smiled at Mario.

"It's a job that makes me happy for now, Mario," I said and I ducked inside to collect Thimble.

Mrs. Clark, her white hair hugging her head in tight curls, a pink bow tucked behind her ear, gave me the small dog as though proffering a precious gift. Thimble too wore a pink bow.

"You'll take good care of my darling, won't you?" Mrs. Clark asked in a trembling voice, the same question repeated each morning.

Each morning I assured her that I would. Her ankles were swollen, broken capillaries mottled her very white skin and, like Thimble, her pale eyes were red rimmed. Invariably, she offered me a fruit from the gold-leafed dish on her table and invariably I refused. I had seen her pay for her groceries at Gristedes with food stamps, carefully setting the fruit on the counter—one apple, one pear, one tangerine.

I collected Lucky at the Catons', letting myself in with the key that had been presented with some trepidation, husband and wife eyeing each other nervously.

"We don't like giving people keys. We would much prefer that the super let you in," Dr. Caton, owlish behind his thick glasses said. "Of course, Lila had a key, but then we knew Lila."

"It'll be a hassle for me to find the super every morning. If you don't feel comfortable giving me the key you can find another dog walker." I tasted the sweetness of independence. No board would meet to pass judgment on what I had said. No angry client would phone a vice president to complain. My decisions were my own; I drew my own borders.

The Catons understood the borders immediately.

"My husband didn't mean any offense." The lawyer wife was swift to extinguish the small flame of incivility her husband had ignited. She wanted his damn dog walked as conveniently and invisibly as possible. She told me, when her husband left, that she had never wanted Lucky in the first place—was she to blame for his deprived petless childhood? She laughed bitterly and handed me the key.

Each morning, I let myself in, and as Thimble and Lucky danced around each other I wandered through the apartment. The golden hardwood floors were covered with oriental rugs, the living-room sofa and chairs were upholstered in nubby pristine white, and a painting of geometric shapes in shades of ochre and green that closely matched the fringed and patterned carpets hung on the white wall. I wondered if they had selected Lucky because the dog's golden coat matched their golden floors.

I opened the refrigerator, studied its contents—the supermarket vegetables sheathed in plastic, expensive cheeses edged with mold, a yellowing loaf of tofu—and imagined their rarely shared meals, their well-ordered life, imagined myself living such a life.

Occasionally, I went into their bedroom, medical books and financial journals on his bedside table, law extracts and the British edition of *Vogue* on hers. The door was always open, the bed always neatly covered with a huge white duvet, oversize pillows in oversize shams. It was a bed that defied intimacy, although once I lay down on it and marveled at how soft and yielding it was. It pleased me to lie there and close my eyes. It surprised me that, as I stretched luxuriously, I thought of Phil and myself lying on a blanket spread across the tall sweet grass of a Suffolk meadow. Wildly, I thought of bringing Phil to the Catons' apartment and making love on their high soft bed. They had been right, after all, to be hesitant about giving me their key. They had not known how I hungered to understand the lives of strangers so that I might choose a life of my own.

Next I went to the Eliots' more modest building to collect Goldilocks. They were, as Lila and Fay had described them, elderly and frail, dignity and delicacy implied in their every gesture. Their cultivated gentleness, their absorption in each other, seduced me.

Clem Eliot's features were honed to a fine sharpness and his thick silver hair was brushed back. Bright blue eyes glinted behind his steel-framed glasses. He had a large collection of silk ascots, which he wore carefully tucked into the collars of his broadcloth shirts, the fabric neatly ironed but worn thin by too many launderings. The crease in his flannel slacks was always impeccable.

Clem had been an archivist at Columbia, content with the silence and solitude of his work because Grace, his beautiful soft-spoken wife, was the only companion he needed. He stood beside her when I arrived to pick up Goldilocks, their frisky cocker spaniel, smiling at her proudly, worriedly.

Grace too dressed each day with casual elegance although she rarely left the apartment. She was ill. The fine fragrant face powder, the coral rouge so deftly applied, did not conceal her pallor. Still, she twisted her soft white hair into a silken chignon and wore linen dresses of muted colors, paisley scarves looped about her too-wrinkled neck, long sleeves concealing her skeletal arms. She glided forward to greet me, awkward as an adolescent in heels that were too high, chosen, I suspected, because she had shapely legs, wondrously free of veins.

I sometimes wondered what it would have been like to have had such parents, so elegant and cultivated, so unconsciously confident and at home in their world. Always, guiltily, I thrust the thought away, shamed because it seemed disloyal to my parents who had not been elegant and confident and who had not seemed at home anywhere.

The Eliot apartment was fragrant with the scent of the flowers that Clem bought twice a week at Melanie's shop. Fresh flowers were as essential to Grace Eliot as the air she breathed; she discarded a blossom at the first sign of decay.

"I cannot bear to see things die," she told me as she plucked a tulip's wilted petal.

Yet she herself was dying. Vials of pills stood on the table beside her chair. Bottles of gem-colored medicines lined a kitchen shelf. I averted my eyes from them as I looped Goldilocks's leash through her collar. I was too recent a refugee from the habitat of near death.

"It's leukemia," Clem told me softly one morning as he bent to offer biscuits to his pet. "She as leukemia, my poor Grace." His hands trembled and his blue eyes were flooded with tears. Again I thought of my parents, who had denied themselves even the luxury of weeping.

Thimble, Lucky and Goldilocks, so used to each other, ambled easily through the park. I relaxed my hold on the three leashes and matched my pace to theirs. The joggers were gone, replaced by children. Toddlers in strollers smiled amiably and clutched their fat purple Barneys, their plastic Teletubbies. Small boys and girls kicked pebbles as they walked, jumped over rises in the path. Fathers in business suits held their hands. Mothers in jeans and loose-fitting shirts waved to each other, shouted arrangements for play dates. "Two at my house." "The playground after lunch." Disinterested nannies urged their charges to hurry. Each day I watched a coarse-looking, heavyset woman in a pale blue uniform that was too tight, drag a small girl who wore glasses along the verge.

"Slow. Why are you so slow?" she hissed.

Older youngsters scurried by, calling to each other, dancing across benches in sneakers that gave them odd, unnatural height, discarding candy wrappers, darting behind trees and bushes. They swung their backpacks with sudden, inexplicable viciousness and darted off, their voices rising in a defiant chorus.

"I didn't."

"You did."

"I won't."

"You will."

My dogs growled softly and I reined in their leashes. I loosened them at Ninetieth Street where two tall women, their skin the color of mahogany, waved to me. Their hair fashioned into head-hugging Afros, their tie-dyed smocks a flash of color over their white polyester pants, they gravely escorted a group of elderly men and women to the benches beneath a row of conifers. The old women slumped on the splintered wooden seats, fingered their cotton dresses with twisted fingers, crossed and uncrossed their legs, revealing dark cotton support stockings knotted below their knees. Their scalps shone infant pink beneath their thinning gray hair. The old men rolled their shirtsleeves up and then rolled them down again. They consulted their watches, polished their glasses, nervously tapped their hearing aids. Sometimes they talked to each other, their heads inclined, their hands moving in rhythm to their words. Sometimes they talked to themselves, lips pursed when a word or a memory eluded them. Sometimes they sat in silence, immobilized by their own sadness.

The aides tried. They tossed a large blue ball to each of them in turn.

"Good catch. See what you can do. Good for you, Mr. Klein."

They offered their arms for a short walk.

"Just to the next bench, Granny. Come on. Let's just try to walk to the next bench."

I, too, tried. I paused and allowed the dogs to wander up to them, to brush against their legs, to lick an outstretched hand. Thimble barked softly, pressed his beribboned curly white head against a thick-stockinged leg. The aides smiled at me.

"Hi, Rochelle."

"Hi, Samantha, Aretha."

We had, after some days, introduced ourselves and now we greeted each other by name, gave the hi sign to messengers on roller skates and bikes, glared in mutual disapproval at a mess of fast-food wrappers left beneath a tree. Samantha lifted Thimble onto her lap, rubbed his back. She was training to be a massage therapist.

"A great field," she said. "I love it. And it pays really well."

Aretha was studying accounting at a community college. Only two courses a semester because she had a baby. "Still, I'll be through in two, maybe three years."

I nodded, vaguely envious and bewildered by that envy.

We always left the park at the same time, the old people shuffling across the street, squinting sadly against the sun's intrusive brightness, my dogs gamboling wildly across patches of shade. Aretha and Samantha waved and I waved back, walked on.

I returned Thimble, Lucky and Goldilocks, picked up the *New York Times* and flipped through it as I sipped a cup of very bitter coffee at a luncheonette. I ignored the business section, which, during my BIS years I had read urgently, impatiently, combing it for mention of a client, psyching out the news releases that appeared as features, checking the stock pages for readings on our clients, readings on their competitors. Brad had trained me well, taught me to be aware of trades and splits, dividends and losses. It was a given that public relations firms like BIS were never thanked when stocks rose and always blamed when they fell.

"Just know about it," Brad had advised. "But don't sweat it. We're okay as long as falls and spurts don't affect our billing hours."

That was, after all, our golden rule—nothing must affect the billing hours. But that was something that no longer worried me and so I left the business section unread on the counter.

Instead, I absorbed myself in news stories with a human-interest angle. I was consumed with a need to know how other people lived their lives, how they managed their day-to-day existences, their decisions, their finances. With a voyeur's intensity I read between the lines, vesting simple stories with long shadows of drama. The *Times* reported on a fire in a luxury high-rise. A fireman (aged forty-one—wasn't that old for a firefighter—why hadn't he retired?) had rescued an elderly widow (aged seventy-eight). Days later there was a photograph of her son, a stockbroker, and her daughter, a fashion designer ("prominent," the *Times* said in lieu of giving her age), handing the fireman a generous check for the fund to benefit the widows of firefighters. Why did the old woman live alone? I wondered. Had she quarreled with her children? Was she fiercely, selfishly independent? How much did a fireman make? What benefits would his family have received if he had been killed? (The rescue had been a daring one, involving an entry into a smoke-filled room, a laborious and precarious descent down a narrow ladder.) Had his wife been angry at him for taking such a risk or had she realized that he could not do otherwise? Such questions intrigued me and I read the paper each day in search of concealed messages, implied guidelines, as though I were a participant in a scavenger hunt and the stories offered clues that would lead me to a promised prize.

My father had given my mother a small brown envelope each week that contained neatly folded bills, but the Catons kept individual accounts. I had seen their separate checkbooks on their separate desks. Would Phil have wanted us to keep our money separate if we had married? Did it matter?

"Yenta!" I chastised myself and went off on my third tour of the morning, this time on the west side. Three dogs, all of them large. Two Afghan hounds, sad eyed, long luxurious fur draping their lean bodies, and a sleek black Lab, aptly named Sir Gawain, haughty and swift, who ignored them, ignored me. I held tight to their leashes as they loped toward the dog run, pausing when they did, reining them in as I scooped up their steamy stinking stools, slid them into a plastic bag that I tossed into a trash can.

They roamed free at the run while I talked to other dog walkers. Sturdy Annette, a divorcée in her forties, leaned against the mesh fence, her thighs bulging out of denim walking shorts, thick unmatched socks sticking out of discolored hiking boots. It was she who had advised me to get myself a long coat and boots, recommending her favorite thrift shop.

"You don't want to dress like that," she said, studying my designer jeans, my T-shirt and the white tennis socks I wore with my very white sneakers. "You look like you're about to hit the courts at a country club."

"Exactly what I used to do," I confessed. "In my other life."

I wondered if Phil had found another doubles partner, if he had taken a share in a beach house, if he missed me. I even dared to wonder if I missed him.

Annette shot me a shrewd, knowing glance.

"But, hey, maybe I'll sell you my coat, my boots. Maybe I'll even give them to you. This is my last season of dog walking. I've had it with the turds and wiping their smelly saliva off my knees." She laughed and then confessed that she planned to quit every summer and was still walking dogs in the fall. She had started doing it to supplement her alimony and continued because the alimony had stopped and there was a daughter in private school, a son in an institution. Autistic. Her husband was ashamed to have fathered such a child. What she really wanted to do was write a novel. She had notes, she had ideas. She even had the beginning of a first chapter. But she was so damn tired when she finally got home. Tired and dirty, but still she would clean up and sometimes even sit down at the typewriter.

"Then the phone rings. An emergency. Someone's dog walker didn't show up. Would I, could I? Double the fee. So I can and I will. A client has to go out of town. Could I baby-sit her beagle? And I need the money. My daughter's class is going to Spain next year. There's a new drug they want to try on my son. Still, next year's for me. Next year's the year I begin to write. Full-time."

"That's right, Annette. Next year's the year. That's when I kiss these mutts goodbye on account of I'll have a starring role on Broadway." Lanky Carl brushed back the long blond hair that tumbled into his eyes, clicked the heels of his boots together and practiced a dance routine, his taps clinking sharply against the soil and feces–encrusted concrete. He was gentle with his dogs, gentle with the other dog walkers, gentle with his lover, Ramon, who came by the dog run to pick up money for lunch, money for drinks, money for dinner. Ramon had to dress nice, had to be seen in the right places, Carl explained, although no one asked him. He was a designer. He had to make contacts. Carl danced again, a neat routine, the many keys to the apartments of his many clients jangling as he moved.

"Poor Carl," Mitzi (whom I always thought of as poor Mitzi) said. She was a wraithlike girl who wore long flowered skirts, loose peasant blouses, the remnants of her Barnard College wardrobe. She came from Minnesota and had not wanted to return there when she graduated ("Do you know how cold Minnesota can be in the winter?" she asked me but did not wait for an answer) and she had not wanted to teach school or work in an office. She had drifted into dog walking as I had, through the friend of a friend. It was something to do until she decided what it was she wanted to do. She had been doing it for three years—or was it four? Anyway, it made no difference. She was happy with it. And she had time.

"Good," I said, and I did not tell her that I had seen her one afternoon, walking her dogs as I walked mine, tears streaming down her cheeks, her lips moving soundlessly. Poor Mitzi.

I left the dog run and returned to the park, populated now by nannies and young mothers who wheeled strollers and baby carriages or raced after very young children. The same small boy darted up to me each day and solemnly, bravely, petted Sir Gawain. Elderly men, their unread newspaper spread out on their laps, looked up at me with grudging approval as I passed. After a few days, one of them doffed his cap and grinned, another commented on the weather. Each day a sandy-haired artist, pastels jutting out of the pocket of his plaid shirt, shifted his oversize sketch pad and leaned forward as I passed. He approached me one morning, a smudge of charcoal on his cheek, the charcoal stick itself balanced elegantly between his paint-stained fingers.

"Listen, I hope you don't mind, but I've been trying to sketch the Lab for a couple of days now and I really need for him to stand still. It's hard to get him when he keeps moving."

"I can manage that."

I kept the dogs on a short leash and stood still as he knelt and swiftly drew Sir Gawain, who stared disdainfully into the distance, his ears pricked, his long body sleek and graceful. He ignored the Afghans, who after a few minutes sank to the ground and lay contentedly in a pool of sunlight. Just as Sir Gawain grew impatient and began to paw at the ground, the work was finished, the sketch pad snapped shut.

"Can I see?" I asked.

The sketch was excellent, capturing the dog's natural grace, the long, lean line of his body.

"That's really good," I said.

"Thanks." He blushed, the color rising slowly to his pale cheeks, suffusing his high forehead. He wiped his hand on his paint-scabbed jeans and held it out to me. "My name is Dave," he said.

"You're welcome," I replied. "I'm Rochelle."

We greeted each other by name after that, although I never paused to chat. When he did not appear for a few days I missed him, but when he returned, working in watercolor now at a small portable metal easel that glinted in the sunlight, we merely resumed that perfunctory greeting.

"Morning, Rochelle."

"Good morning, Dave."

I did not glance at his work. He did not offer to show it to me.

By twelve-thirty I was done for the morning. I wandered over to Melanie's flower shop, sometimes for a brief chat, sometimes for a long lunch at a neighborhood place. Occasionally a college friend joined us. Andrea, who had been our roommate and who had married the July after graduation. The mother of two children, pregnant with a third, she dropped by when she came in from Larchmont for her monthly obstetric checkup, showed us pictures of her children, her house. Sitting opposite each other in a wide-windowed café, we talked too fast, bobbing up and down on those swift clever exchanges so that we would not drown in our envy of each other's lives. We wanted her children; she wanted our freedom.

Brett came by, clever handsome Brett, his fortune made, the window-sash business thriving, his money invested and his marriage punctured by boredom after only two years and threatening to sink. He spoke of taking a year off, maybe doing a graduate degree in architecture, maybe teaching. He was bored, dissatisfied. He needed time off.

"Would that work for you?" I asked.

"Doesn't it work for you?" he countered, annoyed because he had anticipated the sympathy that male friends expect as their due from the women they have entrusted with intellectual intimacy, and I had offered challenge, instead.

"I don't know," I replied slowly, truthfully. His question bewildered and frightened me.

One afternoon Melanie and I picked up lunch at the Food Emporium salad bar and went back to the shop to eat in her workroom. Soil rimmed her fingernails, bright flower petals dotted her freckled hands.

"Clean dirt," she said and leaned back in her bright orange director's chair.

I scrubbed my own hands vigorously.

"Dirty dirt." I grimaced, sniffed my palms. "I've got to get some of those plastic gloves."

"Why not. It's tax deductible. Ask Phil."

"If and when I talk to him."

"Warren went to Michael's Pub with him the other night. Some jazz group they wanted to hear."

I was not surprised. Melanie's brother and Phil had shared a penchant for jazz during their Dartmouth days when neither of them could afford tickets for campus concerts. Now they were young business princes, waving credit cards like scepters, effortlessly paying cover charges and minimums at the best clubs.

"They went alone. No dates. Phil said there was no one he wanted to ask," Melanie added.

I picked up a stuffed grape leaf, put it down and said nothing.

"Rochelle, Shelley, what are you doing? Do you know what you're doing?" She folded a lettuce leaf around an artichoke heart and popped it into her mouth.

"I'm taking it one day at a time," I replied. "As befits a charter member of Orphans Anonymous. I'm fighting my genetic addiction to self-pity. I'm trying to decide what I want to be when I grow up. That's what I'm doing. What about you, Melanie? What are you doing?"

"Getting used to loving Leonard." She smiled shyly, fearfully. "It's really scary."

Her fear was real, woven of the delicate mesh of dark memory, the disparate strands of "almosts" and "might-have-beens," the calls she never received, the calls that went unanswered, the lingering sadness of inexplicable endings.

"I know." I covered her hand with my own and smiled at my brave, gamine-faced friend who grinned back at me and jauntily, defiantly, tucked a long-stemmed daisy into her bright magenta hair.

Occasionally after such a pick-up lunch, Melanie would lock the flower shop and, relishing our freedom, we wandered the city. We visited a neighborhood studio where ceramicists exhibited their new glazes, an Internet bar where we sent messages to distant classmates, a small boutique where we tried on hats, experimented with scarves, each of us occasionally buying something. One afternoon we went to the Museum of Modern Art where I stared up at the *Guernica* as though its tormented landscape might reveal a great truth to me.

Studying Picasso's bold and whirling lines, his dizzying, terrible image of war's devastation, I imagined my parents as young people thrust into a chaos crueler and more incomprehensible than that of the innocent Spanish town. The questions that I had not dared to ask them in their lifetimes flooded my mind. How had they found the strength to survive, the courage to awaken each day, the tenacity to scramble for food and, at last, the grace to walk toward each other, barefoot, skeletal bodies balanced on skeletal legs? What if I found myself trapped in such a nightmare? Would I survive? Would I find the strength, the courage, the tenacity—I who had grown up in the protective circle of their love, who had with such ease claimed all the glittering prizes, never anticipating darkness or danger? Oh, I could never match them, never.

I turned away from the painting, from that landscape of loneliness and terror, grateful that my parents had died in their quiet, orderly home, that I had been with them, that, in the end, their triumph had been complete.

"Hey, Rochelle." Melanie, sensing my mood, linked her arm through mine and with a sudden burst of energy, we sprinted uptown.

By three o'clock I was on the Upper West Side, where I guided a sleek dalmation and a comical-looking chow on a dignified stroll down Riverside Drive. Patient dogs, they allowed me to rest on a bench as they dropped exquisitely shaped golden turds on the scrub grass.

Back on the east side I collected twin bassets and a beagle, careful to move them swiftly toward the park and away from the broad avenues crowded with work-weary pedestrians hurrying home after a day that had been too long and too hot. One afternoon I saw my former colleague, Suzanne, standing on a corner, tapping her foot impatiently as she waited for a light to change. She wore a sleeveless black dress and a loosely knotted turquoise silk scarf. Wasn't it enough that she had my job? I thought wryly. Did she have to steal my wardrobe as well? Still, gripping the leashes, I waved at her but she was talking earnestly into her cell phone and did not see me. Just as well, I thought. She would not have been amused by the bassets' long floppy ears, by the beagle's mournful gaze. I wondered if she had been talking to Eddie Longauer and the next morning I checked the price of Longauer stock. Up two points. Good for Eddie and, I supposed, for BIS. It appeared that I was hardly indispensable. As Brad had known. As I should have known. Not that it would have made any difference. I had done what I had to do.

In the evening I again walked Thimble and Goldilocks, delivering Goldilocks last because the Eliots invariably invited me in for coffee or tea, setting out a cheese tray and crackers, the cutlery arranged on woven place mats, an exquisitely embroidered linen napkin, frayed at the edge, on each delicate milk china dish. I hesitated at first but I soon looked forward to the nightly interlude. They had something to teach me and I was an eager student in the academy of other people's lives.

I watched as he adjusted the pillow on her chair and settled Goldilocks on her lap. I listened as she urged him to tell me an interesting anecdote about the literary critic Lionel Trilling, who had haunted the Columbia archives. It was a story that she had heard often, she confessed when he went to the kitchen to replenish the crackers, but he enjoyed telling it and she did so want him to enjoy himself.

They showed me their photograph album, their lives chronicled in the snapshots artfully placed on black pages crumbling at the corners. A courting couple smiling up at each other beneath the shade of a tree. Bride and groom, she in a gown of ivory satin surprisingly revealing, he in full dress, a carnation in his buttonhole. Their honeymoon, poses at the Eiffel Tower, the Colosseum, the Acropolis.

"We did the grand tour," he said sheepishly. "Everyone did then. I'm sure your parents did the same thing."

"No," I said. "No, they didn't."

I turned the page.

They stood in front of a tent, his arm around her. *Hammonasset, Connecticut,* she had written neatly in white ink. *Camping at the Beach.*

"Oh yes," she said, noting my surprised look. "We loved to camp. We had leather camping stools, folding beds, everything."

They camped as they had done everything always. With style.

Another picture at Hammonasset, this time before a larger tent, his hand resting on a small boy's shoulder, her arm encircling a little girl with a heart-shaped face.

"Our son and daughter, Avery and Eunice." He answered the question I had not asked.

I looked around the room. My own parents' living room had been a photographic gallery, every surface covered with framed portraits or a collage of candid snapshots. I stared out at them, smiling in my white elementary-school graduation dress, a beribboned medal pinned to the collar, in my purple high-school cap and gown adorned with the pins of academic, athletic and service honor societies; finally, in my black college robe, the Phi Beta Kappa key bright against my throat. In smaller prints I sprinted

across the finish line in an intercollegiate race, posed in front of a
booth at a college fair, sat at a desk, my eyes fixed on a heavy text
although my smile denied any real concentration. I had sent them
all those photographs, shopped for the frames that I presented as
Mother's Day, Father's Day, Chanukah gifts, knowing that all their
pleasure centered on my life, my happiness, my achievements. My
mother had even laminated the story that had appeared in *Time* and
placed it in a Lucite frame. But there was no picture of my mother,
no picture of my father, in that room. I was the vortex of their
household, the only player on my parents' small, circumscribed
stage.

In contrast, the only photograph in the Eliots' living room
showed them in a formal pose, Clem in a tuxedo, Grace in a high-
necked silken evening gown, her hair falling in gentle folds about
her face.

I asked them about their children, whose photographic presence
was so conspicuously absent from the room in which they passed
their lives. Eunice was a high-school English teacher, divorced and
living in Oregon. Avery was a scientist. He taught at MIT and had
three children.

"We like his wife," Clem said absently.

"Eileen. That's her name," Grace added quickly, as though I
might think that they had forgotten their daughter-in-law's name.

The children, she observed, all looked like Eileen.

"Oh, no." Clem's voice was firm. "They're such pretty little
girls. They all look like you."

And then he adjusted the pillow behind her back and asked me
if I had read the book they were currently reading aloud to each
other. Edith Wharton. *The House of Mirth.*

"Grace has wonderful insights," he confided proudly. "She could
have taught English on a college level." It was clear that he would
much rather talk about his wife than about their children.

I understood then that their lives revolved around each other, that their children were peripheral, benign intruders on their cherished togetherness but intruders nonetheless. Which was, perhaps, as it should be. Their loving disinterest had granted their son and daughter independence, had allowed them to forge their own lives. Eunice had been free to move to Oregon, to divorce her husband without fearing how such decisions might impact upon her parents. Avery had built a career, established his own life at a comfortable, but not formidable, distance. Surely their mother's illness saddened them, but it had not entrapped them. Avery went to his laboratory each day, I was certain. Eunice had not quit her job and moved back from Oregon. Unlike myself, they had no emotional debt too awesome ever to be repaid.

"But what else could I have done?" I shouted into the darkness as I walked home that night. A young man put his arm protectively around the shoulder of his dark-haired girlfriend and, swiftly, they crossed the street. A woman hugged her brown bags of groceries and sidled closer to an apartment building as though seeking shelter against my madness. Shamed, I hurried on.

At the next corner I saw Mitzi on the opposite side of the street, her light hair and pale skin further blanched by the light of the street lamp, the winged sleeves of her ivory-colored blouse whipped by the gentle summer wind. She held the leash of a sleek white borzoi hound who strained to move forward, and just as I thought to call out to her, she slipped into the park. Like shadows, as delicate as smoke, dog and walker disappeared into the darkness of the tree-lined path.

"Stupid Mitzi," I thought worriedly, almost angrily. She had to know that the park was dangerous at night. I would talk to her. No. Better still, I would have streetwise, life-worn Annette talk to her. "Poor stupid Mitzi."

There were two messages on my answering machine that night. A man's voice (not Phil's), flat and vaguely familiar.

"Rochelle. Sorry you're out. I'll try again soon. I guess."

No name. I played it again and still did not recognize the speaker. The second message was from my cousin Morrie.

"Ruchele, are you all right? Call us. Come for dinner maybe on Friday night. Shabbos. Please, Ruchele."

I did not call Morrie. Instead, I called Phil and listened to his answering machine. He was out, as I had known he would be, and I did not leave a message.

I read some Muriel Rukeyser poems and then settled down with my own pad and pen. I was writing quatrains, then carefully controlled odes to my own searching sadness. I juggled words, balanced cadences and then reread the lines with grudging pleasure. For the very first time I tore the page loose and inserted it into an empty folder.

I heard Melanie and Leonard laugh as they walked down the hall to the studio sublet. Swiftly, I shut the light. They paused briefly at my door and then, talking softly, they walked on, leaving me alone in the darkness.

# CHAPTER
## SIX

Days drifted into weeks. Heat besieged the city. The Korean salad-bar owners sprinkled crushed ice over their strawberries and pyramided bottles of Evian water in refrigerated cases. Dog owners took long weekends and I wandered through empty apartments filling feeding dishes with Alpo and basins with water. As the dogs gobbled and drank, I stretched out on sofas and dreamed my way into lives that were not my own. I scanned mail and calendars. The Catons each made large monthly payments to therapists. I played the answering machine in the elegant penthouse of the Afghans' owners. A woman's breathy voice. "Please call. *I want to explain what I did not explain last night.*" It seemed to me that apartments throughout the city were electric with words unsaid.

I did call Morrie but he told me apologetically that he and Zelda were spending the rest of the season in the Catskills. He had told me once how the gentle mountains reminded him of the mountains that surrounded the village of his childhood and that of my parents—a vanished dreamscape of which they'd rarely spoken. Their memories, I supposed, had been too fragile to withstand the impact of their words.

I went to a party on a rooftop and a party on a boat moored in the Seventy-ninth Street boat basin, my name not yet removed from the Rolodex of the event planner.

"What do you do?" young men and not so young men asked me, their eyes raking approvingly across my face, taking in my Phi Beta Kappa key, my well-cut silk shift.

"I'm a dog walker," I replied and watched their interest flicker, their eyes wander. Phil, of course, was not at these parties although I looked for him. I did see Eddie Longauer leaning against the rail of the boat, awkward and ill at ease. His aloneness, his platform shoes and the way his pale blue designer shirt hugged his body saddened me, but I moved swiftly away so that he would not see me. I had strength enough to sustain only my own loneliness.

I sipped my wine and watched couples chat briefly and drift away from each other, their long shadows falling in velvet swathes across the deck of a ship that would not sail.

Some evenings I spent at Melanie's flower shop and others I sat beside Mario in the small patch of garden behind my apartment building and helped him fill out school applications for his daughter. He wanted her to be accepted at a specialized school that emphasized science. They were the best, he said, and he wanted the best for her, as my parents had wanted the best for me. I generally visited the Eliots at least one night a week when my last dog-walking tour was done. Clem made us tea and now and again read poetry aloud. Once, on such a visit, I clipped Grace Eliot's toenails. Her long slender feet rested lightly on my hand and we both smiled at this odd and necessary intimacy. I tried to remember if I had ever touched my mother's feet before her illness, but I knew, of course, that I hadn't. She had guarded her privacy, perhaps because it had been denied her for so many years, perhaps because she had never wanted me to see the long scars, carved like smiles into the callused flesh of her soles—the reminder that once she had walked shoeless through prison gates.

That night I wrote a poem, the words coming to me in a rush, a series of visual images, chronicling the movements of two barefoot wraiths walking toward each other through a heavy mist. I wrote swiftly, fearful that if I paused, I would cease to see them or that they might elude each other and vanish into a damp miasma. I carried the notebook with me the next day, something I had not done before. In the late afternoon I took the two Afghan hounds and Sir Gawain on a run through the park and then I selected a bench along Riverside Drive, knotting their leashes around the iron rail. The dogs, exhausted by the long run, stretched out in a pale pool of sunlight and I opened my notebook, holding my pen poised over it. Heavy-hearted, I read my own words. The rhythm was irregular, the images obscure. I crossed out one line, then another, my pen ripping angrily across the paper. I was so absorbed, so weighted by my own despair, that I was not aware that Mitzi had glided toward me until I looked up and saw her staring down at my pad.

"Poetry?" she asked and took a seat beside me.

Although the day was uncomfortably warm Mitzi wore high red suede boots and a faded green poplin jacket, its huge pockets crammed with Baggies and dog biscuits, with the heavily laden key ring that jangled when she walked and with paperback books whose titles always surprised me. Mitzi read poetry and art history, philosophic treatises and English detective stories, plucking them from the laundry-room libraries of the apartment houses where she collected her dogs. She gave the books she no longer wanted to Ida, the tall black homeless woman who sat with quiet dignity on a bench at the far end of the dog run. The clothing in Ida's battered shopping cart was meticulously folded, her toiletries shrouded in Saran Wrap and the books tucked neatly into corners. Ida, who rarely spoke, was the ward of the dog walkers. I placed two dollar bills on her cart each afternoon and Carl brought her a paper cup of coffee and a bagel lathered with cream cheese every morning.

I sighed.

"Well, I thought it was poetry last night but today I'm not so sure." I snapped my notebook shut and shoved it into my backpack.

"I used to play at writing poetry." Mitzi sucked a strand of pale hair and reached down to scratch the ears of the silky-haired brown Pomeranian who was her only charge that hour. Its owners paid her double the regular fee because they wanted their dog to have her undivided attention.

"They're obsessive," Mitzi had said dismissively when she told me about them. "All they think about is their precious Peaches— a stupid name for such a cute dog. It's a good thing they never had children. They probably would have kept them on short leashes."

"Possibly," I said and my throat had grown tight, remembering my parents' obsessiveness about my life, their unarticulated expectations always keeping me on a short and strangulating emotional leash. All that had been denied them would be thrust upon me. The unkindness of that unbidden thought had shamed me.

"What kind of poetry?" I asked Mitzi.

"Haiku, free verse, whatever. I was a lit major and I loved my poetry courses. I thought if you loved something enough and worked hard enough at it, you could do it. I was wrong but that's okay. It's just another thing I was wrong about." She stared out at the river, where a scow ploughed through the cobalt water, creating hillocks of foam.

"But how do you know you can't do it?" I kept my tone light, encouraging, to counter the sadness in her voice and in her eyes. The Pomeranian barked and she tossed him a dog biscuit and then gave one to each of my dogs, who turned their heads in acknowledgment but remained supine as they chewed slowly. That was a professional perk, I thought wryly. Instant appreciation, silent companionship. I stroked Sir Gawain's ear and heard the throaty breath of his gratitude.

"Because I went to this poetry workshop at the library. Not up here. A midtown branch. A poet taught it. Constance Reid. And I listened to other people read their work. And some of it was really good. So good. So much better than I could ever be. I knew it. I knew it at the very first session but I kept going for a couple of months. I never read anything of my own. I just listened. Finally, there didn't seem to be any point in going and I just stopped. I do that a lot, I guess. When I don't see any point, I just stop." She closed her eyes, wearied by her own words.

I leaned back and watched Ida stand and wheel her shopping cart to another bench, removed from the glare of the afternoon sun. It occurred to me that I was not too different from Mitzi. When things seemed pointless, I too stopped. Hadn't I done that with BIS? Wasn't I doing that with Phil? Mitzi reached into a pocket for a granola bar and I wondered what she would do when her life in New York reached a point of no return, when she could no longer sustain the loneliness of walking through the park with tears streaking her cheeks. Would she pack her bags and return to Minnesota or would she take off for Europe, for the Berkshires, for Mexico?

"I know Constance Reid's work," I said. "I've read her poems in *Granta*. And she had something in the *Atlantic Monthly* a while back. She's good. Where exactly does this workshop meet?"

"Forty-fourth Street. There are flyers up at all the branches. You have to call, submit work."

She did not ask me if I planned to join the workshop. She did not ask to see the poem in my notebook. Which was not surprising since we did not even know each other's last names. Ours was the situational intimacy of urban wanderers who would, one day, disappear from each other's lives without impact or imprint.

Ida, tall and majestic, walked by us, her laden shopping cart elegantly balanced. Hastily, I thrust two singles into it and Ida nodded and glided on. It was, I knew, entirely possible that we might never see her again. She might migrate to another part of the park, another part of the city.

"Bye, Ida," Mitzi said and the regal black woman nodded and waved but did not look back at us.

"Mitzi," I said, "it's not a good idea to walk through the park alone at night."

"I can take care of myself." She smiled sadly. "I'm a savvy west side gal." She bent forward and, with great deliberation, wiped a sliver of creamy yellow turd from the soft surface of her high red suede boot.

We both fell silent as Annette, with two poodles in tow, came up to us. We would not speak of writing or of poetry with Annette who read and reread the half-completed first chapter of a novel begun four years ago. Instead, we listened to her amusing stories about the owners of the poodles, a man and woman now divorced who lived in neighboring apartments and did not speak although they shared custody of the two white dogs. They walked them in silence to the grooming parlor and in silence they passed each other cans of dog food, water dishes and ointments for the constant infections that caused their pets' pale eyes to ooze.

"Creeps," Annette said and we nodded in agreement. We considered most of our clients to be creeps.

I left as Carl approached. I had used up that day's ration of sorrow on Mitzi. I did not want to hear about Carl's lover, Ramon, who had surely lost yet another job.

"What kind of lives are they living—Mitzi, Annette, Carl?" I asked Melanie later that week as we perched on my kitchen stools and expertly plucked steamed vegetables from greasy white take-out cartons with the elegant lacquered chopsticks that Brad had distributed to every BIS employee when he returned from a trip to China. He had been the beneficent father, gleefully carrying

party favors home to his grateful children. *I should get rid of them,*
I thought. *I should get rid of everything related to BIS.* But instead I
traced my fingers along their smooth and shiny surface and fished
out another piece of broccoli.

"Linear lives," Melanie replied. "One day at a time. No grand
plan. Not even a five-year plan. They're not so different from a lot
of our friends. All the opportunities and probably too many
choices. We're Yeats's generation, Rochelle. *Our center does not
hold.*" She wore a magenta sweat suit that almost matched her hel-
met of hair, and her gamine face was washed clean of makeup, giving her a childlike look. Leonard was visiting his mother in Queens
that night and she listened expectantly to footfalls in the corridor.
The phone rang and she darted nervously forward. It was a tele-
marketer asking if I wanted to switch my long-distance service.

"But I have no one to call, not in this city, not in any city," I told
the hoarse-voiced operator, who swiftly hung up.

Melanie poured more tea.

"Do you have a grand plan, a five-year plan?" I asked and reflected that I did not even have a five-day plan—I, who once kept
a Filofax so crammed with appointments that I could not find a free
hour to go to the dentist.

"Sort of. I want to buy the shop next door and expand. I'd have
one section for plants and another for flowers, maybe even a miniature greenhouse. And I want to marry Leonard and have at least
two children. I'll put a playpen in the workroom and they can
watch me make bouquets and wreaths and play with the fallen
petals."

"They may eat them," I said wryly, but I imagined two cherubic
infants bathed in the ultraviolet light that illuminated that fragrant
work space.

"They may," she agreed pleasantly. "And I want you to have a plan
of your own. Not a grand plan. Just any plan." She hesitated. "Phil
called me. He wants to know what you're doing, how you're doing."

"What did you tell him?"

"I told him that he should ask you. Am I not a good friend?"

"You are." I speared the last snow pea. "And I will reward you. I do have a small plan. A very tiny plan."

I told her then about the poetry workshop. I had called and received an application. I had submitted three poems and Constance Reid had written to me—not on a typewriter or a computer but in an elegant spidery hand, a poet's hand—that I was welcome to join her students.

"Well, that's something," Melanie said approvingly.

My doorbell rang then and she slid off her stool and opened the door to Leonard. He smiled down at her, the collar of his plaid shirt tucked unevenly into his camel-colored sweater. It reminded me of how my own mother had stood on tiptoe to adjust my own collar and an unanticipated wave of grief washed over me. Mourners, I supposed, were not unlike recovering invalids who think their symptoms have abated and are startled when weakness overtakes them. Just so, fresh sorrow ambushed me.

Leonard's large hand rested on Melanie's head, an encircling crown of tenderness. I did not mind that when they left they took all the fortune cookies with them. I hoped that each sliver of paper would promise them success, happiness, mysterious and wondrous journeys. That was what I wanted for my elfin friend whose childhood had been spent with parents who addressed each other in the distant tones of polite strangers, until one day her father had packed a very large suitcase and left, kissing Melanie on the cheek and gravely shaking hands with her brother. A large manila envelope addressed to his wife covered the pillow on the bed they no longer shared. Melanie had studied psychology, intent on analyzing the sad secrets of her childhood. In our dormitory room she had read aloud to me from texts on marital incompatibility, fears of abandonment, case histories of familial dysfunction until she at last decided that there were no answers, that no explanation would be found in those heavy volumes. I hoped that Leonard offered her solace, contentment. She deserved it, my friend, my generous and zany friend, who appeared, despite my initial doubt, to have finally found a center that would hold.

The poetry workshop met on Tuesday evening, which I occasionally spent with Grace and Clem Eliot. When I told them I would not be coming, I saw the disappointment on their faces. We had, over the past weeks, bonded into a surrogate family of a kind; I was the attentive daughter and they were the elegant, cultivated parents. I felt a twinge of disloyalty to my own mother and father as I sat in the Eliots' book-lined living room, encircled by their interest and affection.

"I'm really sorry," I said, "I should have told you earlier."

"But when will you be coming?" Clem asked and the plaintiveness in his voice irritated me. My parents would never have asked such a question. They would have masked their letdown and assured me that they were happy I was doing something that was important to me, that I would enjoy. Always, my contentment, my happiness, had come before their own. *Go, Ruchele. Have a good time. Enjoy,* their love whispered in memory.

"I'll come tomorrow night," I said. "In fact, I'll bring dinner. I've been wanting to make stuffed cabbage and it's stupid to cook just for myself. And then I'll be able to tell you about the workshop."

Clem nodded. "That would be very nice, Rochelle. And I have a nice burgundy I've been saving. That will be nice, Grace. We'll drink that good wine and eat Rochelle's excellent stuffed cabbage. That's something to look forward to."

"That will be wonderful." She smiled wanly and held out her hand, the swollen blue veins taut against the parchment-pale skin that bruised at the slightest pressure. She would, of course, do no more than take a single sip of wine and force a bit of meat into her mouth; but, yes, it was something to look forward to. Had my parents, during the long weeks of their dying, looked forward to anything at all? I wondered, saddened again by all that I did not know about them.

I took Grace's hand in my own, the almost fleshless bones of her fingers sharp within my palm.

"You'll like my stuffed cabbage," I said. "My mother's recipe."

I did not tell her that it was a recipe my mother had learned from an older woman in the camp. Huddled on a crude bunk, she had listened to older inmates speak of their abandoned kitchens, of the joy of cooking for their families. They each had favorite dishes and they listed the ingredients and the secrets of preparation. Thin cabbage leaves. Meat. Tomatoes. Garlic. They pronounced the words lovingly although their stomachs were cramped with hunger, their mouths were dry and their stale breath soured the air of the barracks. My mother, of course, had never told me this but her friend Bella, who had been interned with her, was an infrequent guest and I willed myself to wakefulness during her visits.

Lying in my darkened bedroom, I listened to the two women trade their bitter memories, laugh their uneasy, inexplicable laughter.

"Do you remember, Lena, old Mrs. Abramowitz?"

"Do I remember? It was from her that I got my recipe for stuffed cabbage. The secret, she said, was to brown the meat with the garlic and onions. That was the secret."

And I squeezed my eyes shut and conjured up an image of my mother, Lena, and Bella, her friend, young girls (my age perhaps?) in tattered striped uniforms, listening (as I listened now) to their mentors, imprisoned housewives, dispossessed of their kitchens, bereft of their children, lovingly recite their recipes, reveal their terrible, impossible yearnings.

I glanced at my watch, patted the dog, waved to Clem and Grace with false gaiety and ran for the bus, which miraculously arrived at once and even more miraculously cruised downtown avoiding every traffic light.

Darting into the library, I caught a glimpse of my reflection in the glass door and realized that I should have made time to change. I hurried to the ladies' room, pulled my bright hair back and applied the red-gold lipstick that Melanie had bought for me because she insisted that it so closely matched my hair.

"It's all right," I told myself as I tucked my white T-shirt into my jeans, thankfully finding a tangerine-colored scarf into my pocket that I could drape around my neck. "You'll be fine." After all, hadn't I always been fine? The lessons of all the years of my life would not be so swiftly unlearned.

I pushed open the door of the reading room and felt a tingle of excitement and apprehension. I beamed my smile, that carefully cultivated smile that blended shyness and confidence. Hadn't Brad told me that clients loved my smile?

"Please, please come in and sit down."

The tall, thin woman standing at the head of a long table motioned me to an empty chair. I assumed that she was Constance Reid. Her closely cropped iron-gray hair emphasized the sharpness of her features, the narrowness of her face. She wore a well-tailored navy blue pantsuit, a gleaming white silk blouse and, as she waved me in, I noticed her rings—a large pear-shaped diamond, a midnight-blue sapphire, a golden snake that curled around her middle finger and a small ruby pinkie ring. Constance Reid, who wrote of abandoned beach houses, of aging couples wandering through a barren domestic terrain, of hungry-eyed children calling to each other across cornfields stripped of vegetation, was clearly a wealthy woman. Her prosperity seemed an omen to me.

I took the seat that she had indicated, between a heavyset black woman and a young Korean businessman who did not remove his jacket or loosen his tie, although the room was warm. There were eight of us, three men and five women, around that golden oak table, each of us staring down at a photocopy of a sonnet entitled

"Urban Sunset" by Wilma Harrington. Constance explained the procedure we would follow.

"Each week we'll study one or two poems by participants. I will make the assignment and the poet will bring in enough copies for all of us, as Wilma did. The poet will read the work aloud and we'll go around the table and comment on it. I will hold my remarks for last. And I might as well tell you now that this is not a workshop for the fainthearted. If you cannot take criticism, if you are not pre-pared to rewrite, if you are going to be defensive, you are at the wrong workshop and it would be best if you left now."

There was a brief silence. We all kept our eyes fixed on Wilma Harrington's poem. No one moved, as though the slightest motion might be an acknowledgment of anticipated failure. Constance Reid nodded to the black woman who sat beside me, and Wilma Harrington began to read in a lilting Jamaican accent.

The poem's deceptive simplicity engaged me. Wilma relied heavily on the imagery of color. Her setting sun was a blood or-ange dipping into waters as blue as the bluest sky. Her clouds were fleecy-white baby blankets. Bands of purple danced their way across a darkening skyscape.

She finished reading and I saw that the edges of the paper were damp. Her hands were trembling and she reached for a paper cup of water and drank thirstily. She sat very straight, braced for rejection.

The comments were not unkind. There was some criticism of her rhythm and an observation that the intense concentration on color ignored movement and tension. Wilma listened, her lips tightly pursed. I said nothing. I was relieved that the poem was as good as it was and relieved too that it was not significantly supe-rior to my own work. I had, for so long, been accustomed to being the best that I did not want suddenly to be the worst.

When Constance spoke, she cut through the other comments. Deftly, she showed how a word could be shifted, a single line trans-posed, to strengthen and enrich the poem. She suggested that the clouds be described as "layers of fleecy-white baby blankets" and we saw at once how that added depth to the image.

"Then should I work on it some more?" Wilma asked.

"No." Her reply was abrupt, succinct. "It's not worth it. Start something new."

Wilma put her pencil down.

"Thank you," she said and her gratitude infuriated me, but Constance had already nodded to the next reader. A sweet-faced blond young woman, who had surely escaped her own child to attend the workshop, read a neat and humorous ode describing a single hour of motherhood:

Mommy, he commands, my tiny warrior
And I long to tell him that I am more than Mommy—
I am a woman whose name is Laura.

Constance frowned and spoke without waiting for us to comment.

"It's a real reach for a rhyme that doesn't even work. It kills everything that went before. If it doesn't flow, forget it."

The poet, whose name *was* Laura, blushed.

"I thought it worked."

"It doesn't."

By the end of the hour I felt weakened by the rush of words, the frightened tension of the two readers, the cautious comments of the listeners and Constance Reid's harsh and honest critiques. I myself had contributed nothing, not a word, not a nod. And yet a strange camaraderie had developed in that room, at that table. In this city, where anonymity was a watchword, we knew each other's names and, after a single shared evening, we had a sense of each other's lives. We had balanced ourselves on the treacherous beam of competing talents and we had all survived intact. We were grateful to Constance and united against her.

She herself smiled when she said good-night and we all smiled back.

"Will you read next week, Wilfred?" she asked my Korean neighbor, who clutched his attaché case and nodded assent. "And you, too, Rochelle, Rochelle Weiss."

It startled and pleased me that she knew my name.

Dashing down the library stairwell, I barely avoided a tall, sandy-haired man awkwardly balancing an oversize sketch pad and a paint-encrusted wooden case.

"Sorry," we said in unison and then we looked at each other and laughed.

"Hey, Rochelle," he said. "Rochelle without her dogs."

"Hey, Dave," I replied. "Dave still with his sketch pad."

"What are you doing here? So far south and so far east."

"I just started a poetry workshop that meets here. And what about you? You're not in home territory."

"I teach an art class here Tuesday nights. Part of a senior citizens program. But it helps pay the rent."

"Great. Well, I've got to get home."

"No time for a cup of coffee?" His voice was suddenly serious.

"Not tonight. Sorry," I said and wondered immediately why I had refused. But it was too late. His lips tightened. He hoisted his paint box and whipped his hand through the shock of sand-colored hair that fell across his high forehead. I noticed sadly that the pocket of his plaid shirt was ripped. "But, hey, another time," I amended swiftly.

"Sure," he agreed and though we took the next two flights together, we did not speak, and when we left the building we walked in opposite directions.

I made the stuffed cabbage that night as WQXR played Vivaldi's *Seasons*. My tiny kitchen was brightly lit, the door closed against the darkness of the other rooms. I sealed myself into this luminescent cubicle, its wall hung with copper pots I never used, unscarred kelly green pot holders shaped like cunning fish dangling from the hooks Phil had so meticulously installed. My hands flew across the counter, stripping the cabbage leaves, seasoning the meat, chopping the vegetables. I peeled the onions and wept and welcomed the tears. I crushed cloves of garlic and sniffed my fingers just as I had sniffed my mother's fingers when I was a small girl, intrigued by the scent and sizzle of vegetables. I browned the meat in the onions and garlic, poor Mrs. Abramowitz's secret taken as legacy by my mother and now passed on to me. A deathright become my birthright.

As the envelopes of meat-stuffed cabbage simmered in the fragrant broth, I sat down at the worktable, my notebook open, my pen poised. I wrote, the words rushing swiftly from mind and heart onto the page. I would perhaps cross most of them out the next day. I would rework each line, Constance Reid's insights lingering in memory, and then I would type the final draft, make the requisite copies and next week I would read my poem to the class. "Cooking Alone with My Mother." The title, I knew, I would not change.

The Eliots loved the stuffed cabbage. Grace ate with an appetite and even dipped the crust of the warm Italian bread into the broth. Clem and I drank the burgundy and looked at her with pleasure, tiny beams of hope flickering in our hearts. If she could eat, if she could enjoy the food, then perhaps against all odds, she was getting better. The doctors could be wrong. Remissions, miraculous and inexplicable, occurred. We had read of such things. I wondered that I could nurture hope for Grace when I had so swiftly abandoned hope for my parents. But then they had willed me to that abandonment.

"Your mother's recipe, you said?" Clem asked.

"Yes." I did not elaborate, and they were wise enough to sense that it was a story I did not want to tell.

When I reached my own apartment that night, I looked at the covered dish of cabbage still in my refrigerator. I had overcooked, of course. The next morning I dialed Phil's apartment and left a message on his machine. I would not risk calling his office and speaking to him directly.

"If you're in the mood for a stuffed-cabbage feast, please call."

I spoke with a blitheness I did not feel and put the cabbage rolls in the freezer. When he had not called by the weekend I invited Melanie, Leonard and Brett for dinner. Brett and his wife had decided on a trial separation.

"Nothing wrong with the marriage," he told us. "But nothing right, either. We're both suffering from terminal boredom."

He had hired a manager for his window-sash business and was taking off on a cross-country trip in his newly purchased van.

"I'm pulling a Rochelle," he said, spooning an entire cabbage roll into his mouth. "I'm dropping out."

"I didn't drop out," I protested. "I dropped in."

We all laughed a great deal and grew slightly drunk, polishing off two bottles of wine and passing around the single joint Brett pulled out of his pocket.

"I had a good time," I said to Melanie at the door. My laughter seemed a miracle to me, the evening's lightheartedness a milestone.

I cleared up and washed the dishes. Like my mother, I could not leave even a single dirty cup in the sink overnight. She had fought small battles against a chaotic world by establishing little bastions of domestic order, and I had absorbed the lesson of her life.

In my very clean kitchen, I again opened the notebook, reread my poem and added four more lines. And then I closed my eyes and remembered my mother's hands plunged into soapy dishwater, her rosy-pink fingers swimming through grease and glimmering bubbles to close around a fork, a knife, a saucer, while my father, seated in the living room, read the newspaper in a golden halo of lamplight. I went into my bedroom and passed my fingers across the worn surface of the buttonhole machine. The phone rang but I did not answer it. Instead, I fell into a dreamless sleep and wakened early enough to watch from my window as Mario hauled the building's garbage can to the curb.

# CHAPTER
## SEVEN

Returning from an early Sunday-morning circuit with two energetic spaniels, I found a message from Phil on my answering machine.

"Rochelle, Shelley. I've been away. Just got your message. Give me a call."

I shrugged, took off my boots and scraped the cleats with a nail file, allowing the droppings to fall on the newspaper spread across the floor, a tip from Mitzi, who had also clued me in on which paths and streets to avoid and how to bypass areas where mounted police officers patrolled, their horses spooking our dogs.

"Get the crap off your shoes before it stinks up your apartment," she had said, her dreamy voice almost a whisper.

Good advice. The city's detritus, its dank secrets adhered to our soles as we walked and ran with the dogs, scoopers and Baggies at the ready, each of us maintaining a unique pace and pattern. Mitzi affected a languid stroll. Carl kept a tight rein on his many leashes and moved swiftly—the gangs of kids who lurched aimlessly through the park often gave gay dog walkers a hard time. Annette bobbed along, moving in rhythm to her Walkman. My own gait was determined by wandering thought and memory while the dogs tugged at me, pulling me off course. Which was why so much crap clung to my boots.

I crumpled the newspaper and replayed Phil's message. An unfamiliar edge colored his voice, or perhaps I had not noticed it before. But he had been my lover, my companion for years. I knew everything about him. In the shower I reviewed that knowledge.

*He was tall.* Six feet two to my own five nine. His height had delighted me, delighted my diminutive mother. "So American." To her he was vigorous, optimistic, untouched by the dark history that shadowed our lives. I never told her that he was the child of survivors. *He was unconventionally handsome.* High forehead, narrow mouth, his green eyes heavy lidded, dark browed, his skin sun-burnished from earliest spring, wind-ruddied through autumn and winter, always taut and smooth to my touch. *He was intelligent, confident, a talented dealmaker.* With a single bonus check he had bought his parents a condo in Florida to which they stubbornly refused to move. (They had moved enough in their lifetimes, his father had claimed as he rolled the coins into neat packets. Phil had imitated his voice, his gestures.) But his intelligence went beyond the borders of his professional life. He read the newest books, saw the latest plays, sat through concerts with his face thoughtfully composed although he glanced at his watch too often and, more than once, hurried from his seat in the midst of a passionate movement when his cell phone vibrated. When we went to the theater, he spoke softly and knowledgeably during intermission. *The first scene had been weak. The ingenue emoted poorly.*

It did not matter that he had never been to a concert or a play until he went to Dartmouth. Who would have taken him? Who would have had the money for the tickets? Not his father who stood beside his newsstand from dawn until late evening. Not his mother who twisted and baked the salted pretzels his father offered for sale. During the years that Phil and I were together (not exclusive but together, I reminded myself), I had met them twice. Once at a cousin's wedding and once by chance on the street. Both times they had averted their eyes shyly, almost fearfully. They would not embarrass this tall stranger who was their son. Almost angrily, I rinsed my hair clean, allowing the runaway shampoo to sting my eyes.

*He was ambitious.* The word flew into my mind and it would not be denied. Ambition was, perhaps, the cornerstone of his personality. He loved doing deals, loved the deep leather chairs of power, loved to bark orders into the phone and then to speak conciliatorily on conference calls. It pleased him that headwaiters knew his name and nodded us to prized tables, that concierges smiled at him encouragingly, that receptionists beamed a welcome at him. It pleased him that his commission checks were large and grew steadily larger. He was privy to IPOs, he knew the bright kids who were starting Web sites, he had miraculously survived the dot-com cave-ins.

All this I knew. I knew, too, that he had loved being with me, loved walking beside me into parties and restaurants, aware that we were a much-admired couple, each of us tall and self-assured, our well-practiced smiles radiating confidence. We waved to acquaintances, chatted with false animation, laughed appreciatively. His fingers toyed with the collar of my silk shirt, my hand rested on his shoulder, brushed a speck of lint from the soft cashmere of his jacket. How we loved the expensive softness of each other's clothing, the confident lilt of each other's voices. We were in the rapid lane, traveling well, traveling fast, the brightness of our present distancing us from our parents' separate and terrible pasts.

And then I thought of all the things that I did not know about Phil and all the things I had never told him about myself. We rarely spoke of our parents. We never spoke of their war, which we knew, by inheritance, was also our war, as real and immediate to us as the battles fought in Afghanistan and Iraq. We had watched *Schindler's List* in silence, our bodies rigid, our hands clenched, and we had not discussed the film afterward. I had seen Phil stare into space, rise abruptly to leave a party, a dinner, ensnared by a sudden darkness, but I had never questioned those moods. I recognized them. They were twin to my own dark imaginings. The boundaries of our shared silence were unarticulated but defined and would not be breached.

We were like swimmers, Phil and I, afloat on quiet waters, content with effortless strokes but never daring to dive beneath the surface and hazard the depths. We were fearful of a dangerous emotional undertow, of seabeds where memories, like bits of coral, were often jagged and secrets were concealed in wave-worn outcroppings. We had chosen to tread water and play it safe, as I had played it safe always.

I had never plunged beneath the seemingly calm waters of my parents' proud and protective love. I had never asked questions that I knew they would not have wanted to answer. Instead, I lay awake in the darkness and listened to my mother and her friend Bella speak of vanished years and spectral companions, exchanging the recipes of the dead. I had watched my father study my homework and cover my books with brown paper and rewarded him with high grades, awards, medals, but I had never asked him what he would have wanted to make of his life if his youth had not been ambushed by war. I had never spoken of the screams that pierced the nocturnal quiet of our home when nightmares pursued him. Instead, I had listened to my mother soothe him, speaking softly, softly in a Yiddish I barely understood.

I had never asked them about the families they had lost, parents, brothers and sisters. I knew nothing about Ruchele, for whom I was named. I did know that my parents had been born in the same village and that they had first met after the war while searching for shoes in the storeroom of a displaced persons' camp. Years later, mysteriously, serendipitously, they met again at an evening class for immigrants in Queens and married. Their first miracle. Long years later I was born, their second miracle.

I wished other miracles upon them. It was a miracle when I made them laugh, when I told them a story that briefly lifted the melancholy that veiled their lives. It was a miracle when they smiled at my awards and medals, my Phi Beta Kappa key and my glamorous high-earning job. Easy miracles, achieved by the surface swimmer that I was, accustomed to avoiding the shoals of confrontation, the whirlwind of truth.

*No more,* I told myself sternly. It was time to venture into deep waters. I pulled on a loose white cotton shirt, jeans that hung too loosely. Was I losing weight? Probably. All that walking and an end to expense-account dinners and lunches. I owed Brad a debt of gratitude. I pirouetted before the mirror and laughed aloud. It occurred to me that I had never heard Phil laugh aloud. I thought of how Clem and Grace Eliot laughed together, her gaiety rising above her pain. They laughed when they watched *Frasier,* when the president let loose a malapropism, when Goldilocks dashed playfully between them. I wondered if it was possible to love without laughter. Could Phil and I, master and mistress of the cultivated smile, ever learn to laugh together?

*Why not?* I thought. *Why not?*

I dialed his number. He answered on the first ring.

"No more stuffed cabbage," I said. "But I am free today. At least sort of free. I do have a couple of dogs to walk."

"You can't get out of it?"

"It's my job, my responsibility. My clients don't want to come home to apartments flooded with dog poop and dog pee. Besides, I have water bowls and food dishes to fill."

"And miles to go before you sleep."

"Thank you, Robert Frost." It pleased me that he had so easily tossed a line of poetry at me. Constance Reid would approve. That was one more thing I knew about Phil. He had a remarkable memory for poetry.

"Do you want to walk the dogs with me? Maybe get a taste of my new life?" I asked and I realized that was precisely what he did want.

"Sure."

"Okay. Wear old shoes. I'll be over in an hour." That would give me time to pick up the dogs first.

"Make it a half hour," Phil said.

"Nope. An hour."

I glanced at my watch. I was cutting it close, because I'd have to delay picking up Lucky and Goldilocks. I did not want to have to clean up after Lucky, whose loose green turds too often leaked onto the Catons' black-and-white-tiled kitchen floor. Had the Catons remembered to lock the gate that kept him out of their pristine living room with its white leather couches and geometrically patterned rug? I did not mind Phil walking beside me in Central Park, but I did not want him to see me mopping up the floors of other people's homes.

"I'll meet you outside my building, then," I said.

"Great."

And he was outside, a half hour later, dressed for our trek as carefully as he dressed for a business meeting. Long khaki walking shorts, a faded Yankees shirt, scuffed sneakers, with a battered baseball cap perched on dark hair. I felt a surge of gladness, a familiar tingling of desire. He was talking to Mario and fragments of their conversation wafted toward me. I adjusted Thimble's leash and the poodle yelped in annoyance.

"That stock's a good performer," Phil was saying. "Steady and stable with a good reliable return."

"What percentage?" Mario moved a rag across the railing. He cleaned the outside of the building on Sundays because during the week he worked two other jobs, scurrying from the taxi company where he was a dispatcher to the Food Emporium where he scrambled from aisle to aisle restocking shelves. All this to ensure that his daughter would go to college, become a teacher or perhaps a nurse. All this he had told me, barely masking his disapproval that I, who had gone to college, now dumped Baggies filled with dog shit into his garbage pails.

"Eight percent, nine percent. Start with a couple of hundred dollars and see what happens. There's money to be made even in this weird market."

Mario smiled his thanks, a wide smile, very white teeth glinting against skin the color of terra-cotta.

"Hey, Rochelle, Shelley." Phil's arms encircled me, held me close for the briefest of moments.

"Hey, Phil." I brushed my lips against his cheek and tried to remember when I had last seen him. Perhaps two months ago. We greeted each other across that divide of time with a studied casualness, shy initiates into a new game whose rules were not yet defined.

We waved to Mario whose lips were moving silently. He was, perhaps, calculating how many hundreds he could invest and how much tuition a decent return on that investment would cover.

"So Mario's going into the market?" I asked as we walked toward the park, Thimble tugging at the leash.

"Everyone's going into the market," Phil replied. "The elevator operator in my building. The deli delivery boy. The hostess at Shun Lee. Melanie. Melanie's mom. How about you, Rochelle? I could give you a couple of tips. Plenty of bargains now."

"I'm not quite in that league yet, but I'm inching toward it." I had, after all, balanced my books the previous week and realized that to my surprise I was making a fairly decent profit—not anywhere near the BIS scale but enough to cover my new minimalist lifestyle.

Annette had advised me to report only half my earnings to the IRS.

"Look, this is a cash business," she had confided. "The IRS figures you're making something but they can't track it. Just report a percentage of your take."

But I was my parents' daughter, a good and grateful American, and, like them, I was frightened of government officials. I recorded my fees, estimated my taxes.

"So what league are you in?" Phil asked.

"The break-even league, I suppose. But, hey, why are you in the city on a weekend? No time-share?"

For years we had taken joint time-shares, driving out to the island each Friday in a rented car. Both car and house were ours only for the weekend, requiring no permanence, no ownership, no commitment. The back seat was loaded with groceries from Zabar's and Dean & DeLuca, too swiftly purchased, too swiftly unpacked on the scarred counters of other people's kitchens. Slices of lox slithered out of envelopes of oily waxed paper, olives and mushrooms swam in spicy marinades, sun-dried tomatoes spangled focaccia bread and roasted portobellos formed crusty hillocks.

There was no calm in those many-bedroomed houses. Phones rang, beepers buzzed, doors slammed. We laughed too loudly, spoke too quickly, intent on assuring others and ourselves that we were having fun.

My parents delighted in my weekends at the beach.

"My Ruchele, she goes to the ocean with her friends," my mother told Bella. They themselves had never seen a beach until they were young mothers.

Over the years, Phil and I had shared houses with friends and acquaintances, but inevitably by Labor Day early intimacy collapsed into edgy irritation. Best friends became sly enemies, couples split.

"Never again," we vowed at summer's end, but the next year we were back, chasing sun and fun, fleeing loneliness, acknowledging the perks. Phil networked. I snagged a client for BIS and my finder's fee was more money than my father had ever made from his largest buttonhole order. A reflexive guilt intruded on my pleasure.

"Nope. No time-share this year." Phil spoke without regret.

At the Catons' apartment, he whistled softly as I pulled out my heavy key chain.

"Think of what an unscrupulous dog walker could rip off in this city," he said as we entered.

"Yeah. But dog walkers don't think like that," I retorted as I adjusted Lucky's leash, pleased that there was no mess on the kitchen floor.

"How do they think?"

I recoiled at the stridency of his tone and calmed Thimble by stroking her behind the ears.

"I can't give you a researched profile," I said in my cool presentation voice. "But it's a safe assumption that most of them don't think that whoever has the most stuff when they die wins. They're not into stuff, they're mostly not competitive, not one of them would want the Catons' collection of dark blue Venetian glassware or their unread set of classics bound in pale blue leather that just happens to match the pattern of their carpet. And they wouldn't want the carpet, either. Now, the bed, that's another story."

I led him into the wintry-white bedroom, the deep ivory-colored carpet ribbed with streaks of sunlight, the huge bed with its white spread and enormous pillows shrouded in white ruffled shams, not unlike a high and forbidding snowy field.

"Not for me," Phil said. "I don't like making love on frozen steppes."

"Actually, I don't think they're into a lot of sex," I said. I remembered the entry in her diary. *I must tell him. I must.* What was the urgency of her confidence? Did she mean to tell him that she wanted a divorce, that she was a lesbian, that their life together disappointed?

The Catons' bedside answering machine flickered. One message, two, three. If I had been alone I would have listened to the messages, added them to my fragmented knowledge of this couple whose apartment I entered so freely, whose dog greeted me with wild joy. I wondered what Phil would say if I told him that more than once I had stretched out on that high white bed and fallen into a brief sleep.

At the Eliots' we collected Goldilocks and I introduced Phil to Clem and Grace. Grace looked paler than usual as she sat at the table carefully arranging the long-stemmed yellow roses Melanie had sent over.

"So kind of Melanie to offer us these," Clem said. "An excess from a wedding order." There was no surprise in his voice. He was accustomed to genteel courtesies. I wondered if my parents had ever received a gift of flowers, and then bit my lip in punishment. It was stupid to weigh everything on the scales of their experience, to begrudge others the pleasures they had not known. "It's good to meet a friend of Rochelle's," he told Phil. "She is very special to us."

Phil nodded, looking about at the faded slipcovers, the slight tear on the silk lampshade, the gold drapes worn so thin that sunlight poured through them.

Swiftly, I leashed Goldilocks. I knew that shabbiness disconcerted Phil, perhaps because it reminded him of his parents' apartment and its cast-off furniture. He had slept on a daybed in the living room and listened as his mother and father whispered in Yiddish and counted the coins. Phil had spoken of it at a ski house one night when the conversation had veered into a competitive recounting of unhappy childhoods and dysfunctional families. An account executive who lived on Sutton Place had spat out a description of his impoverished and fractured family. There were tales of divorce and abandonment, emotional deprivation and actual poverty—foreclosure and eviction. Someone suggested offering an "Angela's Ashes Award," a proposal that triggered nervous laughter. I had said nothing that night. I would not turn my parents' lives into a cynical sound bite recounted amid the smoke from joints of what everyone agreed was "really good stuff." Phil had told his story, but he had not mentioned that his parents were survivors.

With the dogs in tow we walked uptown, reveling in the odd serenity of the city late on a Sunday afternoon.

Following the pace of the dogs, I paused at trees and lampposts, waited for them to sniff out a pleasing place and then expertly scooped up their leavings and transferred them to Baggies. Phil watched sourly at first and then, grinning with amusement, asked if he could give it a try, and so we were standing on the corner of Madison and Eighty-third, bent over a pooper-scooper, when I heard my name called.

"Rochelle! Wait up!"

Brad and his partner, Julian, walked toward us, both of them dressed in summer chic, white slacks and pastel shirts, Brad's light blue and Julian's brilliant pink, a close match to his flushed cheeks and his ever-expanding tonsure. Portly, cherubic Julian wore his shirt out and it billowed over his very large belly. I smiled at him and he grinned back.

"I assure you, Rochelle, I am not pregnant. Unfortunately, I'm gender challenged. All that I will be birthing this summer is a book of Tuscan recipes."

"Oh, yes, the BIS client Christmas gift. Brad told me about it."

"Did I?" Brad asked. He was petting Thimble, fingering her blue satin ribbon, managing a graceful crouch so that his white slacks would remain immaculate.

"Yes. At that last lunch," I reminded him. I wanted him to remember how I had told him about my parents' illnesses, to recall the false concern of his reaction. Anger stirred within me. Too quickly, I jerked at Thimble's leash and the small dog yelped angrily. Contrite, I reached into my fanny pack and distributed biscuits to all three dogs.

"A very professional maneuver, Rochelle," Brad said approvingly. "But then you were always very professional. And, Phil, how are you? I remember seeing you at the Chelsea Pier launch party for Cyclops."

"Right. We're researching them and they look pretty good even in this crazy market. Educational stuff. Virtual reality based on mythology. Riding on the coattails of the Harry Potter craze. They might be ripe for venture-capital backing. Does BIS represent them?" Phil kept his tone casual but of course they were milking each other.

"We took them on conditionally. We'll see."

"I've been watching for news of the Longauer product," Phil said and I glared at him.

"We're waiting until the timing is right. Suzanne's on top of it." Brad turned to me. "You know, Rochelle, we're dealing with some new accounts that are just your sort of thing. If you're interested give me a call."

I nodded noncommittally although I was seething with anger. Did he really think it would be as simple as that? A chance meeting, a lunch, a discussion of terms and my welcome back into the BIS family, the prodigal daughter returned? No mention of the security guard posted at my office, the peremptory letter of dismissal, the company's refusal to consider any compromise. No mention of my misery, my loss. I turned to Julian.

"Good luck with the cookbook. Have a great time in Tuscany."

"I'll try." He kissed my cheek and murmured, "Brad does miss you, Rochelle."

I shrugged. I liked Julian. I did not want to tell him that his lover had behaved like an absolute shit, that I did not believe he missed me at all.

"I kind of like what I'm doing now."

"Yes. Very enterprising." Julian was embarrassed and that embarrassment caused him to blush deeply. He did not think dog walking was enterprising. He thought it was disgusting. Throughout our brief exchange he had kept his eyes averted from the Baggie of poop I clutched in my hand. Hurriedly, he and Brad walked on.

"See, New York's just one big small town," Phil said wryly.

"Not big enough."

We retraced our steps, returned Lucky, Goldilocks and Thimble to their owners and headed for the west side. It would be an easy circuit, I assured Phil—just Sir Gawain and the two elegant Afghans.

At Ninetieth Street three elderly residents of the nursing home sat listlessly on the benches. Samantha was alone with them, her white uniform clinging damply to her body. Still, she coaxed them into activity, walking from one to the other, tossing her large blue ball into their laps, clapping when it was caught and held tight by a trembling old woman in a striped housedress, her sparse hair the color of the cloud that drifted overhead.

"Hey there, Rochelle," Samantha called. "Where are your doggies?"

"I'm just heading across town to pick up another lot. Where's Aretha?"

"Her baby's sick. I'm on my own today."

"Tell her I said hi and I hope everything will be all right."

"I'll do that, Rochelle. I sure will." She did not break her pace. Gently, she tossed the ball to the stooped old man, hunched over in his wheelchair, an oversize, faded Harvard T-shirt hanging on his withered body.

"Okay," Phil said as we walked on. "I'm impressed. You're the Gracious Lady of the Park. Saint Rochelle, Walker of Dogs, Friend of the Elderly and their Caretakers. A whole new persona. Beats the Hamptons, any day."

"Oh, shut up." I picked up a twig and tossed it at him and he grabbed my wrist in loving punishment. Laughing, we walked on and collected the dogs, Phil holding Sir Gawain's leash and the two Afghans sauntering leisurely beside me.

Ida sat on her usual bench at the dog run and, as usual, did not look up when I passed her. Mitzi and Annette leaned across the fence in urgent discussion, their faces creased with worry. I introduced them to Phil—no last names because last names did not apply, although I knew that Carl was Carl Sandler. He had handed me a scrap of paper one day with his name, address and phone number scribbled on it. "Just in case," he had said and I had not asked, "Just in case of what?" No need. A dog walker had been mugged not far from Strawberry Fields that day, a gay Hispanic boy whom we knew only as Jose. No identification had been found. Annette, Mitzi and I had speculated, after Carl left, as to whether Jose had been sexually molested. We thought not. He had been surrounded by his dogs when the police found him—an Irish setter and two bulldog pups, all barking furiously.

"Why are you guys looking so serious?" I asked Mitzi as Phil stared out at New Jersey.

"We're kind of worried about Ida," Mitzi said.

"Why? She looks pretty much the same."

"Carl brought her a bagel and a coffee this morning. She didn't touch anything. Not the bagel, not the coffee. And look at what she's wearing."

I looked. Despite the relatively warm weather Ida wore a black wool watch cap and a fleece jacket over a burgundy wool dress, and yet she shivered in the sunlight. Her face was contorted and teardrops, like silver bullets, streaked her dark cheeks.

"Have you talked to her?" I asked.

"We tried," Annette replied. "She didn't answer, didn't even seem to know we were talking. She's sick, really sick. Listen, I've got to get these damn Scotties back to their crazy owners or they'll think they were dognapped. As though anyone would want them. See what you guys can do."

She strode away, her keys jangling, the Scotties yelping.

"What do you think we should do, Mitzi?" I asked worriedly.

Mitzi shrugged. The wide sleeves of her white dress fluttered. She tapped her red-booted foot, tossed her mane of fair curls.

"I don't know," she said. "I'd call the Coalition for the Homeless but I don't want them to scoop her off to a shelter. She'd hate that."

"How about 911?" Phil suggested.

"Same thing. They might send cops or EMT people. To Ida anyone in uniform is like Gestapo. Even if they took her to a hospital she'd think it was a concentration camp." The words fell easily from her lips and shattered our hearts.

Phil and I did not look at each other. *Gestapo. Concentration camp.* Mitzi could not have known that those words were the mysterious unspoken terror of our childhoods. To her they were the clichés of war films and novels. We could not be angry with her. And yet. And yet.

I approached Ida.

"Are you okay?" I asked very softly. "If you're sick I can take you to a doctor, a very nice doctor." Melanie was friendly with a woman doctor, a kindly woman who bought a single iris each morning. She worked at a clinic, volunteered at a shelter. If asked, she would remove her white coat so that she would not frighten a homeless woman who feared all uniforms.

Ida did not answer. I scrawled my name and phone number on a scrap of paper, tucked it into her pocket and added a five-dollar bill.

"Ida, I gave you my name and phone number. If you need help call me. And you have money for dinner. Buy something. Something hot. You have to eat."

No answer. She remained motionless.

"Nothing we can do," I told Mitzi and Phil, who had watched me uneasily.

"I guess not." Mitzi's voice was flat, enervated. She stroked her dog's ears.

"Come on, Peaches. Let's go. So long, Rochelle. So long, Phil. Philip. Hey, do you know your name means love?" She smiled wistfully and glided away.

"She was a classics major at Barnard," I told Phil. "Magna cum laude."

"She's putting her degree to good use," he said tersely.

"As I am." I fingered my Phi Beta key and looked at him defiantly. The ease of our walk across town had vanished.

In silence we retraced our steps, delivered Sir Gawain and the Afghans, and crossed the park. I was oddly grateful that the light of day would stretch into evening.

We passed Melanie's shop, closed now, ultraviolet rays curtaining the window.

"Melanie's got a great guy," I said. "Leonard. He's subletting Lila and Fay's studio for the summer."

"Warren told me." Melanie's brother kept us connected, distributing the bits of information that guaranteed continuity.

"How are Lila and Fay?" Phil liked them but disapproved of them. They had veered too far off the conventional path. Like Mitzi, the uncertainty of their lives was as threatening to him as it was to me. We were the children of parents who wakened in the night and screamed their uncertainty into the darkness.

"They're doing okay, I think. They're in summer stock at the Cape. They'll be coming in next week and staying with me for a couple of days. They have some auditions or something—maybe some TV commercials."

"They're getting old to be fooling around like that."

"They're about our age, give or take a year or two."

"Then we're getting old to be fooling around like this." There was a weariness in his voice that I had not heard before and, surprised, I looked up at him. His eyes, those celadon eyes, were sad, but he smiled at me and I struggled to smile back.

It was that weariness, that sadness, that impelled me to invite him in.

"Just a drink," I said cautiously. "Maybe a pickup supper." I thought of the last meal we had eaten in my apartment—the hastily cooked omelette, the sad words, the angry words, the pleas, the accusations.

"All right. A drink. We'll send out for pizza."

"Deal."

And so we sat in my living room, in the black leather swivel armchairs, as we had sat so many times over the years of our togetherness, and watched the summer darkness gather. Lights flickered on in the building across the way but we made no move disturb the dusk that draped us in its comforting shadows. The bottle of J&B stood on the table and, as we both reached for it, our fingertips touched. Phil tightened his grasp, encased my palm in his own and brought it to his lips. As gently as I had kissed his face in greeting, he in turn kissed my hand.

"I've missed you, Rochelle. I've been lonely."

"Ah. Did you miss me because of you or did you miss me because of me?"

"You're being perverse." But he did not release my hand, nor did I pull it away.

"No. I'm being honest. Phil, we can't go back to where we were. It's not enough that we fit together. We have to—I don't know—belong together."

"And how does that happen?"

"We find out who we are. Without the props and the titles. We find out where we came from. Where we want to go." I spoke hesitantly, my own words surprising me, then shaming me. Simplistic statements strangled by a misery I struggled to articulate.

"So that's what you're doing now? Walking dogs, scraping up their shit and discovering yourself?"

"Sort of, I know it seems crazy to you, Phil. This dog walking. You see it as mindless and yes it is mindless. It's work that I don't have to think about—I pick up the dogs, walk them and let my thoughts flow. I've never done that before. Never allowed myself to do it. I was always so programmed, so damn goal oriented, the good girl, the miracle daughter, carrying home the A-plus report cards, the meals, the Phi Beta Kappa key, the fat paycheck, the stupid promotions—because it was all so important to them, because they had never had anything, anything at all."

"I know that feeling." He spoke very quietly and now, at last, he released my hand, filled his glass and sat back in the chair, swiveling about so that he no longer looked at me but out the window, into the nascent darkness, the charcoal sky of urban nightfall.

"But we've never talked about it."

"It's not something I talk about. It's something I try not to think about. Because where—where will it take me?"

"I wrote a poem," I said. "I'm taking this poetry workshop. At least, I've gone to one session. And I wrote this poem that I'm supposed to read aloud. It's about them—my mother, my father."

"Rochelle. Shelley. Please. I don't want to hear your poem."

Sadness thickened his words and, because I could think of no other way to comfort him, I knelt beside his chair. There, in that half darkness, I put my head on his lap. Gently, gently, he stroked my hair, loosened it from the silk scarf that bound it so that it fell into a silken auburn shawl upon his knee. Together we went into my bedroom and came together as secret sharers, gentle lovers who understood each other's dreams, who soared toward the same oblivion, the same release. We slept then, as the darkness deepened. When I awakened, he was gone. No murmured goodbye, no note.

I went into the living room and saw that he had lit a single lamp.

"Oh, Phil. What now? Philip." I spoke his name aloud and remembered that Mitzi had said it meant love, beloved.

I called his apartment and when he answered, I said, "Oh, you're home."

"Yes. I'm home."

And, because neither of us had any more to say, we both hung up.

# CHAPTER
## EIGHT

The library was crowded that Tuesday evening. The hot desperate breath of the swiftly vanishing season had propelled unlikely patrons to the air-conditioned rooms of the aging thick-walled building. Weary men and women sat at the scarred tables in the main reading room turning the pages of glossy magazines and novels sheathed in clear plastic. A group of bored teenagers lounged on the orange faux-leather couch in the young-adult section, staring down at their copies of *Lord of the Flies* as an earnest young woman in a Barnard T-shirt coaxed them into a discussion. "What do you think of the symbolism in this chapter?" she asked and they slumped deeper into their seats and avoided her anxious gaze.

In the darkened community room a group of middle-aged men and women watched a video of *Yentl*. A group of senior citizens clustered about a computer in the hallway as a bespectacled librarian demonstrated its capabilities. Confidently she pressed the keyboard, and titles, authors and shelf numbers in a shimmering shade of blue danced across the screen. Lines formed at the card catalog as wooden shelves were pulled open and slammed shut. A homeless man crouched on the floor and read the *Wall Street Journal.* Young parents with toddlers in tow moved through the video racks and called softly to each other, "Did we see this?" "Do you think the kids will like this one?"

I went up to the second floor and glanced into the wide-windowed studio. Elderly men and women stood at easels and studied the set piece—a blue bowl of summer fruit and forsythia in a clear glass vase strategically placed on a low table. Some were already at work, sketching the still-life arrangement with stumps of charcoal or, more daringly, with wands of colored chalk. *Dave's class,* I thought with a surge of gladness and realized that I had been looking for him from the moment I entered the building. But instead of Dave, it was an elderly man who moved authoritatively about the room, pausing before one easel then another, now guiding a trembling hand, now demonstrating with a quick slash of chalk how an error in perspective might be corrected.

I was disappointed but not surprised by Dave's absence. He had probably quit—he had been unenthusiastic about the job and perhaps something better had come along. It was possible that he had simply left the city, his plaid shirts and worn jeans crammed into a duffel bag, his pads and paint boxes tucked under his arms as he headed north to Maine or west to a desert expanse. I could imagine him easily in either vista, his eyes raking the landscape. I would simply add him to the roster of casual strangers whose presence in my life I had taken for granted until one day they vanished.

A married couple, both wearing rimless glasses, had boarded my bus every morning during the years I worked at BIS. We had smiled at each other, commented on the weather, and smiled again as they left at a midtown stop. And then one day the wife stood at the bus stop alone, her eyes red rimmed behind those glasses and, after a month, she too was gone. There was the Indian news vendor from whom I bought my paper each morning who grinned at me as he shook his head over the headlines and then one day was replaced by a blond woman who barely looked up at me as she counted the coins I gave her. Melanie and I had mourned the disappearance of the plump Polish waitress at our local deli who had shown us her daughter's report cards, her son's class pictures and who had, according to the deli owner, simply stopped coming to work. Such absences left us feeling oddly betrayed. An urban intimacy had been violated. They should have said goodbye, told us where they were going, although we did not know their names and did not know where they had come from. I tried to remember when I had last seen Dave in the park—not for several days, I realized. Yes, of course he was gone and why, after all, should I care? The irrational sadness I felt angered me.

Swiftly then, I mounted the next flight of stairs to the third-floor conference room. The door was open and almost every seat at the round golden oak table was occupied. I noted, with rueful sadness, that Wilma Harrington, who had written of urban sunsets, was absent. Constance Reid looked up as I entered. She wore a wide-skirted sleeveless white cotton dress, a necklace of coral at her throat, a bracelet of coral on her wrist, coral sandals of soft leather on her slender feet. I was glad that I wore a loose copper-colored linen shift that closely matched my hair, an expensive purchase from the days when I gave no thought to expense. I was pleased to be linked in elegance to Constance Reid, whose satiric sonnet on the plight of the homeless has appeared on the op-ed page of the *New York Times* that very morning.

Wilfred Kim read first, his poem an odd poetic dialogue between a man and a woman, strangers who meet on a train platform—the man a foreigner, his hair glistening black, his onyx-colored eyes almond shaped, his skin sun colored—the woman fair, her blue eyes a match for the summer sky, laughter spilling from full curved lips. Together, they look up and watch a flock of geese take flight. They speak of the beauty they witness, of how that beauty has touched their souls, lifted their hearts. But when the train arrives they enter different cars, his shoulders drooping, her golden head bowed.

I glanced around the table. Laura, the young mother, sat with her eyes closed, leaking breast milk darkening her pale green shirt. Wilma Harrington, who had come after all, doodled on her pad.

"Comments?" Constance Reid invited, her voice dry, noncommittal.

A hesitant discussion about whether a dialogue constituted poetry.

"What separates poetry from prose?" Laura asked tentatively.

I formulated a response, rejected it—too pat, too facile, too reminiscent of the ambitious student I had been. No need to strive for grades, no need to please anyone except myself. And then we were back at Wilfred's work, skillfully guided there by Constance.

"Good strong images," she said and he leaned forward, his chin resting on his clasped hands. "But not enough left to dream on. You see that, don't you, Wilfred?"

She was gentle with him, gentler than she had been the previous week with Laura and Wilma. Was that because he was a man, because he was Korean? Would she be as gentle with me?

"But it's worth reworking," she continued. "If you're so inclined. I'd like to see it again."

"Of course." Sweat beaded his forehead. He smiled and I smiled too and thought to reach out and touch his hand in sympathy, in support, but of course I did not stir.

"Rochelle. Miss Weiss."

They turned to look at me and then dropped their eyes to my poem. I read very slowly. I had written and rewritten those words so many times and read them aloud so often that I should have known them by heart, but I did not. My voice faltered. I stumbled over one syllable and then another, coughed and sipped water from the glass someone pushed toward me. I tried not to listen to my own voice as I released the images I had struggled over, the scrawled and rescrawled sentences that had littered my desk, littered my mind. I was sure Constance Reid's eyes did not leave my face as I read.

I cook with my mother
Just we two
In the kitchen of the dead.
I am alone with my mother
Here. In the kitchen of the dead.
Candles light this room
Where we cook
Together and alone.
We prepare chicken soup
For diners delayed by death
For the grandmother I never knew
For the aunt who willed me her name.
We prepare stuffed cabbage
For a party canceled by history
Golden cracklings sizzle on a low blue flame
Their fat odors fill this room
Where I cook alone
With my mother.

I read on, hesitating when I described "that bubbling pot of apple sauce, its golden sweetness too weak to mask the taste of bitter memory." Breathlessly I read the very last lines.

Here, in the kitchen of the dead
I will cook alone always
But always with my mother.

The room was quiet. Constance sat with her hands clasped.

"That was wonderful." Wilma spoke very quietly.

"You created such a mood," said a slender blond man who had not spoken before. His plummy voice, like Julian's, was saturated with the lilting cadence of the South. "I felt your history."

"Let's not allow sentiment to interfere with judgment." Constance was back in action. Her eyes met mine. "You have to be careful, Rochelle, not to allow content and sentiment to overwhelm expression." Her pen was poised above the copy of my poem. She slashed one line, then another. "'Bubbling apple sauce'—a cliché—it interferes with the sweet-and-bitter concept. And here—fat odors of cracklings—a redundancy."

I nodded, underlined, listened to other comments, did not acknowledge a question about whether the poem was based on personal experience—was my mother, in fact, a survivor?

"That's irrelevant," Constance Reid answered for me. "More than personal experience molds the poet."

We did not have to be reminded that although she herself wore a coral necklace and a diamond ring, her poem, which surely all of us had read that morning, spoke of a homeless woman, "her gray-skinned feet jeweled with ulcerated sores as hard and as bright as amber." The rich could write of the poor. Those unscathed by history could capture its sting. Criticism rimmed her reply yet her eyes rested on me and I felt the curiosity in her gaze.

At last the session was over. At last I could make my way out of the reading room, clutching my folder as Constance called out the names of the students who would read the following week, as Laura, harried and hurried, smelling of soured milk, pressed my hand.

"I know," she said softly, and I wondered what it was that she knew.

I raced down the stairwell, eager to avoid any after class intimacy. There had been talk of going to a coffee shop. Wilfred had lingered to speak to Constance. I wanted only to get away as quickly as possible from those sympathetic strangers to whom I had revealed too much, aware, with sinking heart and sweat-damp palms, that my own revelations bewildered me. At the first-floor landing, I stopped short to avoid rushing into Dave who stood, as he had stood the week before, awkwardly balancing his sketch pad and his wooden paint case.

"Hey, is this getting to be a habit?" he asked, steadying me, smiling at me. A daub of red paint rouged one cheek, and the collar of his blue cotton shirt was hopelessly frayed. Did he have any clothing that was not in need of repair? I wondered, and thought of Phil, so repelled by shabbiness that he gave away perfectly good shirts when a button came loose or a small stain speckled a pocket. Phil, who had not called for days, who, perhaps, would never call again.

"I don't know. Maybe. Watch out next week. I may knock you down. Actually, I didn't think you were here tonight. I passed the second-floor studio and someone else was teaching…some old guy."

"That was the still-life drawing class. I teach painting. A little more ambitious. A lot more money." He dabbed at the paint on his cheek with one hand, balancing pad and paint box with the other.

I reached into my bag for a Wash 'n Dry. My mother had cautioned me to always carry cleansing tissues. "Always be prepared. You never can tell," she had said. She, I knew, had been unprepared for that which could not have been foretold.

"Hold still," I told Dave and gently wiped away the smudge of paint and then, for no reason at all, I smoothed his cheek with my fingertips.

"How about taking the rain check on that coffee we never had last week?" he asked.

"Sure. Why not?"

We left the library, relieved that with the gathering dusk, the

fierce heat had abated. The city was preparing for night.
Storekeepers rolled down the metal gates that protected their display windows. The proprietors of fast-food shops carried overflowing garbage bags to the curb. Buses lumbered clumsily down
the avenue without stopping because no passengers awaited them.
The streets of midtown were eerily empty. A lone dog walker, a
lithe young man in a white tank top and black spandex shorts, led
three white poodles down the street and I saw with some annoyance that he did not pause to clean up after them. Annette would
have shouted at him but I shrugged and walked on. A Chinese girl
and a tall blond youth, their hands linked, moved very slowly
through the new darkness and, briefly, we matched our pace to
theirs.

Dave paused at a coffee shop and read the menu.

"Looks all right," he said.

But I looked through the window and shook my head. Wilma
and three other members of the poetry workshop sat at a corner
table nursing tall glasses of iced coffee and talking urgently.

"No," I said. "Let's find another place."

"Sure."

He asked no questions and on the next block we stopped at a
very small, smoky café.

"More my style anyway," he said, sliding into a booth near the
window.

"Okay then." It was definitely not my style. The Formica table
was greasy, the flimsy paper menu was crusted with dried egg and
the balding waiter whose apron was streaked with ketchup looked
at his watch and glared at us.

"We close in an hour," he said.

"The story of my life," Dave answered easily. "Wherever I go they
close in an hour. Okay. We'll order right away. Rochelle?"

"An iced coffee, decaf." I would have enough trouble falling
asleep that night, I knew. Replays of my reading, the reaction of

the class, Constance Reid's criticism would haunt me as I tossed and turned in the darkness. Oh, why had I written, why had I read?

"What was wrong with that other coffee place that probably wasn't closing in an hour?" Dave asked after he had given his own order for a grilled-cheese sandwich and a cup of coffee. "Did you see an old boyfriend?"

"No. Just a group from my poetry workshop. Probably discussing the poem I read tonight. I didn't want to hear their postmortem or, worse still, see them shut up when I walked in."

"First time you read your work aloud?"

"I haven't been writing poetry for very long. Maybe a couple of months. This was the first time I shared my work with anyone."

"You know what a teacher at the Art Students League told me when I had my first exhibit—and it wasn't even a professional show, just some paintings in a student exhibit at a midtown gallery? Some hotshot critics with a special interest in student work were coming, set to write about us, and I didn't think I could deal with that. I wanted to pull my stuff out but this teacher just stared at me and said, 'Hey, you have to lose your virginity sometime.'"

"So what did the hotshot critic say about your work?" I asked. The iced coffee had arrived and to my surprise it was very good, laced with cinnamon and topped with a coronet of whipped cream.

"They didn't mention it. Not a word. So I didn't lose my virginity for another year. Another exhibit. This time it was a one-man show upstate. The art critic at a Columbia County newspaper was supposed to give it a lot of space in a weekend feature. An influential guy, the gallery owner told me, and I hid in a corner while he looked at my work. Ten, fifteen minutes in front of each painting, shaking his head, taking notes. His review came out on the weekend. I didn't just lose my virginity. I was raped. The prick criticized everything, my technique, my subject matter, my use of color, and he finished up by calling me a 'would-be artist.' Ten years of work and I'm a wanna-be."

"What did you do?"

"I stayed in my room in this crummy motel and tried to figure out what I would do with the rest of my life. Three days later, the gallery owner called. Every painting had been sold. That's when I figured out that it doesn't matter what they say. All that matters is what you do."

"I know that. At least I knew that in another life."

"And what life was that?"

And so I told him about my life at BIS, the frantic scrambling for accounts, the development of campaigns, the all-nighters with fierce arguments over logos and voice-overs, the press conferences. Big debates over releases and giveaways. And then Brad's critique, his morning-after judgment calls.

"I guess it was a little bit like waiting for a review to appear except that at BIS every day was judgment day. 'How am I doing?' we asked each other and we really wanted to know. Were the creative juices flowing—was the client going to like it—were the media moguls going to buy it? And what would a good review mean for us, for our careers, would it move us up or down the ladder, closer or farther from the office with a view, the paycheck with enough zeros at the end? I'd lay awake all night before a presentation, just the way I lay awake all last night because I knew I was going to read my poem—itchy with worry."

"Still, it sounds as though you liked part of the job, as though you found it exciting."

"Oh, there were parts of it that I liked. There were exciting times and it's great to get paid well for doing something you're really good at. But in the end, it was about nothing. Weeks spent on the great presentation, an item in the 'Circuits' section of the *Times* and the next day you're wrapping your coffee grounds in it. I would miss my own TV spots because I went out of the room to pee and by the time I got back to the set they were over. Hours and hours of work and energy swallowed up in a thirty-second sound bite. Sure, egos were stroked and there was sales impact. That's what public relations is all about. But in the end what did it mean?"

"So that's why you left?"

"No. That's not why I left. In fact, I didn't leave of my own accord. I got canned." I spooned a sliver of ice into my mouth, pressed its coldness against my teeth until they hurt. The waiter looked at us sourly.

"Okay." Dave asked no more questions. He tossed a couple of bills onto the table, grinned at the waiter, who actually smiled back. That grin bought a lot of mileage, I thought as we left the café.

He walked me all the way to my apartment and we talked about a movie that he had seen and I hadn't. He was a flick freak, he told me. He loved the crowds, the scent of the theater, the escape into darkness as the sound track boomed and engulfed an audience of strangers in a world that was not their own.

"I started going to the movies when I was a kid, maybe six years old. I'd slip into a Saturday matinee walking between two adults who didn't realize I was there," he said.

"But what about your parents? They didn't miss you if you were gone for hours and hours?"

"They were busy. They owned a drugstore and Saturday was their busiest day. My mom ran the lunch counter, which was a big moneymaker, and my sister helped her. Alanport, Missouri, was a pretty safe town and they knew that I was a careful kid. So they gave me a dollar on Saturday morning and told me to be home for dinner— 6:00 p.m. sharp. Meat loaf and potatoes. Every damn Saturday night."

There was an edge to his voice, but when I looked at him he was smiling, a wistful remembering kind of smile. Probably he missed the meal loaf that had appeared with such irritating regularity on his family's dinner table. Perhaps there was no regularity at all in his current life. As there was none in mine.

"That never would have flown in my family. My parents knew where I was every minute of the day. I didn't even cross the street alone until I was almost ten." I closed my eyes, remembering the touch of my mother's fingers, tight against my own, my father's gentle, restraining touch on my shoulder as, looking both ways, he guided me across Queens Boulevard. Crossing the street was hazardous; all of life was hazardous, their protective gestures reminded me.

Dave and I reached a corner and his fingers curled around my own. Looking both ways, we crossed the street.

"Well, that was life in New York," he said, and I did not tell him that it was life in New York as experienced by parents whose lives were haunted by an unrelenting worry that trailed them—a cloud by day, a pillar of fire by night. My mother's voice quivered when the phone rang. My father stood sentinel at the window until I arrived home each evening. Their past, unshared, unspoken, shadowed my present.

"And what was life in Alanport, Missouri, like?" I asked.

"It was fine if you fit the pattern. Which I didn't. Athletics, team sports were the big thing in high school. The big thing in my life was drawing and painting. Not team sports. So I was a loner and loners everywhere get called names. In grade school they whispered—real loud hissy whispers that everyone heard. Arty-Farty Davey. Sissy boy. Faggot. In high school they yelled them. It didn't matter that my illustration for the yearbook won a statewide prize. It didn't matter that I designed the posters for their games." He paused, studied his hands and then continued. "It didn't matter that I won a scholarship to the Tyler School of Art in Philadelphia. That shook up my parents. They thought that drawing and painting was a nice hobby. They gave me money for supplies and even framed two of my pictures and hung them up—one in the dining room and one in the living room." He smiled wistfully. "But my grandfather had been a pharmacist and my father was a pharmacist.

What was going to happen to the Robeson Drugstore if I didn't become a pharmacist? And what kind of a living could an artist make? So there were arguments and a lot of yelling, and my sister, Cathy, sat on the porch swing and cried and begged me to be reasonable. 'It's not unreasonable to try to live my own life,' I told her, but she didn't understand. She had won first prize in a Sunday-school family values and family responsibility essay contest and she told me that it was my job in life to make my parents happy, to make them proud. 'After all their hard work. After all they've done for you.'" He imitated her voice, high-pitched, accusatory.

"I can actually relate to that," I said.

"Yeah? Well, I couldn't. The way I saw it, the way I still see it, my job in life is to make me happy, to feel that I'm living the way it pleases me to live. I knew that, even when the jocks were calling me faggot—which I'm not by the way."

"I'm relieved to hear that," I said dryly.

"I thought you might be." He flashed that grin again and I smiled. "Anyway, I took that scholarship and went to Philadelphia. And then I went to Paris because that's what you're supposed to do when you're a young artist and you're following the set scenario for young artists. And then I came to New York, studied at the Art Students League and started peddling my canvases to galleries. I'm getting some recognition—not a lot. If it was a lot I wouldn't be teaching senior citizens' workshops at the public library."

"But then again, maybe you would."

"Yeah. Maybe."

"Well, this is where I live."

We stood in front of my building, suddenly uneasy with each other. He leaned forward but did not kiss me. Instead, he brushed a leaf from my shoulder.

"Feel like going to a movie tomorrow night?" he asked. "Bryant Park. A big screen, lawn chairs. The Big Apple's outdoor answer to the Alanport Palace Theater."

"What's playing?" I asked.

"Does it make any difference?"

"No. I guess not."

"I'll meet you out here then. Seven-thirty."

"Okay. Listen, my last name is Weiss. I'm Rochelle Weiss."

"And I'm Dave Robeson."

Gravely, we shook hands.

"Good night then."

"Good night."

Feeling oddly disappointed (why, after all, hadn't he kissed me?), I let myself into my apartment. The red light of my answering machine twinkled in the darkness. Two messages. The first from Lila and Fay, who had been gone for weeks. They spoke, as they often did, in breathless unison. Reminding me they were coming to New York for the weekend. Maybe Friday. Maybe Saturday. They weren't sure. Could they still camp out in my living room? Things in Wellfleet were great but they had to scramble for gigs for next year. "Oh, next year." Lila spoke in a mock moan. Fay's laughter trilled. As always, I envied them their careless optimism.

The second message was from Morrie. He wanted only to know if I was all right. "Ruchele, when we're back in the city, you'll come to dinner. Maybe on a Friday night. When the children come. All right, Ruchele?" When he said my name in Yiddish, his intonation matched that of my parents. My heart turned, my eyes grew moist. Oh, when would my grief subside into predictability? And then I smiled at how he referred to his son and daughter——both of them older than me——as children: Lynn, a psychologist, had two children, and Matt, vice president of an advertising agency, was also the vice president of a gay men's legal aid association.

The machine clicked off. No hang-ups. Phil had not called and his silence oppressed me. Admittedly, I had, on that last evening, plunged him into dangerously deep waters. Unfair, when he was, as I had been for so long, a cautious swimmer. Of course he had not wanted to hear my poem. I had been foolish to offer it to him. I called Melanie.

"The reading was okay," I told her. "And I met this really interesting guy."

"Single? Straight?"

"Single. Straight. Attractive."

"You met him in this city? In New York? That's nothing short of a miracle. Just a second."

I heard Leonard's voice in the background, Melanie's whispered reply.

"Hey, I have to go," I said and gently, too gently. I replaced the receiver.

Dave Robeson and I went to Bryant Park the next night and sat cross-legged on the ragged blanket he had brought. The film was *Giant* and we marveled at how young and beautiful Elizabeth Taylor looked, at the bitterness and vulnerability of James Dean's smile. We had both seen the film on television and gleefully we predicted the good parts, the fierce arguments, the sensual lovemaking. The Bryant Park audience hooted and booed and grew sweetly silent at a tender moment. Elizabeth Taylor's huge violet eyes subdued them, vanquished their brittle sophistication.

"Another great thing about films," Dave said, "is how the young and the beautiful still have their youth and their beauty no matter how many years have gone by."

"Bastards," I said. I had noticed the beginnings of laugh lines about my eyes that morning and I had plucked a single silver strand from my hair two days ago. "It's not fair that we'll have to grow old and ugly."

He looked at me with great seriousness.

"Old maybe. But ugly never. You're beautiful, Rochelle. Really beautiful."

His words embarrassed me and swiftly I turned back to the huge screen where a slender Elizabeth Taylor and a sad-eyed, muscular James Dean walked beneath the vast canopy of the Texas sky, their youth and beauty forever preserved on celluloid.

I saw Dave almost every day that week. I stopped to talk to him as he sketched in the park while my dogs scuffled impatiently, entangling their leashes about my ankles. He was doing a series of illustrations for an advertising agency, tentatively called "Park Wanderers." In charcoal and pencil he drew joggers and cyclists, children at play, elderly men bent over their chess games. I took him to the dog run and he drew Mitzi as she stood leaning against the rail, her thin fragile face turned toward the river, her unironed flowered skirt floating to her ankles. He did not draw Annette.

"No subtlety," he said later. "Just cynical discontent."

I wondered what he would say of Phil's profile, of the tight set of his fleshy lips, his deep-set eyes. *Too closed. He reveals nothing.* I anticipated his judgment, formed it in my mind.

Ida arrived, slowly pushing her shopping cart, thinner than ever, her wide dark eyes sunk deep into the skeletal black mask of her face. She wore an orange baseball cap and a dried clot of white cheese stuck to the collar of her burgundy wool dress. At least she had eaten something, allowed some nourishment into her bony body.

"Hi, Ida." I kept my tone light and she nodded slightly.

Dave lifted his pencil and began to sketch her. She glared at him and shuffled off to another bench. He stopped at once, snapped his sketch pad shut and smiled apologetically.

"It's the first time she's been here all week," Mitzi said. "Carl saw her in Riverside Park, in the playground. The mothers and nannies were moving their precious brats away from her. The bitches."

"Oh, I don't know." Had I been a child playing in that park and had Ida approached, my mother too would have jerked me away. Fear of germs, fear of filth and madness, fear of the contagion of misery. My mother had understood such things.

I placed my usual two dollars on the top of Ida's shopping cart as we left. As always, she ignored them, but when I turned I saw her place them carefully between the pages of a tattered paperback.

Late that Friday afternoon Dave walked across the park with me, waiting as I returned each of the dogs. When we reached the Eliots' apartment building I thought of asking him in to meet them, but decided against it. Grace had been unusually weak that afternoon and Clem was pale with worry.

"The doctor says that sometimes patients are at their worst just before a remission," he said softly to me.

"Sure. I've heard that," I said.

We did not meet each other's eyes and Clem lifted his dog and pressed his face against the warm fur.

"*Remission* is such a stupid word," I said when I rejoined Dave. "I looked it up. Its early meaning was pardon or forgiveness. A cancer patient goes into remission. Is she being pardoned or forgiven? What was the crime? Allowing a metastasis to invade her body?" Tears burned my eyes. Unlike Clem, I had never hoped for remission as my parents died. I had wished only for an end to their pain, an end to their memories.

"Hey," he said. "Easy, Shelley. It's just a word." He touched my arm, threaded his fingers through my hair and then, standing on my corner, he wiped my eyes with his paint-stained handkerchief. He did not ask why I wept.

"Come in for dinner," I said.

"Great."

It was the first time he had been in my apartment and I watched as he studied the living room, the teak furniture, the armchairs that swiveled to face the windows, the low-slung russet sofa. Not what he expected, I knew.

"Mind if I ask some friends to join us?" I asked, and when he nodded assent, I phoned Melanie and asked if she and Leonard were free.

"Sure, but let's make it simple and send out for pizza," she said.

"Good idea."

I ignored the red lights that flickered on my answering machine. It might be Phil and I did not want to listen to his voice while Dave was in the room.

"Aren't you going to pick up your messages?" he asked.

"Later. I don't want to answer any questions from stressed-out dog owners. Sir Gawain's owner calls regularly to ask about the consistency of his bowel movements." Sir Gawain's owner was not alone. I had fielded questions about suspect ticks, one dog's nervousness, another's fatigue? Worry and loneliness haunted the voices of those who called. Like obsessive parents, they were prepared to endlessly discuss the frailties of the animals whom they had woven so tightly into the fabric of their lives.

Melanie and Leonard arrived as the pizza delivery boy left, each carrying a bottle of Chianti. I introduced them to Dave and took the wine from them.

"Two bottles for the four of us. You guys have high expectations," I observed.

Melanie shrugged and put my rather dusty wine glasses on the table. Another gift from Phil, who had washed them carefully after each use.

Melanie was very lively that evening. A yellow rose that exactly matched her lemon-colored overalls was tucked behind her ear and her toes jutted out of clear plastic sandals. A tiny lacquered flower blossomed on each toenail, carefully painted there by the Korean pedicurist on our corner. I remembered how I had cut my mother's toenails during the last days of her illness and noticed, for the first time, that the nail on her big toe was missing, replaced by a calloused knot of skin.

"It happened over there," she had said apologetically. She had not meant to cause me grief, to remind me of what she had suffered. I had thought to kiss each distorted toe but instead I had passed my hand gently over them as now I passed my hand across the garden that sprouted at Melanie's feet.

"Wild pedicure," I said.

"I'm a wild gal and I've had some wild news." She drew closer to Leonard. "The cheese shop next door is closing and I spoke to the guy about buying it. There's a three-bedroom apartment upstairs that would be perfect for us and I could expand the flower shop. Maybe have a book section, sell some equipment—gloves, trowels, ceramic planters, that sort of thing. I could even invite botanists to give talks."

"And serve cookies shaped like daisies," I said teasingly as I handed out slices of pizza.

"I spent a couple of days up at the botanical gardens sketching flowers," Dave said. "I could do a poster for you." He munched his slice, leaning back in the leather chair, touching the scar on his knee that smiled whitely through his ripped jeans.

"I could sew that up," I said, lightly touching the ragged fabric.

"Nope. I'm going to splurge on new jeans when the check from the ad agency for the 'Park Wanderers' sketches comes through."

"How much do you make on a job like that?" Leonard asked.

It was a New York question. Money fueled our lives, defined us, and we spoke about it with indifferent honesty.

"A couple of thou," Dave said and I looked at him in surprise.

"Sorry, Shelley," he apologized. "I'm not a starving artist this week. But that doesn't mean I'm ready to give up my day job. Or rather, my evening job." That grin again, an invitation to enjoyment, to shared amusement.

"Well, I couldn't afford to pay you much," Melanie said.

"Oh, that's all right. For you my fee will be suitably modest. Or maybe I'll just design the posters as a gift. A wedding gift."

Melanie blushed. Leonard refilled his wine glass and stared down at the floor. We did not easily use words like *wedding* or *marriage*, not even when we spoke of three-bedroom apartments.

"Perfect for us," Melanie had said, and those words had been daringly spoken. A nuanced invitation to commitment to which no response had been made.

We fell silent. I moved to the CD player, struggled to find a disc that would counter our mood. Roberta Flack, I thought, but before I could insert it, the doorbell rang. *Phil.* Of course, it had to be him, taking a chance that I would be home to offer him a glass of wine and some leftover takeout. That had been our pattern during my BIS days, when both of us worked late and could not manage a proper dinner. My heart beat too rapidly. I imagined myself introducing him to Dave, imagined Dave's wink of complicity, his inevitable grin.

I opened the door and Lila and Fay burst into the room, bubbling with talk and laughter, tossing their knapsacks to the floor and circling the room with outstretched arms and chirps of delight.

"Melanie!"

"Leonard!"

"Rochelle!"

They grinned happily at Dave when I introduced him and glanced quizzically at me, flashing their "Girlfriend, tell all" smiles. They had both cut their golden hair short and they wore their standard summer uniforms of tight-fitting stonewashed jeans and breast-hugging white T-shirts cut short enough to reveal their suntanned midriffs. When Lila perched on the arm of my chair, I smelled the scent of the sea on her skin.

"Hey, you knew we were coming, didn't you? We left a message on your machine," she said.

"Well, you weren't too specific about date or time," I replied. "But it worked out. I'm glad I was home."

"Oh, Mario would have let us in if you were out." Fay spoke with the confidence unique to those who revel in their carelessness and depend on the reliability of others. There would always be some-

one to open a locked door, to write a check against a vague promise of repayment, to offer the use of an apartment, a car, a beach
house. Unlike me, they tried to please no one because they had
never had anyone to please. They lived by impulse rather than design. I envied them their casualness, their assumption that things
would turn out right when so often, through the years, things had
turned out wrong. They bounced from temp job to temp job,
from audition to audition, from man to man. Often they did not
know their lovers' last names, although they were always careful.
They were uninsured and could not afford illness. Yet they remained unfazed, always on the go, always certain that with this audition, with this encounter, their luck would change and they
would be launched, two southern girls who had made it in the Big
Apple.

"Any pizza left?" Lila asked. "We're starving."

They munched the pizza, downed the Chianti, chatted happily
about the Cape.

"How long are you staying?" Melanie asked, because she understood that I wanted to know.

"A couple of days," Lila answered. "I'm auditioning for a hands
commercial. Rumor has it that my pinkie is particularly photo-
genic. And Fay has an appointment with an agent. We only have
bit parts in the next stock production in Wellfleet."

"A couple of days," Dave repeated and a frown creased his
forehead.

I looked at Leonard. Perhaps he would offer to give up the studio while they were here. He could stay with Melanie, but then I
realized that invariably it was Melanie who stayed with him and,
for the first time, I wondered why.

"No problem with that, is there?" Fay asked me.

"No problem at all," I assured her.

It was Dave who left first, resting his hand on my head as he said
goodbye.

"See you in the park," he said. "Same bench."

"Great."

I wanted him to leave. I wanted them all to leave. The smell of the wine sickened me. I wanted to toss away the empty bottles and the pizza boxes, rip up the paper plates and restore my small apartment to order. Like my mother I would wipe down the kitchen counters, pluck up barely discernible crumbs, exercise some small control over my life. And then I wanted to sit at my lamp lit desk and lift my pen above a sheet of white paper as I waited for words to come. But I could not do that, of course. Lila and Fay were here and they would not leave—not tonight, not the next night and perhaps not even the night after that.

I said good-night to Melanie and Leonard, watched them walk down the hall to the studio, arm in arm. And then I got out the light blue sheets and pillowcases for Lila and Fay to spread on the sofa bed they had already pulled open, all of us yawning with fatigue yet still bantering, still laughing. Finally, I played the messages on my answering machine. One hang-up and then Morrie, calling me Ruchele, wishing me a good shabbos, renewing his invitation for a Friday-night dinner. Perhaps next week or the week after. *Don't be a stranger, Ruchele.*

We went to bed at last. I fell asleep at once although it was not, after all, that late. I wakened at dawn, dream images tumbling through my mind and mingling with the unsettling half thoughts of first awareness. I went to the window and stared down at the sad patch of earth Mario called his garden. A thin smoke-colored cat slept beneath the tangle of stripped tomato vines. His left ear had been bitten away, replaced with an encrustation of dried dark blood.

Suffused with sadness, I wandered into the living room. Lila and Fay, in oversize white shirts, lay atop the blue sheets. Lila smiled in her sleep but Fay's face was sad and serious. I turned and went back into my bedroom, closing the door softly behind me.

# CHAPTER
## NINE

Predictably, Lila and Fay stayed with me well beyond the weekend. Morning, afternoon and evening, I listened as they spoke breathlessly on the telephone to agents and friends, spreading wide the net of their contacts and, like the agile fisherwomen they were, dropping lures as they angled for information. There was an audition at Y & R, a walk-on at Nickelodeon, a cameo for Oxygen. Great. Terrific. They whispered their gratitude, their voices tremulous with optimism. I stepped over their clothing, spread in colorful hillocks on my living-room floor. I gathered up dirty mugs and dirtier plates and dropped them noisily and accusingly into the sink. I slammed the door behind me when I left to walk my dogs and then was ashamed when I returned hours later to find the apartment briefly restored to order and a gift offering from Zabar's or Balducci's in the refrigerator.

Late in the week Dave came home with me. We had met as always in the park, moving toward each other across the long shadow of a giant oak, my dogs yelping excitedly. We had not even bothered to feign surprise at this chance encounter that in fact had very little chance about it. Together we had gone to the library, Dave to teach his class and I to attend the poetry workshop where Constance Reid distributed copies of "Thirteen Ways of Looking at a Blackbird" by Wallace Stevens and skillfully analyzed it. Twice, she had startled me by asking me a direct question about Stevens's imagery and intent and twice I had blushed and declined to answer. My reticence surprised me. What had happened to the effortless A student I had always been, the gal with the facile answers, swift to jump to the head of the class? Perhaps I had dropped out of the race because there was no one on the sidelines to cheer me on, no one to receive medals and ribbons too easily earned. I read the poem yet again, more carefully now and, with sudden clarity, I saw the answers Constance had sought, but I neither raised my hand nor went up to speak to her afterward. It was enough that I had made the poem my own.

I did not talk with Dave about it as we walked through the soft late-summer darkness.

"Hungry?" he asked.

"Oh, there'll be something good in the refrigerator. Lila and Fay can be counted on for that at least."

He glanced at me curiously and shrugged, but I was right, of course. There was a wedge of Brie and a large vine-ripened tomato in the chiller and a deliciously crunchy baguette on the counter.

"See?" I said as I spread the runny cheese across the heel of the bread and held it out to him.

He grinned and bit down.

"They have great taste in food." Crumbs pebbled his lips and he used the cheese knife to slice the tomato.

"Excellent," I agreed. "And no expense spared. After all, what's money to them?" I pointed to the living room where a ragged dollar bill lay on the floor. That morning I had found two quarters mysteriously afloat in the bathroom soap dish, and when I kicked Lila's jeans across the bedroom floor a crumpled, uncashed check had fallen out of the pocket.

Always, my southern friends had been careless about money, playfully cute about cash they could not account for, checks that bounced, bills that were sometimes doubly paid or, more often, not paid at all. Early on, I had recognized that their carelessness was not rooted in indifference or indolence but was an act of defiance, a set proof of their independence, an arrogant celebration of their own values. They would not be caught up in the rat race. They had never been monitored and they would not monitor themselves. And I, the daughter of a woman who had worried about the extravagance of buying nectarines out of season, observed them with anger and with envy.

"Are they driving you crazy?" Dave asked, biting into the tomato, its juice sliding down his chin. I wiped it away with my finger and then licked it thoughtfully.

"They're driving me crazy," I admitted truthfully and I offered no rationalization for their behavior, no excuses for my irritation.

"Then why don't you tell them to get the hell out?"

"It's only for another day or so. They have to be back on the Cape by the weekend. And they're friends. They've been very good friends to me."

I did not, would not, speak of how I had watched their entwined bodies, how their sleep-thickened faces had been awash with loneliness. They were orphan girls in search of shelter and orphans could not, should not, be evicted. And then, perversely, I was seized by a strange and bitter jealousy. Lila and Fay, at least, had the comfort of each other's bodies, of soft white breasts rising to pillow golden heads. I looked at Dave and wondered when he would kiss me, if he would kiss me.

He went to the refrigerator and took out a bottle of sangria—another gift from Lila and Fay, a subtle offering with sliced oranges and lemons encased in an envelope of bright pink cellophane cunningly arranged to dangle from the cork. He poured the wine, set the fruit afloat on its rosy surface, and we clinked glasses and took our first sips. And then, our tongues tingling with the wine's sweetness, we kissed and kissed again. Sliding down from the tall stools, we stood in my very white kitchen, our bodies pressed close, his large paint-scarred hand sliding beneath the smoothness of my hair to find the secret places of my neck, his fingers fondling the lobe of my ear, reaching down the trace the bony knobs of vertebrae.

"Rochelle." He whispered my name as though it was too fragile to sustain a normal register. "Rochelle."

"Ruchele. My parents called me Ruchele," I said, but my words were muted by the shrill ring of the telephone and, with it, the jangle of keys at the door, voices, laughter.

"Damn." He spat the word out. "Damn, damn, damn."

I moved out of his embrace, out of the path of his anger, his disappointment, struggling to contain my own anger, my own disappointment. The phone rang again and then again. I waited for the answering machine to pick up, for Phil's impatient voice to fill the room, but instead the ringing stopped and Fay and Lila, laughing and jostling each other, stumbled into the room.

Shopping bags braceleted their arms, danced at their hips—shiny blue plastic Gap bags, sere colored Banana Republic carriers, stiff white Anne Taylor bags. Body Shop scents wafted through the room. They were in the habit of gliding from counter to counter, lathering their hands with creams, spraying perfume behind their ears, lightly rouging their cheeks, dabbing their wrists with moisturizers that smelled of lilacs.

"Anyone can smell rich in this city," Lila had once told me with satisfaction.

"Hey, Rochelle, you're here," Fay said, dropping her bags.

"I do live here, you know," I replied and immediately regretted the spontaneous sarcasm of my response.

"Yeah. But we thought you'd be out. Walking dogs. Going to a class. Doing something worthwhile."

They laughed. They felt no need to do anything worthwhile. It was not expected of them, had never been expected of them.

"Hi, Dave." Lila beamed at him.

"Hey." He masked his irritation, smiled, lifted his glass. "Thanks for the wine."

"Yeah. It's a good wine. We thought we'd order in Mexican. Do you like Mexican, Dave?"

"Hate it. Anyway, I was just leaving. Have a great trip back to the Cape."

"Oh, we've two callbacks tomorrow. We'll be here another couple of days. That okay with you, Rochelle?" But she did not wait for my reply. She plucked a pink top from the Gap bag and stood in front of the mirror, holding it against her body.

Dave stared hard at me, a judgmental, expectant stare that both excited and angered me. He wanted me to refuse them, to assert myself and please him. I teetered on the sensual brink of indecision. I would submit to him—I would resist him—I would submit to him. My heart beat faster, my hands tingled.

"Sure," I told Lila at last. "No problem. Just clear your junk out of the living room."

And then I walked Dave to the door and spitefully, maliciously, I smiled up at him. Spite and malice were new to me and I tasted them tentatively, as though I had been introduced to a strange new food. It was wonderful, I thought, not to have to please him, not to have to please anyone, except myself.

"Tomorrow then?" I asked him.

"Where? When?"

"Same time. Same bench." Early evening, when the heat of the day slowly evaporated and harsh sunlight faded into smoky urban twilight.

"And then where?" His voice was hard, accusatory. We could not go again to my apartment where doors opened unexpectedly, banishing intimacy, intruding on tender silence. He had spoken only vaguely of his own living arrangement—a loft shared with a sculptor who drifted in and out of the city, sleeping bags spread on the floor, a communal toilet down the hall.

"You'll see. A surprise," I said and smiled up at him.

He pulled me to him, too swiftly, too roughly, and when he kissed me this time there was no gentleness in the force of his lips upon my own. The residue of wine upon his tongue was no longer sweet but so bilious that when he turned to leave I wiped my mouth and struggled against a brief and sudden nausea.

In the apartment Lila was on the phone with the Mexican restaurant on Lexington Avenue, studying the menu she had plucked from the manila folder on my counter in which I kept the brightly colored sheets of paper that appeared with mysterious regularity beneath my door. Such menus were an insurance policy against boredom, a guarantee to the lonely and the lazy that nurture and nourishment were only a phone call away. This, after all, was New York. We could order in anything from anywhere at any hour. Even my dog-walker friends remained connected by cell phone to their favorite take-out places. Mitzi had Chinese food delivered to the dog run. Carl consulted with Ramon and called kosher delis, upscale sushi places.

Lila fanned herself with the menu and pointed at me.

"A black-bean burrito," I said.

"A black-bean burrito," she instructed. "Grazia." Spanish thanks in a southern drawl. "I'm going over to the studio to pick up some stuff."

"You'd better check with Leonard," I said.

She shrugged. She had not been schooled to tiptoe through other people's lives.

I remembered a long ago weekend with my mother at Morrie's summerhouse, how she had rushed me from bed each morning so that we could swiftly tuck away the sheets and blankets, obscure any sign of our intrusion. My parents had been thrust from their homes as children and after the war, liberated but orphaned, they had lived on the sufferance of others, tentative trespassers in the homes of American relations, my father's aunt, my mother's cousin, who were, in fact, strangers to them. Gratefully they slept on pull-out sofas, put their few belongings in single bureau drawers, hung their hand-me-down clothing in the corners of closets that stank of mothballs. My father wakened at dawn so that he could use the bathroom before his aunt and her family awakened. He did not want to disturb them. My mother kept her toothbrush in her purse for years because her cousin's toothbrush holder was full and she was too shy to ask where she might keep her own toiletries.

I had inherited their tentativeness, their unease in other people's homes. Even in rented Fire Island and East Hampton beach houses I made my bed first thing in the morning and immediately cleared away my own dishes. I had noticed that Phil did the same.

Lila darted out of the apartment and Fay poured herself a glass of sangria and began to examine the contents of their shopping bags. She held up miniskirts, sleeveless blouses, a yellow bikini and, surprisingly, a sheer white negligee and peignoir.

"I think Lila spent too much on this," she said worriedly.

"So what if she did? You're not her mother," I replied irritably.

Immediately, I regretted my words. Fay replaced their purchases, her color high.

"No. I'm not her mother. Neither of us, not me, not Lila, had a mother like yours, Rochelle," she said. "I remember the way your mother—and your father, too—looked at you, the way they listened to you, the way they loved you. When you bought a shirt, I'll bet they looked at it, touched it, worried whether or not it was good enough for you. Your mother said your name like it was holy. 'Ruchele'—I can't even pronounce it right, but from her it was like a prayer. You couldn't do anything wrong in their eyes, but as far as my folks were concerned, everything I did was wrong—beginning with getting born. And Lila—she thinks her folks don't even remember who she is."

She was crying now, a narrow rivulet of black mascara coursing down her cheek.

"So Lila and I became like family, sisters. I worry that she might have spent too much. She tells me what looks good on me, reminds me to take my vitamins. We're all each other has. Pseudofamily, maybe. But something."

I understood then that they turned to each other to compensate for their vanished birthrights, in quest of the normalcy of family. I had envied them their independence, the ability to live free of the constraints and expectations of others while they, in turn, had envied me my parents' love, my centrality in their lives.

"Oh, Fay, I'm sorry," I said and, leaning forward, I took her hand in my own. She returned the pressure of my fingers and we sat in the gathering dusk, our hands entwined until Lila burst into the room carrying a load of clothes that she tossed onto the sofa before flicking on the light just in time to accept the delivery of our Mexican food.

Clem Eliot called as we finished eating. He was sorry to bother me, he said apologetically, but Grace was not feeling well and he wondered if I could walk Goldilocks.

"Sure. No problem," I agreed. "Can I do anything else?"

"No. There's nothing anyone can do, Rochelle." His voice was heavy with defeat. The days of hope and denial were over.

"I'm sorry." And sorrow did strangle my words so that I uttered them in half voice. Grace would die as my parents had died, and

Clem and his children and their friends would gather to mourn her and then retreat to recover alone. Recuperation from grief is a solitary process, silent and candlelit. That much my parents had taught me.

On each Yom Kippur eve my mother had stood alone in the kitchen and lit three memorial candles, her eyes dry, her lips moving soundlessly. Always she closed the kitchen door softly behind her as she left. My father entered then, in stockinged feet, a shoeless mourner, and he too held a match to the small wicks that sprouted from the squat wax-filled glasses. He murmured names aloud—his mother, his father, his siblings, the grandparents, the aunts and uncles I would never know. The flames flickered teasingly; he moistened his fingers and extinguished the match between them, but he did not wipe away the tears that streaked his cheeks. These were the memorial lights kindled in memory of the dead, left to burn an entire day.

I had watched from the doorway, a furtive spy, searching for clues that would reveal the secrets of their sorrow. I thought of happy things to say to them, words that would make them glad, triumphs that would diminish their sadness.

When Grace Eliot died I would bring Clem a *yahrtzeit* candle that would burn for twenty-four hours in her memory. Its fragile flame might comfort him, he might read verses of consolation in the circlet of its light.

Lila and Fay went with me to pick up Goldilocks and, although they did not go in, they waited for me and we walked on together. Fay had a callback the next day. A soap opera that was just what she needed. A nice long gig at SAG rates.

"If I get that I won't have to scrounge for other work. No more birthday parties. No more dog walking."

"Gee, thanks," I said. "Nice to know you think so highly of my work."

"Oh, come on, Rochelle. You're not going to be walking dogs

forever. This is just until you get your head together. We all know that." Lila was dismissive and, of course, she was right. I would not be walking dogs forever; but what, in fact, would I be doing?

"We'll see," I said and I waved to Mitzi who rounded the corner just then, holding the thin purple leather leashes of the miniature white poodles who trotted proudly through the darkness. They belonged to an anorexic actress who cautioned Mitzi not to offer them dog biscuits and kissed each of them on the lips before surrendering their leashes.

"A nutcase," Mitzi had said of her as we sat together on the bench in the park run and discussed the vagaries of our dogs' owners. Another professional perk—the freedom to mock our employers, to be totally disinvolved. At BIS I had too often pretended a concern I did not feel.

I watched, worried, as Mitzi turned and took a path that led into a wooded park preserve. A jogger had been attacked along that path the previous week and the police had issued warnings against frequenting certain portions of the park after dark. The message had been clear. Joggers and walkers who ignored the warning were courting disaster. It occurred to me that vague Mitzi, in her gauzy skirts and high red suede boots, her fair hair haloing her delicate face, might be doing exactly that. I would speak to Annette about her. Perhaps we could confront her together.

I returned Goldilocks and walked with Lila and Fay to Melanie's shop. She opened a bottle of white wine and we sipped it from paper cups, talking very softly but never mentioning Grace Eliot.

I wakened early the next morning and moved quietly through the apartment, stepping over Lila and Fay, still asleep in the living room, their bobbed hair gleaming in the pale sunlight, their bare arms entangled. I stood at the window and watched Mario walk his small daughter to school. Her dark hair was neatly braided, her plaid cotton uniform stiffly starched. Mario worked a double shift at the supermarket to pay her summer-school tuition.

"So smart, my Rosa," he had told me proudly.

My parents would never have spoken such words for fear that they might tempt the evil eye. I wondered if Mario had followed Phil's stock tips, if he had made those conservative investments. But that Sunday of our last togetherness, Phil's and mine, seemed distant, illusory; although each time the phone rang I trembled with certainty that it was Phil who was calling, that he was ready to speak of all we had left unsaid. Listening to the routine hang-ups on my answering machine, I told myself that Phil was the mysterious caller whose breathy silence bewildered me. But in darker moments I acknowledged that he would not call, that I had asked too much of him—much more than he was willing to give, that he might ever be able to give.

It would be a cool day, I knew. Late summer that year was treacherous, now hot, now cool. Already the workshop poets wrote of the melancholy of changing seasons, mourning in quatrain and sonnet the vanishing days of warmth and sunlight. Constance Reid was impatient with such efforts. "Seasonal sentimentality," she called them in her distinctive withering tone and she urged us to dip deeper within ourselves, to wrest free the poems that surely lurked in dream and fantasy. "Don't waste my time. Don't waste your time." Her voice was crisp, her judgments, as always, harsh.

Still seated at my window, my coffee cooling, I checked my calendar. I could not risk a mistake. I had made a promise of a kind to Dave and I intended to keep it. Determinedly, I banished all thoughts of Phil and circled the date. Yes. I had been right. The Catons, on a protracted vacation, would not be home for several days. Their apartment would be empty. I felt a surge of excitement, an anticipatory thrill. The daring of my own plan thrilled me. Of course, after it was accomplished, I would drop the Catons as clients.

I had disliked them from the first, those two eviscerated man-
nequins, doctor and lawyer, quintessential yuppies, sucked dry
by ambition and pretentiousness, as sterile as their lives. I had
stolen naps on their bed. I had sat cross-legged on a lambskin
rug and stared at myself in the full-length mirrors affixed to the
doors of their walk-in closets where their clothing hung, encased in clear plastic garment bags—his dark suits, her dark
dresses.

Roaming through those spacious very clean pine-scented rooms
I had often imagined myself living their lives. A few more years at
BIS, an accumulation of fat bonus checks, perhaps even a partnership or a sprint to a start-up with stock options and I could have
afforded an apartment like that with furnishings crafted to order
and a wardrobe of power suits with the right labels. I had played
with the thought while taking showers in their bathroom (blue
tiles, blue tub and toilet, gentians dancing across the frosted door
of the shower stall) and laughed aloud. I would not want to call
such an icebox home. I would towel myself dry with my own
towel—a tip from Mitzi who often bathed in her clients' apartments and was careful always to leave no sign of her presence.

"Bring your own soap, too," she had advised. "They're very savvy
about their soap." I had laughed but I had followed her advice.

I would miss that apartment more than I would miss Lucky, but
meanwhile it was available to me. I checked my key ring and made
sure their keys were all in place—the key to the front door, to the
service entrance outside the kitchen and to the service elevator that
I had never used. The Catons had made it clear that they preferred
I used the service entrance, but I had stared them down, fingered
my Phi Beta Kappa key and shook my head.

"I don't feel comfortable doing that," I said. "I'm not a servant."

I smiled at the recollection, rummaged for a larger bag than I
usually carried and thrust two towels and my soap into it. I was
searching for a hotel-size shampoo when Lila, her face still puffy

with sleep, wandered into the kitchen, poured herself a cup of coffee and wiped her eyes with the hem of her sleep shirt.

"Listen, Rochelle, if you want us out of here today we can stay with Melanie. She said it would be okay. I know that Dave guy was pissed we were here and if you guys want some privacy, you know..." Her voice trailed off and she concentrated on her coffee, inhaling its fragrance, taking very small sips.

"No. It's fine for you guys to stay. It would be stupid to schlep your stuff over to Melanie's for what—another day, two days?" I dismissed her offer with casual ease. Their leaving would signify a change in our friendship and I did not want that. There had been too many changes in my life in too short a time.

"I wanted to ask—what's with you and Phil? Is he strictly past tense?"

"I don't know. If you see Phil, ask him. And let me know what he says."

"But meanwhile, are you and this Dave person an item?"

"I don't know, Lila. I don't know anything. I don't even know what an item is." I fought the irritation her questions triggered and turned back to studying my schedule. I would have to fit Goldilocks in. I was certain that Clem could not manage to walk his dog today.

I completed my morning circuit at a rapid pace. Moving through the park, I waved to the three old women who wearily tossed the large blue rubber ball to a smiling and energetic Aretha. They each wore a crocheted pastel shawl, the delicate pink, light blue and lemon yellow of a baby's layette, and, seated beneath a giant oak, leafy shadow dappling their faces, sunlight gilding their thinning hair, they themselves looked like aging infants.

"How's it going, Rochelle?" Aretha called.

"How's it going, Aretha?" I asked in return—a Manhattan interchange, a question answered with a question, the contact, the calling out of names more important than the words.

At the transverse, where the park opens to city streets, I met Annette, who held the leashes of three very small dogs in one hand and the long leads of three very large dogs with the other. Keeping perfect balance, she glided toward me, the smaller dogs sniffing each other urgently, the larger dogs loping ahead, although a collie moved more slowly, her large thick-lashed golden eyes mournful. I patted her. I loved collies and I was feeling mournful myself. Annette smiled.

"Rochelle, can you walk a couple of my mutts this afternoon?" she asked. "I have to get my daughter to the doctor."

"Gee, Annette, I'm sorry. I can't." And I was sorry. I would have liked to help Annette, who struggled to pay her daughter's tuition and juggled her schedule to fit in visits to her autistic son who stared up at her with empty eyes—a six-foot-tall seventeen-year-old who crouched on the floor of his room in the residential facility that had been his home since childhood, building and destroying elaborate Lego constructions. But Annette, gutsy and determined, forged on. She spoke of the novel she had been trying to write for years. An outline and a chapter captured on paper, the plotline dancing through her mind as she walked her dogs. Another good thing about our job, she claimed. The dogs don't give a damn about what you're thinking and they never ask questions or volunteer opinions. She talked aloud as she walked, creating characters, inventing plotlines, occasionally staring down a passerby who looked at her disapprovingly, writing her off as another Central Park crazy.

"You know they think all dog walkers are nuts," she had told me. "And I feel like telling them I'd rather talk to myself or one of their mutts than have one of their stupid cell-phone conversations—you know, 'The decorator didn't come—where do you want to have dinner—but we had Chinese last week—just fax me that memo.' Assholes." I had laughed at her mimicry.

"Ask me another time." I amended my refusal and she nodded.

"No problem. I'll ask Mitzi. She can always use the extra money."

"Annette, I saw Mitzi going into the park last night. She went off the main path." I spoke hesitantly. Dog walkers were careful not to intrude on each other's lives.

She shrugged her shoulders, frowned as the golden retriever she kept on a long lead squatted and then swiftly bent to scoop up the large turd, which she dropped into a Fairway shopping bag.

"Carl mentioned it and she gave him one of her smart-aleck answers about being able to take care of herself, and probably she can. Underneath all that Alice in Wonderland vagueness, she's pretty savvy. The one I'm worried about is Ida. Have you seen her around?"

"Not for a while."

"Maybe she checked into a shelter."

"I hope it was a hospital."

"Yeah. Whatever. I just hope she's okay."

I was eager suddenly to be on my way, to think of Dave instead of Mitzi and Ida, about whom I could do little. As though sensing my impatience, Annette released the leads on the dogs she had been holding in check.

"Take care, Rochelle."

"Listen, I'd really be glad to help you out another time. It's just that today I have these plans," I said.

"Sure. I understand."

And she was off, rounding a corner and then pausing briefly beneath a tree where her three large dogs lifted their legs as the smaller ones danced excitedly.

I completed two circuits and stopped to grab a hot dog at a Sabrett cart. As I stood munching it, a downtown bus lumbered down the avenue and halted at the light.

"Rochelle!"

Suzanne, who now sat at my desk at BIS and dictated memos to my assistant, smiled at me from the open bus window. She was, as always, carefully made up, her dark hair cut fashionably short, pearl buttons glinting on her tailored black shirt. I smiled back, grimly conscious of my soiled jeans, my sweat-stained green Dog Daze T-shirt, the tattered fanny pack stuffed with keys, Baggies and dog biscuits that sagged at my waist. The bus continued on, carrying Suzanne back to the life that had once been my own. I wondered how long it would take her to head for the coffee corner and report her Rochelle sighting, right down to the dog shit on my boot and the smear of mustard on my chin.

"Why should you care?" I asked myself angrily, but I could not deny that I did.

I picked up my next gaggle of dogs and walked them too swiftly, briefly falling into step with Annette and Mitzi, speaking again about Ida.

"Nothing we can do," Annette said and Mitzi and I nodded sadly.

"Well, I'm off," I said apologetically. "I'm in kind of a rush today."

They shrugged, indifferent to my departure. We were, after all, free to create our own schedules, to alter them at will, independent contractors, all of us.

I delivered my dogs to their homes, dutifully filled food dishes and water bowls, secured the gates that kept them out of living rooms and bedrooms, not pausing to glance at the books that rested on bedside tables or to riffle through mail and magazines. With only Lucky in tow, I returned to the park.

Dave sat on the bench where we usually met, his pad open, a clump of charcoal between his fingers. He was sketching two squirrels who scampered up and down an oak tree, their bushy tails swirling importantly, their golden eyes hard and bright. They carried bits of twigs and clumps of grass in their mouths, depositing them amid the branches and then scurrying down for more.

"Do you know what they're doing?" Dave asked as I sat down on the bench beside him and tossed Lucky a biscuit.

I shook my head. "I'm not into squirrel culture," I said lightly.

He did not even glance away from the swiftly moving rodents. I watched as he captured them in broad strokes across the thick white paper.

"They're building a nest. There's a sick squirrel up there and they're building a nest for him. Look up. You'll see." He spoke seriously, ignoring my flippancy.

I craned my neck and there, amid the leafy branches, a very thin gray squirrel crouched, his rheumy eyes half-open.

"Are you going to draw him, too?" I asked.

"I already did."

He flipped the pages of his pad to the drawing of the frightened animal. I thought of Grace Eliot and closed my eyes.

"I have an idea for a children's book," he said. "*The Friendly Squirrels. The Caring Squirrels.* Something like that."

"Interesting. But it's different from your other work, isn't it?"

"You don't know a damn thing about my other work," he said and I understood that he was still angry about the previous evening, angry that I had allowed Lila and Fay to interrupt our sudden closeness, angry perhaps that I had not left with him, that I had abandoned him at the peak of his desire.

"All right. I don't know much about your work. I don't even know much about you," I retorted, my tone echoing his. But my words rang false. I knew more about Dave than I had ever known about Phil. I knew about his yearnings, his ambition, about his sister who sat on a porch swing and wept because he was leaving his home, betraying his parents' legacy. Phil had not shared as much with me.

"Well, there's always time to learn." Dave's tone softened. He closed his pad, put his arm around me, allowed me to rest my head on his shoulder. There were charcoal streaks on his khaki T-shirt; it was frayed at the neck, and the cuffs of his paint-spattered jeans were ragged.

"You're free this afternoon?" I asked.

"I'm free when I want to be. So yes, I'm free this afternoon."

"Not anymore."

I took his hand and pulled him to his feet. With Lucky trailing behind us, we headed eastward across the park.

"Are we going to your place?" Dave asked. "Or are the DuBois twins still squatting there?"

"The DuBois twins?"

"You know, those southern blond waifs who have always depended on the kindness of strangers." He imitated Lila's accent so accurately that I had to laugh.

"No. We're not going to my place. The DuBois gals may indeed be there," I replied. "But I have a plan."

"Rochelle the mysterious."

"It beats being Rochelle the predictable," I answered. "I played that part long enough." Predictably, I had been the good daughter, the successful student, the successful athlete, the successful career gal on the rise, making my parents proud, the brightness of my present banishing the darkness of their past. But their deaths had liberated me. I was free to walk through the park on a workday afternoon, hand in hand with a man whom they would view with puzzled disapproval. Why then, I wondered, did that very liberation fill me with an inexplicable sadness?

I struggled to rid myself of that entangling net of melancholy as Dave and I left the park and maneuvered our way across the crowded broad avenues of the Upper East Side. I listened as he told me the story of the children's book he planned, one small volume in a contemplated series on urban animal life. A literary agent had approached him, suggested books on squirrels, pigeons, sparrows.

"Rats," I offered.

"Rats," he agreed. "The city rat and the country rat. Why not?"

"But what about your painting. Will you have enough time?"

"The books will make the paintings possible. The royalties will be an annuity of a kind and there are all sorts of animation tie-ins, according to this agent. I can give up the teaching and maybe the advertising stuff if I know there'll be a check in the mail—a steady check. It might be almost as secure as running a pharmacy. My parents would be proud."

"But I thought you liked the teaching," I protested. His elderly students trailed after him when we left the library and more often than not he stayed for an extra half hour to offer advice on a completed work, demonstrate a brushwork technique.

"You thought." He pulled at my hair, an affectionate tug, a teasing promise commingling tenderness and roughness.

The doorman who guarded the Catons' apartment building glanced at me quizzically. Although he had seen me often as I picked up the dog and returned him, no one had ever accompanied me before. I smiled at him and moved forward with authority—another BIS lesson. "Act as though you belong and no one will question you," Brad had instructed his junior account executives who were charged with attending the news conferences of rival firms so that BIS might have a jump start on their campaigns. "A little professional espionage," Brad had said. "Not illegal." *Only unethical,* I had thought then as I smiled myself into rooms where I definitely did not belong and smiled my way out again, a competitor's program committed to memory. I trained that smile on the doorman who smiled in turn and told me in a conspiratorial tone that it would rain later that afternoon. A weather anchor for a cable station who lived in the building had told him so.

"Does that count as insider trading?" Dave asked. "Divulging weather secrets before a broadcast. Shame on him."

I laughed and my laughter reassured me. There. I was not sad. I was having fun, I told myself. This was an adventure. This was exciting. I was a good girl being bad. At last. Finally.

We reached the Catons' apartment and I unlocked the door and led the exhausted dog into the kitchen. I filled his food dish and his water bowl and snapped the metal gate behind him. He would not bark. His bladder was empty, his bowels evacuated, he would be neither thirsty nor hungry. I even plumped up the mattress in his sleeping basket.

Dave wandered through the apartment, glancing at the unread books in their pale blue leather binding that almost exactly matched the painting that hung above the sofa and the color of the carpet.

"Do they wear only pale blue when they sit in this room?" he asked.

"Yes. And when they hold parties they ask their guests to dress accordingly. Pale blue dresses for the women, pale blue jackets for the men." We laughed maliciously.

Dave paused in the doorway of the guest bathroom.

"Maybe I'll take a shower," he said.

"Later," I replied. "After."

"After what?" he asked and pulled me to him, slipped his hands beneath my shirt, cupped my breasts, his eyes narrow slits, his face a mask of expectation.

My excitement mounted. This was, I told myself, the most foolish and the most dangerous thing I had ever done. It was, in fact, the only dangerous and foolish thing I had ever done. I laughed at my own innocence, congratulated myself on my absurd courage and led Dave into the bedroom, that pristine-white expanse dominated by the high bed with its snow-white counterpane and duvet that Phil had likened to the frozen steppes.

It startled me to recall that I had been in this very room with Phil and that he and I, practiced lovers, veterans of so many shared vacations, so many shared houses and bedrooms, had not even touched each other. And yet here I stood with Dave and already I was kneeling to remove my walking boots and socks, and already he was sliding down his jeans, kicking off his sandals, arching his back to remove his tattered khaki T-shirt.

Naked, he turned to me and slowly, very slowly, he undressed me, sliding his hands knowingly across my body, encircling my waist, his eyes raking my face as though he was committing each figure to memory.

"Stop! I am not posing for you, I protested, my voice faint, a new tightness fast about my heart. Fear and excitement gripped me. I fought free by taunting and teasing him. I would not be his model, passive and obedient. I would be his lover, his passionate equal.

"Of course you're not posing for me." He flashed me that engaging smile. "But you will. I'll do your portrait in oils. An impasto. Layers of reds, oranges, browns and yellows until I get the exact color of your hair. Firelight." He pulled the scrunchy that held my wild curls in a thick ponytail and they tumbled down my back, fell to my shoulders.

He gathered up our clothing and shoes, tossing them carelessly beside the bed, and pulled me toward him. We kissed and kissed again, his hand upon my head, as though we were continuing the interrupted tenderness of the evening past. I ran my fingers across a small scar on his neck.

"A dog bite, a cousin's dog. Just a nip. When I was two."

"Poor baby," I said. "Poor little boy. Poor Davey."

I laughed and he laughed. Then with sudden urgency he leaped onto the bed and pulled me up. Startled, I uttered a small cry and thought for a moment that I might weep. Who was I? What was I doing in this strange room with a man who was all but a stranger to me? He calmed me, kissed me gently, stroked my hair, my back, the length of my legs and I, in turn, touched him, felt and smelled his skin, so strangely soft, licked the pale, shell-shaped scar. He was not a stranger. I knew him. He was all that I was not. He was free. No one had any claim on his life. His clothing was ragged because he traveled with very little baggage and because he honestly and truly did not give a damn.

"Rochelle, this is crazy," he whispered. "Crazy."

Laughter swelled within me. I had never done anything crazy before. I would tell Melanie about it as we sat bathed in the soft ultraviolet light and we would giggle at the silliness of it, the daring silliness.

"Crazy and weird," I agreed and moved closer to him so that I might feel the rise of his desire.

And then the dog barked, a sharp excited series of yelps and I heard the sound of the door opening, then closing.

"Hey there, good dog. Did you miss us?" Dr. Caton's voice, falsely affectionate, overwhelmed the staccato barks.

"The Catons," I whispered to Dave. "The damn Catons. They weren't supposed to be home for another week."

We scrambled off the bed, frantically plucking up our clothing.

And then Elise Caton spoke, her irritable voice rasping through the apartment.

"How stupid. We forgot to ask the doorman for the mail."

"All right. I'll go down to get it."

"No. You go to the car. I left my makeup case in the trunk. I'll get the mail. Why does this always happen?" Her voice was plaintive. Always she was ambushed by petty disasters. A forgotten case, a garment ruined by a careless dry cleaner. Telephone solicitors who called during a dinner party.

"All right then. Stop whining and come on."

He was angry, impatient. It was an anger and impatience that would cause them to lie in silence on this high white bed until at last she reached for her journal so that she might record her loneliness in ink the color of a robin's egg.

"I'm coming." The door slammed behind them.

Dave and I wasted no time. Still naked, we retrieved our scattered garments and Dave grabbed his sketch pad. I pulled the duvet back onto the bed and we dashed through the apartment, into the kitchen, ignoring the furious barking, and out the service entrance. Safe in the darkened hallway, we pulled our clothing on. I had lost a sock and I wondered what Lynn Caton would say when she found it. The thought made me laugh and Dave too burst into laughter. The service elevator arrived at last and we rushed into it, ignoring the stare of the delivery boy from the Food Emporium.

"I'm sorry," I said breathlessly.

"Me, too. I never got to take that shower. There was no later. There was no after," he said ruefully.

"But wasn't the before terrific?" I asked as we left the building. "And it wasn't my fault that the Catons came back early."

And thus absolving myself of guilt, I lifted my face skyward and was astonished to feel the gentle drops of a sudden rainfall.

# CHAPTER
## TEN

Dave walked me home but would not come in. The rain worried him. He had left the windows of the loft open and his roommate would be pissed if the floor got wet. He'd see me the following evening at the library. Maybe we could grab some dinner after his class, my poetry workshop. I shrugged.

"Maybe." The laughter that had convulsed us in the Catons' stairwell had been stilled. Disappointment, irritation, slowed our steps, muted our voices. A light kiss on the cheek, a desultory wave and he was gone. I shivered against the early September chill.

As always, I glanced at my answering machine. Three red lights flickered, electronic fireflies aglow in the autumnal dimness. I sat in the darkness and listened to my messages.

The first was from Lila and Fay, calling from the Port Authority, speaking in breathless unison and passing the phone back and forth. They were waiting for their bus to the Cape. They had things to take care of there, someone important with whom Lila had some deal going. I might be surprised. They giggled. They were sorry not to have seen me before they left but it was really great of me to give them a place to flop and they'd be back soon. Two weeks, maybe three. The beginning of October. Fay had landed a part in a soap and would begin shooting in November. It was at least a three-month gig and she had a signed contract. I smiled. To Lila and Fay, three months was forever. Who could plan further ahead than that, who would want to? The operator demanded another quarter. "See you soon, Rochelle," they cooed and hung up, leaving the automatic voice insisting on payment.

I closed my eyes and thought about the coming months. The beginning of fall, the onset of early darkness, early frost. I had not yet walked my dogs into the wild chill winds that churned up the inky waters of the Hudson nor had I raced with my graceful Afghan hounds through the falling leaves that rattled along concrete city blocks and expanses of parkland. The park benches would slowly empty, the children and their nannies seeking shelter in the recreation rooms of large overheated buildings, the old men and women planted in front of the oversize television sets that dominated the common areas of nursing homes. I would not see Samantha and Aretha again until the spring and then their places might be taken by new aides who would gently toss the big blue ball to new residents. Should I care? I knew by now that these casual urban encounters were as fragile as the brittle autumn leaves. And yet I would care. The absence of the familiar diminished me.

I wondered if Dave would continue to sketch in the park when it grew cold or if he would simply pack up his gear and head west after he had finished the drawings for his children's book. Briefly, I worried about Ida whom Mitzi had spotted downtown. Would she huddle in a doorway, keeping a firm grip on her neatly packed shopping cart or would she scout out a corner for herself in a church basement?

I sighed and willed my thoughts away, scolded myself for submitting to the melancholy that always overtook me at summer's end. Autumn was the season of sadness, September and October the cruelest months, mingling shadows and longing. I had never been deceived by brightly falling leaves or colorful gourds. I was my parents' child. I knew that bright autumn was grim winter's opening act.

The second message whirled onto the tape.

"Ruchele, do you know who this is?" I smiled. Of course I knew. Who else called me Ruchele, the diminutive Yiddish name my parents had favored? Morrie, returned from his Catskill bungalow, extending his inevitable invitation to a shabbat dinner. Why not? His children and grandchildren would be there. And he didn't have to tell me what a cook his Zelda was. I thought of Morrie, generous hearted, large bellied and florid faced, his bright blue eyes sunk deeply between his too-high forehead and his too-fleshy cheeks. He had wept at my parents' funeral, wept and embraced me, holding me so close that I had inhaled the scent of his sorrow, the enormity of his loss. My mother and father had been among the few who shared his secrets, who understood what he had endured, who, like him, lit memorial candle on Yom Kippur eve for parents and siblings who had no death dates. It was he who had explained their finances to me, who had said, "Please, Ruchele, if you need anything you'll come to me, please, Ruchele." He had implored me to depend on him, pleaded with me to take what he could offer. His wife would offer me steaming bowls of chicken soup, he would write a check, as many checks as I needed. "So you'll call me, Ruchele." He did not say goodbye.

Of course I would call Morrie I promised myself. Of course I would go for dinner, not now, not yet, but soon. I did need something from him—a leasehold on his memories, glimpses into the past he had shared with my parents, which they had not shared with me.

The third message played. Melanie, her voice muffled, her

words oddly vague. Could I have dinner? Chinese would be good. And there was a party somewhere in Chelsea. Warren, her brother, had told her about it. Good music and an open bar. A launch for some new software. "It'll be fun," said Melanie who hated parties, who never thought they were fun. "Anyway, call me when you get this message, Rochelle. Rescue me from this disgusting order for bridesmaids' wreaths—purple roses and baby's breath. Ugh."

I called her.

"Chinese sounds good," I said. "Lila and Fay are gone, so there won't be any surprise goodies in the fridge. But about the party—I don't know. I don't think I'm in the mood."

"Oh, come on, Rochelle." There was an urgency in her voice. We'll have a good time. New people. Dancing."

"The new people will be just like the old people. And I thought Leonard hated dancing."

"No Leonard. I'm on my own tonight. Come on. Dig out your leather miniskirt."

"All right." There was no longer any question of refusing. Melanie needed to go to this party—probably to any party—and she needed me to go with her. "Just give me time to shower and get dressed. I'll meet you at Li Chan's in an hour."

"Thanks, Rochelle." The relief in her tone embarrassed and frightened me.

I took a long shower, washing my body free of any trace of the Catons' lilac-scented sheets, soaping away sour moisture, erasing Dave's touch, realizing how angry at him I was. He should have come in with me. He should not have left me at the door of my building. I layered myself again with fragrant bath gel and struggled to calm the rage that I knew to be irrational. Probably, he had thought that Lila and Fay would still be in my apartment. That, after all, was the reason for going to the Catons in the first place. I myself had been surprised to find them gone. But still, he could have come in, had a drink, a cup of coffee. His abrupt departure cheapened me, cheapened us.

Unforgiving, I toweled myself dry and dressed swiftly. Black leather miniskirt. Long topaz silk tunic. Dangling copper earrings. My hair newly washed and blown dry, held loosely in place with a patterned scarf that matched its brightness, the auburn burnished by long hours in the sunlight. I slipped on a pair of thin-strapped, thick-heeled sandals and applied makeup more carefully than usual. It felt good to get dressed up, good to feel the touch of silk against my skin, good to spray my neck and my wrists with the scent Phil had brought back from his last trip to Paris. "It smells like magic," I had told him then and he had nodded, although I did not think he had really heard me. His laptop had been open and his beeper had been bleating. I cast that memory aside and smiled at myself in the mirror, waved to the girl who only an hour ago had pulled her clothes on in a stairwell, laughing because a sock that probably smelled of dog shit had been lost beneath a high white bed. The phone rang but I did not answer it. There was no point. I was off to have fun. I deserved some fun.

I waved to Mario who was mopping the lobby and he nodded at me approvingly. I looked the way a college-educated woman was supposed to look. His small daughter stood beside him. Shyly, she brushed my skirt with her finger. She was a pretty child who would, one day, be beautiful, a bright child who might well turn out to be brilliant. I hoped that she would not disappoint. For Mario's sake. As I had not disappointed. For my parents' sake. Immediately, I revised that mental wish. I hoped that she would not disappoint for her own sake. Impulsively, I bent and kissed her on the forehead. There was no doubt—she would be beautiful.

Li Chan's, a very narrow neighborhood place that specialized in takeout had only a few tables. A blind man sat at one, deftly maneuvering sweet-and-sour beef onto his chopsticks, dropping a piece now and again for his dog. Two men shared a dish of fried rice and silently passed soy sauce to each other. A girl in a black tracksuit ate an egg roll, an open book propped against her water glass, her eyes dangerously bright. "Hi," she said to me and I returned her greeting, knowing that she wanted only to hear the sound of her own voice.

Melanie had settled into the only booth and had already ordered for the both of us. A tureen of hot-and-sour soup was on the table and she ladled the hot liquid into the plain white bowls as I slid onto the cracked red leather seat across from her.

"For someone who didn't want to go to a party you look terrific," she said.

"I'm not sure that's a compliment," I retorted, "coming as it does from someone with green hair."

"Green-tipped hair," she corrected me and smoothed her chartreuse-fringed bangs into place, the magenta covered now by a dark brown dye that gave way to green. Green sparkles studded her dark eyebrows. "It all matches my outfit. Do you like it?"

I studied her bright green close-fitting sweater, her skort of the same color. Her thin wrists were heavy with narrow silver bracelets and a celadon bangle hugged her pale arm.

"It looks like we both resurrected uniforms from previous lives," I said.

Melanie had not worn the psychedelic outfits she had once been partial to since she and Leonard had been together.

"But I do like it," I added quickly. "But will Leonard? Isn't it a little extreme for him?"

"Oh, yes. Leonard." Melanie began to eat her soup, its steam rising to meet the tears that drifted down her cheeks. I leaned over and wiped them away with my napkin, a familiar gesture because Melanie had always been an easy weeper.

"Hey, Melanie, what's going on?"

The girl in the blue tracksuit looked at us, Melanie's misery had dulled her own.

"I wish I knew. I thought everything was great. Leonard and Melanie. One couple indivisible under God. This was it. Love and marriage going together like a horse and carriage."

"Then what happened?"

"Nothing happened. Leonard says he loves me, I'm fabulous, we're fabulous together."

"So?"

"So I don't know. He worries about his mother in Queens and he wants to break away from that worry. That's what the sublease on Lila and Fay's studio was about. One small step for Leonard, one giant step for Leonard and Melanie. Bye-bye, Mama, I'm a big boy now. And I can't blame it on his mother. She's independent. She dyes her hair blonde and wears great suits and plays bridge twice a week with her friends who all look like Mama Gabor. She goes to an exercise class and plays mah-jongg at the senior center. And she likes me. She likes me a lot. She calls me Melli. *Gone With the Wind* is her favorite movie and she thinks I look a little like Olivia De Havilland. But then she hasn't seen my green hair."

She laughed harshly and divided the sesame chicken the waiter had set down. Melanie loved ladling out food, planning menus, shopping for vegetables. Her own mother had stopped cooking after her divorce and had instead lined up frozen dinners like library books on the shelves of her freezer.

"She should have had a Dewey decimal system," Melanie had said, while assuring herself that her own life would be different. Fragrant soups and stews would simmer atop her stove, freshly baked breads and cakes would cool on her counter as she arranged her flowers. And with Leonard that long-held fantasy was hurtling toward reality.

"Look," I said reassuringly. "He's getting there. He probably just needs time."

I bit into the chicken, wondered briefly where Dave was having dinner and decided, too swiftly, that I did not care.

"But there is no time. The tenants above the shop are leaving and the landlord offered me a deal on the building, a chance to buy. He likes me and he's an old man who just wants out, no showing the property, no haggling. It's a Manhattan dream—a place to live, a place to work, all of it coming together at the right time. I thought it was simple. Leonard and I buy in, get married and get on with it. Like adults. We scrape floors, paint walls, buy furniture that doesn't come from IKEA. I thought he would jump at it. I worked up the figures and it's doable. If we both put money in and my brother gives us a loan it would all work out. So when Leonard met me for lunch today I showed him the figures, explained the deal. I was flying, Rochelle. I thought I had it made." Her voice was very low and she began to tear her napkin into narrow strips.

"What did he say?" I asked.

"The usual. Everything was happening too fast. He loves me, he can't imagine life without me, but he's not sure he's ready. And then he began to talk about his mother, which, I think is a lot of crap. She wouldn't give a damn if he got married as long as he left her the bridge table. Oh, yes. Just like you said, he claimed he needed time. And then, Rochelle, he began to cry. *He* cried, not me."

Melanie refilled her plate. The memory of Leonard's tears had staunched her own.

"Sounds like he needs a therapist," I said, sending us both into sudden fits of laughter.

Therapy was the panacea of our friends, the inevitable and convenient repository of all their pain, all their yearnings. Melanie and I had listened to them with wry amusement, winking at each other as the code words clicked on. Always they were in the process of "working things through," gleaning "insights," dealing with "issues," achieving "closure," confronting their feelings. The expensive fifty-minute sessions structured their emotional lives, relieved their loneliness, quashed their feelings of impotence. They were doing something, weren't they? They were trying. They left mounds of damp tissues on deep leather chairs and faded couches. They downed antidepressants designed to take the edge off their anxiety—a temporary measure against the day when they could really cope with their "issues," their repressed anger and expressed melancholy. They sought solace from sadness, anodynes against disappointment. Zoloft. Paxil. Prozac. The very names of the drugs had a soothing cadence, but Melanie and I, proud independents, would have none of it.

Several friends had tactfully suggested that I see a therapist after my parents' deaths, advice that I had disregarded with ease. I had, after all, watched my mother and father light memorial candles for their vanished dead and I had understood that bereavement brings sorrow, a grief that is neither unhealthy nor pathological. I mourned as they had mourned, withdrawing into the cocoon of solitary anguish and gossamer memory. I would not rely on tiny gem-colored pills or fifty-minute sessions in dimly lit rooms.

"Okay then," I told Melanie who was methodically breaking open fortune cookies and crushing the messages without reading them. "I understand where you're coming from, I think. Therapists are out—not for you, not for him. So what are you going to do? Are you going to go on seeing him? Or are you resuming the hunt?"

We spoke the secret language of our smug college years when our own phones rang incessantly and we made dates that we did not keep, offered our classmates' names to men who called us for dates. We were pretty and popular, just zany enough to be interesting and completely removed from the desperate hunt that sent the other girls out to mixers at neighboring medical and law schools, compelled them to accept every blind date in their zeal to find the right man, to relax into the security that came when a diamond flashed on the ring finger of their left hands. Our own sights were fixed higher.

But we were ten years out of college now and the hunting grounds were no longer the lounges of professional schools, lecture halls or campus cafés. We went to bars and coffeehouses, product launches and book parties. We took shares in beach houses and ski lodges, flew off on not-so-spontaneous junkets to the Caribbean. We did not have boyfriends. We had "significant others" who too quickly or too easily became insignificant. I wondered suddenly if Phil would be at this party we were going to but I did not ask Melanie who, having shredded her own white paper napkin, now began ripping mine.

"Oh, I don't know, Rochelle. I'm so tired. I was so happy with Leonard. It was so good. I don't want to begin again. All the stupid small talk, the stupider games. The sexual charades. I'm too tired to start that again. And I'm not going to get over Leonard as easily as you got over Phil. I loved him. I love him." She fanned the ragged napkin strips across the table and stared at them as though they were mysterious tarot cards.

"Did I get over Phil? And were Phil and I even close to having what you and Leonard had?" My own words surprised me, tumbling out as if they had been waiting for an opportunity to escape. "Maybe it was just that we fit together so well and it was all so easy. We were on the same wavelength, high earners, high livers. We liked the same things, we looked good together and we even had the same energy spans. But we never really shared feelings. Not the way you and Leonard do. Phil couldn't utter the word *commitment,* couldn't even talk about not being ready. That would be an admission of weakness and vulnerability, and being vulnerable is something that people like Phil and me can't deal with."

"You mean because of your parents?" Melanie asked softly. She understood that she was trespassing into dangerous territory. I had never spoken of my parents' war experiences except in the most general terms. How could I have? What did I know of them?

"I suppose so. I suppose that's what I mean." I turned away, sig-

naled to the waiter for the check, fumbled in my purse for my lipstick. "But listen, let's forget Phil and Leonard for tonight. Let's
have some fun. Actually, I almost had fun this afternoon." I spurted
out the tale of my late-afternoon adventure, the Catons' unexpected arrival, painting a vivid verbal picture of Dave and myself
running naked to the service elevator and twisting into our clothing.

"Dave even put his underpants on backward," I reported and this
struck us both as riotously funny. Laughing and giggling, we paid
our bill and, laughing and giggling, we hailed a cab and sped south
to Chelsea.

"Fun. Let's have fun," Melanie gasped, and the driver, a delicate-
featured Indian stared at us through his mirror and smiled shyly.

The party was in an old loft building, newly resurrected and
gentrified. We glided out of the elevator into a huge space awash
in silver light. Strobes, set into the high-beamed ceiling like giant
stars, beamed their rays onto the hardwood floor. Dancing couples, the women in loose dresses the colors of wildflowers, the
men wearing soft collarless shirts and wonderfully tailored blaz-
ers, moved slowly, dreamily, through drifting beams of pearl-toned
glimmerglass. The music was soft, restrained. An Asian string
quartet played "I'll Be Seeing You" and a Chinese vocalist in a close-
fitting jade-green gown swayed languidly as she sang. A sushi station had been set up in the far corner of the room and small
ceramic cups of saki were lined up on a lacquered bar.

This was, I knew, a low-key but high-end product launch and
the product itself, a disc wrapped in silver paper and weighted by
a miniature silver rocket, was pyramided on a display table beneath
a sign that read, A Gift for You—Test our Moonbeam Memory.

Melanie zipped off to the bar and I studied the room and thought
of how I might have set it up differently. More hype, more color,
more prominent display of the Moonbeam discs. I would have set
them into mobiles dangling between the strobes.

Suzanne danced by with a short bald man whose too-prominent breasts bulged against his closely fitted white silk turtleneck. She wore a pink miniskirt, a black velvet top and she had dyed her hair rose gold. A dead giveaway, a desperation measure, I decided maliciously. Women who thought themselves off balance as they climbed the corporate ladder inevitably colored their hair or discovered an urgent need for orthodenture. Suzanne had settled for cosmetic whitening. She smiled brightly as her partner talked, holding her too tightly. Immediately, I felt better. Dog walking beat dancing with fat, sweating clients.

"Don't worry, Rochelle. He's a vending-machine account. I wouldn't have given it to you." Brad stood beside me, his skin bronzed by the Tuscan sun, his tinted glasses a match for his loose raw-silk shirt. Chubby Julian, wearing the same shirt, wending his way to the sushi station, turned to look at him and waved to me. Brad held up two fingers and Julian, the obedient lover, nodded.

"It's not an account I would have taken," I retorted. "Although I guess you guys need stuff to replace the dear departed dot-coms.

"Is this a BIS product launch?" I asked, eager to change the subject.

"Does it look like a BIS launch?"

I shook my head, knowing that Brad would have aimed at something more creative, more sophisticated. If there was enough money he would have booked the planetarium, the one at the Hudson River Museum, with a luxury bus carting guests north from the city as the moon came up. You couldn't forget a product called Moonbeam if the launch was at a planetarium.

"You would have taken it to the Hudson River Museum," I said.

"See. I wasn't wrong about you, Rochelle. You've got the instinct. You've got the eye."

"Yeah. Unfortunately, I also had these dying parents." My tone was accusatory but Brad did not flinch.

Julian joined us then, carrying plates laden with sushi and Cal-

ifornia rolls. He kissed me on the cheeks and popped a glossy bit
of raw tuna wrapped in glistening seaweed into his mouth. He
smiled contentedly, his pink cheeks striated by the silver wands
of light.

"How's dog walking, Rochelle?" he asked.

"It beats dancing with big-breasted fat men," I replied and we
all laughed as Suzanne whirled by. She glanced at us and her eyes
narrowed with worry.

"She thinks we're talking reconciliation, a deal. She's worried
that I'm going to reclaim my office, my window," I said.

"That could be arranged." Brad lounged against a pole, curled a
bit of ginger about his finger. "We could use some help on the
Longauer account."

"No. Thanks, but no thanks."

"You mean 'not yet,'" he countered and smiled the seductive
smile of the skilled manager who could effortlessly read his subordinates' minds.

I shrugged.

"Thanks for the sushi," I told Julian. "I'm going to try the saki."

"Join your friend Melanie," said Brad. "She hasn't moved from
the bar."

I had forgotten that about him—his ability to survey a room and
assimilate small details, threading them together into a netting
that he could untangle at will, strands of malice that might prove
useful one day. He was right. Melanie had been drinking steadily,
turning each ceramic cup in her hand before draining it, as though
admiring the design. I made my way toward her, but before I could
reach her she had glided onto the dance floor. Dancing alone, hugging herself, head tossed back, she moved with rhythmic ease
through the wands of light.

"Rochelle?" Phil's voice, hesitant, questioning.

"Phil." My own voice trembled.

Instinctively, I held my hands out and he took them in his own.

He looked tired. In the silvery light, his face seemed ashen. Strands of gray streaked his hair, jutted out of his heavy eyebrows. I recognized the oversize navy blue cotton shirt he wore. We had bought it together on a junket to the Bahamas. I wondered if he remembered that.

"This must be old-home week," I said. "Brad and Julian are here too."

"I know. I saw them. How are things going for you?"

"Okay. Business is good. Dog walkers are much in demand. I could incorporate, maybe even franchise out." I laughed so that he would know I was not serious, so that *I* would know I was not serious. "How about you?"

"I've been busy. Lots of rescue work from the market fallout."

"I figured." I was careful, intent on keeping casual. I did not ask him why he hadn't called. I did not say I had missed him. I played by the old dating rules—disinterest incites interest. Insouciance teases, even wounds. I wanted to tease. I wanted to wound. "What else is going on?" (By which I meant, "Have you met someone else? How does she do at doubles? Do you like her, really like her?")

I braced myself for his answer but he surprised me.

"I've been pretty involved with my parents. They're not doing well and the time has come to make some decisions."

"They're ill?" I asked and wondered at my own concern. I knew that they had stumbled out of the darkness of postwar Europe and had somehow made their way to a new life in a new world. Their needs had been modest, their fears overwhelming. They measured their day sin the nickels, dimes and quarters that passed across the counter of their newsstand. They submitted to nights of sleeplessness, of terrifying awakenings, half remembered dreams. I knew this because Phil visited health food stores in search of sleep aids, valerian, Saint-Johns wort, peppermint blends. He bought obscure herb blends from a healer on St. Thomas, a seratonin compound in an upscale alternative-medicine boutique in Vail. And whatever he bought, I bought, each of us handing over our credit cards for identical purchases, each of us hopefully carrying home remedies for festering wounds of memory that would never heal.

"Did the valerian help them?" he had asked me once, his only acknowledgment of the twinship of our worries.

"No. Nothing helps them."

He nodded.

"I know."

I pieced together scraps of knowledge. His parents had met in a displaced persons camp in Italy and, like my own mother and father, they had been startled by a child born so late in their lives, amazed by his strength, his competence, his good grades, his athletic prowess. He had shown them how to sign his report cards, his college loan and scholarship applications. They had brought sandwiches wrapped in waxed paper to his Dartmouth graduation. This he had told me with amusement. They nagged him because his clothes were too expensive, his rental too high, his investments too risky. This he told me with anger. Carefully observing our unspoken contract, I had asked no questions, offered no advice although I did tell him how my father had covered my books with brown paper, examined my test papers. Each A was a triumph, a validation of his survival. Phil had turned away from my use of the word. It was not a word to be used casually.

Even now, his eyes raked the dance floor, as he answered my question. It would be too revealing to meet my gaze.

"My father had a small growth removed from his back. It was benign but the surgery took a lot out of him. He's tired, depressed. His doctor says he should stop working. And my mother's exhausted. Her fingers are so twisted with arthritis, she can barely move them. Her doctor says a warmer climate. Florida. Arizona. They can't manage the newsstand, not even with the kids they hire to haul in the magazines and newspapers and set them up. And they're forgetful. My father forgets to lock the front door. My mother leaves a pot of water boiling on the stove. She buys so much fruit that it rots and then they don't take the garbage out because the trash cans are two flights down, so the apartment stinks. The truth is, they can't cope on their own." He spoke in a monotone as though he had so often turned the words over in his mind that they were committed to memory.

"A nursing home. Are you thinking of a nursing home?" The words curdled on my tongue even as I uttered them.

"No nursing home," he protested vehemently. "They'd feel like prisoners there and that's something they've already lived through. I could never do that to them. But if they went down to Florida, bought a small condo, I could hire an aide, someone to do the cooking, the cleaning. Maybe even sleep in."

"That sounds right," I agreed.

"But they don't want that. Even that frightens them. A new place. Who would they know? My father says he's already lived in too many places in one lifetime. But the way I see it, it's the only choice."

"Maybe." I kept my tone neutral.

"But it's not what you would do, is it, Saint Rochelle?" he replied.

"You know what I did," I replied. "But that was different." My parents had been ill, the days of their lives finite, the days of my devotion limited. I had factored all that in. I had made only one mistake. I had misread Brad. But perhaps, in the end, that had not been a mistake.

"I read these ads," he said musingly. "There are agencies in Florida who send people to visit the elderly. Just to talk with them, maybe take them shopping, to restaurants, handle their bills."

"You mean sons and daughters for hire. You pay someone to do what you should be doing and that makes you feel better. Maybe I could do that instead of dog walking. The same principle."

He blanched under the impact of my sarcasm, my scorn.

"Don't be so damn self-righteous." His fists were clenched, his knuckles white.

"I'm not being self-righteous. Look, Phil, you can be in Miami in two hours. If you told your parents you'd be flying down every week, they might feel better about the move. Why the hell should you pay a stranger to be their surrogate son?"

"I thought you would understand what I'm going through." He countered his own anger with accusation.

"Why should you expect my understanding? A summer of silence. And before that, what did we have—years of silence, of not talking about what we were feeling? You know, Phil, this is probably the most intimate conversation we've ever had and we're probably having it too late." I spoke too quickly. My cheeks were hot and I feared that I might cry. I reached for a cup of saki and held it to my lips with trembling fingers.

"I'm sorry." And he was sorry. His face collapsed in shame. "I should have called but I didn't know if you wanted me to. I felt like an intruder in this new life you're building. I thought I'd give you space, give myself space. And then all this stuff was coming down—with work, with my folks. But I shouldn't have laid it on you tonight. I had no right." He drew closer and smiled a half smile. "Hey, you're wearing that perfume I brought from Paris. You're right. It does smell like magic."

He had heard me then, all those months ago. The knowledge calmed me. I even managed to smile at Suzanne, who managed to smile back at me before she was danced away.

The music was faster now, the string instruments replaced by sweet brass with a rapid beat. The company reps had stepped up the pace. They circled the room passing out the silver-wrapped Moonbeam Memory discs and news releases on thick cobalt paper dotted with silver crescents. People glanced at their watches, began to make their way to the door. The next day was a workday and everyone in that room had meetings scheduled, conference calls to set up, presentations to coordinate. This was a crowd in a hurry. They pounded their way across the dance floor, beating names and numbers into their Palm Pilots, speaking urgently into their cell phones.

"It's all right, Phil. I overreacted. Do you see Melanie?"

"Over there with Warren. He's playing big brother. She looks a little looped. Everything okay with her?" He liked Melanie, but then it was hard not to like Melanie.

"She's just getting a buzz on. There's some kind of miscommunication with Leonard but they'll get it together."

"Sure they will. She's a great gal. And he's a nice guy."

"Right. But it has occasionally happened that great gals and nice guys finish last. Look at us," I added. "I'm a great gal. You're a nice guy. Most of the time."

He smiled. Peace was restored, or at least the surface calm that had always passed for peace between us.

Melanie glided up to us just then. She was in her small-girl mode. Standing on tiptoe, she kissed Phil on the cheek, grabbed her brother's arm for balance, shielded her eyes against a swirl of silver light. Warren looked at her worriedly.

"Rochelle, how about you and Melanie taking a cab home? Come on downstairs. I'll hail one for you. Coming, Phil?"

Phil looked at me but I said nothing and he shrugged.

"No. I think I'll hang here for a couple of minutes. I want to get some data from a Moonbeam rep. There's a rumor that they're putting together an IPO."

"Take care, Phil." I concentrated on Melanie, my hand on her fragile elbow just as Warren's arm was about her waist. Gently, we guided her to the exit. I waved to Brad and Julian, accepted a Moonbeam disc from the cute blond rep whose smile now seemed frozen on her face, and dropped it onto the floor of the elevator.

Melanie wept in the cab all the way uptown, her head resting on my shoulder, droplets of chartreuse sparkle dust drifting from her eyebrows onto my blouse.

"Stupid of me to drink so much," she murmured.

"Then why did you?" I was skilled at attacking Melanie's grief.

"Because I'm scared. Because I'm sad. Because I'm tired. Because I missed Leonard. Because I wanted to be with him."

"Melanie, it will be all right."

"No. It won't be all right. Not without Leonard. I love him, Rochelle. I want to make a life with him. A real life. I don't want to go to parties and smile hopefully and discuss my flower shop with strangers. I don't want to eat take-out Chinese with you and Lila and Fay. I don't want to lie naked on some high white bed that isn't my own with someone I just met."

"I met Dave weeks ago," I corrected her. "I shouldn't have told you about it. I just thought it was funny, that it would make you laugh." My face was hot with shame.

"I suppose it was funny. And it was sad, too. Silly and sad. Oh, Rochelle, we're getting too old for stupid games like that. And I'm too tired, too alone."

"A lot of us are alone." My words were harsh, my voice soft. I thought of Dave hurrying away from me through the light drizzle to the loneliness of a studio that was not even his own, of Phil going back to his empty apartment, so expensively furnished with pale woods and woven fabrics, to struggle silently over his parents' future, his parents' past. And I, within minutes, would enter my own apartment, light a single lamp and look down at the blank page of my open notebook and wait for words that in the end might never come.

"Hey, this side of the street all right?" The cabdriver pulled up across the street from the flower shop. "I turn around and it's another buck on the meter if I don't catch the light."

"No. This is fine." I pulled out my wallet and noticed that a picture of his family was perched on the dashboard. Two small boys. Dark-haired twin girls in white communion dresses. His hand rested on the shoulder of his fat frowning wife. Good for him, I thought, and added an extra dollar to his tip. He sped away as soon as I slammed the door, turning the corner as the light changed and traffic began to flow down the street.

I stared over the tops of the swiftly moving cars and saw a tall man standing vigil in front of the flower shop, his long pale face a mask of misery, his hands sunk deep into his pockets. He turned his head toward a taxi that had stopped to discharge passengers, to the bus that lumbered to a stop on the corner, stepping forward expectantly, stepping back, his shoulders sloped in disappointment.

"Melanie," I said, still grasping her arm because she had leaned against me unsteadily as we got out of the cab, "there's Leonard. Looking for you. Waiting for you."

"Where?" She stood on the curb and peered across the intersection and then, before I could hold her back, she dashed into the street.

"Leonard. Oh, Leonard," she sang out, her arms stretched wide, thin pale wings fluttering in the urban darkness. She would soar above the moving traffic, fly toward him, bury her head against his chest, smooth away the misery etched about his eyes, his mouth. "Leonard." Her voice rang with relief and with love.

"Melanie. Be careful." He and I shouted in dissonant chorus as a black gypsy cab sped down the street, its headlights beaming on her so that when it struck her she soared skyward in a radiant glow and then tumbled heavily onto the street. She lay motionless, a broken gamine-faced doll; her arm rose briefly, the celadon bangle still in place, and then folded itself against her exposed breast.

I opened my mouth to scream but there was no sound. I sprinted toward her, knelt and cradled her head on my lap, despite all the frenzied warnings not to touch her, not to move her. Leonard, his hands trembling, covered her with his jacket. He looked at me, but we dared not speak.

# CHAPTER
## ELEVEN

Melanie was not dead. Perched on the narrow metal bench in the ambulance that careened toward Mount Sinai, its siren screaming, its lights flashing, we listened to her shallow breathing. My hand blanketed her icy fingers as the EMS technician monitored her pulse, her blood pressure, her heartbeat, all the while tossing comforting words out at us.

"She's holding her own. Too early to know anything. Don't you be thinking the worst. It's in her favor that she's so young."

He himself was perhaps twenty, lithe and fine featured. His long mahogany fingers, the skin beneath his very clean nails strangely pink, danced gracefully across Melanie's frighteningly still body.

His gentle singsong reassurances muted Leonard's sobs, interrupted his anguished repetition of her name.

"Melanie. Mellie. Melanie." His voice was a whisper. His hands flew to his face.

Together, Leonard and I waited outside the curtained cubicle where Melanie lay on a white-sheeted gurney. Together we listened to the bespectacled young resident with thinning hair who warily described her condition. I focused on his long white coat, blood spattered at the collar, the pebbled stains of a tragedy already some hours old, not Melanie's blood.

He proffered the standard clichés of hope.

"Too early to know anything. We've ordered a battery of X rays. We want to watch for internal bleeding. No discernible fractures, not external traumatic injuries, so we're cautiously optimistic. We'll monitor her closely. We have a great team, great resources. She's unconscious but there was no long-term loss of oxygen."

Gratefully, I remembered the police officer who had knelt beside her and breathed into her mouth until the ambulance arrived, his own face red with strain and effort.

"Then she'll be all right?" I asked.

"Like I said, it's too early to tell. We're cautiously optimistic, but we don't have enough information to give you a realistic prognosis."

I nodded. He was a kind man. He wanted to raise our hopes but he did not want to raise them too high.

I called Warren, willed myself to keep my voice steady as I told him what had happened to his sister. I repeated the words of the doctor. "She's holding her own. It's too early to really know anything. They're cautiously optimistic." The words became a mantra. I repeated them to myself as Warren told me that he would call his mother, that he would try to reach his father.

"I can't believe this," he said. "Oh God, Rochelle." He was crying, I knew, and I thought it strange that my own eyes were dry. But then, I could not afford to weep. Not yet.

I returned to sit beside Leonard who hugged Melanie's soft green leather evening bag to his chest, passed it across his cheek. I went to the vending machine and brought him coffee, which he spilled on the floor. I wiped up the mess, pleased to be doing something, anything at all, relieved to avert my eyes from the gurneys that passed before us. I did not want to see the face of the diminutive Chinese man I had seen minutes earlier in the admitting area. I did not want to hear the weeping of the young mother who had held her swaddled infant out to a nurse, an aide, a clerical worker. "He's not breathing. I don't think he's breathing." Her voice shrilled in desperation.

When Warren and his mother arrived, I embraced them. They were very pale, their faces frozen in startled masks. They put their arms about Leonard's quaking shoulders, they held each other close, locked into a circle of grief, intimate and exclusive.

"Can I do anything?" I asked, but I knew the answer. No one could do anything.

"You'll get home all right, Rochelle?" Warren's eyes were riveted to the cubicle where his sister lay. The nurse had told him he could see her before she was wheeled down to X ray, meaning that he could see for himself that she was still alive.

"I'll be fine," I assured him.

"We'll call you as soon as we know anything."

"I'll be back tomorrow. Oh, I'm so sorry."

Leonard kissed me. His breath was sour.

"Thank you," he said and I wondered why he thought he should be grateful to me.

I walked home very slowly, moving like a sleepwalker down the deserted streets, ignoring the stares of curious doormen, the taxis that slowed as they neared me. Halfway home I removed my shoes and walked barefoot on the hard concrete. Who would be called, I wondered, if I was suddenly taken to a hospital emergency room? I had no parents, no siblings, no husband or lover. My tears came then and I did not know if I was weeping for Melanie or for myself.

I was numb, heartsick, the next day and the day after that and the day after that. I adhered to my schedule and walked the dogs on my roster, never varying the routine, smiling at those clients who were at home, leaving short notes when necessary for those who where not. I reminded the Afghans' owners that their sack of dog food was almost empty. I warned the owner of the small Yorkie that a vet should check her pet's eye where an infection was beginning. Such precautions comforted me. I was still in control. I did not cancel my arrangement with the Catons but picked up Lucky at the usual time and picked up my check from its usual place on the kitchen table. I walked Goldilocks every morning and evening. Clem Eliot touched my hand sadly. He had heard about Melanie, as had everyone in our neighborhood. Warren had put a simple sign in the window of the flower shop—Closed Indefinitely—but everyone knew what had happened. Melanie's regular customers paused at the shop hopefully. The young mothers leaned against their strollers, nodded to each other and bent to adjust a child's blanket, a hat. They crossed the street very slowly, looking both ways, racing to the opposite curb even though the light had not yet changed.

Each evening, before going to the hospital, I collected the mail at the flower shop, watered the plants, trained ultraviolet light on the African violets, the miniature orchids, the dwarf rose bushes. Benny, the mildly retarded adolescent whose father, Fran, was a security guard at BIS met me there and swept the floor, carried away the litter.

"Don't worry, Miss Weiss," he said. "She'll get better. She's a good person."

For him the equation was simple. Sickness and death were punishments visited on those who were evil—the boys who sometimes taunted him, the girls who laughed as he lurched down the street. They were bad. They might suffer. Melanie was good and therefore she would not die. She would get well.

"Sure she will, Benny," I agreed.

"My dad said to say hello to you and that he's sorry. He says you're a good person."

"Tell him hello from me and thank you," I replied gravely and, because a gesture of respect was called for, I shook Benny's hand.

Three days passed, four days. I called the hospital from pay phones during the day, trudged there each evening. Melanie's condition was stable. She was breathing on her own, the X rays did not show any internal bleeding, her vital signs were good but she had not wakened. They could offer no explanation. A plump nurse who talked too much told us of a young man who had fallen from a ladder. He had remained comatose for almost ten days and then awakened suddenly and demanded his breakfast. We turned to look expectantly at Melanie but she did not waken. She lay very still, her dark hair, washed free of the green tint, framed her pale pixieish face.

"She looks like a baby, a little girl," her mother murmured.

"Like a little girl." Her father's voice was husky. He looked at the woman who had been his wife and nodded. On that much they could agree.

Leonard, gaunt and soft eyed, moved nervously from bedside to window to doorway. He brought fresh flowers each day, played Melanie's favorite tapes, bent his pleading face toward her. He wanted love, forgiveness, exoneration. He remained at the hospital and could not be persuaded to leave when I did. I stayed awake until I heard his footsteps in the hallway, until I heard him turn the key and enter Lila and Fay's apartment.

Phil called. He was in constant touch with Warren but he wanted to know if he could do anything for me.

"What exactly do you think you could do for me?" I asked, irritated and exhausted. Immediately, but too late, I regretted my words. His voice turned cold, abrupt.

"Okay. Forget it. My beeper is going. I'll be in touch."

"Sure. Thanks for calling." But I doubted that he would try to reach me again and I knew that I could not blame him if he didn't.

Constance Reid called very early one morning, her voice professorial, monitorial. I had missed the poetry workshop. Surely I knew that absentees were supposed to call, offer excuses. She had been quite explicit about that. She could not reserve a place in the workshop for anyone who was not sufficiently interested in attending. There was a waiting list, as I knew.

"I'm sorry," I said, and I explained about Melanie's accident, my involvement.

"I hope your friend recovers soon, Miss Weiss." Sympathy softened her voice. "I would like to arrange a conference with you. No. That sounds too formal. Perhaps we could meet for a cup of coffee. When you have some free time. I will understand, of course, if you are not at the next workshop. But do call me when you can." She gave me her home phone number and asked me not to call between ten and twelve in the morning or three and five in the afternoon. Those were her working hours. I envied her discipline, her organization, her rigid schedule. I envied her beautiful clothing, her interesting jewelery, her sense of self. I wanted to be like Constance Reid. I wanted to know who I was.

I did not hear from Dave nor did I see him in the park, although I purposely took the path that led to the bench where he usually worked. It was possible that he was sketching in a different part of the park or perhaps along the river. He had told me that the editor of his projected children's book had suggested that he include drawings of the gulls that clustered along the city's waterways and we had spoken of stealing an afternoon and walking, in search of them, along the Palisades. It was also possible that he had left the city. Autumn depressed him, he had confided during our walk to the Catons, a day that now seemed lost in a distant past. It was more likely, I decided, that he was trying to avoid me, embarrassed by our last encounter. What a stupid idea that had been, I chastised myself, but it did not matter. Not now. All that mattered was Melanie's recovery. I knew that with each passing day her prognosis grew more ominous.

By Saturday afternoon, I felt weak with worry, weighted by a melancholy I could not overcome. Wearily, I sat down on the bench where Dave sometimes worked. I was walking two Labs and a pointer that day, all of them on long leashes that I could rein in and out by adjusting the metal coil I held. They were easy dogs, content to frolic and then stretch out on the sere grass, lifting their paws lazily to swat at the falling leaves.

I lifted my face to the pale, late-afternoon sunlight, closed my eyes and felt my body relax, my jaw unclench. One by one, willfully, consciously, I banished all troubling thoughts, emptied my mind of shards of worry just as the small boy and girl playing nearby emptied their pails of pebbles, lifting them out one by one. I did not think of Melanie. Thoughts of Phil and Dave, memories of my parents drifted away. In their place came fragments of poetry, Auden, Stevens, Rukeyser, a Housman verse that I remembered in its entirety. I murmured it aloud and smiled because I remembered how beautifully Meryl Streep had spoke the words in *Out of Africa*. "'For rose-lipped maids,'" she had said. "'And lightfoot lads.'" I had seen the film with Melanie and Phil and yes, Warren had been there, too. We had all gone out for pizza afterward. I remembered that evening without sadness, with the stirring of joy. A happy evening, a happy time. There had been happy times, no matter what.

I leaned back, blanketed in a heavy pleasantness. How wonderful it would be to fall asleep right here, on this bench, its wood blanched by sunlight and wind. I understood now why Dave had chosen this particular bench as his workstation. Set back from the path, it faced two young oaks, planted so close to each other that their branches entwined in leafy embrace. On the small space between them, a fragile dwarf conifer had sprouted. In the gentle breeze, the green-needled sapling swayed now toward one oak, now toward the other, like a small child seeking reassurance from two powerful parents. I myself had never sought reassurance from either my father or my mother. Instead, I had sought to reassure them. *Look at me, let me make you happy. I am pretty, successful, I earn medals and high grades, bonuses and recognition. Let my brightness fight the darkness of your dreams, the dreams you will not share.* They had not asked that of me. It was a role I had created for myself and one that I could now abandon. Their death had released me, replaced pity with sorrow. I was free to sit on a park bench, my face brushed by rays of sunlight. I was free to fall into a sleep as light and fine as silk.

A pull at my wrist wakened me, swiftly, harshly. All three dogs stood, straining at their leashes, their moist nostrils nervously snorting and sniffing. Their delicate ears quivered, their bodies tensed, their muscles pulled tight. They lifted their narrow heads skyward. They were hunting dogs, skilled at discerning scent and movement, bred to wariness, and they were wary now, poised for action against a threat. The pointer barked a warning, a howl that mingled fear and fury. He arched backward, his eyes fixed on the golden-leafed crown of the young oak.

I followed his gaze and my heart stopped. A huge black bird veered toward us, his wings spread wide, his head pointed downward, plunging so close that I could see the golden sharpness of his beak, the ebony slits of his eyes. I stood, pulled my dogs close as he continued to descend, landing at last, with a great thud. He stared at me, and I, breathless and paralyzed with fear, stared back at him. Then, as suddenly and gracefully as he had descended, he soared skyward, a gray squirrel forked in his talons, curled about the cruel dark nails. The small rodent's blood drizzled onto the path in scarlet droplets. My dogs barked furiously. A child cried—the small girl who had been so earnestly and peacefully collecting pebbles.

A small crowd had gathered, observations and opinions were offered.

"It was a hawk. There was one here last summer. He got one of those little dogs, leash and all," a bike messenger reported.

"A good thing your dogs are so big," a Jamaican nanny told me.

"They say there's a hawk's nest way west, over near Strawberry Fields."

"They should clear it out. The park's no place for wild birds." A young mother spoke indignantly, flushed with excitement. She pulled the blanket tightly around her sleeping toddler, vigilant and protective.

"Sure. He could grab a baby." The bike messenger grinned maliciously and pedaled away, riding with one hand lifted. He was not afraid of winged predators. He could ride more swiftly than they could fly.

The women pushing carriages and strollers glanced anxiously down at their charges.

"Listen, hawks have a right to live. This is a park." A long-haired blond student in torn jeans and a faded T-shirt glared at the others, shifted his book bag.

"Yeah, what about squirrels? Don't they have the right to live?"

A counterattack had been launched. Sides were being taken, alliances formed. The small boy and girl crouched beside their tin pails, stilled and silent. Death had invaded their game, shadowed them with dark and terrible wings. They did not protest when their mother arrived. They emptied their pails, allowed her to take their hands and left the park that had so suddenly ceased to be their playground.

I too left, leading my dogs along a dirt path, pausing to open my fanny pack and give each of them a biscuit. Slowly, very slowly, we made our way west.

I delivered the dogs to their homes and then decided to walk down to the lower path. I did not deceive myself. I was actively looking for Dave who often walked that way. I wanted to taunt him with what I had seen, with what he had missed. I knew that a sketch of the hawk and the squirrel would be perfect for his sequence on urban animal life.

But Dave did not appear (nor had I realistically expected him to). It was Mitzi I met. I walked with her to the Central Park South apartment building where the thin silver-haired actress waited anxiously for her three miniature white poodles, snatching red leashes from Mitzi's hand. She bent to caress her dogs, lifting one of them into her arms. But she glared at Mitzi.

"Look, I told you to bring them back on the hour. I don't want them to get exhausted."

Mitzi nodded, smiled her vague smile, fingered her gauzy skirt, blue shot through with silver threads.

"Screw her," she said as we turned. "I was, like, five minutes late. Maybe ten. She's an obsessive nut."

"Well, you have to worry about small dogs. A hawk might have gotten them." I told Mitzi about the hawk and the squirrel, welcoming her amused laughter because it dispelled my own superstitious fear. The hawk was not, after all, a messenger of the Angel of Death but merely a hungry predator.

"You want to grab something to eat with me and Annette?" Mitzi asked. "I'm meeting her at the burger place."

I hesitated. But I knew that I did not want to go to the hospital, that I did not want to sit beside Melanie's bed and offer words of false comfort. Death had winged too close to me that day.

"Sure. Why not?" I agreed. "It'll be fun."

I called the hospital and spoke to Warren.

"I'm going to skip tonight," I said. "I'll be there tomorrow."

"We'll see you then, Rochelle. She's going to be all right. You know that, don't you?"

"I know that," I said and shut my mind against the memory of the hawk, his sharp talons gripping the broken body of the squirrel.

Mitzi, Annette and I actually did have fun that night. The little restaurant was smoky, the air thick with the smell of very good coffee and overcooked hamburgers. We leaned toward each other over the triangular red topped Formica table and told tales of our clients, their eccentricities. Mitzi's actress could not sleep unless all three of her dogs were in bed with her. Annette had a client who fed his Irish setter duck eggs. I told them about the Catons and our narrow escape.

"You went a little too far, Rochelle," Annette said.

"No. She didn't go far enough," Mitzi interjected and we all laughed.

"I'm surprised they didn't fire me," I said.

"They probably didn't even notice you'd been there," Mitzi assured me. "You know dog walkers are anonymous. We're invisible servants, ghosts with keys and pooper-scoopers, sliding in and out of their houses, doing a job they can't be bothered with. We're their human appliances, like their garbage disposals and dishwashers. We get their crap taken care of and they couldn't care less about who we are and what we do. I walked a dog for this couple for, like, three years. A Jack Russell. And then it died, so of course the gig was over. Three months later I pass them on the street and say hello and I swear they had absolutely no idea who I was. That's why it really doesn't matter what we do in their apartments. It doesn't matter if we drink their bottled water, watch their videos or get laid—although it's a good idea to make the bed and not to leave a condom."

We laughed, a sorority of conspirators, superior to those who paid us. We knew their secrets but they were stupidly indifferent to ours.

"I've got this client out in Hoboken," Annette said. "He pays my fare to go out there and double time including travel time. A nice guy. I go out there twice a week when he has to be in the city for a meeting. He's some kind of freelance designer. The dog's an Italian greyhound, very sensitive, very nervous. I used to walk him when they lived in the city, before he moved to Jersey and he knows me. So I go out there. This guy has a terrific town house and after I walk the dog I soak in his Jacuzzi and after that I take a nap on this great bed he has in the guest room or maybe I go to the den and watch a video on his state-of-the-art DVD. He knows I like Brie and he always leaves me a big wedge. It's my three-hour gift to myself, my little vacation. Why not? Who am I hurting?"

"No one. I would say you are absolutely guilt free. Wouldn't you say that, Rochelle?"

"I would say that." We clapped softly, applauding Annette for her daring.

We ordered second cups of coffee, studied the check and counted out singles to tip the waitress. Dog walkers were good tippers, our generosity a professional conceit.

"What's happening with Ida?" Annette asked as we left.

Mitzi shrugged. "I haven't seen her."

"Me, neither." I did not say that I thought we might never see her again.

"Listen, Rochelle, I hope Melanie will be okay," Annette said and I nodded and touched my heart.

I went to the hospital on Sunday, relieving Leonard who went home to grab a shower and a nap. Her mother and brother gratefully went out for lunch. I played the tapes I had brought and talked to her. The doctors encouraged us to do that. I reminded her of college escapades, of books we had read together, of friends who had alternately amused and angered. I ran out of chatter and read aloud from the Styles section of the *New York Times* which Melanie had playfully dubbed the Sports section for gals. There was an announcement of a marriage—the bride a student at Harvard Med and the groom a cook in a homeless shelter.

"How long do you give them, Mellie?" I asked, and the two nurses who had come into the room to fill her IV bag, adjust the catheter and press bits of ice between her parched lips raised their eyebrows.

"I give odds they split in the middle of her residency," one of them said and we all laughed.

"You're doing the right thing," she told me, suddenly serious. "The talking, the tapes. All that helps." She smiled brightly at me, but I saw her glance at her friend and shake her head. They left together, walking too swiftly.

Melanie stirred but I knew that the movement was what the nurse called an "involuntary" response, a mere reflex.

I left the hospital late in the evening.

"Rochelle, you look beat." Melanie's mother touched my forehead, smoothed my hair.

Tears stung my eyes. The tenderness of her touch overwhelmed me.

"I am. I'm very tired," I admitted.

I felt totally depleted, each movement an effort, each word an exertion. I dragged myself home, forced myself to eat a yogurt, to glance despairingly at an unfinished poem. I summoned all my energy to run a bath, and as I lay prone in the warm fragrant water, I feared that I might fall asleep. I toweled myself dry, put on my softest nightgown and crawled into bed. Almost immediately I fell into a deep and dreamless sleep.

The harsh ringing of the telephone jarred me awake. Bewildered, I groped through the darkness, my heart beating loudly, rapidly, a clammy sweat filming my body. I lifted the receiver, my hands shaking, my mouth dry.

"Hello. Hello." My voice was thick, my tongue coated with fear. I strained to hear the voice at the other end, obscured by clatter and a ringing bell. But I heard the word *nurse* and I heard the word *hospital*. No, I thought wildly. It can't be. Dizzied, I gripped the phone and listened to the nurse who was surely calling from Mount Sinai to tell me that Melanie was dead. A name was spoken but I did not hear it. The voice grew impatient.

"Are you her next of kin? Are you a relative? If not, do you know how we can reach a relative?"

"No. I'm her friend. But she has a mother, a brother. You have

her chart. Surely you have their names and phone numbers. Phoebe
Asher. Warren Asher. They filled out these forms." I had watched
them fill in their names, their addresses, their phone numbers. I
had seen them blanch when the very young resident had asked
them whether Melanie had a living will, whether they had thought
about a "do not resuscitate" instruction.

"We have no chart. She was only brought in minutes ago. We
have no identification of any kind. No handbag. The only thing we
found was your phone number in her jacket pocket." She spoke
slowly, wearily. She was a professional, experienced at coping with
nocturnal misery.

"I'm sorry. You must have a wrong number. I don't know who
you're talking about. I thought you were a nurse calling from
Mount Sinai. I have a friend there who's very ill." I was restored to
calm, prepared to hang up.

"You are Rochelle Weiss?"

"Yes. I'm Rochelle Weiss."

"Look, I'm Lorna Cole, the charge nurse at St. Luke's emergency room. We have a patient who was just brought in. She collapsed in an alleyway. An African-American woman, very thin, late
middle age, I'd say. She's in respiratory distress, unconscious. She
was wearing a fleece jacket and we found your name and phone
number on a scrap of paper in the pocket."

"Ida. It has to be Ida," I said, my voice dull. I had thought myself home free, reprieved, but the call after all was for me and I
sank again into sadness, into grief for Ida whose voice I had scarcely
heard. I remembered how I had scrawled my name and phone number on an index card and thrust it into her pocket all those weeks
ago, that last afternoon Phil and I had spent together. He had
watched me disapprovingly, almost angrily. So stupid, so naive, to
give my name and number to a half-mad, homeless woman. I had
not argued with him. What would have been the point?

"Ida." Lorna sounded relieved. She had a name. She could open a file, the wheels of hospital bureaucracy could start turning. "And what's her last name?"

"I don't know."

"Do you know where she lives?"

"Does she look as though she has a home?" Immediately, I regretted my sarcasm. Lorna was simply doing her job, probably going beyond her job description by taking the trouble to call a faded phone number in the hope that she could locate a relative, a friend. It could not be easy to call strangers in the dead of night and tell them that this was the phone call from hell.

"Look," I explained, "I'm a dog walker. Ida is a homeless woman who hung around the dog run. A couple of us kind of adopted her, brought her stuff to eat, slipped her some money. We worried about her. I put my name and phone number in her jacket pocket weeks ago and she looked pretty sick even then. That was the last time I saw her."

"Then you wouldn't have the authority to sign her in, to authorize treatment." Lorna was disappointed.

"No, of course I wouldn't. But look, she always pushed this shopping cart and she had some papers in it wrapped in Saran Wrap. She was very neat." I added this so that Lorna would know that Ida had standards, that she folded her clothing, kept her toiletries in Saran Wrap, arranged her tattered paperbacks artfully.

"No shopping cart. The paramedics probably left it where they found her and I imagine it's gone by now."

"I imagine you're right," I agreed and we sighed in unison. We understood the dark side of our city, the hazards of homelessness.

"Well, thanks for your help, Miss Weiss. I'm sorry I wakened you. I'm sorry I frightened you." She was defeated and regretful.

"No. Thank you for calling. Look, is there anything I can do for her? I could come down to St. Luke's."

"I don't see what that would accomplish. She's not conscious. She wouldn't know you."

"Yes. But I would know her."

It seemed important to me suddenly that Ida be granted some measure of dignity, that someone who knew her name would actually stand by her bedside. I remembered the nocturnal whispers of my mother's friend Bella as they talked about the guards who had patrolled their barracks. "It was so terrible that they didn't know our names. It is a terrible thing not to be called by a name." Bella's words traveled back to me across the years.

"Do what you want." Lorna Cole's voice grew cool. She was a busy woman. She did not have time to waste on foolish whims.

I leaped out of bed and pulled my clothes on. I glanced at my wristwatch. It was 2:00 a.m. Was I nuts to dash through the city at such an hour? Yes, I was nuts, I decided, but it did not matter. Magical thinking had overtaken me. I would go to Ida, identify her, whisper her name, perhaps tuck some money into her pocket. Bella's words propelled me. And if I did all that, Melanie would get better, she would open her eyes and reclaim her life. The columns of a mysterious ledger would somehow be balanced. I knew that I was being irrational but I could not stop myself.

Miraculously, a cab cruised down the street, slowed when the driver saw me. I darted in.

"St. Luke's. The emergency entrance," I said.

"You're okay?" He looked at me nervously. He did not want blood or vomit on his rear seat. He did not want me to be nine months pregnant.

"I'm fine," I said. "It's a friend. A friend who's in trouble."

He nodded and drove swiftly down the empty streets, whizzing through yellow lights, ignoring stop signs. He sped into the ambulance bay and I counted out the fare in the whirling red lights of a MedEvac unit, counted my change in the glare of a police car that pulled in beside it, its siren shrilling.

Lights blazed in the admitting area. A baby cried in the arms of a teenage mother. Two elderly men and two elderly women dozed in molded orange plastic chairs. A man, his arm in a sling, glared at the grossly overweight woman who sat beside him.

"Bitch," he muttered. "Fat bitch."

Two men crowded the desk insisting on information about someone named Dinah.

"She come in two, maybe three hours ago."

The nurse shrugged.

I edged my way forward.

"Can I speak to Lorna Cole, the charge nurse?" I asked.

Miraculously, I was buzzed in. Even more miraculously Lorna Cole appeared before me. She was a nurse of the old school. She wore the classic white starched uniform—no bright pink smock for her—and a black-banded white cap perched on her neatly bobbed iron-gray hair.

"Rochelle Weiss?" she asked.

I nodded.

"I figured you'd come. Although I don't know what you've come for. This way."

I followed her into a curtained cubicle, turning away from the empty-eyed old woman, her tiny body lost in an oversize flowered housedress, who lay on a gurney in the hallway. The housedress was unbuttoned, revealing the triangle of sparse gray vaginal hair and her concave, smoke-colored abdomen bisected by a pale scar, perhaps from a cesarean section. I shivered to think that once life had been lifted from that deathbound body. I was grateful to Lorna Cole, who instinctively pulled a sheet up to the old woman's shoulders before leading me to Ida's bed.

Ida, much emaciated, her skin dangling in dark folds because there was no flesh to sustain it, lay on a narrow bed wearing only a coarse white hospital gown. Her feet were bare and an ulcerated sore at her knee oozed pus that drifted in a thread of liquid yellow down her matchstick-thin leg. Even with the aid of a facial oxygen mask her breathing was shallow and uneven. I gagged against the stench that emanated from her body but still I drew closer.

"Ida," I said. "It's me. Rochelle. From the dog run. We've all been worried about you. Annette. Mitzi. Carl. We hope you'll get well. We'd like to see you sitting on your bench again. I have some nice paperbacks you can put in your shopping cart."

She did not stir although it seemed to me that her lips moved. I repeated her name.

Lorna Cole watched me.

"She can't hear you, you know," she said, but her tone was not unkind.

"I guess I do know that." I reached for my wallet, pulled out a twenty-dollar bill. "Look, can I leave this for her? In case she wants something."

"She's not going to want anything. She's barely breathing on her own. The pneumonia is pretty advanced and her general condition is so deteriorated that she doesn't have the strength to fight the infection. Her immune system is shot. We see this a lot with the homeless." Her voice was flat. She wanted me to understand that Ida would soon be dead.

Defeated, I replaced the money.

"I guess you're right. I guess this was sort of crazy. My coming here."

"A good kind of crazy. We see a lot of the other kind here." Her smile was thin, tired.

I drew closer to the bed.

"Goodbye, Ida," I said, but there was, of course, no response, no reaction. Still, I had said her name. It was important that I had said her name.

Silently, we left the cubicle. The old woman on the gurney was gone.

For the second time that night I left a hospital and returned to my apartment. For the second time I dimmed the lights and crawled into bed. Again, sleep came swiftly and I wakened only when morning light flooded my bedroom, accompanied by the familiar metallic chorus of Mario pulling in the emptied garbage cans and the distant atonal whine of a car alarm. I felt refreshed and oddly at peace.

I dressed hurriedly and dashed out to pick up the dogs I walked on my first round. The day was bright, the air edged with an autumnal chill. I walked briskly, now running with the dogs, now slowing my pace, stooping to pick up after them. Goldilocks, the last dog to be delivered on that morning circuit, chased a chipmunk and I ran after her, through mounds of golden leaves, laughing and calling her name. I reined in her leash when she grew too close, holding her in check until her prey darted into a hedge. She looked at me accusingly, a dog betrayed and then, immediately forgiving, licked my hand. Still laughing, I rewarded her with a dog biscuit and leaned against a tree to pluck a bramble from the cuff of my jeans. I paused at a fountain, bathed my flushed face and tucked my unruly hair into a bright green bandanna.

When I delivered Goldilocks, Clem Eliot invited me in for coffee and I gratefully accepted. Grace, very thin, her skin parchment pale, her white hair plaited into a French braid and wearing a violet silk robe, sat erect in the straight-baked chair she favored. She smiled at me, noting my surprise.

"It appears I've had a reprieve," she said dryly. "The doctors call it a miracle because they're afraid to use the word *remission*. That apparently raises expectations. But we have chosen to have expectations in any case."

"Whatever they're calling it, you certainly look better," I said. I stirred my coffee so that I might hear the chime of the silver spoon against the delicate china.

"How's Melanie?" Clem asked.

"I haven't called the hospital yet today. Her condition was pretty much the same last night but I have the feeling we'll have good news today."

"Why?" Intuition, instinct, interested him. He sought to understand it in poetry, in the dreamy short stories and the complex novels he and Grace read aloud to each other.

"No reason." I would not tell him about the mystical equation I had fashioned, the magical seesaw on which I had balanced Melanie and Ida.

"Rochelle, we wanted to tell you that we'll be moving to Cambridge. Avery and Eileen, our son and daughter-in-law, want us to be with them. Now. Especially now." His voice faltered. "They have a wonderful yard. Goldilocks will love it and our grandchildren are delighted with the idea of a dog. In fact, we think they'll tolerate us only because of Goldilocks." We all smiled, greedy for any scrap of humor.

"You've been wonderful," he continued. "We'll miss you." Goldilocks pressed her damp nose onto my upturned palm.

"And I'll miss you," I said sadly.

Their book-lined living room, shabby and elegant, dim lights sheltered by worn silk lamp shades, ancient carpets, faded and soft beneath my feet, had been my refuge, a world removed from my own sharp-angled modern furniture, the black leather chairs on stainless-steel swivels, the red wink of my answering machine. Our shared hours of reading and talking had been a respite from the rolling city streets, a relief from the vigorous walking, relentlessly pulled by or pulling my dogs, that marked my days. In their courage, their soft and caring voices, the love that linked them, I had found surrogates for my parents, so newly lost to me.

"I'm very glad I came to know you." My voice broke. Grief had found its way to clarity.

"We'll stay in touch," Clem promised. "We wanted you to have this."

He handed me the slender volume of Hardy's poems, the red leather binding worn thin, that I had once admired.

"Thank you." Tears filled my eyes and, because there was nothing else to say, I kissed each of them on the cheek, felt their own dry lips brush my forehead. I patted Goldilocks and, clutching my gift, I hurried out.

I did not collect the dogs scheduled for my second circuit. It would not matter if I was an hour late. Gripped by a sudden urgency, I headed uptown to Mount Sinai.

The corridor outside Melanie's room was deserted. The door to her room, always open, was closed. A student nurse stared at me and hurried off, as though fearful of meeting my eyes. I trembled, breathed deeply and tapped tentatively. I waited. Footsteps moved slowly, too slowly toward it.

"Just a minute." Melanie's mother's voice, soft, muffled.

The knob turned, the door swung open and she swept me into her arms.

"Rochelle. You got my message. Who would have thought it? Who?"

She stepped aside and I looked at Melanie who sat up in bed, a mischievous smile playing at her lips.

"Melanie. My God, Mellie." I rushed toward her, sank into a chair, rested my head on the bed, felt her fingers toy with my hair. "When? How?" Questions raced through my mind. Could I be imagining this? Was this the way people awakened from comas, smiling in amusement as though a successful prank had been played out? The swiftness and completeness of her recovery delighted and bewildered me.

"This morning. Very early. It was dark and I woke up and couldn't figure out where I was, why there was a tube in my arm, a steel guard on my bed. I screamed, I think, and a nurse came running and then a doctor and another doctor. They kept asking me questions, my name, my address, my telephone number, who the president was, and then what had happened to me. I couldn't remember what happened although my mom told me. A car, an accident. The car hit me and I've been asleep—for how long? For days and days. That's right. For days and days." She leaned back against the pillows and plucked at her hospital gown. "Uch, I hate this fabric. It's so coarse."

I smiled.

"I'll bring you a nightgown later. And yeah, that's what happened. It's been a really bad time but you're okay now. Nice flowers," I said, looking at the vase overflowing with long-stemmed yellow roses interspersed with tall irises.

"Leonard was here. He brought them." She smiled, the proud smile of a woman whose lover knew her favorite flowers and how to arrange them.

"Great." I kissed her cheek. "I'll be back later. I've got dogs to see, poop to pick up. I'm a busy dame. Obligations. Responsibilities. Alpo to distribute, water bowls to fill."

She smiled weakly. I embraced her mother and hurried off. She had awakened in the darkness, she had said. Could it have been just when I stood beside Ida's bed? I dismissed the thought. Magical thinking did not survive morning light or the passage of danger. Melanie was restored to us and that was all that mattered.

# CHAPTER
## TWELVE

I sat opposite Constance Reid in the café of the Upper West Side Barnes & Noble. It was two in the afternoon, an hour we had agreed upon because it did not interfere with her work schedule or with my afternoon round of dog walking. The alcove was crowded and noisy: the voices of toddlers shrilled above the hum of intimate conversations, and those clustered at the coffee bar called out their orders imperiously. "Two lattes!" "A decaf cappuccino!" Exhausted young mothers shared tiny triangular tables and spooned hot chocolate into their toddlers' mouths, fed them bits of biscotti. The children clutched newly purchased books, wriggled on their booster seats and whined. "Read the story, Mommy. Read it now." One small boy, thick straw-colored bangs almost brushing his very wide hazel eyes, thrust a pristine copy of *Red Fish, Blue Fish* against his mother's pulsating pregnant abdomen and shouted, "Book me, Mommy. Book me."

The mothers continued talking to each other. They were skillful warriors in the daily battle for constant attention, surrendering only under the assault of tears or when disapproving glances radiated from other tables. A pale young woman, her dark hair plaited into braids, sat in a corner lightly rocking a stroller. Tears streaked her cheeks as she sipped her coffee, a book open but unread on the table in front of her. The other mothers, as though fearful that her misery might be contagious, ignored her. Constance Reid stared hard at her and turned away.

"Every time I see a woman like that I feel vindicated, certain that I made the right decision," she said in that cool clipped tone that I both feared and admired.

"What decision was that?" I asked daringly, although I understood that she had invited my question.

"The decision not to have children," she replied. "I knew what having children would mean in terms of my work, of what I wanted to do with my life. I knew that I had to prioritize."

She lifted her coffee cup to her lips, so carefully colored and outlined, the light coral color a match for the polish that coated her manicured nails. The rings on her fingers glinted in the harsh fluorescent light. They were all of graduated shades of green— a malachite chip on a narrow gold pinkie ring, a large jade stone in a platinum setting on her middle finger, a ring of celadon rimming her wide marriage band. They had been chosen, I knew, to subtly coordinate with her pale green sweater set. I had taken note of the jewelery she wore to each workshop, the gemstones usually of a color that matched the loose linen dresses she favored, sapphire when she wore blue, garnet on the evenings when she wore mauve or lilac. Those beautifully crafted rings, the polished pendants that dangled from heavy chains, set her apart from her students, compounded her authority. They defined her, gave proof of her success, her taste, her wealth. I had wondered about that wealth—surely it had not been derived from two slender volumes of poetry published by a university press or from the occasional pieces she published in the *Atlantic Monthly* or the *New Yorker*.

She tapped her jade ring against her coffee cup, toyed with her necklace of braided gold and waited for my reaction to her words.

"Your husband didn't mind not having a family?" I asked, because I wanted to know about that husband whose checks and credit cards paid for her exquisite jewelery, her designer sweaters and suits.

"He didn't mind. He had three children of his own from his first marriage. All of them grown and married, parents themselves. In fact, one of his granddaughters is getting married this month." She saw the surprise that flickered across my face, the rush of color to my cheeks, and smiled. "Don't bother doing the arithmetic, Miss Weiss, Rochelle. I hope I may call you Rochelle. He is, of course, much older than I am. We've been married for fifteen years. I was thirty-two when we met—a bachelor girl. He was in his late fifties and a widower. There was no sordid divorce, no affair. It sounds shocking, I suppose, but our arrangement was reasonable and equitable. He wanted an elegant young wife, a talented hostess. I wasn't elegant and I didn't know how to be a hostess but it was clear that I could learn very quickly. And I wanted to be free of every obligation that might interfere with my writing. I wanted never to have to worry about money. I wanted the leisure that I needed for the dreaming of my poems, for the writing of my poems. I needed the freedom to teach and to study poetry, to talk about it, to discover it. And it was good that he loved me and that I respected him and cared about him, cared for him. In my way, my own way. The romantic poets would not have approved but then we don't live in romantic times, do we?" She raised her eyebrows quizzically, inviting argument, awaiting my shocked disapproval.

I did not offer an argument. I did not express shock. I stirred my coffee and glanced again at the pale young woman who no longer wept, who now held a beautiful dark-haired infant girl on her lap, encased in a cocoon of soft pink fleece. I wondered how old the young mother was. I wondered why she had wept. I turned to Constance Reid.

"I'm thirty-two," I said.

"I imagined that you must be around that age. I'm not going to say that you remind me of myself when I first came to New York. You don't. I was much younger than you and I didn't even know what a Phi Beta Kappa key was. I'd never been to college. All I had was a certificate from a mediocre midwestern secretarial school and two hundred dollars."

I toyed with my golden key, pleased that she had noticed it, hopeful that she did not think that I was flaunting it.

"What do you do, Rochelle? How do you make your living?" Her tone changed abruptly.

"I'm a dog walker," I replied and smiled with satisfaction at her surprised expression, the subtle lift of her pale eyebrows. "I walk dogs whose owners don't have the time to do it or can't be bothered. I clean up the mess they make, make sure that they've urinated at least once and that the larger dogs have had a run. I make sure that they have enough food and water. That about covers the job description. Oh, don't worry," I added, because she was looking at my hands, "I always wear latex gloves. It's all very hygienic. Just a little disgusting. But it pays the bills. I'm my own boss, set my own hours. It works for me. For now. And what did you do before you married?" It was only fair that this should be an even exchange.

"I was a secretary in a brokerage house. A very quiet brokerage house. I filed, typed letters, took dictation. Moronic work. But there was a lot of downtime, empty hours that meant I could write the poems that came to me when I was filing. No one cared what I was writing as long as the typewriter was clattering. That's where I met my husband. He was a client. Are any of your dog owners wealthy widowers?" She flashed me an amused smile. She would write my scenario to match her own.

"Mostly yuppie couples. Or old ladies. Or elderly people." I thought of Grace and Clem Eliot and wondered if I would ever see them again.

"Not much of a career for someone with your academic record, is it? Is that what you've been doing since you graduated?" Sarcasm and implied criticism tinged her question. Armed with my credentials, she would have forged a career, established herself professionally, earned enough money to buy herself the linen dresses, the cashmere sweaters, the beautiful rings and pendants.

"No," I replied defensively. "I was an account executive at a public relations firm that specialized in high-tech clients." I described my work at BIS, surprising myself because I recounted it with pleasure.

"It sounds as though you enjoyed it," she said. "Why did you leave?"

"I didn't leave. I was fired. My parents were very ill and I needed time off to care for them. Instead, I got my walking papers. With regret, but without excuses. No time-out in the corporate world for compassion. But it was just as well. I was able to take care of my parents and I didn't try to go back after they died, although I kind of guessed that the door was open. I needed the time to sort myself out, to work things through, to live without worrying about pleasing anyone except myself—just taking things one day at a time—actually, as it turned out, one dog day at a time."

We both laughed uneasily. Our conversation was going too fast, veering too suddenly into a dangerous whirlpool of revelation. We feared that we might not easily return to the safe harbor of casual, restrained exchanges, that we would no longer be able to sit across from each other at the scarred golden-oak conference table in the library, hesitant student, authoritative teacher.

"And have you worked things through, sorted yourself out?" she asked.

"In some ways, I think I have. In other ways, no." I spoke slowly, holding her question in my mind, weighing my answer. She had forced an emotional accounting and I wanted the debit and credit columns to be accurate. "I have slowed down. I'm not racing for approval. I've given myself time to think, to feel. I've come back to things I care about. The pressure's off. I'm not placing my achievements on the altar of my parents' sadness. Not that they demanded it of me. I demanded it of myself. That much I've come to understand. But I'm still unclear about what I want to do. Obviously, I'm not going to be a dog walker forever, but where do I want to go from here? I don't know. Yet. The only thing I do know is that I want to go on reading poetry, writing poetry." I sat back. My answer pleased me. It was honest. It was concise.

"Yes. Your poetry. That is what I wanted to talk to you about today. I wanted to know a little more about your background, how much you have studied, how much you want to study, whether poetry is going to be more than a casual hobby for you."

She offered me, at last, the real reason for this meeting and then fell silent, waiting. I was meant to go on, to discuss my work, perhaps to evaluate the workshop, to speak of how I wanted my writing to develop. This was a test of a kind, although I could not imagine what the reward for excelling might be.

Constance sat back in her chair, her coffee cup empty. The young mothers prepared to leave. They dressed their exhausted toddlers in sweaters and jackets and talked to each other too loudly, making play dates, lunch dates, baby-sitting arrangements. They spoke softly, reassuringly, to their children. They would have to hurry. The school day was over. There were older sibling to be picked up, shopping to be done, frenetic shepherding to dance classes, to piano lessons. Constance studied them with the eye of a tourist. Their lives and concerns were alien to her but she was a keen observer. She might, even as she sat there, be writing the scene or committing the angelic face of a small girl with gossamer golden hair to a lockbox of memory to be opened weeks or months later when she sat at her desk in a dimly lit room. She turned back to me, looked at me expectantly.

"Well, I took the requisite lit classes in college and I was always drawn more to poetry than to the other required reading," I began. "I memorized poems, kept them in my head, recited them to myself at parties. I would be dancing and smiling but my head would be full of Wallace Stevens. I even wrote some poems, but I didn't show them to anyone, didn't submit them to the literary magazine. It was a kind of secret life. I wasn't supposed to be writing poetry. I was an athlete, a long-distance runner. And I didn't even think of majoring in lit although I squeezed in as many electives as I could. I was practical. I majored in economics and wrote my senior thesis on the emergence of electronics. That's how I earned my Phi Bet key and that's how I got my job at BIS. Once I was swept into the whirlpool of working, of meetings and conferences and jetting from place to place, getting and spending, then getting and spending some more, the poetry faded. I would still try to read it sometimes but never with the same intensity, the same involvement. There was no time. No dreaming time, no writing time. Until this spring when my life kind of emptied itself. My parents were gone. My job was gone. The man I had been involved with for four years was—is—almost gone. There was room then for the poetry, for the reading of it, the writing of it. I'm not sure how good my work is but I want to go on writing, if that's what you're asking. I want to develop whatever small talent I have." I paused, startled that I had revealed so much. "And I do feel a new depth, a new way to weave words and thoughts," I continued. "That sounds kind of pretentious, I know, but that's what I feel. A lot of it comes from the workshop and a lot of it comes from just having the time, from being able to submit to a mood, to allow the thoughts and words to drift. Walking dogs through a park doesn't require any concentration. You're on automatic pilot. They take a crap. You get it with your scooper and get rid of it and all the while a poem could be dancing through your mind."

I sat back, exhausted. My own words had surprised me just as the poem I had worked on late into the night had surprised me. I had been unprepared for the slow unrolling of the imagery of death—the hawk, midnight black, plummeting toward me, Ida's frail dark body on the white-sheeted bed, her lids trembling as though to resist the "dying of the light." I had threaded those word-scapes with a description of my parents' pale granite gravestone, shaded by the slender thick-leafed trees that grew in such profusion in the Long Island cemetery. I did not know how good the poem was. It was only a first draft, hastily trapped onto paper, not a word altered, but I knew that it went deeper than anything I had written before. It had come to me unbidden and that, in itself, was a triumph. Constance Reid would understand that if I shared it with her, but I remained silent. I had said enough, given her enough.

She smiled that thin enigmatic smile. My words had passed her test. She tendered the reward in a cool and reasoned tone, restored to the role of dispassionate mentor.

"You may know, Rochelle, that I hold the position of writer in residence at Richmond College. I've been there for some years, a rather unusual arrangement because I don't even have a bachelor's degree and I'm surrounded by faculty flaunting their Ph.D.'s. But exceptions are made for what they call 'creative staff.' It was my publishing record that attracted them. Alumni tend to be impressed by faculty members who publish." She smiled, added cream to her coffee, studied my face and resumed talking. "Richmond recently received an endowment from such an alumnus designated for a fellowship in poetry. The terms are specific—it must go to a poet rather than a scholar. It offers a small stipend—about fifteen thousand dollars a year, perhaps twenty—clearly not enough to live on in a city like New York, but it can be supplemented. The recipient of the fellowship would be expected to act as a teaching assistant in my poetry seminar and to take courses that would eventually lead to a master's of fine arts. I had thought to recommend you for the fellowship if you're interested. If you're not, I completely understand."

I stared at her in disbelief. I had never contemplated graduate school. I had never thought to make poetry the center of my life.

She glanced at her watch, adjusted the fine silk scarf that caped her green cardigan. It was after three. Our meeting had impinged on her writing time. My silence impinged on her patience.

"When would you have to know?" I asked at last.

"Within a few weeks. The fellowship will commence in the spring semester but there are formalities. I would have to submit your credentials for consideration."

"I don't have any credentials," I said.

"Your academic record, your membership in Phi Beta Kappa will impress them. I'll also include a sampling of your work. By the way, I did want to suggest that you submit 'Cooking with My Mother' to Lamplights. At the risk of sounding insensitive, I should tell you that there is a great deal of interest in Holocaust writing."

"You were very critical of that poem when I read it in the workshop," I countered.

"It was good. I wanted it to be better. And you did make it better. I read your revision. That's one reason why I want you to have this fellowship. You're prepared to learn, to rework, to revise. I wonder—have you other poems about your parents, about their experience?" She coughed, as though embarrassed by her choice of words.

"Please understand," I said quietly, "my parents almost never talked about the war. They didn't want to burden me, or perhaps it was just too painful. But no, I think the real reason was that they didn't want their history to diminish me, to shadow my life. They shielded me and pampered me. They didn't want their darkness to stain my life. So I have no poems, no stories, no memories. I can't cash in on the great interest in Holocaust writing." I heard the anger in my voice, saw the color rise to her cheeks.

"That wasn't what I was suggesting," she retorted stiffly.

"I have other poems though," I continued. "I'll show them to you. And, of course, I'll think very carefully about the fellowship. No matter what I decide, I want to thank you for considering me. It means a great deal to me."

We both stood. Oddly, we shook hands. Her large emerald ring bit into my palm.

"I'll look forward to hearing from you, Rochelle. And, of course, what I shared with you about my life, about my marriage—I can assume that you will not discuss it with anyone." There was fear in her voice. She had revealed too much, rendered herself vulnerable. She twisted her rings nervously and it shamed me that her discomfort brushed me with pleasure.

"Of course not," I assured her.

She left then but I returned to the coffee bar and ordered a cappuccino. As I sipped it, I studied the poem I had written so late in the night, thrust into my purse because I had flirted with the thought of showing it to Constance Reid. I read my own words and again I saw the hawk plummeting toward me and heard the violent beat of deathbound wings. I gripped my pen and, with great concentration, I crossed out one word and substituted another, added a line and read and reread it, knowing that I had broken the rhythm, not knowing how to restore it. I sipped my coffee and watched the café fill up again. Music filled the store. Vivaldi. Autumn. Sadness seeped through me and I hurried out before the melancholy movement segued into winter.

At the next poetry workshop Constance Reid studiously ignored me. A week had passed and I had no answer for her; although I had visited Richmond College, walked down its cobbled paths, stared up at its wide-windowed buildings and visited its very modern library, trying to imagine myself seated at a table in the reading room, a sharp light focused on my open book.

Only one student poem was scheduled to be read at that workshop and copies had been distributed. It was a painfully structured sonnet by Wilma Harrington, the heavyset Jamaican woman who had read the very first time I attended the workshop. She read very slowly, her voice trembling. That first poem, I remembered, had been about an urban sunset, but this new sonnet concentrated on the subtle changing of seasons, the turning of the leaves, the too-early darkening of the sky.

She had struggled for rhyme, struggled for simile. The Korean businessman made rapid notes on his electronic pad. *Contrived*, I read. *Graceless*. I hoped that he would not use those words in a critique and he did not. Laura, the young mother, who was always so tired and always so sweet, raised her hand.

"I liked it, Wilma, really I did." She spoke in the practiced tone of a teacher who has been trained to offer positive reinforcement before zeroing in on a weakness, a technique I remembered from a BIS management seminar. "But I think that maybe you chose the wrong form. A sonnet is so structured, so demanding, so confining…"

Her voice trailed off. She liked Wilma. They went out for coffee together after every workshop before Wilma began her journey back to the Bronx, an hour's journey after a wearying workday. Laura's criticism, so gently offered, had been protective. Unlike Constance Reid's harsh critique, which came next. It was not her job to protect her students. It was her job to be honest.

"You worked too hard, Wilma," she said briskly. "And the real difficulty is that your effort shows. We can't read comfortably or listen easily. We read knowing that you reached for every word. There is no flow. No beauty. The sonnet is contrived. Graceless."

I looked at my neighbor and watched him delete those very words. He smiled. His judgment had been vindicated.

"But you say, you always say, that we should work at our poems, rewrite, revise," Wilma protested.

"Of course I say that. But the secret is to rewrite and revise and leave the reader unaware that you did just that. Laura was right. You selected a form that is too difficult for you."

"Maybe all poetry is too difficult for me," Wilma said sullenly.

"I think, frankly, that that may be the case," Constance agreed. Her tone was not harsh. It was matter-of-fact. She was telling the truth. She was doing her job.

I did not look at Wilma who gathered up her papers, her notebook, and shoved them into a discolored green plastic case that she could not close because papers thrust their way into the teeth of the zipper. I did not have to look at her to know that she was crying. She lurched from the room, a heavy woman who moved clumsily because she was blinded by her tears. She left, not slamming the door, not even closing it, and sweet-faced Laura hurried after her.

"Our first casualty," Constance said dryly. "All right. Let's get back to work."

She distributed copies of poems from Sylvia Plath's *Ariel*. She presented her own analysis and invited our comments. Laura returned, her eyes red, her cheeks flushed. Constance motioned her impatiently back to her seat.

I realized then that I did not like Constance Reid, that as difficult as it was to be her student, it would be even more difficult to work with her. I imagined myself teaching a seminar under her supervision—if that indeed was what a teaching assistant did. Supposing a student not unlike Wilma read a poem, a poem as inept, as clumsy and, yes, as contrived and graceless, as Wilma's had been. Would I be able to be as honest and thus as cruel as Constance had been?

I riffled through the sheets of paper, indifferent now to Plath's passionate and fluent words, indifferent to Constance Reid's reminder that the "Ariel" poem spurted from what Plath herself had called "the bloodjet of poetry." And even as she spoke, she stared across the table at me, her lips curled, as though my thoughts were clear to her. *Deal with it. Make decisions. Take control of your life as I took control of mine.* Her hard stared was relentless. She twisted an amber ring, almost the exact color of her narrow eyes.

"Next week I'd like you to read, Mr. Kim," she said. "And Rochelle Weiss."

We were dismissed. The photocopies of Wilma Harrington's poem littered the table. A sheet fluttered to the floor and we stepped on it as we left the room.

I did not join the others who lingered in the hallway, discussing where to go for coffee. I hurried away, angry at myself for not joining Laura, for not offering Wilma a word of regret, a word of comfort. I raced down the stairwell, but on the second landing my way was blocked. Dave Robeson planted himself on a wide step, his arms outstretched, and then, with lithe swiftness, encircling me, holding me prisoner. His body pressed against mine and he drew me into his studio, slammed the door behind us.

"Where the hell have you been?" he asked, his grip on my shoulders still tight.

Angrily, I shrugged free. "I could ask you the same thing," I replied.

"I was here last week and the week before that. I looked for you, waited for you. I even went up to the room where your workshop meets and they said you hadn't been there. I thought you were avoiding me."

"And why would I avoid you?" I asked.

"I don't know. Second thoughts about what almost happened between us. Maybe you were relieved that things turned out as they did. Maybe you didn't want to get more involved with a guy like me—an artist, a drifter. I sleep on a sleeping bag in someone else's loft. You have leather chairs, polished floors."

"Or maybe my closest friend was hit by a car and was in the hospital and for a while it looked like she might never wake up. And maybe I spent every free minute with her, with Melanie," I retorted. "Here's a big secret for you, Dave. Things go on in other people's lives that have absolutely nothing to do with you."

"I'm sorry." He released me and looked at me sheepishly.

"You could have called," I added. "You have my number."

"I'm not the kind of guy who makes calls like that."

"Calls like what? Like I'm worried about you and I'd like to see you? Is that too conventional for you?" I asked bitterly. "I was worried about you and I did want to see you but I don't have a phone number or an address for you. So I went by the bench where you usually work and you weren't there. And I followed the path that you sometimes take and I didn't meet you there, either. So I guess I decided that you were the one who was relieved that things turned out as they did. After all, that whole scene at the Catons' apartment was my plan and maybe you were angry with me. And then I thought you might have left the city. You did talk about how much you hated New York in the winter, how you wanted to go out West."

"I wouldn't have gone without seeing you. I haven't been in the park. I've been finishing the illustrations for the children's book, sketching at City Island. Gulls circling sailboats, egrets on the wharf, even a swan cruising the boat basin. Then there were these stupid editorial meetings in an office without windows, phones ringing, fax machines spitting out memos on toilet paper." He sighed, inviting me to commiserate.

"I'm familiar with New York office life, Dave," I said dryly and suddenly we both began to laugh, all vestiges of mutual anger and disappointment swept away in the spontaneous wave of hysteria that washed over us. We laughed as we had laughed in the hallway outside the Catons' apartment, acknowledging our own foolishness, a perceived absurdity.

Still laughing, he encircled me again in his arms, but this time his embrace was tender and the touch of his lips on my own was gentle.

"So where do we go from here?" he asked.

"First we get something to eat," I replied. "Because I'm starving. And then, maybe we should see about finishing our unfinished business."

We ate at the coffee shop, served by the same surly waiter who again reminded us that the shop closed in an hour and added extra pickles to our sandwiches.

"That compensates for a lot," Dave said, sliding the pickle into his mouth, "an extra pickle—the ultimate New York gesture of acceptance."

We walked uptown, hardly talking, but with our hands touching. Dave carried his battered wooden paint box and I clutched the folder that contained the draft of my poem and poor Wilma's sonnet. The night was cool, and when I shivered, Dave took off his gray sweater. He pulled it over my head and gently thrust my arms into the sleeves, like a father dressing a small girl. The gray wool was unraveling and loose tendrils brushed my neck. I rubbed the sleeve against my face. It smelled of paint and sweat. I inhaled deeply and gripped Dave's hand very hard.

We reached my apartment building and, without discussion, he followed me inside and held my folder as I fished for my keys and unlocked my apartment door. I ignored the flickering lights on my answering machine, pulled down the shades and drew the drapes. Dave lit a single lamp and we left the dim light burning in the living room and went into the bedroom. He went at once to the window and stared out at the small courtyard, at Mario's small urban garden, abandoned now, the tomato stakes pulled up and neatly piled, the trellis stripped of cucumber vines. He pulled the shades and glided toward me through the darkness, pressed his face against mine, freed my hair from the tortoiseshell barrette that held it back and allowed it to drift through his fingers.

He undressed me as tenderly as he had arranged the sweater about my body, pausing when he had removed my shirt and bra to touch my breasts, to kiss each nipple, to trace his fingers across my abdomen; sightless in that darkened room, he relied on touch to recognize me, to know me. I stepped out of my jeans, out of my panties and he pressed his face to my thighs, slid his hands down my legs, caressing one foot and then the other.

And I, in turn, unbuttoned his worn plaid shirt, pulled his paint-scabbed jeans down about his knees, his ankles, and watched as he stepped out of them, startled by the grace of his slightest movement. And then, all rhythmic slowness vanished. We were on the bed coming together with small gasps, tears—mine, because, mysteriously, I often wept during lovemaking—and laughter—his, triumphant and exuberant—mingling until at last we lay side by side, my head resting on his shoulder.

"Don't talk," I said.

He put his finger to my lips.

"Of course not," he promised and I was lost in a sweet half sleep, exhausted and content.

I wakened to find that he had pulled the covers up about me, slipped a pillow beneath my head. He knelt beside the buttonhole machine that stood beside my bed, draped still in the chintz cover my mother had fashioned for it.

"Hey," I said.

"Hey, good morning." He did not turn away from the machine. "This a sewing machine?" he asked.

"No."

I pulled on a robe and knelt beside him, removing the cover to show him the mechanism, pointing out the minuscule scissors that carved their way through fabric and could be adjusted to different sizes, the pedal that controlled the speed, the needle attachment used for finishing.

"A buttonhole machine," I explained. "It belonged to my fa-

ther's aunt. She did piecework for garment manufacturers at home.
It was supposed to occupy her, calm her nerves. When my father
same to stay with her, after the war, she taught him how to use it.
It gave him a skill, a way to make a living."

"And that was his job?" Dave asked. "That was what he worked
at?" He stroked the wooden frame of the machine that my mother
had kept polished to a high gloss.

"That's what he worked at. He helped his aunt fill her piecework
orders, then he got a job in a factory, children's pajamas, I think.
He worked the buttonhole machine there and saved until he had
enough money to rent space in a loft and buy his own equipment,
to hire workers. He worked at home very rarely but his aunt gave
him this machine and he always kept it in the bedroom. A reminder, I suppose, of early days, new beginnings. When I closed
my parents' apartment, this was one of the few things I brought
here. And I can't figure out why I did that. Probably because it was
so important to him and to my mother. It brought them independence. It helped them to build a life in a new country. He had a
skill, he could own a business, live a normal life, provide for my
mother, keep a college account for me. He could be proud of the
life he had made. An ordinary life but to him it was a miracle of a
kind."

"And he was proud of you?"

"I worked hard to make him proud of me. To make them both
proud of me. I made it my job. I wanted to make them happy, to
somehow balance the scales. So I did all the right things—great
grades, great scores, terrific job, promotions. My friends smoked
pot, dropped courses, quit jobs, but I don't think I ever did anything that they might disapprove of."

"They wouldn't have approved of me, I suppose." Dave did not
pose a question. He stated a fact.

I laughed.

"They definitely would not have approved of you. You're the

wrong religion. You don't have a steady job. You will probably never have a steady job. You wear torn clothing and you don't have a permanent address. I'm not even sure that I approve of you."

"That's all right," Dave said. "My own family doesn't approve of me. Although that may change. I spoke to my sister last week and we agreed that it was time I went home for a visit. My parents aren't getting any younger. I've never seen my sister's kids. I want to show my father the contract I signed for this book. I want to show him the check I got as an advance. Hey, do you want to see the contract, Rochelle? It might boost my approval rating."

"No. I've seen contracts before. I've seen checks before. But congratulations." I went back to bed, my good humor evaporated, my mood deflated.

He was leaving then, traveling to Alanport, Missouri, to confront his family with his success, the prodigal son, the attentive uncle, and then heading west to Colorado, Arizona, to the vast expanses of mountain and desert that he ached to paint. I had no reason to resent his departure. He was transient in my life and I had known that from the beginning. I had no hold on him nor did I wish for one. And yet his leaving filled me with sadness, with an odd and muted sense of abandonment. I turned my face to the wall. He lay down beside me, gently rubbed my back.

"You could come with me," he said softly.

"Come with you where? To Alanport? Do you want me to sit beside your sister on the porch swing? Do you want me to have Sunday dinner with your parents? Perhaps I could help your mother carry covered dishes in from the kitchen. Your father might take me downtown to see his drugstore." I drew away from him but he drew me back and continued to press his fingers deeply, rhythmically, into my flesh with practiced certainty. I wondered where he had learned it, in how many beds he had wakened in cool autumn mornings.

"No. I'm not suggesting a visit to Alanport, although I don't know what you have against covered dishes. Don't Jews put hot food in covered dishes?" He was not afraid to make light of our disparate backgrounds, to joke about religious differences that were meaningless to him. "But we could meet up after I see my family. Maybe in Boulder. You've never been out West. We could travel together, get ourselves a beat-up station wagon and some camping equipment, sleep out, cook over open fires, maybe rent a cabin. You could write some poems to go with my sketches. My next project is a children's book on desert wildlife and my editor is interested in original text. Why not poetry—your poetry? We'd work well together. I know it." The pressure of his fingers on my back intensified but I remained tense beneath his touch.

"How can you say that? We hardly know each other," I protested.

"Then what better way to get to know each other? Come on, Rochelle. We're not talking long-term commitment here. We're talking about a couple of months."

"Sure, a couple of months of being wafted about like tumbleweed with the wind blowing us this way and that. No plans. No itinerary. Do you really think I could do that, Dave?" I asked.

My resistance was instinctive. I would be like Lila and Fay, rolling restlessly away from my own loneliness, my own rootlessness. But wasn't that, after all, what I had been doing for the past several months as I followed that vague, daily routine...of my own design, pulled by my dogs now eastward, now westward, indifferent to direction, resistant to destination. Perhaps Dave's idea, in some weird way, might be the logical end to all these months of walking and walking that had not, so far, brought me any answers to questions that remained ephemeral. No. I knew the basic question. Who was I, now that I was freed of the obligation to be my parents' daughter?

"Why couldn't you do it? I've done it. In Europe. In the States. In Canada. Going where I please, when I please, how I please."

I thought his smile smug, self-congratulatory.

"But I haven't," I responded.

I thought of how Phil and I had traveled, our airline tickets booked, rental cars awaiting us at airports: hotel reservations confirmed. Our parents, refugees from chaos and upheaval, had taught us the importance of orderly planning, constant vigilance. Dutifully, we had followed a straight path, always knowing where we were going and how we would get there. I wondered what Phil would think of Dave's proposal, but of course I knew.

"Then perhaps you should try it. See if you have the nerve to do it." He tossed out the challenge and pulled me toward him, rubbed his unshaven chin harshly across my face and then twisted my hair into a knot that he held high above my head. And then, abruptly, he released me and began to dress, picking his clothes off the floor, ferreting beneath the bed for a missing sneaker.

"Look," he continued. "Just think about it, about meeting me in Boulder. What's the big deal—what would you be leaving behind? You can pick up a whole bunch of new dogs to walk when you come back if that's what you want. You can sublet this place. It's your choice, Rochelle. Our adventure." He flashed that enticing grin at me and I rolled across the bed to mess his hair, to playfully pummel him, to demonstrate that I was not rigid and rejecting, that I was fun, capable of spontaneity. I imagined meeting him in the Boulder airport, running toward him, both of us bathed in sunlight.

"Hey." He grabbed hold of my wrists in playful restraint. "Give yourself some time to get used to the idea. Then make your choice. No pressure. I promise."

"So many choices," I murmured, but he did not hear me. I realized that I had not told him about Constance Reid's offer and I congratulated myself on my silence.

He kissed me lightly on the lips and I walked him to the door. He was leaving so early, he explained, because his easel was in place at the western window of his loft and he was at work on a skyscape set in the half light of dawn. He did not want to miss the river mist that shimmered in the slow-breaking brightness. He had a new brush, expensive sable, bought especially to capture the droplets of moisture in swift, pointillist strokes.

"I'll call. We'll talk," he said and walked swiftly down the hall, eager to return to his work, to concentrate on capturing that elusive light.

I returned to my bedroom but I did not return to bed, although sleep tugged at me. Instead, I removed a piece of flannel from the drawer of the buttonhole machine and pressed my foot down on the treadle. It purred into life and I listened to its gentle whir, the comforting mechanical lullaby of my childhood. I put the flannel in place, adjusted the scissors and slowly moved the fabric as they carved small ovals, each exactly formed. I fashioned row after row and then I unplugged the machine and covered it again with the chintz cover that still carried the faint scent of the hand cream my mother had used.

"Mama. Papa," I said aloud and then I did go back to sleep. I dreamed of drifting clouds and a wind that rustled the branches of newly barren trees, whispering my name. *Ruchele. Ruchele.* No. Not a single wind but twin breezes swirling softly toward each other.

I wakened, feeling oddly comforted and surprised that my sleep had been so brief, that I would not be late, that I could adhere to my schedule. I went to the window and lifted the shade. The sky was gray and the ground damp because a light rain had fallen, a very brief autumn shower. The park would be grim and deserted. The smaller dogs I walked would slip on mounds of leaves. I moved slowly then, reluctant to face the sunless morning, reluctant to begin my rounds.

I dressed in layers, following Annette's seasoned advice.

"You never know when some damn dog is going to break into a run and you end up all sweaty and disgusting," she had said. "Especially this time of year."

"I feel disgusting every time of year," Mitzi had countered. "How can you not feel disgusting when your clothes are covered with dog hair and your hands smell of their shit?"

I sniffed my own hands, pulled on my thin woolen gloves and pulled latex gloves over them, fighting back a surge of nausea. I rushed out, resisting the urge to return to bed.

I cut my circuits short that day, keeping a firm grip on the leashes. By midafternoon, I had worked my way west and, as always, I took the Lab and the two Afghans to the dog run. Annette, Mitzi and Carl were there. I munched the last slice of cold pizza from the pie they had shared and told them about Ida.

"She's dead then," Mitzi said, her voice flat.

"I would guess. She had pneumonia. She was all skin and bones, a skeleton." The pizza turned sour in my mouth and I spat it out.

"Like a concentration camp survivor, it sounds like," Carl said and I cringed but they did not notice. Why should they, why would they?

"Well, we tried to help her." Annette fed a dog biscuit to a small terrier, her favorite, I knew just as Goldilocks had been my favorite.

"It's too damn hard to help anyone in this city."

Carl looked helpless himself—a man who clung to boyhood, tight jeans hugging his slender hips, boots polished to a high gloss although the soles were caked with muck. Sadness veiled his eyes, masked his face. He was fear haunted. Two bulldogs crouched beside him, large black and whites, innately gentle despite their fierce ugly faces. Carl preferred large dogs that offered a semblance of protection. He carried a canister of Mace and avoided side streets. He feared to linger in the park and he feared to go home because Ramon, his lover, might be gone. It had happened before and it might happen again. We had all overheard Carl's anxious cell-phone conversations. "Ramon, should I pick up Chinese? How about the Zen Palate?" "Ramon, please don't go out. Wait for me.

I have two more dogs to drop off. That's it. Wait. Please." Once we had seen him cry as he shoved his cell phone back into his pocket.

Like all of us, Carl had been drawn to Ida because her vulnerability, her neediness, surpassed our own. Our generosity to her reduced our own marginality, defined us as caring people. It relieved us that she accepted what we gave, a couple of dollars, a sandwich, bagels, without acknowledgment, and that she never asked us for anything, that she rarely spoke. We wanted contact. We did not want connection.

It had been Annette who had asked Ida her name, months earlier and had been surprised when she hesitated for long minutes and then answered.

"Ida. I was called Ida," she said and smiled as though she had pried her name loose from an abandoned mine of memories.

We had watched as Ida ate the food we offered her, as she arranged the battered paperbacks we saved for her atop her shopping cart. Our concern for her briefly dissipated our own aloneness. Because of her we had bonded and become an informal family of caring strangers.

"Listen, Carl, at least we made the effort," Mitzi said. She took her beret off and her fine fair hair tumbled about her shoulders. Briefly she had the look of an angelic flower child. "That's something, I suppose."

"Not much but something," Annette agreed.

"You walking east, Mitzi?" Carl asked. He did not want to be alone. He could not bear to be alone.

"Sure. I could do that. It doesn't matter." Mitzi arranged the leashes of the three poodles, pulled at them gently. The dogs yelped indignantly and I wondered if Mitzi would deliver them home to their actress mistress at the appointed hour. Not that Mitzi worried about that. If she lost that job she could easily get another. Dog walkers were in demand, particularly during the winter months. Job security was not among our problems.

Annette and I stared after them as they exited the park.

"Well, at least they're together," Annette said. "Which means that Mitzi won't take one of her stupid shortcuts."

"I thought she had stopped doing that."

"No, I saw her the other night around 98th Street, ignoring the path, going straight toward that wooded area that doesn't even have a streetlight. But I've stopped warning her. I'm not her mother. Listen, Rochelle. I want you to do me a favor. Remember, you promised me a rain check when I asked you to take on my dogs a couple of weeks ago."

I groaned.

"I remember," I said.

"Well, the thing is, my son's school is having a parents' day next Saturday. His therapist thinks that it's important that I be there, and I don't want to disappoint him. Even though half the time I'm not even sure that he knows that I exist. If you know what I mean.

"The problem is that months ago, I promised this guy in Hoboken that I would go out there on Saturday and take care of his dog. You know, my crazy gig out there. The nervous dog, the great house, the Brie. Plus, I really like this guy. He's been great to me and I know he's got a really important conference going. So I wondered—could you cover for me? I've asked everyone else and they all have stuff going on. And it's really good money."

"I suppose," I said reluctantly. "And I guess I could use some really good money. I'm thinking about going out West for a while." I listened carefully as I spoke the words, wondering if they had the ring of truth, if I believed them myself.

"Terrific," Annette said. "Thanks." She did not ask me about my plans. We observed the careful parameters of privacy. It occurred to me that I did not even have her phone number, or Mitzi's or Carl's. I did not know where they lived. "Listen, I'll meet you here tomorrow about this time and I'll give you the address, the directions and the keys to the house. Or I could do that now."

"Tomorrow," I said. I did not want to loop another set of keys onto my laden key chain. I did not want yet another heavy metal reminder that I was doing something else that I really did not want to do.

I stopped at the flower shop to tell Melanie that I could not go shopping with her as we had planned. We were looking at wedding dresses. Leonard had given her a small sapphire ring as they left the hospital, sliding it onto her finger as they descended the steps. A ring, but no wedding date; yet we had decided to look at white suits, at simple silk A-lines, maybe even try our luck at a vintage boutique.

"It's a bummer," I said. "I really don't want to go to Hoboken. I don't want to look at another dog. I'm tired of their drool and those damn mournful eyes."

"Then why did you say you'd do it?"

"It was easier to say yes and not struggle with the pros and cons. I'm just not up to another decision."

Sitting opposite Melanie, our faces lit by the ultraviolet light, I told her about Constance Reid's offer, about Dave's suggestion.

"Rochelle at the crossroads," she said.

"I wish I knew which road was less traveled," I added, "because that might make all the difference."

We both laughed and Melanie reached into a drawer and removed two bottles of nail polish. She switched the radio on and with great concentration we painted our nails a pale pink as we listened to a clarinet solo.

# CHAPTER
## THIRTEEN

The weather turned cold that week. An early-autumn frost threaded the newly barren tree branches with a silver filigree and the toddlers in the park lurched gleefully and clumsily toward each other in brightly colored snowsuits. The frozen earth, hard and unyielding, did not absorb the dogs' urine and the steaming golden puddles glittered in the harsh light until I blanketed them with brittle leaves. My dogs walked slowly, reluctantly, and because my mood was dark, I tugged them impatiently along, pulling cruelly at their leashes, speaking to them with an unfamiliar harshness. A red-cheeked, white-haired woman, scattering crumbs for pigeons and squirrels, glared at me as I passed her, walking so rapidly that the dogs on their shortened leashes yelped miserably.

"Watch how you treat them," she shouted, the shrillness of her voice a surprise after the gentleness of her gestures.

Tight-lipped, ashamed, I nodded to her, lengthened the leashes and walked more slowly.

At the dog run I met Annette who gave me the keys to the Hoboken house, directions on how to get there and a description of the routine she followed with the Italian greyhound who was called Fabrizio.

"He's a great dog but crazy nervous. Really high-strung. He twitches. But then so does Len, his owner. It's crazy how some of our mutts are just like their owners in temperament," she said.

"In looks, too," I agreed. I thought of Thimble whose curly white coat so closely matched Mrs. Clark's cluster of thinning snow-white curls, of my soulful Afghans whose large sad eyes and shaggy russet coats so closely resembled their master, a tall melancholy psychoanalyst whose chestnut-colored hair fell to his shoulders.

Annette laughed and switched her red woolen mitten from one hand to another. The borzoi she walked only one day a week had snatched the other mitten from her hand and chewed it through.

"Now I'm going to walk him no times a week," she had said. "And I'm going to get his cheap bastard of an owner to pay me for a new pair of mittens."

But I knew that she would continue to walk him and that she would not mention the mittens to his owner. Confrontation was not part of the dog walker's profile.

"But Fabrizio doesn't look like Len," she mused. "He's long and lean with a great sleek coat and golden eyes. Len's a great guy but he's short and fat, almost bald, and he squints. Maybe Fabrizio is his wanna-be. You know, if I can't be sleek and handsome at least my dog's all that and more."

"A trophy dog, like a trophy wife. Why not? What does this Len do?" I asked.

"He's the creative director of some big ad agency. He has great taste. The house is like to die for in this gentrified stretch of Hoboken. You'll see. A Sub-Zero fridge loaded with great cheeses and bottled water. Fabrizio drinks only bottled water. Give him anything from the tap and he twitches. On the second shelf there'll be a dish of chopped sirloin. That's what you put in Fabrizio's dish. He eats it raw."

"Not good for dogs."

"Len goes to a top vet. A vet's vet, and that's what he recommends. Fabrizio also eats fresh liver—beef liver."

"No foie gras?"

"Maybe on Christmas. Or his birthday."

Annette laughed and I did, too. It was necessary that we dog walkers laugh at the excesses of our employers, that we recognize the nonsense quotient of our work. Unlike the men and women who strode purposefully past us, clutching their briefcases and laptops, speaking urgently into their cell phones, we had no pretensions about the job we did. We recognized both its absurdity and its necessity.

A sudden wind gusted and Annette shivered and wound a scarf around her neck.

"Feel this and it's not even winter yet. You're smart to be going West, Rochelle," she said.

"If I go."

"Yeah. If you go." It was acknowledged between us that all plans were fluid. Tickets were not booked until the last minute; decisions could be altered as swiftly and spontaneously as they were made. We had heard Mitzi speak vaguely of returning to her home in the Midwest, of heading for Alaska or maybe California. Once she had spoken of becoming pregnant, having a child. Always her voice was soft, tentative, each idea loosed like a child's balloon that might soar beyond sight or deflate sadly, suddenly. We did not challenge her. Her indecision matched our own.

Annette sighed.

"Anyway I told Len you'd be there about two o'clock. There's a kind of esplanade along the Hoboken waterfront where Fabrizio likes to walk." She stroked the borzoi hound's neck and he stood and shook himself free of the leaves and earth that clung to his coat.

"Well, I certainly wouldn't want to disappoint Fabrizio," I said and recoiled inwardly from the cynicism in my voice.

"Hey, are you okay, Rochelle?" Annette asked and there was real concern in her voice.

"Yeah, I'm fine. Aside from the fact that I don't know what I'm doing or what I want to do, I'm fine."

I tried for a reassuring smile. Annette shouldn't be worrying about me. I wasn't the one with an autistic son and a backlog of tuition bills. No such heavy obligations anchored me. I was free, no one's daughter, my decisions my own. I could stay East, go West. I might spend months reading and writing poetry or I could stare out at a desert landscape, look up at a star-crowded sky. Hey, I could even sleep with one man and fantasize about another, then spend a whole afternoon wandering through Body Shops, smoothing pastel creams across my eyebrows, spraying my wrists with the scent of lilacs and apple blossoms. I thought of Fay and Lila and a sadness as cold and amorphous as the autumn air settled about my heart.

"Okay, then," Annette said and she broke into a run, the graceful hound sprinting ahead of her, his paws scattering the dry leaves in a fine necrotic spray.

I thrust the keys to the Hoboken house into my fanny pack and hurried to collect my next group of dogs. I walked them too swiftly and, for the first time, I did not scoop up the noxious mound dropped by the Labrador retriever but hurried guiltily away. I wanted to be home, to sit in a circle of lamplight, pad on my knees, pen in my hand as the evening darkness gathered.

But the phone was ringing as I entered my apartment and I hurried to catch the call, tossing the mail onto the table.

The familiar voice, tinged with my parents' accent, boomed into the phone and with that deep intonation, my childhood sprang to life.

"Ruchele. Ruchele. It's me. Morrie. Your cousin. Ruchele, can you hear me?"

I tucked the phone beneath my chin and peeled off my earth-encrusted work boots, wiping my hands against my sweatshirt.

"Yes, Morrie. I can hear you. Is everything all right?"

I waited. I wanted to hear him repeat my name, spoken in the tender Yiddish inflection that seemed always to rise from heart to throat, forming a soft word capsule of love. My mother had never said hello when she heard my voice on the phone. She used my name as greeting. "Ruchele. Ah, Ruchele." My name, the name of her vanished sister, melted in her mouth. My father's voice trembled when he spoke it. *Ruchele.* For him, my name enunciated survival, triumph. Miracle of miracles, he had a daughter, a tall American daughter with flame-colored hair who ran races, who won prizes. His pride, his amazement, spurred me on. I could not disappoint a father who said my name with such awe, such joy.

Morrie laughed into the phone.

"Such a question. Something has to be wrong for me to call you? No, everything is fine. I'm calling to invite you to come to us on Friday night. For dinner, for shabbos dinner. You can come on Friday night, Ruchele?"

"Friday night? Well, my weekend is sort of complicated. I have to work in Hoboken on Saturday," I said. My reluctance puzzled me. I liked him, loved him. He was my last link to my parents. There were things I wanted to say to him, questions I wanted to ask. And yet. And yet.

His booming voice overcame my excuse.

"So Friday night isn't Saturday. You'll come. Your cousins will be there. My Lynn and her Herbie, their children, the twins. And Matt. Come, Ruchele. We haven't seen you much since the funeral, the *shivah.*"

His tone did not alter as he spoke those last words. *Funeral. Shivah.* Facts of life, facts of death. He was an old man. He had attended so many funerals, visited to many houses of mourning. His grief at my parents' deaths, at my loss, was profound but it was pragmatic. Alone among the mourners, he had wept and had not even bothered to wipe away the tears. Alone among the mourners, he had murmured the Hebrew words *"Baruch dayan emet,"* which I had not understood but which Phil, to my surprise had translated "Blessed be the true judge."

"I know. You were away. I was busy." I fumbled for excuses.

"So now we're home and maybe you're not so busy. You'll come, Ruchele?" Again he wrapped my name around my heart.

"I'll come. Of course I'll come," I agreed. I felt the same stirring of excitement that had always overtaken me when Morrie visited our quiet apartment, often with Zelda and their children, overwhelming us with his gifts—stamps from foreign capitals, silk scarves for my mother, brightly colored ties for my father, lox wrapped in slick oil-stained paper, cake in rectangular boxes tied with red string that I used for games of cat's cradle. I remembered the thrill of weekend visits to Morrie's bungalow in the Rockaways, the scent of sea air, the explosions of talks and laughter, of children fiercely quarreling and then tumbling into shared play. Like all only, lonely children, I marveled at their swift angers, their raucous glee, and waited shyly, patiently, for them to draw me into the magic circle of their togetherness.

"Good. So you'll come. And, if you want, you can bring someone. Maybe that nice tall fella who was at the funeral, at the shivah."

"Phil?" I was surprised that Morrie remembered him, even more surprised that the idea of inviting Phil to that Friday-night dinner did not seem absurd to me.

"That's right. Phil. You remember how to get to our apartment?"

"I remember. And Morrie, thank you."

"Ah, Ruchele, our Ruchele. No need to thank."

I hung up, saddened because when Morrie died, no one would call me Ruchele.

I turned to my mail. The manila envelope held a note from Dave clipped to a charcoal sketch of mountains outlined in broad strokes shadowing a valley striated with ribs of sunlight. The scrawled message told me he was going to be tied up for a while organizing an exhibit at a gallery in Massachusetts. The drawing was to remind me of the trip West we had talked about, but that was up to me. "No pressure," he wrote and underlined the words. I studied the sketch. The mountains looked ominous, the valley inviting.

There was a postcard from Lila and Fay of the Wellfleet beach, a message scrawled in purple Magic Marker—"Miss you a lot, Shelley girl. Lots to tell you." And, amid the flutter of bills and magazines, a Jiffy bag from Constance Reid that included a description of the Richmond College Poetry Fellowship, a slender journal entitled *Writers at Richmond,* a course catalog and an application form. On thick ivory-colored notepaper, embossed with her initials in steel-gray raised lettering, she wrote, "I thought you might be interested in the enclosed." She, of course, ever an economical writer, had not added "no pressure," nor had she bothered to sign her name.

I glanced at the fellowship application. An essay question: *Please explain in 250 words or less why you are applying for this poetry fellowship.* Answers sprang to mind. *I am applying because I can't think of anything else to do at this point in my life. I am applying for this fellowship because I am in love with wordcraft and need time to work at it. I am applying for this fellowship because it's time for me to move on—even if I don't know where I'm going.*

I thrust aside the application and dialed Phil's number. He answered on the first ring.

"Hi," I said. "It's me." My own calm surprised me.

"Hi, you." He himself was unsurprised, his voice even, almost subdued. I wondered if I should apologize for my harsh tone when he had called in the aftermath of Melanie's accident. But I did not.

"I'm kind of surprised to find you home," I said, instead.

"Well, it's Wednesday night. *West Wing* time. And I'm tired. There's a lot going on."

I did not ask what was going on. I did not want to know about deals that had fallen through, about friends who had disappointed, about the complexities of caring for his aging parents. Warren had told me that Phil had arranged for them to move to an assisted-living facility, but I had not asked where. Not knowing, I reasoned, was the first step on the road to not caring.

"I'm calling because I wondered if you were busy on Friday night."

"I'm not busy on Friday night."

"My cousin Morrie, you met him at the funeral, I think and then at the shivah…"

"I remember him. The chubby man with very red cheeks."

"That's right. Anyway, he remembered you. He wants me to have dinner with his family on Friday night. He said it was okay if I brought someone—actually, if I brought you."

"He wants us to get married," Phil said. "He wants me to give you an engagement ring when his wife serves the gefilte fish."

"Okay. If you don't want to come it's okay. It was stupid of me to call you. After all these weeks."

"No. It's nice that you called me. After all these weeks. I'll come. But no engagement ring."

"It's a deal. I guess we should leave about six-thirtyish."

"I'll pick you up."

"Great. Bring flowers. If we're not going to get engaged, we have to do something to make them feel good."

"Right. I'll tell Melanie to make up a shabbat bouquet."

"Deal." I hung up and cleared away my papers.

I put the Richmond application on my desk, Dave's note and drawing over it.

* * *

I finished working early on Friday. Mitzi had agreed to walk my last group of dogs. When I turned my keys over to her she looked thinner. Dark circles shadowed her high cheekbones and her skin was alabaster white. She wore a hooded scarlet cape she had found in a thrift shop on Madison. Dog walkers haunted those resale shops tucked in between upscale boutiques. In such a store I had found the long black vinyl duster I wore on rainy days and the quilted army jacket I might wear in the winter if I didn't go West. Or even if I did go West. And for ten dollars I had claimed a black mohair sweater coat, suitable for walks along the paths of a wintry campus. But I would never had dared to buy Mitzi's cape.

"Listen, I appreciate this, Little Red Riding Hood," I told her. "And stay away from the Big Bad Wolf."

"Don't know what you're talking about," Mitzi retorted. "This park is wolf free. The mayor says so. Don't you believe your elected officials?"

"Of course I don't. But Mitzi, seriously, be careful."

"I am careful. Besides, I'm getting out of this lousy city soon. I can't face another winter. Dog turds frozen onto the snow, the mutts shivering and whining. Me shivering and whining. I know this guy who's sailing a sloop from Florida to some Caribbean port and he needs a crew. That sounds pretty good, doesn't it, Rochelle?"

"It sounds great," I agreed. I reflected that Mitzi was one of those wistful girls who always found a rescuer. Evicted from her illegal sublet early in the spring, she had been invited to house-sit in an East End Avenue co-op with a wraparound terrace and a river view. Friends lent her cars, offered her frequent-flier miles for a swift trip to London. Like a practiced skater, she glided through the seasons of her life, but the ice beneath her feet was treacherously thin and it was always possible that it might split open and drag her down into frigid darkness. I shivered at the thought, but when I spoke, my words were playful.

"Listen, Mitzi, you'll be walking the Catons' dog. If they're home and ask how come you're filling in for me, tell them I'm sick, and if they're not home sneak a look at their bedroom. The boudoir as operating room. Everything high and white and sterile."

"Ah, the bedroom where the evil deed was not quite done." Mitzi grinned. Barnard had not been wasted on her. "I'll be careful, Rochelle. I promise not to get raped while I'm walking your dogs."

"Thanks. I appreciate that." I smiled, too. Smiles were all right. Anything deeper was suspect.

Back in my apartment I luxuriated in the work-free hours and showered slowly, concentrating on what I would wear. I decided on a brown silk turtleneck and a long tan skirt, an outfit that Phil liked, understated and expensive, appropriate for poetry readings on a small campus, out of the question for a rambling journey through the West.

I toweled myself dry and, standing before the mirror, I brushed my hair and twisted it into a loose chignon. Stupid to obsess about clothes, I told myself. What, after all, was revealed by the way women dressed? But mental images persisted. I thought of Mitzi's long skirts, her red, hooded cape loose about her shoulders, the soft red suede boots flapping about her pale legs—a vulnerable flower child, an innocent en route through a dangerous woodland; Constance Reid, her well-cut linen dresses, the double-weave cashmere sweaters that matched her heavy rings and heavier pendants advertising her success in the life she had chosen for herself; Lila and Fay, provocative nymphets in their oversize snow-white T-shirts.

And, I—how did my outfits advertise my persona? In jeans, sweatshirt and work boots I was the earthy, crunchy poet-cum-dog walker; in silk and soft wool I was reinvented as the safe date slated to become the safe mate, the dutiful daughter to parents who no longer were, the willful, whimsical lover, lying naked on the high white bed of strangers. *Rochelle. Ruchele. Shelley.* I smiled quizzically at myself in the mirror and went into the bedroom where I dressed very slowly, pulling the brown silk top down around my hips, carefully adjusting the kick pleat on my skirt, sliding into the wide-heeled Ferragamo pumps I had not worn for months.

The doorbell rang as I applied the last of my makeup and I frowned. Odd for Phil to be so early. Still, I was ready. I blotted my lipstick on a tissue that I passed across the rise of my cheeks, my mother's trick, so gently taught.

"Why should I waste money on rouge?" she had asked. Of course. Why should they waste money on anything that was not meant for me, their late-born baby, their miracle child?

The bell rang again and I opened the door, but it was not Phil who stood there. Leonard Quinton, holding the bouquet of long-stemmed white roses and graceful blue irises that Phil had arranged to bring to Morrie and Zelda, smiled at me.

"Melanie asked me to bring this over. She said you needed it for tonight."

"Great. I was planning to stop at the shop on my way uptown but this saves me some time. Do you want to come in?"

"Sure. Why not?" He blushed. We had not been alone together since our vigil at the hospital when Melanie lay locked in a netherworld of unnatural sleep, bordered neither by night nor dawn.

"So things are going well?" I asked as we sat opposite each other on my black leather chairs.

He slouched, as tall men often do, as though their height embarrasses them. But then Phil did not slouch, nor did Dave. I congratulated myself on their posture. It demonstrated their superiority to Leonard.

"Seems to be. Except that Lila and Fay are coming back. Next week maybe or the week after. Which means I lose their apartment."

"What will you do?"

He shrugged. "I don't know yet," he said.

"Oh?" My question was not a question. My voice was cold. Melanie was shopping for a wedding dress, holding white silk A-line dresses against her slender body, allowing her hair to grow long enough for a garland of asphodel, while Leonard Quinton did not know what to do. I walked to the window and looked down at the windswept street. Leonard spoke slowly now, as though his words might be unintelligible to me.

"You know that we're negotiating to buy the space beside the flower shop and live in the apartment above it. What I don't know is whether we should get married before, after or during the renovations. And I don't know where I'll live if we decide to wait until after—with Melanie, with my mother? But that's not what you thought I was going to say, is it?"

I stared at him in surprise.

"You thought I was going to dance around the question of marriage. That I was going to disappoint. Because that's what you do, Rochelle. You wait for people to disappoint. You place the bar way up high and you think no one is going to be able to scale it. You think you're the only high jumper, the only long-distance runner, the best of daughters, the best of friends, the most diligent of professionals. So good, so valuable. Unmatchable." His voice was not harsh. It was calm, matter-of-fact.

"You don't like me very much, do you?" I asked. The very question was alien to me. I had been conditioned, from earliest childhood, to be liked, to be admired, to be sought after by friends and classmates, colleagues and clients.

"I like you. You're Melanie's best friend. But it's hard to be in the orbit of your judgment. It's hard to watch you judge yourself."

Wounded and ambushed by the unexpected pellets of truth in his words, I said nothing. He rose to leave and then, quite suddenly, he knelt beside me and his lips brushed my forehead.

"You look very nice, Rochelle. Have a great time tonight."

The door closed softly behind him and I sat quite still. After all these months, I understood why my zany friend Melanie, who brushed magenta coloring into her hair and danced solo in rays of violet light, loved grave-eyed Leonard Quinton, so quiet and reserved, who had lived for so long with his mother.

Phil's rap on the door, moments later, was light and tentative. We stood awkwardly in the doorway, our words of greeting colliding with each other, lovers become strangers.

"You look terrific, Shelley," he said.

"Thanks."

I did not tell him that he looked terrific because it was not true and he would not have believed me. He had lost weight and his tweed jacket hung too loosely on his newly angular frame. Always he had retained his carefully cultivated summer tan, the "good color" we had both avidly pursued on the beaches and tennis courts of Fire Island and the Hamptons, into the late autumn, renewing it during wintry getaways to the Caribbean and the slopes of Aspen. We were united in our courtship of the complexion of success. But now his skin was sallow, slack about his cheeks and there was a dullness in his narrow green eyes, as though some strange sadness had extinguished the playful glint I remembered.

"You okay, Phil?" I asked.

"Sort of okay."

"The market bumming you out?"

"No. For me the market's fine," he added and held out my coat.

And for him and his clients, it was fine. He told Mario as much when we met him in the hallway where he was plucking up the flimsy menu of a recently opened Chinese restaurant.

"I say no menus. I have a sign," he muttered. "But do they care, do they listen?"

Still, he smiled when he saw me with Phil. He approved of Phil. He approved of the way I looked.

"Hey, Mario, your stocks are doing great," Phil said and his face came alive. "I checked your account just a couple of hours ago and you're in good shape. I'm glad you didn't go for that dot-com crap."

"I did what you told me to do, Mr. Phil. So thank you. Next year my daughter goes to a new school, more tuition, more uniforms." He shook his head. He worried obsessively about his pretty daughter's schooling, her texts, her classroom supplies, but for now he beamed at us and continued to thrust the scattered menus into the black plastic bag.

"You see, there's some redeeming social value in what I do," Phil said.

"I never said there wasn't," I replied, pleased to see that he was smiling, that the aura of sadness had briefly lifted. I tucked my hand into his and we walked to the subway.

As the train careened north, he asked me about Morrie.

"Well, he was my father's cousin. Their mothers were sisters. He and Zelda, his wife, and my father grew up in a village near Warsaw. He and Zelda got to New York after the war and he stumbled into the import-export business and did pretty well. He knew how to live. He laughed a lot, kibitzed with his kids, bought a phonograph and danced around the living room with Zelda. They played cards every Saturday night with a group of friends and then they all ate kosher deli. They tried to teach my parents how to play rummy, canasta, pinochle. They never learned."

"What about his kids? Where are they now?" Phil asked.

"They were years older than me. Leo, their oldest son was a superstar. Bronx Science, debate team, varsity swimmer at Cornell, straight A pre-med. He died of meningitis his senior year. Awful. I paid a shivah call with my parents, and Zelda said to my mother, 'Well, I guess God's not done with us yet.' My mother gripped my hand so tightly that I thought she was trying to protect me from God. Their daughter, Lynn, is a psychologist, her husband Herb's a pediatrician and they have twins, Abie and Annie. Matt's their youngest, an ad executive, gay, with a terrific partner, a Korean guy." I turned to him. "I'm glad you're coming, Phil. Thanks."

"I wanted to come," he said gravely. "Lots has happened. I've wanted to talk."

I waited, but he was silent until the train rumbled into our stop.

Morrie and Zelda lived in the same apartment where they had raised their children. At my ring, the door was flung open and the family came forward to greet us. Morrie hugged me, Lynn kissed me and took Phil's coat and urged us into the huge living room that overflowed with history. Portraits marched across every dark polished wood surface, along the breakfront cabinet and the credenza. There were framed graduation pictures and wedding portraits, photos of shyly smiling children, grave adolescents. There were family groupings, shots taken at the beach and at weddings and bar mitzvahs, a photo of myself and my parents at my college graduation. Why weren't we smiling? Were we fearful of tempting the evil eye, of being thrust back into the darkness of my parents' yesteryears?

I looked around the living room with its thick oriental rug, the long sofa and oversize armchairs upholstered in faded gold, the coffee table on which a heavy cut-glass bowl squatted. There was permanence in this room, stability. It was a home where no one had ever huddled on the floor and wept into the darkness.

"Ma, Rochelle, Ruchele, is here. With her friend," Matt called.

Zelda came out of the kitchen, threw her arms around me, shook hands with Phil and buried her flushed face in the flowers he offered her. A flurry of activity as she searched for a vase and then placed the flowers on the beautifully set table, and we gathered around, sang the prayers that welcomed the sabbath, chanted the benedictions over the wine, the braided challah.

During the meal, Phil was affable, complimenting Zelda on the food, joking with the children. It puzzled me that during all our years together I had not thought to invite him to such a dinner. I tried to imagine Dave at the table and dismissed the thought. I was playing too many mind games with myself, too much was converging in what Leonard had so shrewdly called "the orbit of my judgment."

Matt told me that BIS had published a disappointing annual report.

"I hope that won't impact on you, Rochelle."

"No. I'm no longer with BIS."

"I didn't know you'd gone to another firm."

"I didn't. I kind of went into my own business."

"What sort of business?" Lynn asked.

Phil reached for a piece of strudel and frowned.

"Dog walking. I'm a dog walker," I said.

I looked around the table, anticipating their shock, their disapproval. But they were not shocked. They were not disapproving. Lynn smiled.

"Good for you," she said. "A real breakout. Fresh air, exercise. No rat race."

"How much money do you make?" small Abie asked.

"Such a question. You should be ashamed." Zelda bristled.

"Oh, come off it, Ma. I'll bet you're dying to know," Matt said.

"It varies," I replied honestly.

Morrie said nothing. He continued to build small snowy hills of challah crumbs as Lynn's family prepared to leave.

"I'll go with you," Matt said. "Kim's got the flu."

"Wait, I'll give you soup for him. Chicken. Potato pudding." Zelda hurried into the kitchen.

Lynn leaned toward me.

"It's a new world, Rochelle," she said. "My mother is sending shabbos dinner home to my brother's Korean partner. Who would have thunk it?"

"Everything's being rethunk," I replied dryly. "Listen, let's stay in touch."

"Come for dinner. Bring Phil," she said.

"Thanks. We'll see."

But what would we see? I wondered. Would I be bringing Phil to other family dinners? Would I ever seem him again after this evening had passed, after he and I had traded revelations?

I returned to the table where Phil and Morrie sat in an oddly companionable silence. Phil's fingers, splayed across the wine-stained cloth, were bathed in the soft golden light of the sabbath candles. Morrie looked up.

"So you have yourself a new job, Ruchele. You walk dogs. You clean up after them. That's what you do?"

"That's what I do. You don't like it?"

"What difference if I like, if I don't like? Do I like that Matt lives with a Kim? Do I like that my grandson, Abie, wears an earring? But I'm not Matt, I'm not Abie, I'm not you. Should I tell you how to live? If this job, this dog walking suits you, if you can support yourself from it—so I like it."

"Would my parents have liked it—my mother and father?" I did not ask a question. I threw out a challenge.

"Your parents only wanted that you should be happy, Ruchele."

"And I only wanted to make them happy. To make them proud. I thought that I had to do that for them, after all they'd gone through."

"That wasn't your job. What they suffered, what they lost, you couldn't give back to them. Their lives were their lives. Your life is your life."

"But I never knew what they suffered, what they lost. They never talked about it, about a those years. Not to me."

Phil stared at me as I spoke and nodded, as though my words gave voice to his thoughts. I moved my hand toward his, across the wine-spattered cloth, but our fingers did not touch and the moment passed.

"They wanted to spare you. They wanted to spare themselves.

Like I wanted to spare my children. Should I give them nightmares? Should I tell Annie and Abie how Leo died? Do I want them to dream of death? Your mother and father, they wanted to keep you safe from their *tsuris*. So they didn't speak of it. They were quiet people, gentle people, but strong, so strong."

"And brave," I said.

"Brave?" Morrie repeated the word as though it was new to him. "Brave, I don't know. There is one story about your mother. I heard it from Bella, her friend who was in the camp with her. You remember Bella?"

"I remember Bella." It was Bella whose stories embroidered the nocturnal fantasies of my childhood, whose whispered memories threaded my poems.

"She told me that in the barracks where she and your mother slept, there were girls even younger than them. One day a German woman officer got angry with one of the very young girls and she lifted her hand—maybe with a whip, maybe without a whip—to hit her. Your mother moved in front of that girl and stared hard at the German woman. She could have been hit, she could have been killed. But in the end nothing at all happened. That officer just walked away—ashamed maybe. All the prisoners gathered around your mother. Oh, you were so brave, they told her, but your mother said, 'No. I didn't even think about what I was doing, about what could happen. I just did it.'" Morrie's voice trembled.

"She was brave," I said. "I don't think I could ever be that brave."

"You shouldn't ever have to know from being that brave." Zelda was in the room now. "Morrie, why such talk, such stories? What was, was. But, Ruchele, listen to me. Winter is coming. Snow, ice. To walk dogs in such weather—it will be hard. Maybe you should think about going back to school, to study to be a teacher. Oh, what a good teacher you would make. Always you had the highest marks. Your mother showed me your report cards—A, A, A plus." She smiled at me and I smiled back.

"Actually, I have been thinking about going back to school. Of doing graduate work," I said. "But I'll see."

Phil looked at me in surprise then glanced down at his watch.

I read his gesture and rose to leave.

"This has been wonderful," I said. "But I have to be up early to-morrow. I'm working out in Hoboken and I don't know how long it's going to take me to get there."

"You see, teachers don't have to work on weekends. Summers they have off." Zelda was persistent. "You'll come again, Ruchele. Soon, you'll come again. And you, too." She enfolded Phil's hands in her own, her small bright eyes studying his face.

He nodded.

"I'll be glad to," he said. "And thank you."

"Nice people," Phil said to me as we rode back downtown.

"Really nice," I agreed.

We were silent then. I closed my eyes and thought of my mother, so short, so slender, stepping forth to shield a younger girl. I tried to imagine the tilt of her head, the defiance of her gaze, her pale brown hair, close-cropped, hugging her head, narrowly framing her thin face. Oh, she had been brave and that courage did not surprise me; it only filled me with sadness. I rested my head on Phil's shoulder and slipped into the lightest of sleeps. He shook me gently awake as the train pulled into our subway stop.

Hand in hand, like the practiced lover-friends we had been for so long, we walked to my building. I unlocked the door of my apartment but did not enter until Phil flicked on the living-room lamp and the room was bathed in a soft light. That had been his habit from our very first date when I told him that I feared to enter darkened rooms. It was a fear inherited from my mother, who had always hesitated in the doorway when we returned home after dark. She waited then for my father to turn on the lights and even then she entered cautiously, sometimes opening and closing a closet door as though to assure herself that no threatening presence lurked in her home. I did not tell Phil that my own fear of that homecoming darkness had vanished when my parents died. It comforted me to know that he remembered my irrational terror and sought to counter it.

Wordlessly I hung our coats side by side on the brass hooks that he had screwed into the wall years ago and, without asking, I brewed our tea, the sweet peppermint that we both favored. I too was bonded to the memory of shared habits, shared preferences. He studied my CDs and selected *The Goldberg Variations,* lowering the volume so that the complex chords faded and soared and faded again.

I carried the tea into the living room and, with twin gestures, our hands circled the cups—not mugs because we, both of us, had grown up in homes where china cups and saucers were prized. We would wait long minutes until the tea cooled and only then would we drink, my teaspoon resting on the napkin, Phil's balanced against the cup. All these small things we knew about each other, a trove of trivia accumulated during our years together.

Phil smiled at me.

"This feels good. It's been a long time, Shelley."

"A while."

"When did we see each other last? Oh yeah, that product launch at the end of the summer. For some memory chip. What was it called—Starlight, I think. I meant to follow it, but I don't think I did."

"Moonbeam. That was the name of the chip. That was the night of Melanie's accident."

"Yes. I remember now."

"Not easy to forget."

"But Melanie's okay now?"

"She's fine. She and Leonard Quinton are buying the store beside the flower shop and they're going to get married and live happily ever after. So that's okay."

"That's very okay." Melanie's unorthodox zaniness amused him. Her courage delighted him. Gutsy to run her own business, to haunt the flower market, place her orders and shrewdly market her fragrant wares.

"I think so." I acknowledged that I thought it was more than okay. I was happy for my friend but I ached with envy. Had Leonard Quinton perceived that, too?

The tea was cool. Simultaneously we lifted our cups, took long sips and set them down again, a perfectly timed, delicate duet of china upon china.

Phil looked at me, his gaze sad and steady.

"Do you remember that at the party, that Moonbeam launch, I talked to you about my parents?"

I stiffened. Here it came then. The confidences I did not want to share, the check tendered at evening's end, owed him because he had been understanding, accommodating, pleasant to my cousins, kind to me.

"I remember," I said. "You were worried about making new arrangements for them. I don't think I was very helpful. In fact, I remember that I wasn't particularly nice. I recall sounding awfully self-righteous." I also remembered sounding cruel but I did not say that.

"Actually, everything you said was right on target. You made sense. And in the end I listened to you. I decided against getting a place for them in Florida, against paying someone for doing what I should have been doing. I found an assisted-living facility in Riverdale, a nice place, a little upscale. I wouldn't dare tell them what it costs. They think their social security covers it. But it's worth it. The management works hard to keep the place from being depressing, institutional. There are lots of windows looking out on the Hudson, wall-to-wall carpeting, good lighting, good prints on the wall. It turned out to be a really good decision for them and for me. I actually visit them a couple of times a week, something I never did when they lived in their old apartment. I hated walking into those cramped rooms where I grew up. I used to think that the kitchen smelled of every meal my mother had cooked there. Every closet stank of camphor. Once, on my way to see them, I actually got off the subway and went home."

"And now?"

"And now it's no big deal for me to drive up to Riverdale. And it's not just an aesthetic thing. The fact is that in Riverdale, in Pleasant Manor—that's what they call it—there are no memories. I was never a boy dressed in clothes that were too big for me, bought to last for two seasons—that boy never lived in that nice river-view apartment where they live now, where everything smells new and clean. When I visited them in the old place my stomach would clamp up. I'd see myself in elementary school, in high school, wandering through those dark rooms, dark because they always used the smallest-wattage bulbs. Electricity cost money and their lives were dedicated to saving money because you never knew when you would need it and how much you would need. Who knew that better than they did? And it was quiet in those dark rooms. The phone never rang and they were never home. They were at that damn newsstand from early morning until late at night. Who knew when someone might want to buy the late edition of the *New York Post,* the early edition of the *News?*" His brow furrowed, his eyes darkened. "I'd do my homework and listen to the radio and watch television. I'd eat the cold dinner my mother always left for me and I'd go back and forth to the window watching for them, waiting for them. I'd see them come up the street, carrying those plastic shopping bags heavy with coins, covered over with old clothes so no one would know what was in them. And then I'd run into the cubicle they called my bedroom and make believe I was asleep so I wouldn't have to talk to them, so I wouldn't have to help them separate the coins into separate mountains of dimes and quarters and nickels and wrap them in the wrappers they got from the bank. I didn't want my hands to turn black. I'd concentrate on this damp spot on the wall near my bed and I'd fall asleep. There are no spots on the wall in Riverdale. It's a memory-free zone."

He sighed. There was a pause in the music, an interval between movements. A siren wailed in the street below. A door down the hall slammed. I saw Phil as a small boy at the window; I saw myself as a small girl seated opposite my father at the kitchen table.

"I know how you feel, Phil. I always found it easier to visit my parents once they moved from Queens to Suffolk. But it's great that the Riverdale place is working out so well."

"That's what I thought until two weeks ago. My mother had a ministroke. At least that's what they called it. She was hospitalized for a couple of days and now she seems to be functioning fairly well but she's scared. And so is my father. They cling to each other. Her hand claws his arm. He wakes her up in the night to ask if she's okay. She knocks at the bathroom door if he's in there for more than a few minutes, calls to him. 'What are you doing? Come out already.' And me, I'm as bad as they are. I wake up in the night trembling. I call first thing in the morning to make sure they're all right. I have dreams. I see them wandering away from me, bent over, carrying those damn shopping bags and I want to call out, 'Come back! Show me what you're carrying in those damn bags. Show me who you were before the war and who you were during the war and what happened and how you became what you became.' I want to tell them that I'm sorry that I didn't help them count the coins, that I pretended to be asleep because I couldn't stand the sound of their sadness. But before I can say anything, they disappear. They vanish into shadows. What did your cousin Morrie say?—he didn't want to tell his kids about his war because he didn't want to give them nightmares? But I want to lay claim to those nightmares. If I don't know who they were, how will I know who I am? If I don't know where I came from, how will I know where I'm going? I need substance, history. My own history. Am I making any sense, Rochelle?" Sorrow thinned his voice.

I leaned toward him, took his hands in my own.

"You're making sense," I said. "You're asking the same questions I wanted to ask and never could. We want to get back something that never was ours. I wrote this poem—it's about something I saw in the park—a hawk swooping down, seizing a squirrel in its talons. An angel of death soaring through a balmy blue sky. Celestial violence. I wanted to shout after him, to ask him why he killed, why blood dripped from his claws. I wanted to understand my parents' deaths, the deaths of their families, of my aunt Ruchele, the deaths they surely witnessed but never spoke of. But all I have is my poem and all you have is your dream. That's what's left to us." Tears ambushed me. Surprised, I lifted my fingers to my cheeks, brushed them away.

Phil placed his hands on my head, pulled me toward him, crowning me with comfort.

"We're disinherited then, you and I," he said.

"Maybe. But your parents will be okay, Phil. They'll adjust. They'll grow less frightened. Can they cope in Riverdale, in Pleasant Manor?" The name made me smile and Phil smiled, too.

"Yeah. That'll be fine. They anticipate this sort of thing. They're prepared for it. I've spoken to them." He leaned back and for the first time that night, his face was relaxed. "Maybe you'll come with me when I go up there sometime."

"Maybe." We had crossed a border. We had, after all these months of separation, after all our years of restrained togetherness, tumbled into the intimacy we had, for so long, denied ourselves. I imagined driving up the Henry Hudson with him, a bouquet of flowers in my arms. I imagined how his mother would smile to see me, as my mother had smiled to see him.

"What's this about graduate school, Rochelle?" Phil asked. It was my turn now. He declared his readiness to listen. Would Dave have been so ready? I thought not.

I told him about the poetry workshop, about Constance Reid, about the offer of a fellowship at Richmond College. He listened attentively, patiently, as surely he listened to clients and pitchmen. His observation was incisive.

"You'd be working pretty closely with this Constance Reid and it doesn't sound to me as though you particularly like her."

"I don't. She's calculating. She's cold. But I do admire her. She's an excellent poet. She made hard choices. She didn't just let life happen to her. And the program at Richmond seems like a good one. Although the stipend's not great."

"You couldn't live on it." His answer was curt and accurate. I couldn't live on it. I had figured that out for myself.

"Well, maybe I can work something out. The Richmond catalog and the application are on my desk if you want to look at them." Suddenly, I felt too tired to move from my chair. My body felt heavy, weighted by a luxurious languor. It pleased me that Phil would walk across the room for me, that he would fumble through my bills and letters.

"My desk is a mess," I said as he crossed the room, flicked on the desk lamp.

"Your desk has always been a mess." I heard the rustle of papers and then an uneasy silence.

"Rochelle, what's this?"

I turned. Dave's drawing fluttered in his hand, that graphic invitation to climb forbidden mountains, to wander through pleasant valleys, so deftly sketched in charcoal. Phil was looking down at Dave's note, reading it because he automatically scanned desktop papers. And I, after all, had given him leave to do so.

"It's a drawing. The artist is a friend, someone I spent a fair amount of time with this summer." That was all he had to know. That was all I would tell him.

"Dave." He tossed the name at me. It was caught in a swirl of Bach.

"Yes. Dave."

"A fair amount of time or a lot of time?"

I did not answer.

"Did you sleep with him, Rochelle?" An inquisitorial note edged the question. All ease, all tenderness vanished, the fragile intimacy of the moments just passed shattered.

"You have no right to ask that." I moved toward him. My face was hot. My hair whipped about my face. "But if you want an answer I'll give it to you." I seized the drawing from his hand. The rough paper ripped, severing mountain from valley. "The answer is, yes. I slept with him. Once, only once, I can't even tell you why. It just seemed that it was something I had to do that one time. I had to cross a border into previously forbidden territory and then I would be free. I'd have a clean passport, unstamped by the expectations of others. I don't expect you to understand. I'm not sure I understand it myself."

He turned away from me, took his coat from the hook, buttoned it carefully. He left without speaking, closing the door softly behind him. The disc came to an end. The music faded into silence. I stood quite still, holding the torn drawing, and then I sat down at my desk and carefully taped it together.

I left the living-room light on and prepared for bed, setting the alarm because I did not want to oversleep. I had to be in Hoboken by early afternoon.

# CHAPTER
## FOURTEEN

I did not oversleep. At dawn, swathed in a tangle of bedsheets and blankets, I lay back against my much-pummeled pillows and watched the pale autumn sunlight streak the sky. It had been a night of wild serial dreams interrupted by surges of unwelcome wakefulness shadowed by a confusion of thought and memory. Sourmouthed, heavy-limbed, it seemed to me that I had not slept at all.

I stared at the phone and wondered if it was too early to call Phil. I lifted the receiver and immediately replaced it. It would now always be too early or too late to call him. And what, after all, would I say to him? There were no words to cancel out those I had spoken in answer to the question that he had had no right to ask. My anger had not been misplaced. We were not married, we had ceased to be lovers.

Even when we saw each other constantly, traveling together, scheduling opera and theater subscriptions, we had played by the rules, so familiar to other couples we knew with whom we shared beach houses and ski chalets. We were well matched, both of us savvy and upscale, careful to observe parameters, protective of privacy, wary of exclusivity, all compounded because we knew ourselves to be the rootless children of the uprooted. I had not asked him the name of the woman who had helped him select his green blazer all those months ago. I had not asked him outright if he had slept with her. We were free agents, linked but not locked. Now, it seemed, he had changed the rules, or perhaps the game was over.

I thought back to the previous evening, to the intimacy that charged us as we talked and sipped our tea in the glow of the lamplight, speaking quietly, listening carefully, our shared understanding almost palpable as we tried to understand our parents' silence, the mystery of their lives in a country we had never seen. Our eyes had locked, wordless messages telegraphed. *"Yes, I know how you must have felt." "Yes, I felt that, too."* For those moments I had thought that we were balanced at the edge of a new beginning, an open and honest coming together. I had not anticipated that he would leave in silence, closing the door so quietly behind him.

I broke free of the bedclothes and wandered through the apartment, washing the teacups, putting coffee up to brew while I showered. Wrapped in my father's tattered gray bathrobe (what odd things I had salvaged from that home that had never been my own), I sipped the coffee as I riffled through the pages of *Writers at Richmond*. The words blurred and danced before my eyes. I lifted my fingers to my cheeks, startled to find them wet with tears. I slammed the slender journal shut and put it on my desk, sliding it between Dave's note and his sketch, an odd positioning that I did not alter. I studied that sketch, imagined myself strolling through the peaceful valley he had drawn, struggling to reach his flower-blanketed mountaintop.

The phone rang and I ran to answer it, my heart leaping with sudden hope. But it was Melanie, wispy voiced and irritable.

"Today we have to schlepp out to Len's mother in Queens. Then tomorrow it's drinks with my father, dinner with my mother. The whole weekend parent-visiting routine."

"I remember," I said, recalling my own long Sunday drives out to Suffolk County, the rush to embrace my mother who always waited at the door, her mouth puckered in anxiety. Her arms had encircled me, her lips had touched my forehead, as though seeking out my emotional temperature. Was I happy or sad, dispirited or contented? I had to be happy. I had to be contented. I was her bright-haired child, born to soar above the ashes of her losses. Then my father would come forward, a smile wreathing his thin face. I made him glad. I brought him joy. He wanted to hear about my week, my work, accounts rescued, campaigns applauded. My success sustained him, validated him.

"Oh, Shelley, I'm sorry." Melanie was swiftly and needlessly repentant.

"It's all right," I assured her. "I'm getting used to their being gone."

And that was true, I realized. Slowly, through the weeks and weeks of walking, through the long and repeated circuits of park and street, through the evenings of reading and writing, I had confronted the reality that they were gone, vanished from my life, lingering only in my longing. Lifting my face to wind and sun, my arms straining against the pull of the leashes, I had mourned the sadness of their lives, the sadness of their deaths. I had grown used to ghost-haunted, fragmented dreams in which black-winged hawks circled narrow white-sheeted beds and brown wrapping paper was smoothed and smoothed again by caring hands. I had worked hard at polishing shards of memory and stringing them into necklaces of words—my mother's smile, my father's touch, Bella's whispered memories—my poems written with trembling hand, read softly, too softly—yet written and read aloud, small triumphs but my own.

"Listen, come for brunch tomorrow," Melanie said, her voice newly, falsely bright. At Leonard's place. It's our last chance—Lila and Fay descend next week. Leonard's going to Zabar's. Do you want to ask Phil?"

"No. I won't be asking Phil to brunches. Not in the immediate future."

"Okay." Melanie was too good a friend to ask questions. "Hey, aren't you supposed to go to Hoboken today?"

I glanced at the clock.

"You're right. I'll see you tomorrow. Elevenish."

I was glad now that I had agreed to take over for Annette, that I had a defined destination, a job to do. I would not have wanted to be in weekend limbo, aimlessly wandering through shops, buying things I did not need, calling friends I did not want to see, slowly killing the hours of the long and empty day.

I dressed quickly, thrusting my notebook and a newly published anthology of contemporary poetry that contained two poems by Constance Reid into my worn black knapsack. Annette had spoken of a park with a dog run that overlooked the Hudson, and if Fabrizio, the nervous Italian greyhound cooperated, I might manage an hour or so of reading and writing. I added a bath towel. I had not forgotten about the Jacuzzi. The phone rang just as I was leaving and I answered it impatiently. It was Clem Eliot, calling from Massachusetts, his cultivated voice restrained, sorrow deadened.

"Rochelle, I thought you would want to know that Grace passed away last week."

"No!" I wanted to tell him. *"I do not want to know. I want to be done with death."*

Instead, I spoke gently, offered my condolences, soothed his sadness with my own. Guiltily, I remembered how I had envied their children, the distant son and daughter on whom they had made no claims. Ridiculously I asked about Goldilocks and listened patiently as Clem told me how the cocker spaniel missed Grace, how he slept beside Clem and refused to leave his side.

"We take long walks," Clem said. "I have plenty of time for long walks."

"Clem, I'm so sorry. But things will get better." I heard my mother's accented inflection in my own voice.

My mood lifted as I boarded the subway and rocketed down to Christopher Street where I would catch the PATH train to Hoboken. I felt a stirring of anticipation. It was a relief to break my routine and leave Manhattan even for this short journey to an unfamiliar riverside city in a neighboring state. I willed myself to stop thinking about Dave (whose silence puzzled me—his note and drawing lacked the intimacy of a phone call, voice touching voice), about Phil (whose silence, I knew, would be long and uncompromising), about the choices that teased me. Leaving the subway, I stopped to buy a large latte and a croissant, which I laved with butter. Who would pamper me if I did not pamper myself?

As I waited on the PATH platform I remembered my only other journey to Hoboken for my meeting with Eddie Longauer, my last BIS assignment. That morning crowds of impatient travelers had peered down the track, glanced impatiently at their watches, whispered tersely into their cell phones. It had been a weekday, workday crowd. Clutching briefcases and laptops, wheeling document cases, they rushed into the train. Minutes lost were dollars lost, billable hours ticking ruthlessly on.

I, too, on that distant day, had dashed down the stairwell—no time for the escalator—my high heels clattering, my silk shirt moist with sweat, feverishly reviewing the ideas I would pitch. But for this dog-walking gig I walked leisurely on to the train, comfortable in my serviceable boots and jeans, my bright orange scarf jauntily knotted about the frayed collar of my thrift-shop army jacket.

The train was disproportionately crowded with men. Casually dressed, toting shopping bags from FAO Schwarz and Barnes & Noble, they stared straight ahead, avoiding eye contact, as though mutually embarrassed by a shared dark secret. They were weekend fathers, I decided, en route to collect their children at the homes of ex-wives who had been exiled to this small New Jersey city where the rents were lower and the streets were safer. On arrival they would shake hands stiffly with new husbands, new lovers, standing at an awkward remove from the women they had once held close. All intimacy, I knew, was fragile, all relationships vulnerable. Always, one had to be prepared for silent departures and doors closed with excessive softness.

Hoboken was said to be a haven for the newly divorced. Suzanne, who now sat at my desk at BIS, had considered an apartment there but had decided against it.

"Too isolating," she had said. "I don't want to live on a reservation inhabited by singles and latchkey kids. Too grim."

But exiting the train, I looked around and did not find Hoboken grim at all. The low-rise buildings allowed for a clear skyscape, an unobstructed view of a canopy of unthreatening clouds in playful, wind-tossed drifts. It occurred to me that in the Southwest I would awaken each morning to a changing sky and sun-bright air. Why not? I thought, my eyes fixed on a gull that soared and dipped and soared again. I was not forever bonded to the city where skyscrapers strangled light and the air was thick with gaseous fumes spewed by cars and buses. I was free, unfettered by family and job. About that, at least, Dave had been right.

I rummaged in my knapsack for Annette's directions and, following them, I walked along the broad expanse of Washington Avenue, passing brightly curtained gourmet-food shops, elegant boutiques, whimsical antique shops. I turned up Garden Street, found the house and, even as I turned the key in the lock, I heard the dog's fierce protective barks, the sound of his sharp clawed paws across the hardwood floors. I opened the door and he raced toward me, his teeth bared, his eyes narrowed.

"Hi, Fabrizio. Calm down, boy. It's all right. It's me, Rochelle. I'm here to take care of you," I said softly.

And Fabrizio did calm down. He stopped barking and moved toward me, his long-lashed golden eyes glinting in his narrow vulpine face, his silver coat sleek against his long muscular body. I held my hand out and he placed his paw in it, knelt and moaned softly. We were friends.

He followed me as I moved about the designer-perfect, expensively austere room. I studied the books on the shelves of the free-standing white bookcase. Biographies and weighty histories in unfrayed jackets, probably all unread except perhaps by Annette who often borrowed books from her dog owners with or without their permission, sometimes returning them, sometimes not.

It was part of the deal, she insisted. After all, they invited us into their lives, gave us keys to their homes, assumed our diligence and discretion, which we rarely violated. We did our jobs and did them conscientiously. Hey, they went away for weekends or even for weeks and knew that we would care for the pets whose pictures stood on their desks. We were unobtrusive and made no demands. Often we did not see our employers for weeks on end. We picked up the dogs, collected the envelope that contained our fees, rarely bothering to count the loose bills. It was okay to add a few perks.

"Whom do we hurt?" Annette had asked challengingly. "So we take a bath, we take a nap, watch a video, maybe eat some cheese. Do they care? Does it matter?"

I had not answered. How could I? I, who opened drawers, read letters and diaries, examined photo albums, insinuated myself into other people's lives, even into their beds, while exhausted dogs whimpered in adjacent rooms. Unlike Annette, I did not excuse myself. I acknowledged that I was filling a void, compensating for much that had been denied me. It was not books I wanted to harvest from the apartments of strangers. It was knowledge. I wanted to know about families, normal families, with aunts and uncles and grandparents. I turned the pages of photo albums and stared down at white-haired women cuddling infants and thought bitterly that only my mother and father had reveled in my childhood. I was twice bereft, orphaned by my parents, abandoned even before my birth by those whose lives were only noted in the flickering candles lit on Yom Kippur eve, whose names were seldom spoken.

I did not even open Len's desk drawer, nor did I glance at his appointment calendar. With Fabrizio padding after me, I went into the huge kitchen with its birch cabinets and matching butcher-block island, ringed by high chrome legged, leather cushioned stools. In the Sub-Zero refrigerator I found the lean red chopped meat and a wedge of Brie. I filled Fabrizio's dish, cut myself a slice of cheese, poured Perrier for both of us. We ate in companionable silence, Fabrizio's jaws moving rhythmically, his long tongue sweeping away granules of meat, lapping at the water. When his dishes were empty, I took his long blue canvas leash and linked it to his collar. The phone rang as we headed for the door. Len, wanting to make sure that I had arrived, that Fabrizio had eaten well, reminding me to allow him a good run in the park. His concern did not surprise me. I had grown used to men and women who worried about their pets as anxious parents worry about their children. Their dogs were their barriers against loneliness, sentient creatures that absorbed their love, provided a focus for their concern, surrogates for all that had been denied them. And unlike children, dogs did not disappoint. They did not turn hostile and withhold affection. They returned kindness with kindness, wagging their tails, offering licks with their long rough tongues.

"Fabrizio will be fine," I assured Len. "I'll refill his dishes before I leave."

The phone rang again. A neighbor who had told Len she would make certain that I had arrived, that Fabrizio was taken care of.

"Everything's under control," I told her and patted his head.

"You know, *signor*," I told him, "more people are concerned about you than are concerned about me."

He barked softly and I opened the door. Ears pricked high, his damp black nostrils sniffing the fresh air, he glided into the bright autumn afternoon, paused to urinate on a carefully selected spot in the garden and gracefully buried the small pool with balletic kicks.

I retraced my steps down Washington Avenue and turned into Stevens Park. The playground was crowded with children who careened down the slides, soared skyward on swings, clambered across multicolored jungle gyms. A father balanced his twin daughters on an orange teeter-totter. Zipped into dark green hooded snowsuits, their blond hair petaling their oddly serious narrow faces, they looked like flowers surprised by the dying season.

"Doggie," they shouted in unison.

Fabrizio surged forward and I reined him in, shortening his leash and smiling apologetically to the young father. I steered him onto the path, loosed the leash and followed as he ran, his hind legs kicking up a cloud of dried leaves and pellets of earth. Hurtling down, we reached the river and I looked across the water to the Manhattan skyline. Sunlight gilded the roof of the Chrysler Building, spangled the windows of the Empire State Building, brushed the sky-hugging towers of riverfront condos. The river itself was a silvery expanse, a glacier smooth and calm on this windless day. My life lay across the river, my book-littered apartment, my friends and lovers, and yet standing on the Jersey shoreline I felt no connection to the urban island that was my home. Fabrizio tugged at the leash and we walked on, my eyes averted from Manhattan.

An artist had set up his easel along the protective barrier. He was a silver-haired man who wore a heavy wool shirt and well-pressed khakis. He stared out at the river, his brush poised, and then he moved it, slowly, carefully, across the paper. He paused, waited and moved his brush again, and I saw that he was concentrating on two mallards who floated regally by. Dave would have captured them in swift bold strokes, his eyes never wavering, intent on capturing the light, the movement, the mood. But then, Dave was not a middle-aged weekend watercolorist. He was an artist, totally absorbed in his own work, a believer in his own talent. In its service he had abandoned home and family, in its pursuit he rushed from early-morning intimacy, from the afterplay of love, to capture light on a newly stretched canvas. It was important that I remember that about him.

I led Fabrizio past the easel, glanced at the watercolor and smiled at the artist who did not smile back. His work was, as I had known it would be, precise and amateurish.

We followed the path up an incline, toward a group of dog walkers, a tall graceful African-American youth, a short plump woman whose mousy-brown hair was brushed with gray and a slender blonde. Their dogs danced playfully about them, their multicolored leashes entangled. Three Irish setters who looked so much alike that they surely came from the same litter, a frisky spaniel, two comical dachshunds and a limping black pointer. The walkers chatted with collegial intimacy, now and again pausing to separate out the leashes, to pull one or another dog back, to utter a command that was ignored. Fabrizio raced toward them and barked in greeting.

"Hey, Fabrizio." The blond woman stroked his neck and smiled at me. "You filling in for Annette?" she asked.

"She had a meeting at her son's school."

"Oh, right. Her son."

They would know about her son, as Annette would know intimate details about their lives—auditions that had not gone well, lovers who disappointed, parents who were too demanding. These were the confidences dog walkers shared although they seldom knew last names and addresses.

"I'm Rochelle," I said.

"Mike."

"Kay."

"Leticia." The blond woman gave her name hesitantly, stumbling over the syllables as though practicing its utterance. Her hands were smooth, her boots Timberland's best, her green jacket, white sweater and gray slacks classic Anne Taylor. A runaway suburban housewife who had reinvented herself—easy enough for a dog walker. No résumés were required, references could be easily faked by cooperative friends. *"She walked my dogs for a year. She was very honest, very reliable."*

We chatted easily as we walked along the broad path. Mike was a dancer, a refugee from the Alvin Ailey American Dance Theater.

"Got tired of the traveling," he said. "But it's been a long time between gigs. I haven't hooked up with anyone."

"You've hooked up with me," Leticia said cloyingly and linked her arm through his. Fine lines were etched about her mouth and even beneath the carefully applied mask of her makeup, shadowed circles beneath her eyes were visible. An odd couple, walking their dogs, transient lovers marking time until he signed on with another dance company and she went back to her home in Tenafly.

Kay was a teacher who supplemented her income by walking dogs on weekends.

"I like it," she said. "I think maybe I like it more than teaching. Dogs are easier than kids."

We all laughed in recognition. Dogs were easier than kids, easier than people. At the dog run, the three of them waved goodbye. They were done with their circuit and the dogs had already run free that day.

"Another crew of walkers should be coming by soon," Kay said.

"That's all right," I said honestly. "I don't mind being alone."

In fact, I wanted to be alone. I needed time to think, to sort out old memories, new knowledge, to open a book and read it or not as I chose.

I opened the gate, secured it and removed Fabrizio's leash. He sprinted from one end of the run to the other, yelping happily. I settled down on a bench, took the poetry anthology from my knapsack. Sharply angled rays of sunlight brushed my face and formed a radiant pool at my feet. Fabrizio lurched wildly up and down the run and then stretched out in the golden pool of warmth and fell asleep, his lean aristocratic head resting on my boot. I opened the book and found Constance Reid's poems, one long, one short.

The longer one was an elegant fantasy. A woman sifts through her jewel case and remembers how and when she came to own each bracelet, each pin, each necklace. Pearls drip through her fingers, smaller and more lucent than the tears that inexplicably fall from her eyes. She pricks her finger on a ruby pin. The tiny drop of blood matches the color of the stone. I read it through once and then again, admiring the cadence, the graceful use of metaphor and wondering why it was that not a single line moved me. I whispered the words, as I often did when I read poetry, bending forward to stroke Fabrizio's warm sleek neck, to feel the slowly beating pulse of his throat.

"Rochelle, Rochelle Weiss, is that you?"

A man's voice shattered the silence, broke my reverie. Fabrizio jerked awake and growled. I turned. Eddie Longauer, wearing a long brown leather coat and matching platform boots, waved at me, blinking wildly because the sun shone directly into his eyes.

"Eddie. Hi. Yes, it's me, Rochelle. Although I don't know how you recognized me from out there." My back was to him. All he could have seen was the incline of my head.

"Oh, I don't forget hair like yours so easily. Or ideas like yours. And I noticed at that meeting we had that you had this way of holding your head when you were reading—stuff like that sticks with me. And then I see this gal with great hair sitting right her in Stevens Park, holding her head just that way, chin forward, a little at an angle, and reading. I figured that maybe, just maybe, this was my lucky Saturday and it was you, Rochelle. And I was right. Congratulate me."

I laughed.

"I'm flattered that you made the connection. And surprised. I don't know a soul in Hoboken and then someone calls my name. Come on in."

He opened the gate, secured it and sat down beside me. Fabrizio stared at him, then licked his hand and stretched out again.

"So you just came out for the day. You and your four-legged friend. What kind of a dog is he anyway?" His voice was raspy, still edged with adolescent uncertainty.

"He's an Italian greyhound and his name is Fabrizio. And we didn't come to Hoboken together. He lives here. I came out to walk him and feed him because his owner's tied up today."

"That's being a good friend." Eddie sat down beside me on the bench, stroked Fabrizio and withdrew his hand too quickly.

"Nothing to do with friendship. I'm doing it because I get paid to do it. That's my job now. I'm a dog walker."

"You're kidding." Eddie Longauer, unlike the polite men I met at parties who drifted away when I told them I was a professional dog walker, did not bother to hide his surprise. But it was an accepting surprise, laced with interest, devoid of contempt.

"I'm not kidding," I assured him. "It's what I've been doing for months."

"Since you left BIS?"

"No. Not since I left BIS. I spent some time taking care of my parents who were very ill."

"They're all right now?"

"No. They died. My mother and my father." How easily I said those words, how detached my tone. I could speak of death calmly now, accept its incomprehensible reality, its ghostly companionship. Bitterly, silently, I congratulated myself.

"I'm sorry."

"Thank you." I had learned too how to accept condolence and acknowledge compassion although I could not and perhaps never would be able to say, "Baruch dayan emet," "Blessed be the truthful judge." When Phil said those words, I wondered, did he mean them? But then I remembered that he had not said them, he had simply translated when Morrie spoke them. I had thought to ask him how he knew what they meant but I had not, and now, perhaps, I never would. Sadness swept over me, but I remembered to smile when I turned to Eddie, the smile that clients loved.

"So that's why you left BIS?" he asked.

"Well, I didn't leave by choice. Actually they fired me. I needed time off to care for my parents or at least the option to work from home or half time. They felt that you needed a full-time account executive and I guess they were right."

"No. They were wrong," he said emphatically and I looked at him in surprise. "I needed you. A part-time or a quarter-time Rochelle Weiss. Oh, Suzanne's all right. She's a hard worker, conscientious, ready to come out here at the drop of a hat. She makes a good pitch. But her pitches don't work. They don't translate into campaigns that generate any heat, any excitement. I told that to Brad. I like him. I want to stay at BIS but I'm in business, I'm not looking for friends and fancy lunches and Tuscan cookbooks. I'm looking for public relations campaigns that will make people smile and nod when they see the Longauer name. I smiled and nodded myself when you told me your ideas and I'm not even supposed to believe my own propaganda." He sat back, shoved his hands into the pockets of his leather coat and licked his lips.

"I'm sorry it's not working out," I said. "And I'm flattered. But maybe you can still work something out. Did Brad have any suggestions?"

"He said the door was open for you to come back to BIS, that you knew that."

"Sometimes when a door is slammed hard against you, it's hard to go through it again." I would not tell Eddie how a security guard had escorted me from the building that last terrible morning at BIS. But neither would I allow him to think that I had left peaceably, with dignity. Brad had really screwed up. Eddie had wanted a half-time or quarter-time Rochelle Weiss. That would have worked for me. But then these past months had more than worked for me. Inadvertently, Brad had done me a favor.

"Do you come to this park often, Eddie?" I asked.

"I walk through it on my way to Stevens Tech. Those red buildings over there."

I followed his gaze. I had been so absorbed in looking out at the river, so lost in my own thoughts, that I had not realized that the redbrick buildings that bordered the park were part of the engineering school.

"I hire a lot of Stevens kids for research, data validation, that sort of thing," Eddie continued. "And I rent out lab space near there. That's one of the reasons why I located in Hoboken."

"Education and industry—the ideal partnership. Excuse the PR speak," I said. "I do it automatically. The words are yours—a gift." I smiled.

"See—that's why I wanted you on my team. I tell you something and you come up with a slogan. One, two, three." He grinned at me. "Listen, come walk with me to the factory, to my office. I want you to think about an idea that I have."

"I don't have too much time," I said hesitantly.

"We don't need too much time."

"Fabrizio would have to come, too."

"Fabrizio is welcome."

"Okay then."

I followed him to Sinatra Park, where we turned and climbed the redbrick stairway, overgrown and graffiti scarred, that led us back to Washington Avenue. A middle-aged couple, wearing

matching navy blue windbreakers, walking silver-coated fox terriers, passed us. Fabrizio sniffed at the dogs, danced flirtatiously
around them until I pulled his leash back.

"I wouldn't want to be walking him when he sees a female dog
that turns him on," I said.

Eddie Longauer blushed. I marveled at his naiveté, at the incon-
gruity of his innocence. He was a man who negotiated million-dol-
lar deals, who conceived of ideas that would make even more
millions, yet he blushed at an oblique sexual nuance. A skillful pro-
filer could structure a terrific feature around the story of an elec-
tronics-empire builder who managed to remain as unsophisticated
as an impish Harry Potter. I wondered what it would take to get
J. K. Rowling to come to Hoboken. Perhaps, in exchange for a huge
donation to an education project in which she had an interest, she
would sit beside Eddie Longauer and autograph copies of her
books that would be given to the children of Hoboken, assembled
for that photo op beneath a banner with the logo of Longauer In-
dustries. I smiled at the idea.

"What's so funny?" Eddie asked.

"Funny?"

"Well, you're smiling."

"Oh, just an idea I had, a crazy idea," I said and realized that I
was smiling because the concept pleased me and I knew that it
would be fun to make it happen. I had always loved choreograph-
ing an event, watching it slowly develop, become a reality, however ephemeral. And I had been good at it, really good.

We reached the factory and he guided me past the workstations
on different floors. His original computer chip had progeny, each
capable of a different function, all of them selling in fantastic quan-
tities to major companies. There was an entire floor for packing
and shipping, opening on to his own loading deck. And he was marketing a new software package that he had designed to monitor
Web pages. He couldn't keep up with orders from universities and

hospitals. A floor of the factory once used for research and development had been turned over to production of that one package.

"Which is why I rely so heavily on Stevens," he said. "Eventually, of course, I'll have to buy another property and expand."

In his glass-paneled office, he pulled over a black leather Eames chair while he perched on the ladder-back wood chair, probably scavenged from his boyhood room. Fabrizio, loosed from his leash, loped through the room and then stretched out beside me. Eddie took off his leather coat. He wore a torn MIT sweatshirt and chinos. He glanced at his battered wooden desk with the worried gaze of a student with a term paper due. I unbuttoned my quilted army jacket, loosened my orange silk scarf.

"Coffee?" Eddie asked and then blushed. "I don't know how to make it," he confessed. "The assistants do it."

"It's all right. I don't want any coffee," I assured him. "But what's this great idea you're going to pitch to me?"

"I want to hire you to be my public relations person. Half-time, full-time, quarter-time, working from home, whatever. Your call."

"I'm not looking for a job, Eddie. I have a job. And with the way your operation is going, I don't know why you need a PR person at all."

"I need a PR person to keep my name in the papers and on the TV screens, to remain visible so that venture capitalists will always know it. And you don't have a job. What you have is a time filler. Okay for now maybe. It's something you can do while you're thinking about other things. Gives you income, sure, but that's it. It's like this job I had when I was at MIT—custodial staff, midnight shift, mopping up office, classrooms, toilets. I kept a pad in the pocket of my coveralls, worked out ideas, thought about how I could get far away from Brockton, from my brothers' bullying and my parents' fighting. Some nights I didn't think about anything at all. I get the feeling that's what you're doing these days, walking your dogs and letting ideas float through your head."

His shrewdness, the accuracy of his perception, surprised me. I had underestimated him.

"Ideas. Poems," I admitted. "I've been writing poetry, going to a workshop. And now I'm thinking about going to graduate school, getting a master of fine arts."

I did not tell him about Constance Reid and the Richmond fellowship. Enough of my privacy had been invaded.

"What's to prevent you from working for me part-time and beginning your graduate work?" he asked. "You'd have enough money, enough time. I'm not BIS. I'm not going to send you on cross-country trips or schedule marathon meetings. No all-nighters. I just want you to be my idea person, maybe a press conference now and again. Suzanne can deal with the presentations, the product launches, the events."

"You mean you'd remain a BIS client?"

"That's what I mean. You wouldn't have to worry about poaching on Brad's territory or being disloyal to your friend Suzanne. Who isn't your friend, by the way."

"By the way, I know that. But she's really good at the organization stuff. Bookings, reservations, catering." I took a perverse pleasure in the thought of handing Suzanne a list of assignments, calling her to make sure they'd been followed up, chastising her for some small error. Payback time—but then it wasn't Suzanne who was to blame for the BIS decision. I bent to pluck a dry leaf from Fabrizio's sleek coat, shamed by my instinctive malice.

"Then you'll do it?" He leaned toward me, prepared to smile, to shake hands, to acknowledge that a deal had been done.

"I don't know. I'll think about it. But it would have to be part-time. Very part-time." Of that much I was certain.

"You'll call me when you decide? When will you call me?" He was unused to delay.

"Soon. As soon as I sort some things out, make some choices. It's not something I can decide right away."

"Okay. Call me when you know what you want to do. We'll talk hours, money, perks."

I smiled at his assumption that I would agree, his certainty that money and power could persuade anyone to do anything.

"Eddie, don't tell Brad about this idea. Not yet."

I did not want Brad to insist on taking me to lunch at the Four Seasons, his restaurant of choice for a subtle turning of the screws, for gentle manipulation. He might even invite his partner, Julian, to join us because he knew that I liked the chubby, mournful gourmet cook who had remembered to send me a postcard from Tuscany.

"All right, I won't tell him. Not yet. Not until I hear from you."

"Thanks."

At the side entrance of the building, we separated, gravely shaking hands. Fabrizio and I walked back along Washington Avenue and then raced back to Garden Street to the yellow house with the wrought-iron railings.

There Fabrizio followed me into the kitchen, panting excitedly as I filled his water bowl, his food dish. There were messages on the answering machine and I played them back as he noisily ate and drank, careful to press the save button.

A small girl's voice: "Daddy, where are you? When are you coming? I'm waiting."

A woman, her light tone breathless, hesitant: "Len, are we on tonight? What time will you be here? Call me. Please."

So Len had a child and Len was dating and Len had renovated and decorated this Hoboken house, transforming it into a single guy's fortress, sterile and clean angled. Any lovemaking would be done on the bed of the woman with the breathless voice.

I wandered through the house. I opened a closed door and looked in at a child's room. Sunshine-yellow walls, the ceiling painted blue and stencilled with sparkling stars, stuffed animals arranged on the bed, toys and books on scalloped shelves. I opened the bureau drawers. A pair of pink pajamas, two changes of underwear in the Barbie pattern. Two dresses hung in the closet, one white, one green. I wondered how often his small daughter visited Len, how often she stayed over, whether the dresses had been purchased by her father or her mother.

Eddie Longauer, for all his astuteness, could not have guessed at this dimension of what he so accurately called my "mindless job." Without anchor myself, I explored the hidden intimacies of others so that I might learn how their lives were secured and held fast.

I closed the door to the child's room and went into Len's bedroom, opened his bureau drawers, glanced at the neatly stacked shirts, the carefully folded piles of underwear, the three sets of pajamas in light blue cotton, his monogram on the pockets. Who monogrammed pajamas? Was he afraid that he would lose his identity while he slept? I smiled, feeling myself tolerant and superior, and went into the huge bathroom with its tan ceramic fixtures and mirrored walls. I turned on the Jacuzzi, adjusted the temperature of the rushing water and stripped off my clothes. Naked, and amused to be walking naked through this stranger's home, I went into the living room, took my towel from my knapsack, patted Fabrizio's head, allowed him to lick my knees and follow me back into the bathroom. He sprinted across the tiled floor, then stretched out beside the womb-shaped tub, a patient sentinel, emitting soft growls.

I sank into the warm, whirling water and closed my eyes, allowing image and memory to form and fade in gossamer collage. I saw my father's large hands folding brown wrapping paper, feeding fabric in and out of the buttonhole machine, touching my hair, my face. "*Ruchele.*" My mother's whisper of love, my tiny brave mother, her courage a wonderment, a mystery. The whisper vanished and tears squeezed their way through my unopened eyes, dampening my cheeks with sorrow. "*Mama!*" Half-awake, half dreaming I saw the hawk, saw him and then did not see him.

The phone rang, jarring me out of my reverie, shattering my half dream. I lay back and listened to the insistent recurring rings with luxurious indifference. It could not be for me. I was wonderfully out of reach of anyone who might make a demand on me—Dave, Constance Reid and Phil, even Phil. And what I wondered, would Phil demand of me? And almost at once, the answer came to me.

If ever we spoke again he would, in his probing executive voice, demand to know why I had asked him to go to my desk, knowing that he would see Dave's drawing, read his note. Because that, I realized, with absolute clarity, was exactly what I had done. I knew how I had positioned the Richmond College materials, knew that he would automatically scan whatever covered them. And I understood, with that same clarity, why I had done it.

I was, in fact, offering Phil equity of a kind, balancing his revelations with my own. I wanted him to know that with Dave I had crossed a self-set border, written my own declaration of independence. Dave had not known me when daughterhood and job defined me. It was my unbound self I had offered him, unfettered by the expectations of others, defined only by my own needs, my own yearnings. And it was that unbound self that I had wanted Phil to know and accept. I had wanted him to step away from the roles we had played during our high-living, high-loving years together, to shed the costumes and forget the dialogue of the well-matched couple, interests and income in sync. But I had, of course, asked too much, not knowing what I was asking, and expected too much, not knowing what I was expecting.

The phone stopped ringing. The answering machine picked up. The small girl, plaintive now.

"Daddy, you're so late. Please, Daddy. I'm waiting and waiting."

"Me, too," I said. "I'm waiting and waiting." Waiting and waiting for a decision to be taken, for a road to be marked. "Soon. Soon."

I turned lazily, hugged my knees to my breasts, allowed the churning waters to rise and fall across my body.

I emerged from the tub, dried myself and carefully wiped the tub with my towel. I dressed, tied my hair back, refilled Fabrizio's water and food bowls, cut myself yet another wedge of Brie and brewed a cup of hazelnut coffee. I decided that even if I did not take Eddie Longauer up on his offer, I would teach him how to use his Mr. Coffee.

I took Fabrizio for one more circuit around the block, waited patiently as he paused beside favored trees and bushes, and bent to scoop up his leavings.

"Hey, why is a gal like you doing a job like this?" A good-looking jogger paused and ran in place as he watched me. Dog walkers, I knew, were considered to be easy pickups. Lila knew a girl who had married a man who had asked her that exact question.

I looked up at him and shrugged my shoulders.

"You know something—I don't know, but I'm trying to find out. Really."

His smile faded. He shot me a look that said he didn't need any crazies in his life and ran on.

I led Fabrizio home, wrote a note to Len giving him my hours of arrival and departure and patted the dog who trotted after me, his golden eyes pleading with me to stay.

"Sorry," I said. "Sometimes you got to do what you got to do."

I closed the door behind me, made certain that it was locked and headed for the PATH station.

# CHAPTER
## FIFTEEN

$S$now freakishly falling in late October. Large lazy flakes driven by a sudden wind into a dizzying dance then landing softly on mounds of russet-colored leaves. I watched from my window as Mario's small daughter, her arms outstretched, dashed happily through the yard wearing oversize black boots and a white flannel nightgown sprigged with violet flowers. Crystal droplets sparkled in her sleep-tangled black curls.

"*Nieves*, Papa. Snow, Papa," she called excitedly and darted away from Mario who scowled at her from his doorway.

"Rosa! You want to catch cold? Rosa, come in now!"

"No," she answered with the happy assurance of an overloved child who knows that a parent's anger will be brief and forgiving. I, surely, could testify to that.

Mario sprinted toward her, deftly scooped her up and she laughed into the warmth of his neck.

Shivering, I went to the closet for my robe, but when I returned to the window the snow had stopped and a pale sun melted the last remaining flakes, dissolving them into narrow ribbons of water.

"Like a dream," I said aloud and pressed my face against the cold windowpane. The snow, however brief, however unseasonal, was a reminder that winter was approaching, that a seasonal border would soon have to be crossed. I wondered if Dave had watched the swift, balletic flurry, if he had rushed to capture it in his sketchbook. I went to my desk and studied the charcoal drawing he had sent me, tried to imagine how he might paint snow descending on his imagined mountains and valleys.

"Have you heard from your Dave guy?" Melanie had asked me during Sunday brunch. She was too smart to ask about Phil.

"The Dave guy went to Massachusetts. Some deal with a gallery doing a show of his work. At least that's what he said in his letter."

"He wrote to you?" Leonard asked sharply.

"There are still people who write letters. The entire world is not enslaved to e-mail."

"I wasn't thinking e-mail. I was thinking a phone call." Leonard did not back down although Melanie shot him a warning glance.

"Yeah. Well, a phone call would have been better," I admitted. I would not deceive my friends as I did not deceive myself.

Dave's silence did trouble me. It might be that he had had second thoughts about inviting me to join him, that he had decided, after all, that he did not want to be burdened with a companion on his trip through the Southwest. He was used to operating alone, skilled at severing ties. He had had no compunction (nor should he have had, I reminded myself) about leaving his family, his weeping sister, his worried mother, the father who felt himself betrayed. He would have no compunction then, about canceling a suggestion rashly made in the aftermath of our coming together. Days later, he might have reconsidered, seen our traveling together as a drag.

"Never trust anything a guy says immediately after making love," Lila had once said and her words, spoken in that southern drawl that blended naiveté and cynicism, came flashing back to me, suspended in memory, bathed in ultraviolet light.

I put Dave's drawing away, careful this time to place it in a file folder, and dressed quickly, pulling heavy socks around the cuffs of my jeans and lacing my work boots all the way. That early brief snow meant that the dogs would leap through piles of wet leaves and I would have to dash after them. My cousin Zelda was right. Winter was a lousy time to be a dog walker.

As always, I checked my roster before leaving. Lucky was the first dog to be picked up. That would be swift and painless. The Catons were seldom at home, not in the morning, not in the evening. They had no time to make small talk with the hired help. There were billable hours to fill, power breakfasts, conferences that extended past the dinner hour. I checked the calendar that hung in their kitchen, each square neatly filled. They did not rely solely on their Filofaxes. They could not afford mistakes because a missed meeting meant money lost and they deeply believed that they needed every dollar they could make. And perhaps they did. They had expenses—the rent on the apartment that they did not own (I had found their lease in a desk drawer), the cost of the housekeeper who made sure that dust did not settle on their pale furniture, and that their rugs were vacuumed, their snow-white linens and duvets laundered regularly. Sterility and style did not come cheap. I wondered if it had been the housekeeper who had found my dirty sock. Had she blinked, chalked it up to an uncharacteristic kinkiness and tossed it into the trash? Probably. She would not have wanted to annoy Elise Caton, Esq., so compulsively orderly herself that she could not tolerate the disorder of others. Dr. Caton had other problems. He wrote notes to himself, concealing them throughout the apartment. Post-its in the medicine cabinet reminding him to take his Zoloft, a pad in the refrigerator listing the calcium-rich foods he needed in order to survive, the cholesterol-free foods that would keep him from an early death. Beneath the phone on his bedside table he had taped the name of his own physician, the fraternal medical order that would handle his funeral, the number and location of his life insurance policies.

It was a relief that I would not see either of them, that I would not have to answer the questions other dog owners occasionally asked. The owner of the Lab, my noble Sir Gawain, needed reassurances that he was not gaining weight, that he had had a good run. Others worried about their dogs' appetites, their energy levels. The too-thin young widow who owned the golden retriever worried about the mysterious lump behind his ear, there was concern about the watery bowels of the older Afghan hound. But the Catons, the few times I saw them, never asked me about Lucky. They did not welcome him or pet him. I had more than once wondered why they had bought him. Probably it had seemed the chic thing to do. And, of course, he was less trouble than a baby. No mess, no diapers, no midnight feeding. And dog walkers were cheaper than nannies.

The doorman smiled slyly at me as I entered their apartment building. That smile was relatively new, dating back to the afternoon I had brought Dave there. He had, on that day, enlisted himself as my coconspirator, a guardian of my secret. We were colleagues, each of us providing a service to the building's tenants. I smiled back. Why not?

"She's home," the doorman, whose name I suddenly remembered was Ruiz, confided.

"She can't be," I protested. I did not add that I knew for a fact that she had a breakfast meeting at the corporate headquarters of a large company her firm represented, information I had gleaned from her kitchen calendar. It was not a meeting she would miss, not with a three-thousand-dollar bill from her psychotherapist on top of the bills so neatly piled beneath the crystal paperweight on her delicate white desk. I had, of course, studied each bill, noted what was owed to the personal trainer, the decorator, the spa, the garage.

"Hey, she is," Ruiz insisted and left me to whistle for a cab for an elderly tenant who wore a purple suit with a matching pillbox hat perched on her snow-white hair. She fumbled in her purse for his tip. Coins, I knew. I was wise to the ways of the very rich.

I escaped into the lobby, stared at myself in the ornate gilt-framed mirror. Too grubby-looking, I decided, and pulled a tie-dyed scarf from the pocket of my black vinyl thrift-shop coat to tie around my hair.

"When I am old," I murmured, "I shall wear a purple dress." I struggled to remember the next lines of that poem and I was still thinking about it when I reached the Catons' apartment. I pulled out my heavy key chain, but before I could sort out the keys the door swung open. Elise Caton, wearing a white satin robe with an oval red stain on the pocket stared blankly at me, as though trying to recall who exactly I was and why I was standing outside her door. Without makeup, her face was very pale and her jet-colored hair was pulled back into a punishing bun that emphasized her sharp avian features.

"Oh, yes. Rachel," she said at last.

"Rochelle," I corrected her. "I came to collect Lucky."

"Well, Lucky doesn't live here anymore," she said and tears flooded her eyes, streaking her cheeks with furrowed lines of black mascara. She stood perfectly still, then turned abruptly and walked back into the apartment, leaving the door open.

I hesitated and then followed her, trailed her into the kitchen. The dog's gate was gone, as were the feeding bowls and the cushioned basket that had been his bed. Several long golden hairs clung to the white-tiled floor and the extra blue leash dangled from its hook. Elise Caton whipped it off and tossed it onto a counter.

"He'll want that, I suppose," she said, leaning against the sink. "He took him. He doesn't live here anymore, either."

"I'm sorry." I did not know what to say to this woman I had never liked but whose misery now settled like a weight on my own heart.

"I'm not. I wanted him gone. I wanted the damn dog gone. It's better this way." But she continued to weep, lifting her arm to wipe away the tears with her sleeve, the mascara muddying the white satin.

I dug into my pocket and gave her a tissue. She stared at it as though it were an alien object, then lifted it to her eyes.

"We split," she said. "Or rather he split. He preempted me. That's what kills me." She laughed harshly. "Listen, I'm sorry. I shouldn't be acting like this. I shouldn't be talking to you like this. It's none of your business. I should just pay you and let you get the hell out of here. What do I owe you?"

She went into the living room and sat down at her delicate white desk with the drawers that pulled open with ivory handles. Her checkbook was in the middle drawer, I knew. I even knew her balance—$4700 as of last Friday. She found it, flipped it open. I took out my notebook.

"It comes to seventy-five dollars," I said. "That includes two days from the week before last. Your husband didn't leave enough money."

"Seventy-five dollars." She wrote the check swiftly and handed it to me. "That ends your business with us. With him. He has someone else to walk Lucky and he doesn't even have to pay her. She can walk his dog, make drinks for his friends, pick up his dry cleaning. I don't give a damn. I never liked his friends. In fact, I'm not sure I ever liked him." She slammed the desk drawer shut and looked hard at me.

"What are you staring at, Rachel, Rochelle? What's so interesting?"

"There's a stain on the pocket of your robe," I said.

She glanced down, touched it, licked her finger. "I know. It's ketchup. I made myself a ketchup sandwich because the only thing in that damn Sub-Zero fridge was a bottle of Perrier, half a loaf of brown bread and a bottle of ketchup."

"I'm sorry," I said because I didn't know what else to say.

"I'll bet you are." Her face was contorted; the anger, briefly staunched by her grief, was released in a sudden torrent. "I'll bet you really give a damn. I know what you're doing, what you're playing at. You're marking time between jobs, trying to decide where you're going to twirl your Phi Beta key next. Figuring everything out. Just make sure you know what you're doing before you make your next move. Scenarios can get fucked up. Look at me. I thought I knew exactly what I was doing. I had my terrific career, this great apartment. I was married to Dr. God. And I end up making myself a ketchup sandwich at three in the morning. Pathetic, isn't it?"

"I don't know." I inched away from her. I did know that I wanted to leave that apartment, to turn away from her grief-striated face. I did not want to hear the intimate revelations she would soon regret and which were definitely none of my business.

"Oh, I know what you're thinking, Miss Dog Walker." She moved closer to me, her breath sour. "And I know what you've been doing here in this apartment, in my apartment."

A cold sweat coated my body. My hands trembled. She knew then that I had opened her drawers, her closet, napped on her bed, showered in her bathroom. She knew, too, that I had brought a lover onto her high white bed and that we had lain naked upon her silk sheets. I shivered with shame and turned to leave, to escape the accusations made more terrible because they were true.

But she was not done. She followed me.

"I know that you used my bathroom. I know that you ate fruit from my refrigerator, even leaving the pits on my counter. You're a sneak. A slob. So get out of here and give me back my keys."

I willed myself to calmness and slowly, deliberately, I released her keys from my chain and put them down on the coffee table. I did not look at her but made my way out, relief coursing through me as I closed the door quietly behind me. I did not wait for the elevator but ran down the stairs, avoiding Ruiz, who stared after me in puzzlement as I ran through the service entrance and down the broad avenue.

I paused at the corner and looked back at the apartment building, staring upward to the fifth floor. I half expected Elise Caton to be standing at the window, but of course she was not there. It was more likely that she would be lying on her bed, her hand pressed against the stain on her robe, tear shaped and blood colored.

At the dog run later that afternoon, munching a pretzel and looking across the river, I described the scene to Mitzi and Annette.

"The funny thing is, I never ate her damn fruit," I said. "Sure, I used her bathroom but I was always careful to flush, wipe the sink. I even dried my hands with paper towels. I mean, we have to pee somewhere. We can't walk their mutts with a full bladder." I was in the rationalization mode, struggling to eke out a laugh from that which was not funny.

"It was me," Mitzi said. "Remember I filled in for you that Friday? So I checked out the apartment and yeah, I ate a peach and left the pit on that marble counter. And I used her bathroom and didn't flush. On purpose. I thought it would be good to get some dirt and stink into that sterile operating theater they call a home. Don't worry about her, Rochelle. She'll be fine. She'll find herself another upscale husband. Not that I give a damn. And neither should you."

"Okay. If you say so." I reached for a hot chestnut from the sack Annette had bought from a vendor. Late October, too early for chestnuts, but then this seemed to be a year for jumping the seasons—snow at dawn, roasted chestnuts in the afternoon. The weather toyed with us, mocked us.

"Listen, I hope Lucky likes his new digs. He's a cute dog. And I hope Dr. God likes his new squeeze. Not that we'll ever know," Annette said. "But who cares? That's the good thing about our gigs. You never get emotionally involved with the clients. They're ghosts, leaving our money on the kitchen counter, notes on the table. 'Don't come on the weekend.' 'Make sure there's enough water in the bowl.' And we're ghosts to them. No. Not ghosts. Convenient robots. Invisible. They pay us and we go into motion. Walk the dog, fill the bowls, wipe the floor, toss the poop. And that's okay. Who needs to hear their problems?"

"Oh, I don't know. Sometimes it goes beyond that," I protested. I thought about the Eliots, about the quiet evenings in their death-haunted apartment, sipping tea and reading aloud, Goldilocks curled against my legs. I had infiltrated their intimacy, envied them the innocence that allowed them to think of Europe as the continent of honeymooners rather than the vast dark territory of nightmares. I still received postcards from Clem, but my replies were desultory. I no longer had a need for surrogate parents, not now when I could write my own mother and father into my heart.

"Are you still thinking of taking off for the Southwest, Rochelle?" Annette asked. "Boy, would I like to get out of the city."

"Me, too." Pain and wistfulness mingled in Mitzi's voice.

I nodded. Everyone in New York talked about getting out of the city but very few left.

"It's an option. But right now I have to get these guys home. I hate walking across the park in the dark." I looked pointedly at Mitzi, who ignored me, as I knew she would.

I left the Lab on Riverside Drive and walked the Afghans farther downtown through the park. The pale melancholy sunset of autumn brushed the sky with streaks of pink and violet. Elderly players dropped their chess pieces into cigar boxes and shuffled off. Exhausted toddlers wept in their strollers and pummeled their tear-streaked cheeks with mittened fists. The small girl who wore thick-lensed glasses and always played alone sat desolately on a bench while her nanny, the stocky woman, coarse featured, her badly dyed blond hair clinging to her head, talked into a cell phone. "*Nein*," she said in an irritated voice and then again "*Nein*."

I had marked the little girl's awkwardness before and the painful shyness that caused her to cringe when other children drew too close. Always I had smiled at her and received only a frightened glance in return.

But today the little girl approached me.

"What are the dogs' names?" she asked.

"Zita and Fella," I told her. "You can pet them if you like. They're very gentle."

She placed her hand on Zita's neck and smiled to feel the dog's silken chestnut hair against her skin. And then, very gently, she placed her other hand on Fella's head.

"Lauren, what are you doing?"

The nanny stomped over to us, her fat legs straining pinkly against her black vinyl boots, her pale blue eyes narrowed. She grabbed Lauren's wrist and held it tight within the thick-fingered vise of her fist.

"I'm just petting the dogs." The protest was a whimper. The grip tightened but Lauren continued to stroke Zita.

Flushed with anger, the woman pulled at her but the child stood firm although tears glistened behind her glasses.

Not releasing her grasp on Lauren's wrist, she lifted her other hand and brought her fleshy palm down hard on the child's cheek.

"You could get germs, you could get bitten. And then they'll blame me. They'll blame me, your mother and father, because you don't listen." Spittle rimmed her mouth and this time when she pulled at her arm, Lauren, blinded by her tears, did not resist.

I trembled with anger.

"Hey," I said. "What do you think you're doing? You can't hit a kid like that."

Zita barked, perhaps frightened by the fury in my voice.

"It's none of your business what I'm doing. You, what are you doing, talking to strange children in the park. You think I don't know about people like you, about women who chase after little girls?"

A small crowd gathered, children and their nannies, curious young mothers, two old ladies.

"You can't be too careful," one said to the other.

"Of course not. Not in this city. Not during times like these."

My cheeks burned. I stuttered in protest, struggled to think of a punishing reply but she was already hurrying away, pulling Lauren by the arm, her steps firm, her back straight, braced by her authority and her power.

I looked around, saw the pointing fingers, heard the muttering voices.

"These dog walkers," a young mother told her friend. "They are so weird."

I turned away and walked on, ignoring the accusing glances, the malicious murmurs. The Afghans kept close to my side as though to comfort me.

"Good dogs," I said. "Good dogs."

I was calmer by the time I delivered them, calm enough to smile and report on the firmness of their bowel movements, Zita's renewed energy, to promise to pick them up earlier the next day. My wave was jaunty, my voice cheerful. But alone again, my face lifted to the wind, I was suffused with shame. I should have freed Lauren's hand, thrust myself between her and her tormentor. I should somehow have gotten Lauren's name and phone number so that I could tell her parents about their nanny's abusiveness. I should have brought my hand down against that disgusting cow's fat doughlike cheek, scratched at those narrow slits that were her eyes. Or I should have simply stood still and stared her down, my dignity challenging her cruelty. I thought of my mother, only a girl then, staring down that camp guard. She had risked death. All I would have risked was a brief moment of embarrassment, if that. But I had stood mute, paralyzed. I did not have my mother's courage. I could not have survived her life.

I thought of Phil and wondered if such parallels assaulted him. Were he and I, the late-born children of parents who screamed out in the night in a language that we could not understand, who lit memorial candles for the grandparents and aunts and uncles we had never known—were we scavengers of imagined miseries, twinned in our ignorance, ever grasping at the memories that had been denied us? I felt weighted with words unsaid, questions unasked.

"Oh, Mama. Oh, Papa."

I stared skyward into the gathering darkness, and turned east.

I loved the park at this hour, when night hovered close and the frenetic rhythm of the day was slowed. The pretzel and chestnut vendors packed up their carts and wheeled them past me. Students with bulging backpacks munched slices of pizza and murmured to themselves, leisurely repeating conjugations, snatches of poetry, arguing softly with absent lovers. An in-line skater in a business suit glided by, smiling with a pleasure he knew to be foolish. I smiled back but he took no notice.

As always, the rhythm of the walk soothed me. Left, right, left, right. My feet fell lightly along path and pavement. I controlled my pace, swung my arms, held my shoulders straight. I listened to the sound of my steps, so steady and purposeful, and welcomed the sudden wind against which I thrust myself, never slowing, veering only to allow a cyclist or jogger to pass me. As always, my thoughts flew free as I walked, scattering like the wind-driven leaves. I walked myself into calm, into self-forgiveness and by the time I reached my apartment building I was caped in a pleasant fatigue.

In my darkened living room I removed my boots and heavy socks. Not bothering to turn the lights on I played the messages on my answering machine. Two new clients who described their dogs as though they were candidates for admission to exclusive private schools. "My beagle is very bright." "Our miniature terrier is exceptionally well trained." I smiled and jotted down their phone numbers. If I didn't add them to my roster I could always pass them on to Annette or Mitzi. There were two hang-ups. *Phil? Dave?* I could imagine each of them listening to my recording and remaining silent. It was Melanie's theory that hang-ups were a power game of sorts. The person who did not leave a message did not have to wait for the call to be returned and did not render himself vulnerable. Leonard, she had reported proudly, always left a message.

"Saint Leonard," I said aloud and decided that the hang-ups were probably wrong numbers.

I listened to Eddie Longauer who asked me to call.

"I just wanted to catch you up on a couple of things. A lot has happened since you came out here for BIS."

"Yes. A lot has happened," I murmured.

I jotted his number down although I knew that I would not call him. Not yet.

The last message was from my cousin Lynn, inviting me to a dinner party. "And bring that handsome Phil guy," she said so casually that I knew that her mother had put her up to the call, to the dinner party. "We liked him. We really did."

"I really liked him too," I said. *Liked.* A dumb word, a dormitory word. "Did you like him—really like him?"—meaning, "Would you go out with him again, would you sleep with him, would you marry him?" Would anyone have asked Anna Karenina if she "really liked" Count Vronsky? I added Lynn's number to Eddie's on a Post-it that I stuck onto my refrigerator door. I wouldn't call her back, either. Not yet.

I rummaged through the refrigerator and found a container of mango yogurt—a Lila/Fay leftover. The phone rang as I pulled the lid off. Constance Reid's cool voice took me by surprise.

"I wanted to remind you that you're scheduled to read at the workshop tomorrow night," she said.

"Yes. I know."

"I'll see you then."

"Thank you for calling." I hung up, feeling strangely unsettled. Such a call was unusual, I knew, and I wondered why she had singled me out. I realized that I had not thanked her for the Richmond College material, nor had she asked if I had received it.

I imagined the poet returning to her own work in her elegant book-lined study, the door closed against any intrusion by the wealthy elderly husband she had scripted so successfully into her life. Elise Caton was wrong. There were scenarios that did work out, people who could program their own lives, who imagined that they could program the lives of others. Constance Reid was proof of that. I wondered if she needed me to validate her own decision, an acolyte to prove her right. I grimaced and shrugged, impatient with myself. I was attaching too much importance to the interest she had shown me. It was more likely that she needed an academic slave to keep her attendance records, to grade her students' papers, to do her scut work. Selecting me meant that she would not have to weed through piles of applications—it was probably as simple as that.

I turned off my phone, disconnected my answering machine, flicked on the floor lamp and sank back in my leather chair, the mango yogurt in one hand and the much-reworked poem that I planned to read in the other. I scanned it, noting typos that would have to be corrected, a sentence inadvertently deleted, but I did not read it through. I finished the yogurt, tossed the container into the kitchen garbage, which I took out to the hall incinerator.

"Hey, Rochelle." Leonard, heading toward the studio, stopped me. "We're ordering in Thai. Interested?"

"Sorry. I'm doing some paperwork tonight."

"Okay. Catch you another time."

"Great." But I did not think it was so great. I did not want to be the single friend included out of pity or guilt. I would have to talk to Melanie about that, a conversation certain to be awkward.

Back in my apartment I changed the towels in the bathroom, wiped down the kitchen counters and then, when I could delay it no longer, I took up my poem and began to read it aloud.

My voice trembled as I spoke the words I had written, the metaphors over which I had labored, writing and rewriting. The poem had haunted me for weeks. I had leaped from bed to substitute one word for another, turned a single line over and over in my mind as I walked my dogs, returning home to rework it with a cold calm, as though I were passing a thread through the eye of a needle, a thread that could be made to fit if I concentrated hard enough, long enough. My head had ached, my eyes had grown tired but I had continued to work. But now, as I read, my heart sank. It was terrible. It was worse than terrible. The words I had written were obscure, pretentious, embarrassingly bad. My own voice seemed fluted with fakery. I would not read it in the workshop. I would not submit myself to the criticism of the others, to Constance Reid's cruel but inevitably accurate insights. What made me think I could write poetry? I imagined Constance Reid listening to my revisions. She would curl her lips, toy with her necklace, twist her rings, each gesture signifying disappointment, contempt.

I closed my eyes, breathed deeply and forced myself to read it again, this time silently, slowly, allowing the words to wash over me. And suddenly, strangely, each line soothed, the cadence pleased, the imagery engaged. I had painted a word picture of the death-seeking urban hawk, the winged predator, the avatar of sudden danger and aching vulnerability. On my poetic canvas the squirrel's dark blood and a child's lucent tears mingled and congealed into puddles of sorrow. Flames burned deep within mounds of gray ashes and pale stone graves were covered with autumn leaves. My imagery was drawn from the year's long sadness, from the compounding of losses, inexplicable and irretrievable. The poem was all right, after all. I would read it and bear the reactions and the criticism.

Swiftly but carefully, I entered it into my computer and printed it out. I would drop it off at Kinko's in the morning, collect the copies in the afternoon.

I took up my pad and began a new poem impelled by a single visual image. A young girl stood very still in a circlet of sunlight staring up into the fat-cheeked, narrow-eyed face of evil. She did not flinch. She did not speak. Nor did she weep.

# CHAPTER
## SIXTEEN

I hurried home the next day. I had planned my afternoon walks carefully so that I finished on the east side. I shortened Thimble's walk, which also saved me some time. Schedule changes were another perk of dog walking. I could never have told Brad that I wanted to leave a BIS conference or pitch early because I wanted time to prepare for a poetry reading. He would have stared at me in disbelief and arranged for my transfer to a windowless office. Would Eddie Longauer react any differently? I wondered. But then my arrangement with him would be totally different. "We'll do it your way," he had said. Easier said than done, I told myself. I was my parents' daughter, well schooled in distrust and vigilance. Something else I had shared with Phil who surely, and as it turned out, correctly, distrusted me.

I welcomed the quiet of my apartment and ran a bath, sprinkling the steaming water with lilac-scented bath salts, a freebie plucked from the bathroom of a Four Seasons hotel in the Caribbean where I had stayed during a product launch. Phil had liked the aromas, I remembered.

"You smell expensive," he had said the first time I used it and we had both laughed.

I relaxed slowly, in the sweet-smelling water, willing the rare luxury to banish my mood so newly dark.

I had thought a great deal about what I would wear to the reading—a yellow silk blouse, loose tan slacks, a jacket of soft golden wool, narrow brown leather pumps that matched the portfolio in which I placed my poems and the copies I would distribute. I brushed my hair to a high burnish, allowing it to cape my shoulders, and applied a subtle amber-tinted blush to my cheeks and eyelids. I wanted to offset the darkness of my poem with my own carefully manufactured radiance, a skill perfected during my years at BIS.

"Dress for the pitch," Brad, the skillful manipulator, had advised his trainees. "Look like a slob and you won't get the job."

We had all laughed, mocked his rhyme and followed his advice. I followed it now, fingering first one scarf, then another. I settled for the copper-colored length of silk that so closely matched my hair, remembering that I had bought it the day of my last lunch with Brad. Not a good omen, I reflected as I draped it over the jacket, and, to my annoyance, heard a sharp, insistent knock.

Reluctantly, I went to the door.

"Who is it?" I called.

"It's us, girlfriend!" they replied in unison.

I opened the door and Lila and Fay burst in. Blond dervishes in their long flowered dresses and bulky cardigans, they whirled about me, thrust gifts into my hands—bouquets of bittersweet, bundles of Indian corn, dethorned sprays of beach plums. They danced into the apartment, bubbling over with talk, finishing each other's sentences, their bulging duffel bags and backpacks forming a small mountain in my doorway.

I struggled to conceal my irritation at their invasion of this hour I had so carefully scavenged. I had wanted to read my poem aloud once more. I had wanted to check the Kinko copies for typos. But I was trained to acceptance, acquiescence, the dutiful daughter become the dutiful friend. I did what was expected of me. I smiled, hugged each of them in turn.

"Come on. Let's schlepp these in," I said and bent to hoist a duffel bag.

Fay stopped me.

"No. We're taking everything over to our studio. Didn't Leonard tell you?"

"I saw him just last night. He didn't mention anything."

"We called him this morning and he was cool with our moving back in today. He said he'd stay at Melanie's. He knew it was important for us to move back in right away. We told him that we had to plan the wedding."

"The wedding?"

"Yes. The wedding. A twilight wedding. At a hotel. A good hotel. The Plaza maybe or the Pierre. I once had a walk-on for a commercial that was shot at the Pierre and I loved the lobby. We thought champagne and caviar to begin with and then a buffet supper after the ceremony. Is that classy, Rochelle? Is that the way to go? And, of course, flowers by Melanie, lilacs and roses." Fay was aglow. She hummed, "Here comes the bride," and mock waltzed into the living room, collapsing on the couch.

"Very classy," I said. "But who's getting married?"

"Guess," Fay commanded.

"Lila?"

They nodded and broke into a laughter so contagious that I had to join in.

"Sit down," I said. "And tell me everything, beginning with the mystery groom. But tell it quickly because I'm late."

I plucked three mini bottles of Perrier from my fridge and we sipped them as Lila told me that she was marrying a terrific guy, Morton Adamson, the chairman of the board of their repertory company. Divorced, but no children. Older but not that old. A financial planner with a thing for the arts. An apartment on Park Avenue, a summer home in Orleans. And nice, really nice.

"You've known him all season?" I asked.

"He came up on weekends but we weren't together. I just kind of watched him watching me. And then, maybe three weeks ago we began to talk. And talk." Lila blushed.

"He's a great guy. Smart, sophisticated. He has a terrific face. And he just adores Lila." Fay spoke with the enthusiasm of an agent promoting a new client.

"And do you adore him, Lila?" I asked and glanced nervously at my watch. I did not want to be late. Constance Reid often embarrassed latecomers, sometimes halting the discussion and more often making a wry comment.

*Constance Reid is a bitch.* The thought, unbidden, made me smile and suddenly I was no longer in a hurry.

"Adore? That's not my kind of word, Shelley. But I want to marry him. I want to marry him more than I've ever wanted anything in my life. I feel so protected when I'm with him, so safe. I know that he would never let anything bad happen to me, that he will always take care of me. He says that I'm the center of his life. I love knowing that he's watching me. I knew he was watching me all summer, even before he said anything about the way he felt. It was as though his caring shielded me." She spoke with a shy hesitancy that was new to her, the color rising to her cheeks.

"Good for you, Lila." I leaned toward her and kissed her lightly on the forehead.

I remembered Lila's wistful envy when she came with me on a visit to my parents, how accurately she had calibrated their love for me, my dominion over their lives. She had spent her childhood in foster homes, had been thrust too early into an involuntary independence. Neither she nor Fay had a safety net. Nervy acrobats in a nervy city, they maintained their balance, always smiling too brightly, always on the move because it was too dangerous to stand still astride a tightrope. Her marriage would change all that. It would offer her the encompassing, protective love that had been mine until my parents' deaths. She would be treasured and cosseted by her older husband, guaranteed security by his wealth, gravitas by his social position. I predicted the psychobabble that would be used to describe their relationship. It would be said that she saw him as a father figure, a compensation for the parental love she had never known. He would be perceived as the caregiver who would infantilize her as she had, in fact, infantilized herself. There would be malicious speculation, sly laughter. But none of that mattered. What mattered was the new calm that had settled on Lila. Her hands no longer fluttered as she talked, the nervous giggle that had punctuated her words was stilled. She had found a safe harbor.

"I'm going to stay on in the studio," Fay said. "Morton's going to buy up the lease or make some sort of deal with the renting agent." She, too, had sailed into the orbit of his protection. She would not be alone. Lila would not have allowed that. Theirs was a special friendship, a sisterhood that needed no blood tie, uncomplicated by childhood jealousies or adult resentments. I envied them. I had no friend like that, no sister of either blood or choice.

I emptied my bottle of Perrier in one long swallow and rose to go.

"Great news," I said. "But I have to take off. I'm reading my poem at the workshop tonight. Get your stuff into the studio and we'll touch base tomorrow."

They leaned back in my leather chairs, languid blond nymphs in the flowered gowns that fell to their ankles, exhausted by their journey, aglow with their good fortune. Soon they would seek out

Mario and he would smile at them, help them with their bags as he told them about his small daughter's achievements in school and listened to their murmurs of approval, their soft and gentle laughter.

The library was much less crowded than it had been during the summer. We were in the season of early darkness, a time when city dwellers hurried home and lowered their shades against the starless skies. As I dashed up the stairs I passed empty rooms, their doors left ajar. The door to the art studio was closed and I resisted the temptation to peek in and see if Dave was teaching. Somehow I knew I would see him that night.

The poetry workshop was in session. Constance Reid, sleek in black slacks and a black satin tunic, fingering a long chain of fretted gold, cast me a withering look but did not pause in her analysis of a poem that had appeared in the *Colorado Quarterly*. She had distributed copies and I slipped into a seat beside Laura who was, I noticed, newly pregnant. Laura slid her reprint toward me so that I could read it easily. It was simple and skillful, a series of quatrains, the words shifting and scattering like bits of colored glass in a kaleidoscope, the same phrases repeated and then juxtaposed, each stanza concluding with the same line: *You would have me understand but I cannot.* The poet was haunted by premonitions of a war yet to be fought, a musing wonder that wars were fought at all.

"Why the constant repetition of the refrain?" Constance asked.

"Perhaps the poet wanted to emphasize his inability to comprehend the wars that haunted his life," Wilfred Kim suggested. "To restate it for that emphasis."

I wondered if war had haunted his life. He was in his early forties. It was more than probable that he had not even been born in Korea, had never lived there. His English was fluent and without accent. Still, if his parents had been affected, their war would have shadowed his childhood as my parents' war had shadowed mine. Perhaps he, too, had lain awake at night and listened to voices thick with sorrow and memory. Did Koreans light memorial candles? Had he, too, stared at flickering flames kindled for the never-known dead? I stared at him with a new sympathy.

"A reach," Constance Reid said dryly. "You give yourself away when you use the word *restate*. Poets do not make statements. That is for essayists. Perhaps you are working in the wrong genre, Mr. Kim."

"I am working in the right genre," he retorted sharply and I marveled at his courage. But then all of us knew that Wilfred Kim was the best poet in our workshop. His work was subtle, multilayered, deeply felt and carefully crafted. His poems had appeared in the *Kenyon Review* and *Poetry,* and the poetry editor of the *Atlantic Monthly* had written him a detailed letter critiquing a submission and asked to see more of his work. We had passed it around the room, reading it with admiring envy.

"If you say so." She would grant him no quarter. It occurred to me that she might be jealous of him, of his nascent success. She wanted protégés, not peers. "Does anyone else have any comments?"

There were one or two mild observations that she did not comment on.

"All right then. We have two participants scheduled to read tonight. I'll ask Rochelle Weiss to read first. Do you have copies of your poem, Miss Weiss?"

"Yes, of course." I opened my portfolio, slipped out the Kinko's folder and gave it to Laura, who took one and passed it on. I waited until everyone had a copy and looked at Wilfred whose pen was already poised.

Slowly, in the cadence I had practiced in my lamp-lit living room and then spoken aloud throughout the day, as I walked my dogs, I began to read. My voice gathered strength, rose and fell to the rhythm of the words and images. I read of black-winged death, sudden and inexplicable, swooping down in a quiet park where children were at play, of country meadows and urban plazas transformed into crematoria. Softly, I read the lines that described how ashes flurried through the air and fell to earthlike flakes of soiled snow, my voice gathering momentum as I read of the hawk who flew on and on, the still-bleeding squirrel clutched in his talons as he soared over pale stone graves blanketed in bright autumn leaves.

The room was silent when I finished. I set my pages down, toyed with my scarf and tried to smile although I feared that I might weep.

"It is a competent mood piece," Constance Reid said at last. "You did have us with you in the darkness."

"I don't understand," an older woman, a children's book author, said plaintively. "Why the ashes? The crematoria?"

"That's just it." Wilfred turned to her impatiently. "The symbol of crematoria in our own lives, our own times. Real and imagined. Ground Zero. Kabul. Jerusalem. The hawk sees them and flies above the ashes with his prey. He is death's messenger, kin to the dark angel, capricious and unexpected. We visualize him just as we visualize Wallace Stevens's three blackbirds sitting in a tree. Again we are of three minds, or perhaps more than three minds. That's it, isn't it, Rochelle, Miss Weiss?"

"Yes. Oh, yes." My voice trembled with gratitude. He had understood so well what I had struggled to convey.

A thin youth who had never spoken before leaned forward.

"I liked it," he said simply. "I liked it very much." The gentleness in his voice caused my heart to turn.

And then Constance Reid rose to add her comments. My stomach clenched.

"It is an extremely good effort. But I would caution Miss Weiss and all of you against the use of too many images, of too heavy a reliance on natural phenomena. Pare back, less is more. Concentrate on a single visual image. In the Stevens poem the blackbirds imprint themselves on our imagination, our memory. Don't lose your soaring hawk in a shower of metaphors."

"I see," I said but I didn't see. Her use of the word *effort* wounded me. Dismissed, I stared at the words I had written, diminished now in my own eyes. I would rewrite, of course, but not yet, not at once.

"I thought it was very good," Laura whispered to me. Her eyes were heavy lidded, her long light brown hair hung lank. The flowing sleeve of her pink maternity shirt had been ripped and inexpertly mended. Still nursing, her breasts heavy with milk, she was newly weighted by this pregnancy, unplanned, I suspected, and unwelcome. She had told me that motherhood overwhelmed her, that the poetry workshop was the small island of time she could claim as her own, two hours a week when she was free of her whimpering infant daughter, free of the phone she answered, pad in hand because her husband was a salesman and orders were often phoned in. I had heard her read twice, painful poems, clumsily phrased, small cries of loneliness and longing that had embarrassed us and caused us to be gentle and sparing in our criticism.

"Thanks," I said and covered her hand with my own. Her fingers were ice cold to my touch.

There was some additional discussion, references to poets who struggled with the theme of death. Gerard Manley Hopkins, John Donne, Sylvia Plath. Diverted from my own work, I relaxed and listened. These interchanges added a dimension to the workshop experience. They invigorated our memories of words that touched heart and mind, igniting our determination to read poets long neglected. We jotted down the names of poets who were unfamiliar to us, of newly published collections. A portly, retired physician quoted Dylan Thomas, spontaneously and sonorously. "'Do not go gentle into that good night. Rage, rage, against the dying of the light.'" I was suffused with a new calm, at home in this room where words mattered and were remembered.

Constance Reid interrupted, her voice sharp. She would not rescind control. She had an agenda to complete.

"Thank you. All this has been very useful, especially I am sure to Rochelle Weiss. But we do have to follow our schedule. We will now hear from Laura Somers. Do you have copies of your poems, Mrs. Somers?"

Laura remained seated, her eyes cast down, her voice barely audible.

"I don't have anything to read tonight. My baby was sick all week and I didn't feel so well myself." She passed her hand across the low rise of her pregnancy and smiled, inviting our sympathy. "I'm really sorry but I just didn't have time to work on the poem I wanted to read."

Constance Reid stared at her, her face frozen into a mask of contemptuous disapproval. She twisted her gold snake ring, folded back the cuffs of her black satin tunic.

"You understand the rules of this workshop, Mrs. Somers. You know that everyone enrolled must follow our procedure. Assignments to read must be met. You have an obligation to everyone here. You have an obligation to me. I work at the schedule. If you feel you cannot do the work, I assure you that there is a waiting list of writers who would gladly take your place."

We shifted in our seats knowing that what she said was true.

Constance Reid was much admired, much in demand. Laura Somers's place could easily be filled.

"It was up to you to plan your time, to make certain that you were prepared. Your sick baby, your fatigue, is not our concern. This is not a counseling center," she continued. "This is a workshop for serious students of poetry."

Her voice was clipped, and as she spoke she looked around the table as though seeking our agreement. No one spoke. No one looked at her or at Laura who slumped in her seat, her eyes half-closed, pain and shame contorting her face. She too was quiet. She could not defend herself. She could not apologize for having a sick child, for not being able to afford child care, for being pregnant. She could not explain her life to Constance Reid who wore satin and cashmere, whose time was meticulously planned, just as her life had been meticulously plotted. And then my own voice, too loud, too harsh, splintered the silence.

"You know, Ms. Reid, no grievous crime was committed here. So someone didn't have a poem to read according to your schedule. But she had very good reasons. We're not part of some earth-shaking seminar where every session counts because there are credits to be earned, grades to be recorded. We're just a bunch of people who love poetry, reading it, writing it. But we have other things in our lives, other obligations. It's no big deal to us that Laura Somers couldn't read tonight. So she'll read another time. I don't think anyone has to be humiliated because you can't see that."

I trembled. My own daring thrilled me. I had not meant to speak, but a spontaneous anger had triumphed over caution. I had not thought my words through but spurted them out with a reck-lessness that startled me. My cheeks were hot and rivulets of sweat trickled down my arms, dampening the yellow silk blouse I had selected with such care.

Again the room was silent. Wilfred Kim coughed, opened his briefcase, placed my poem atop his spreadsheets and snapped it closed. The children's book author nodded at me and smiled in ap-proval, in assent.

Constance Reid did not flinch and when she spoke her tone was cool.

"Thank you for your input, Miss Weiss, although it is a reaction I don't understand. We meet here for a serious purpose. It should be obvious to you, with your emphasis on other obligations that the little time we have together is precious and must be carefully allocated. I thought you accepted that, but I see that I was mistaken. We will meet again next week, of course. I take it that those who are assigned to read will be prepared. Shall I reschedule you, Mrs. Somers?"

"I don't know. I'm not sure," Laura said miserably.

"All right then. You'll let me know."

She tossed a bright red cape over her shoulders and swept from the room without once glancing back at us.

The others followed her, pausing to smile sympathetically at Laura, to congratulate me on my poem, to wave to Wilfred Kim who had moved to sit beside us.

"Listen, Laura," I said, "don't take all this too seriously. It was a lousy night. Stay on in the workshop."

"Why should she?" Wilfred Kim asked. "There are other workshops, other poetry classes. Our Madame Reid is good but she's not that good. She's a control freak. She wants her values to become yours. She sees herself as sacrificing her life on the altar of poetry and she wants you to do the same. Never mind that she made calculated choices and turned her husband into her patron. She should have lived in medieval times so that Cellini could create gold pens for her and send his bill to the lord of the manor. But given that she lives in the twenty-first century, she only has absolute power in this workshop and she wants us all to emulate her. That's how she validates herself."

I nodded. His words gave voice to my thoughts.

"How do you know all this?" I asked.

"Oh, I was her protégé. Briefly. Very briefly. We met once for dinner, more than once for coffee. She couldn't understand why I looked at my watch while we were talking. She couldn't understand that I have a wife and three kids that I had to get home to. She couldn't understand that I'm an accountant and there are nights when I bring work home and nights when I have to work late because I support a family and I help my parents out, make life a little easier for them because they had a rough time when they were younger."

I had been right then. He was kin to Phil and myself; he, too, was the child of parents whose suffering could never be redeemed, but like us, he would try to compensate them for all they had lost.

"That's why I had to turn down the poetry fellowship she offered me," he continued. "She thought I could supplement it with some part-time work. Imagine me telling my boss I want to be a part-time accountant, in these times, at my age!" He laughed harshly.

"The poetry fellowship at Richmond College?" I asked.

"That's the one. She began talking about it last year after I'd been in the workshop for a couple of weeks. I wouldn't have taken it even if I was younger and single. Because she would have had demands, expectations. Her teaching assistant would have to publish, win prizes. She'd want people to say, 'Oh, the winner of the Yale younger-poets prize studied with Constance Reid.' And she'd want me to do all the work she puts aside, to grade her papers and keep her records. She doesn't have the time because she has to play hostess to her rich husband and she needs hours and hours to do her work, sitting over a single line like a patient jeweler, beveling and rebeveling it. She wants you to do that to your poem, Rochelle, and you shouldn't. You'll craft out all the feeling. Go with your gut." He looked at me, a new shrewdness glinting in his almond-shaped black eyes. "She offered you that fellowship, didn't she, Rochelle?"

"Yes."

"Well, it might work for you. But don't forget what she'll expect."

"I won't." I did not add that I was used to living up to the expectations of others, real or imagined. I had been my parents' golden girl, Brad's rainmaker, Phil's undemanding lover. But all that had changed. I had opened other people's drawers and closets, read letters and diaries. I knew now that there were other ways to live my life. It pleased me that I had angered Constance Reid and jostled her expectations of me.

"All right then."

He turned to Laura, still huddled in her misery.

"Listen, Laura. You do what's good for you. If you want to keep attending this workshop, fine. But if not, give me a call and I'll steer you to some others."

He gave her his card. He was a kind man, so slender and well groomed, his attaché case always so organized, his poems laced with an unembarrassed tenderness. I envied his wife and children. I envied his parents.

"Thank you," Laura said. "And thank you, Rochelle." She walked swiftly to the door. I have to hurry. The baby. It's late."

"Yes. It is late."

We watched as she left and wondered if we would ever see her again.

"Good night, Rochelle."

"Good night, Wilfred."

We have never before called each other by our first names.

I remained seated at the table after he left, gathering up the scattered sheets of my poem, reviewing the quatrain we had analyzed so thoroughly. I made my way out only when the closing bell sounded, reluctant to return to the silence of my apartment. The chasm between a cultivated solitude and loneliness is very narrow and I knew that I hovered perilously close to it.

Hurriedly, I descended the stairwell where the lights were already dimming. And there, in the half darkness of the landing, Dave Robeson waited for me, as I somehow knew he would, gripping his battered wooden paint case, an apologetic smile playing at his lips.

"Hi, Rochelle. I was waiting for you," he said.

"I think you've got that wrong," I replied. "I've been waiting to hear from you."

"Hey, I wrote you that I would be away. Things up in Massachu-setts took longer than I thought they would. And you know, I'm not a phone person."

"No. I don't know that. I'll add it to the list of things I don't know about you." My own ignorance shocked me. How had I en-tered into intimacy with a man who was a virtual stranger to me?

"Look, let's not talk here. How about coffee, a hamburger?"

"Fine."

We went to the coffee shop and ignored the surly grimace of the waiter who looked at his watch as he handed us the grease-streaked menus.

"Grilled cheese and coffee," Dave said automatically.

"The same." I was hungry, I realized. I hadn't eaten since early afternoon, when I had grabbed a hot dog from the Sabrett cart near the dog run and gulped it down before Sir Gawain caught the scent and leaped up, planting his muddy paws on my black vinyl coat.

An occupational hazard, Annette called those greedy sprints. She tapped her dogs' heads as she ate. "Down! Down!" Her dogs obediently crouched. Annette always smiled at their response with cynical satisfaction. She could not control the mysterious behav-ior of her autistic son, her ex-husband's unpredictable rages, the assault of unexpected bills, but she could control her dogs. That, at least, was one small certainty in her uncertain life.

Mitzi always tossed half her frank to her dogs. She ate very lit-tle. Her clothing hung loosely on her wraithlike body, her heavy silver bracelets slid dangerously down her thin wrists. She was so slight that she seemed lost in her hooded red thrift-shop cape. That afternoon she had taken a single bite of her frankfurter and handed the rest to me. I had looked at Annette, who had shrugged hope-lessly. Mitzi did not want our advice. She wanted to be left alone.

I thrust Mitzi from my thoughts. Our food arrived and I bit into my sandwich.

"You look great," Dave said.

"Well, I read tonight. I thought that if I couldn't charm them with my words, maybe I could dazzle them with my beauty."

"And did you?"

"Did I what?"

"Charm them, dazzle them."

"People in this city don't get charmed, don't get dazzled. But I think the reading went fairly well. They liked the poem. There were a couple of helpful suggestions. And the usual incisive dissection by Madame Reid. Unfortunately, there was an ugly scene." Briefly, I described the exchange with Laura Somers.

"I don't know if your Madame Reid was so off base. She's a serious poet. Her work is her priority. She expects the same of the people in her workshop."

"Does that give her the right to be cruel, to be insensitive to other people's priorities? Laura has a baby. She's pregnant. She and her husband don't have a lot of money. It's a struggle for her to find time to write, a struggle to get to the workshop every week."

"Then maybe she shouldn't be coming. And if writing was important to her, maybe she should have thought about all that before she got married and had kids."

The waiter slammed down our coffees. I took a sip. It was lukewarm, the acrid remnant of an early-morning brew that had been reboiled throughout the day.

"You'd never let anything interfere with your work?" I asked.

"My work comes first. I don't think about anything or anyone when I'm painting or when I'm involved in a project like the book, the exhibit."

"I've noticed," I said dryly.

"Hey, Rochelle, if you're mad about something spit it out."

"What would I be mad about?"

"You're pissed because I haven't called you. But I did write you. And I sent you a sketch."

"Not the most personal way to communicate."

"Suppose we stop dancing around each other. Suppose you tell me exactly what's bothering you."

I took a deep breath.

"I guess I'm bothered, as you put it, because we shared something important. At least it was important to me. I'm not a *Sex in the City* gal. We made love, which to me implies a relationship or, at least, the beginning of a relationship. And then you disappear, creeping out early in the morning because you're working on a skyscape and you need the first light. But before you go, you talk about our going out West together. A serious suggestion that I took seriously, that I thought about, although there were no logistics like when we would go, where we would go. And then I receive your note and your sketch, followed by nothing. No phone call. No note, no picture-postcard. So, yes, I'm pissed." I bit into my sandwich, strangely relaxed, satisfied that I had said what I had to say. It was my night for venting.

"That's me," he said. "That's how I operate. I'm not going to apologize. That's the way I lived. It doesn't mean that I didn't think about you, that I forgot about our plans. But I was involved in setting up my show in the gallery, getting the lighting right, hanging the canvases to the best sequence. It's an important show. They're expecting collectors, curators. And then I took off for the Cape because the gallery owner told me that the season there was spectacular. And it was. The autumn scene blew my mind—the solitary beaches, the foliage, the birds. Gulls and terns perched on rocky outcroppings, gray birds soaring against a gray sky. I began to paint and that was all I thought about. I struggled to capture that gray against gray. I mixed and scraped and mixed again. My palette was a mess. Titanium white with Brunswick black. Strontium white and chrome black. I got silver, I got steel, I got shell gray and smoke gray. One dab looked like ashes, another was pearly. I painted and I scraped and painted again. I wanted those birds, that sky, and I wanted to get them right. So that's why you didn't hear from me. All right?"

"Maybe."

He reached across the table for my hand, flashed me his grin. He would charm me into forgiveness. "So let's talk about our going West together. What do you say?"

"I've thought about it."

"And?"

"And I don't know. Things have been happening."

He did not ask about what had been happening and I did not tell him about Eddie Longauer's offer, or the possibility of the Richmond College fellowship, which I had probably effectively removed from the realm of possibility. Constance Reid would not easily forgive my words, nor did I want her forgiveness. Still, the thought of the probable loss of that opportunity saddened me. I did not mention Phil. What, after all, would I say? That I had been thinking about the man with whom I had shared so much over the years and had only now begun to understand what had brought us together and what had kept us together—now that it was too late.

We sat on in silence, stirring the coffee neither of us wanted.

"So you have to decide about these things, these things that have been happening?" he asked.

"I have to decide about a lot of things."

"You'll let me know?"

"How will I let you know? I don't know your address. I don't know your phone number." I did not list all the other things I didn't know about him.

He rummaged in the ripped and paint-scabbed pocket of his denim shirt, found a pencil, a scrap of paper and scrawled a number.

"My cell phone," he said. "Call me."

"Okay." I thrust it into my portfolio.

He paid the bill and we left.

"Walk you home?" he offered.

"Halfway. I sort of need to be alone for a while."

"I understand."

And strangely, I knew that he did.

We walked uptown, our arms brushing, our faces turned upward to the wind. Halloween pumpkins grinned at us from store windows and bouquets of Indian corn shivered on the railings of brownstones. By the next week they would be gone, replaced by paper-cut turkeys and early Christmas wreaths.

Dave took my hand. Fingers entwined, we walked to the transverse where we would veer off to the park and continue on to the Upper West Side. We paused at the gateway to the park.

"You're sure you'll be all right?" he asked.

"I'm sure."

But he did not walk on. Instead, he set his paint case down and drew me close. I felt the rapid beat of his heart, the roughness of his face against my cheek. I inhaled the scent of his body, a commingling of paint and sweat. He brought his mouth down on mine, his kiss punishingly hard. His arms encircled me so tightly that I staggered for balance and gripped his shirt, clawing at the ragged pocket until it came loose in my hand. Steadied, I clutched the paint-spattered denim square.

He stepped back, lifted his paint case and stared wordlessly at me just as he had all those weeks ago in the Catons' apartment. His gaze was professional, I realized. He was an artist committing my face to memory. I turned away.

"We'll talk," he said as he brushed my cheek with his lips and started up the park path.

"Dave!" I called after him. "I want to ask you something."

He paused and turned to me.

"I wanted to know if you ever got that perfect shade of gray, for the gulls, for the sky?"

"No. No, I didn't," he said gravely and then continued on, disappearing into the darkness.

I walked on, my gait matching my mood, my measured steps reverberating against the nocturnal quiet. Slowly, slowly, I stepped over blocks of pavements and concentrated on not touching the line, the game of my girlhood strangely remembered. *"Step on a crack, break your mother's back."* I spoke the words aloud. A city bus lumbered by. A cruising cab slowed and then sped on when I shook my head. Two dog walkers stood in the orb of light cast by a street lamp, his arm resting on her shoulder, loosely holding the leashes of their dogs, his a large Irish setter and a jet-black Scottie, hers two miniature white fox terriers. She bit into a pretzel, then broke a piece off and fed it to him. His tongue licked her fingers and they both laughed, the soft companionable laughter of untroubled lovers. One dog barked and then another, a fierce contagious yelping. The Scottie and the terrier bared their teeth and had to be separated. Deftly, they pulled the leashes in and, still laughing, walked on.

I stared after them, my game abandoned, and walked briskly, barely pausing at each corner to watch for approaching cars. I did not want my steps to lose their rhythm, my night-wandering thoughts to be interrupted by a break in pace. And I wanted to be tired, very tired, when I reached home.

I waited impatiently for a bus to maneuver a cross street. It passed and through its veil of belching exhaust fumes, I saw someone on the opposite side of the street dart into the park. I registered the scarlet hood cape, the turquoise cotton skirt that brushed the red suede boots. Mitzi. Mitzi plunging herself into darkness and danger. *Stupid girl. Foolish girl.* Anger and annoyance spurred me to move more quickly, to distance myself. She had to know better. This was an area where joggers had been assaulted, a dog walker raped, a Columbia student stabbed and found bleeding beneath a tree. Mitzi had been warned, more than once. I was out of it. I had said enough.

But even as I hurried on, a scream pierced the quiet night. One scream and then another shrilled from the park onto the street, the sound of terror muted by a wind that whistled with sudden fierceness through the trees. A cab slowed. The driver's window was open. He had heard the screams.

"Get a cop!" I shouted as I sprinted across the street and into the park. I raced along the path, following the sound of the scream into the underbrush. Twigs cracked beneath my feet, a low-hanging branch scratched my face. The screams had stopped, replaced by a plaintive pleading.

"Don't, please don't." Mitzi's voice tremulous with sobs.

"Mitzi!" I shouted. "It's me, Rochelle. I'm coming. And the police, the police are right behind me."

"Bitch!" He bellowed his fury.

I rushed on and I saw him, I saw her. She lay on the ground, sprawled across a pile of leaves. Her red coat was thrust open, her skirt pulled up to her chest. Her cheeks were bruised, her shirt ripped and blood trickled from cuts in her exposed shoulders. He was astride her, pinning her down, fury distorting his face. A black woolen watch cap did not quite cover his matted hair. The blade of a knife protruded from the rear pocket of his faded jeans.

"Bitch. Liar," he said, spittle rimming his mouth. He plunged his knee into Mitzi's stomach and reached for his knife as she moaned in pain.

I lurched toward him and seized his arm so that he loosened his grip on Mitzi, who rolled herself free. He came at me and I smelled his fetid breath, his sour sweat. I felt the adrenaline surge that had sent me soaring over finish lines when I ran track. I kicked him in the groin and he clutched himself in pain and then, recovered, whirled toward me, smashed his fist into my stomach and sent me sprawling onto the ground. I inhaled the sickly sweet odor of rotting leaves and tasted my own tears.

"Hey. Hold it right there!"

Two police officers ran toward us, their guns drawn. He swiveled around, saw them and dashed through the trees and underbrush, disappearing into the darkness. One officer pursued him, the other knelt beside us. The cabdriver stood behind him, nodding his turbaned head, his teeth very white against his dark skin.

"You okay, lady? You all right, lady?" he asked anxiously.

"I'm fine," I said. I managed to get to my knees before bilious vomit filled my mouth and spurted out, spackling my shoes, my portfolio.

"Easy. Easy," the officer said and pulled me gently to my feet.

Instinctively, I reached for the portfolio.

Mitzi stood, put her arm on my shoulder.

"You're sure you're okay, Rochelle?"

"Worry about yourself," the policeman said. "He messed you up real good."

She reached into her pocket, found a wad of tissues that she pressed to her face, her blood-streaked shoulders.

"I'll be all right," she said dully.

"What the hell were you doing in the park?" he asked.

"Walking. Just walking home." My tone was apologetic, regretful. I smiled ruefully, my apologetic smile, expressing what he wanted to hear. *We were sorry to have caused so much trouble. We really should have known better. We would be more careful in the future.* I had a full repertoire of smiles.

The officer who had given chase returned.

"Lost him," he said. "Like I knew I would."

He turned to us.

"You gals nuts or something?" he asked and there was real anger in his voice. We could have been killed. He could have been killed. He could have had a heart attack, running like that.

He pulled out a pad.

"Anyway, we have to get a statement."

We stood together in the darkness, a single light trained on his pad as Mitzi described the assault. She had been taking the short-cut through the park as she often did and he had come up behind her, knocked her down, pulled at her clothing. He had a knife and he had cut her lightly about the shoulders.

"I don't know why," she said and her voice broke.

"But he didn't rape you."

"No. Because Rochelle came."

"Pretty brave of you." His admiration was grudging.

"I didn't think about it," I said. "I heard her scream and I just ran. I didn't know what I was going to do."

"You inherited some pretty good instincts, lady."

"Yes. Yes. I guess I did."

He turned to Mitzi.

"You were lucky," he told her severely.

"I know." But she fixed her gaze on the ground. It was the opposite of luck that she had been seeking on her reckless nocturnal jaunts into danger. She had been demonstrating her indifference to life, demonstrating her ability to live on the edge. I knew that and she knew that; and both of us knew that, in the end, she had discovered that she was not indifferent at all. The violence, the near violation had jolted her into a new reality, had shattered the vague-ness she had cultivated as carefully as I had cultivated my smiles. We were, both of us, stripped of our defenses.

"Would you recognize this guy if you saw him again?" he asked us.

"Maybe. Probably," we said in unison. He jotted down our names, addresses, phone numbers.

"You may hear from us. If we get lucky, you may hear from us."

He turned to Mitzi.

"We'll take you to the E.R. at St. Luke's. You'll want someone to look at those cuts. You'll need a tetanus shot." Already his annoy-

ance was tempered into compassion. Mitzi nodded gratefully. She
had a talent for finding people who would take care of her.

"What about you?" he asked me.

"I'm fine, really. Unless you want me to come, Mitzi."

She shook her head.

"You've done enough, Rochelle."

"I take you home, lady," the Sikh cabdriver said. "Not to worry.
I take you."

"Thanks." I did not resist. A heavy exhaustion weighted me,
slowed my steps, and I took the arm he offered me. He did not
turn on the meter but I pressed a twenty-dollar bill into his hand
as he helped me out of the cab when we reached my apartment
building.

"You're sure you're all right now?" he asked and his gentle concern moved me to tears. But then, at that moment, anything might
have caused me to weep. Shock had set in. I was amazed at what I
had done, weakened by the thought of what might have happened
to me, to Mitzi.

"I'm fine," I assured him, but I was grateful that he remained
parked at the curb until I was safely in the lobby.

My hand trembled as I turned my key and trembled still more
as I slid the bolt into place. I did not turn on the light but stumbled into my bedroom. Kicking off my shoes, I sprawled across the
bed and did not bother to wipe away the tears that streaked my
cheeks. I drifted into a sleep so light that I felt suspended between
slumber and wakefulness. My brief sequential dreams seemed a
gentle collision of fantasy and reality, not unlike the unbidden, vagrant thoughts that glide through the half light of dawn.

Images swirled through mind and memory in a dizzying flurry.
Constance Reid, her face smooth, her eyes hard, her too-red lips
moving rapidly but emitting no sound, toyed with a lasso of fretted
gold. Dave hefted his battered wooden paint case, waved a brush, its
sable tip leaking droplets of silver, and lunged toward me, his mouth

hard upon my own. My half-wakened self licked my lips, surprised that they were unbruised, that no blood blistered my tongue. I was sure that he had hurt me, but that certainty belonged to the dreamer. I lapsed back into the safety of sleep and saw Mitzi, her face obscured by her red hood. She turned to me but now she wore the face of Lauren, the solitary child. Frightened eyes glinted behind thick lenses.

I was not at rest in those fragmented dreams. I darted from one ephemeral vignette to another, now an observer, now a participant. Anxiety compounded. I was fearful that I would be late for a mysterious meeting, fearful that a door would shut before I could slip through it. I ran through shivering shadows, now toward Phil who vanished just as I reached him, now toward two barefoot figures who turned to me, their arms outstretched. "Mama, Papa," I called but I sprang into wakefulness before they could embrace me.

Strangely calm, I undressed, took a long hot shower and slipped on a fresh nightgown. I returned to bed, certain that I would sleep deeply, certain that I would not dream because I knew exactly what I meant to do.

I followed my regular routine the next morning, walking my dogs, stopping in the park to chat briefly with Aretha.

"It's getting too cold for the old folk now," she said as she tossed the large blue rubber ball first to a frail woman in a wheelchair, then to a stoop-shouldered white-haired man whose vacant expression was transformed into a smile when he caught it. "We won't be coming out here in the winter."

"Good luck then," I said.

"And good luck to you, too, Rochelle."

Back home in the early afternoon, I nestled deep into my leather chair and made one call after another. I called Constance Reid. I called Dave Robeson. I called Eddie Longauer. I thought to call Phil, but I replaced the receiver after I dialed. I was not ready, not yet, perhaps not ever.

That evening I sat with Lila, Fay and Melanie in the flower shop workroom, bathed at that hour in the soft violet light of the warming lamp. We plunged our chopsticks into white cardboard cartons and spoke of Melanie's wedding in the spring, of Lila's wedding in the winter, of Fay's new gig on a soap opera. I told them about the calls I had made, about the decisions that now seemed so clear to me. Our lives, for now, were on course, our agendas set.

Melanie brewed tea, turned the radio on. FM Lite, the music slow and languorous. Roberta Flack, her rich voice laced with sadness.

We danced. Melanie and myself. Lila and Fay and then the four of us linked arms and swayed, our voices joining hers in tender chorus. The phone rang but Melanie made no move to answer it. We lifted our faces to the lovely light and breathed in the mingled fragrance of lilacs and roses.

# EPILOGUE

Melanie's wedding day and the first anniversary of my parents' deaths. In the half light of late afternoon, I lit two memorial candles. They flickered bravely and gathered strength until they burned with a steady glow. I thought of how my parents had lit such candles each Yom Kippur eve, striking the long wooden kitchen matches and holding them to the fragile wicks. Their lips had moved, not in prayer, but in a whispered recitation of names. *Mendele. Chaya Rivka. Hirshel. Leah. Shmulek. Ruchele.* The grandparents I had never known. The aunt whose name was my legacy. I had read somewhere that the flame of the yahrtzeit candle captured the soul of the person remembered and in that light that burned from sundown to sundown the remembering living and the unforgotten dead were united.

"Mama. Papa," I whispered as I held my hands over the flames, their warmth brushing my fingers.

I set the candles in a Pyrex dish filled with water and stole one last glance at myself in the mirror, threading my fingers through my newly cropped hair. The hairdresser in Boulder had been reluctant to cut it but I had insisted. I was traveling and it would be easier to keep, I explained. I had not told her that I needed a new hairstyle for the new me. It had grown since then, but I kept it short and layered.

The wedding was held in the formal garden of a mansion north of the city, timed for the twilight hour. The fragrance of young grass and early lilacs filled the air, and as Melanie and Leonard exchanged rings, a pale crescent moon appeared in the cobalt sky. The flautist played, a soft heartbreaking melody, and just as I thought that I might weep, Leonard brought his foot heavily down on the white-wrapped glass, cries of "Mazel tov" rang out, bride and groom kissed and raced joyously into the garden, magically lit with fairy lights.

Music played, a wild hora, a gentle debka, slow fox-trots, rapid rumbas. I danced and danced, laughing, changing partners, retreating at last in exhaustion to the buffet table.

"You know, this gladiola almost matches your hair."

Familiar words, first spoken before we even knew each other's names. Phil stood beside me, holding out the amber-colored blossom. There were new lines about his eyes, sprinkles of silver in his hair. I noted that his body was firm in the blue cord suit he had always favored in the spring, that his skin was bronzed against the snow-white shirt. He must have gotten an early start on the season. I wondered where—Fire Island or the Hamptons—or perhaps he had grabbed the last rays of sun glinting on a Vermont ski slope. We had often skied until early spring.

Smiling, I took the flower from him, brushed its petals across his cheek.

"And it almost matches your complexion," I said.

"My parents were in Florida for a lot of the winter. I spent last week with them."

"How are they doing?"

"Better. Relatively speaking."

"That's good." I plucked two carrot sticks from the bouquet of crudités and handed one to him. "I didn't know you were going to be here."

"Melanie invited me. Last minute. Warren's doing, I suppose. But I was glad to come. I always liked Melanie."

"And she always liked you. Me, too," I said daringly. "I always liked you. At least most of the time."

"I should hope so." He smiled and my heart turned. I had forgotten the rueful-small-boy expression that swept across his face when he smiled. "So catch me up, Rochelle. What have you been doing?"

"I was in the Southwest for a couple of months."

"I see." His words were abrupt, almost angry. He averted his eyes, looked out at the dancers.

"I went alone," I said. "It was a time to be by myself, to travel on my own to places I hadn't seen before. To get some distance, to figure out for myself what I really wanted to do."

That was what I had told Dave when I called him that afternoon, all those months ago.

"I want to follow my own rhythm," I had said.

"Sure. I understand. I'm cool with that. Maybe I'll catch you when we're both back in New York." His voice, edged with impatience, had shown no disappointment. I guessed that even as we spoke he was staring at his easel, twirling a paintbrush. I had been incidental to his life as he had been incidental to mine.

Phil turned back to me, lightly touched my hair. A gesture of relief, of forgiveness? I could not tell.

"I thought Warren would have told you that I was traveling alone," I said.

"I didn't ask Warren about you. I didn't ask anyone about you. But did you figure it out—what you wanted to do?"

"I figured it out. For now. I'm in an MFA program. I applied before I left. Very part-time. Just two courses."

"At Richmond?"

"No. At Columbia. Not a fellowship. I'm paying my way. I didn't want to be in anyone's debt."

But according to Constance Reid I would always be in her debt. It was she who had introduced the idea of graduate work to me, she who had first taken my poetry seriously, who had taught me that I had to make a choice, as she herself had done. She had said as much in our last conversation, her voice brittle with anger. And she had been right. But there were debts that had to be canceled because there was no way to repay them.

"You're not paying Columbia tuition with what you earn as a dog walker."

"I'm also a very part-time dog walker. A couple of hours a week. Thimble out of pity and my west side Lab and Afghans because they're great dogs and because the walking is so wonderful and I might not do it if I didn't know they were waiting. They set my routine. My real income is from the work I do for Eddie Longauer. In-house PR, setting my own hours, with BIS doing the scut work, the photo ops, the event scheduling, location scouting for launches or press conferences."

"Brad must love that."

"Brad doesn't care. It's a down market. I bring money in and he doesn't have to pay me. The best of all possible worlds for him. A blow to Suzanne's ego, but I don't care. In fact, I'm glad. You see, I've learned how to be nasty."

"Nasty can be good," Phil said and now his smile was mischievous. He took two stuffed mushrooms from the tray offered by a passing waitress and dipped them in mustard. "The way you like them," he said. It pleased me that he had remembered that. It pleased me that he popped them into my mouth, one at a time. I thought of the dog-walking couple who had stood encircled by lamplight, he eating the pretzel she held in her hand. I had seen them again several times after that evening and then they had disappeared from my radar. A not unusual Manhattan occurrence. Now I see you, now I don't. It did not even seem strange that Mitzi had vanished from my orbit. I had asked Annette about her when I returned from the Southwest and she had shrugged. "She said she was going home, but who knows? She gave Carl an address, I think." But I had not asked Carl about her. There would have been no point.

"Well, you're a busy gal," Phil said. "I've missed you, Rochelle."

"I missed you, too."

"I acted like an asshole."

"I wasn't too swift myself."

"Can we start over?"

"We can just start."

A waiter passed with a tray of champagne glasses, strawberries floating on the bubbling golden wine.

We each took a glass, clinked them wordlessly and sipped slowly, very slowly.

The band struck up another hora and lively dancers quickly formed a circle. Melanie and Leonard, seated in chairs at its center were lifted high. They each held a corner of a white napkin and they smiled happily down at their dancing friends, their faces radiant.

Phil took my hand and pulled me into the circle. Round and round we swirled, our fingers intertwined until we were separated by other dancers who wove their way between us. Phil mouthed something to me as, exhausted, I left the circle, and I nodded in reply although I could not read his lips.

Fay and I traveled back to Manhattan together and danced our way through the lobby of our building into our separate apartments. I opened my door and stood briefly in the entry, staring across the room at the small pool of liquid light cast by the memorial candles. I carried them into my bedroom, placed them on the golden wood surface of the buttonhole machine and fell asleep, my face bathed in their gentle glow.